A COLD
DAY IN
HELL

A COLD DAY IN HELL

A Cold Case Investigation

LISSA MARIE REDMOND

MIDNIGHT INK
WOODBURY, MINNESOTA

FIRST EDITION
Second Printing, 2018

Book format by Bob Gaul
Cover design by Kevin R. Brown
Editing by Nicole Nugent

Midnight Ink, an imprint of Llewellyn Worldwide Ltd.

Library of Congress Cataloging-in-Publication Data
Names: Redmond, Lissa Marie, author.
Title: A cold day in hell / Lissa Marie Redmond.
Description: First edition. | Woodbury, Minnesota: Midnight Ink, [2018] |
  Series: A cold case investigation; #1
Identifiers: LCCN 2017029344 (print) | LCCN 2017038984 (ebook) | ISBN
  9780738754529 | ISBN 9780738754109 (softcover)
Subjects: LCSH: Women detectives—Fiction. | Murder—Investigation—Fiction.
  | GSAFD: Mystery fiction.
Classification: LCC PS3618.E4352 (ebook) | LCC PS3618.E4352 C65 2018 (print)
  | DDC 813/.6—dc23
LC record available at https://lccn.loc.gov/2017029344

Midnight Ink
Llewellyn Worldwide Ltd.
2143 Wooddale Drive
Woodbury, MN 55125-2989
www.midnightinkbooks.com

Printed in the United States of America

To my husband Dan and my daughters Natalie and Mary Grace,
who have watched me hunched over my computer
for so many hours: anything is possible.

Author's Note

I was born and raised in Buffalo, New York. I have never lived anywhere else and hope my great love for the city shines through. This book takes place in Buffalo, but it is a work of fiction. In the spirit of full disclosure, I took many liberties with locations in this novel. The gated community Lauren lives in does not exist. Garden Valley resembles a neighboring town south of the city, but you won't find it on a map. Real roles, such as mayor, Erie County district attorney, and the police commissioner are populated with fictional people who in no way resemble any living person. I took great pains to create fictional characters to populate the very real Buffalo that I love. Hopefully my fellow Buffalonians will forgive the literary license I took.

1

"**Y**ou got a man here to see you, Lauren."

Detective Lauren Riley put her coffee cup down on top of a mound of paperwork that was inching its way toward the ceiling. It swayed there perilously for a second as she juggled the receiver, then settled. "Did he ask for me? By name, specifically?"

Linda, the round little secretary who manned the front desk, handled the walk-ins, but she never called upstairs unless she absolutely had to. "Yes, you. By name."

"Who is it?"

She could hear Linda covering the mouth piece with her hand, and then, "He says if I tell you who he is, you won't see him."

Lauren frowned into the phone. "That's odd. Hold on. I'm coming down."

She grabbed her stained *World's Greatest Grandpa* coffee mug off its perch before it fell and got up from her desk. She had stolen it from her partner, Reese, who had taken it from Eddie Finestein when he retired. Lauren always made sure to leave a ring of lipstick on it so Reese wouldn't steal it back. She knew he was too lazy to wash it.

She walked past the old Homicide files that lined the room, some in boxes pushed against the wall, others in crumbling manila folders written on in fading ink. Stuffed into three rooms on the second floor of Buffalo, New York, police headquarters was thirty years' worth of unsolved murders in disintegrating files. *Ridiculous*, she thought as she maneuvered through the clutter. *These should all be digitized.*

Other, more modern, departments had been scanning them into computers for years. They had cross-referencing databases, geographic computer software programs, and unlimited travel expenses. In her office, they had duct tape holding the chairs together, mounds of decomposing paper, and computers that were new when Lauren Riley first came on the job sixteen years ago.

"What's up?" Shane Reese asked from across the room where he was running a suspect's record. He had a red Buffalo Bison's baseball cap turned backwards over his short dark hair. Very unprofessional, but he claimed the hat helped him to think. Lauren knew he was just a baseball fanatic and that the thinking part was questionable.

"I don't know. Some guy downstairs won't give his name and wants to talk to me."

"You specifically?" They'd become so in tune as partners that they even asked the same questions.

"That's what Linda said." She absently tucked a strand of blond hair that had come loose from her ponytail behind her ear.

Walking by him, she looked at the dry erase board where they recorded appointments. High tech it was not, but it allowed everyone in the office to know who was coming or going and when. There was nothing scribbled on the calendar. Monday, June 26th: a total blank. "You could come down and investigate this with me, you know?"

He smirked as he turned back to his computer. "Good luck with that. I'd love to help you, but I'm overwhelmed right now."

"You're waiting for a pizza," she pointed out.

"A man has got to eat. You should try it sometime, slim."

"And get that nice middle-age belly you already have?" She poked him in the gut as she walked by. "No thanks. Are you going to help me solve this mystery or not?"

He shrugged. "I need my pizza. You're a big girl. Do your own homework. I'll save you a slice."

"Thanks a bunch, partner," she called as she walked past the hand-lettered COLD CASE sign adorning the door to their overstuffed office.

"Anytime," he assured her, typing away.

She mulled over who would come to headquarters but wouldn't want to give his name. An old witness who crapped out? A snitch? Someone ready to confess to an old homicide? That would make her day. It was rare, but it happened.

The part that really mystified her was why it was her, in particular. There were only four detectives in the Cold Case Homicide office. Reggie Major and Stanley Polanski worked opposite of Riley and Reese, so there were always two detectives on duty. They all had their own cases that they were working on, their own witnesses and snitches. There were more than enough old homicides to go around. There was no good reason for anyone not to identify themselves.

As soon as she passed through the door to the main lobby, everything became abundantly clear. The door hadn't even closed behind her and she was already reaching for the handle to go back upstairs.

Frank Violanti was standing there, briefcase in hand, like the evil little troll Lauren regarded him as.

"Wait! Lauren, five minutes," he called. "All I need is five minutes of your time."

3

She paused, door still open. "Why don't you just pull my gun out of my holster and shoot me in the face? It would be quicker and less painful."

"Lauren, I know we've had our moments across from each other on the stand, but that's really pretty dramatic. Even for you."

She turned to face him, but they weren't really face to face, since she had a good two inches on him. "You called me a liar with a badge in your last summation."

"I was trying to save my client's life."

She let the door fall shut. "You called me a sloppy cop and said you wouldn't trust me to make you breakfast, let alone handle a homicide."

He was backing away from her now, hands up. "Courtroom banter. It's not personal."

She thrust a finger out and poked him in the chest. "You said I tried to seduce your client to get him to confess."

"That was his perspective on the meeting..."

"You got a lot of balls to come here, to my office, and ask for five minutes of my time, Mr. Violanti."

"Just hear me out, Lauren."

"That's Detective Riley. And I don't have time for you." She swiped her ID card and the door clicked open. "And by the way, I don't care how much hair gel you use to spike it up, you're still not five foot six."

———

Frank Violanti found himself standing in the lobby of police headquarters with the secretary frowning at him from behind her glass-encased counter. Riley had shot him down, but he hadn't come this far as a defense attorney by taking no for an answer.

4

2

At the age of thirty-eight, Lauren Riley was a twice-divorced mother of two college-aged daughters, working cold case homicides. Raising the girls alone had been hard, but somehow she had managed. Pregnant at eighteen, again at nineteen, and divorced by twenty, her daughters never knew their dad. Ron Riley told her he was going to Florida to work construction when she was six months pregnant with Erin. Said he'd send his first paycheck to cover her travel expenses. Lauren never heard from him again, except to sign the divorce papers. Two years later she got a call from his sister saying he died in a motorcycle accident. No great loss in the long run, but at the time she had struggled. Struggled hard.

The look on her mom's face when she moved back home steeled her resolve that she would never again depend on a man for anything. That resolve had been eroded and tested over the years. She made more mistakes. But she had also learned from them, right?

Now she was single, both her girls were out of state in college, and she was getting restless. She missed having to rush home and help Erin with her science project or take Lindsey to soccer practice. Her life consisted of the job. She suspected finding a good man was highly unlikely. She loved losers. Every single man she'd ever dated was damaged.

Not that Lauren didn't look good. She wasn't beautiful, not in the classic sense. She had natural blond hair that had not darkened with age, the pale skin that came with northeast winters, and only a few lines around her sharp blue eyes. Except for the tiny scar on her forehead where she had been hit with a fishing pole on a call when she first came out on patrol, she had remained pretty much unscathed on the job.

Her attractiveness came more from the way she carried herself. A quiet confidence that stemmed from shyness as a child and evolved into a cool aloofness that intrigued men as an adult. She'd been blessed with a slim build, verging on skinny at times. She just never ate much. Her mother was the same way, existing on tea and toast down in Florida.

The pool of eligible men was shallow at her age; everyone came with baggage. In her mind, she repelled good men. Her track record proved that. She figured she was better off waiting for her daughters, now eighteen and nineteen, to meet their own Mr. Rights and do the whole grandma thing. Maybe adopt that golden retriever puppy she never had time for.

Retire, dog walk, baby-sit. A nice reward after all the difficult years. *And never run into slimy Violanti again*, she mentally added as she walked back to her office.

That was her plan.

But in Lauren Riley's life, everyone else had plans too.

3

"**G**et off my car, Violanti."

He was leaning up against her Taurus, his expensive suit making him look like a little boy who'd raided his dad's closet. Short, impossibly young-looking, Frank Violanti was a forty-one-year-old cocky Italian who'd made it big as a defense attorney despite the handicap of his height and youthful looks. Since he had already tried and failed with eye-to-eye, he was obviously giving a shot at toe-to-toe. He peeled himself off her car and stood in front of her.

"I was just admiring the lovely, economical blue Ford you drive. I would've pegged you for a nice, chic foreign job."

She tried to maneuver around him. "Wrong again, Counselor. My dad was an autoworker. Now go away." When he continued to block her door, she considered throwing a shoulder into him and forcibly pushing him off to the side. He must have seen the storm brewing in her face and stepped back.

"Come on. Just listen," he pleaded with her. "Do you really think I wanted to come here and be abused by you? Do you think I would be here if I didn't have to be?"

Lauren clicked the unlock button on her key fob and threw her duffle bag into the backseat, then slammed the door for effect. "Okay. I'll bite. Why are you bothering me?"

"I want to hire you as a private investigator."

"You cannot be serious."

His demeanor immediately flipped to grave, as if he knew this was his one and only chance to convince her. "As a heart attack."

Her eyes narrowed. "Why me?"

"Do you really need me to say it?" All around them cars were backing out of spots and pulling out of the lot, engulfing them in exhaust fumes. The oppressive summer heat made it worse. Buffalo was in the midst of an unprecedented heat wave. Apparently, hell had done the opposite of freezing over.

She crossed her arms against her chest. "Yes, because for the life of me, I would think you'd rather stick pins in your eyes than have to deal with me on a professional level."

"Nicely put, but the fact is we've had three hard-fought trials together."

"And you lost every one," she pointed out with some satisfaction.

"Exactly. Because you're good at what you do, and more importantly, juries trust you. When you get on that stand and say why you think someone is guilty, they believe you, no matter how many holes I punch in the case."

"They believed me because your clients were guilty."

"Maybe," he conceded for her benefit. "But I just got retained to represent a young man and I'm convinced he's not guilty. And I think you will be too. I just want you to meet with the kid. That's all. I think once you meet him, you'll want to take his case."

"What's he charged with?"

"Murder second."

"I can't investigate a case for the defense in a murder. I work in the Homicide squad, stupid."

"She was murdered in Garden Valley, not Buffalo. Not your jurisdiction. I know you have your private investigator's license. I would hire you under that." His face tightened up. "Come on, Lauren, there's a lot of pressure for the county attorneys to nail this kid. You don't think I know I'm sticking my neck out by even asking you for this? I'm not asking as a friend. I'm asking in the interest of justice, because I think this kid is being railroaded and the real killer is still out there."

She was disturbed by the genuine display of emotion he was putting on. It threatened the delicate balance of hate and disgust they had for each other. "Way to play to my soft spot."

"I have to use what I can." Knowing he was making progress, even a little, he grinned his little-boy smile at her.

Lauren drank him in with the eye of a seasoned bullshit detector. She wasn't buying it. He had to have an angle. Violanti always did.

"Who's the victim?"

"Katherine Vine."

"Whoa, now I get it. Her murder was all over the radio this morning when I was driving in. She was found strangled behind a toy store." She held up her hands as if to ward off the bad mojo. "You fell into a media shit storm and want me to join you. No way. I wouldn't touch that case with a ten-foot pole, even if you weren't the kid's defense attorney."

She opened the driver's side door to her car and started to get in when Violanti grabbed onto the handle. "Please. Lauren, I'm begging you. Just talk to David. If you think he did it, walk right to the prosecution. Go right to the Garden Valley detective, Joe Wheeler, with everything he says."

She paused. "It's Joe Wheeler's case?"

Violanti's swagger seemed to fail him a little. "He made the arrest this morning."

She mulled that over in her head for a second. "Joe Wheeler is an even bigger scumbag than you are. And you can get disbarred for saying things like that to me."

"That's how strongly I believe in David. I'm willing to risk it. He's just a kid, Lauren. Eighteen years old. Just talk to him."

She studied the look on his face for a moment. Sincerity. That was something new. "Why do you care so much about this kid?"

"Because he's my godson."

4

The county holding center was conveniently located across the street from Buffalo Police Headquarters and kitty corner from the county court building. The two made their way from the parking lot to the corner, where they dutifully waited for the light to change. Violanti had to take two steps for every one of Lauren's long strides. The pair turned a couple heads of county court workers. Their rivalry was well-known around the local law enforcement community. One court officer stopped and watched them curiously as they crossed the street together. Lauren looked straight ahead, ignoring the gawkers, as she climbed the stairs to the holding center. *Maybe they think he finally pushed me too far,* Lauren thought as they entered the double doors, *and I'm locking him up.*

More curious glances followed them into the jail. Violanti signed them in while Lauren stowed her gun in the lockers that were kept for visiting law enforcement. Instead of signing her name in the police book, he had written her name in the attorney's book. The deputy on duty took it from Violanti and looked up at Lauren, arching an eyebrow. "Defense counsel?"

"For now." She signed the book and got her visitor's pass.

The deputy put the book back on the shelf behind him and typed something into his ancient computer. "I'll call him down. Room 5."

Violanti led the way through the metal detectors toward the holding area.

The fat, old deputy who kept watch at the lockup entrance wanded them both in silence. He had been the keeper of the gate since Lauren was a rookie cop. The same round man, the same stained uniform, the same facial expression. The heavy metal door behind him was rigged to close slowly. No loud slam like in the prison movies, but a soft, sure snap. It was less dramatic, but the message was just the same: you only get out when he let you out.

They passed through that portal, only to wait for another heavy door to pop open and take them into the hallway that led to the lawyers' visiting rooms. It was a complex labyrinth by design. Lauren always felt so suffocated in the holding center, breathing in the recycled air that smelled like cheap industrial disinfectant.

Room 5 was all the way at the end. The small six-by-six room had two doors opposite each other, a table bolted to the floor, and one chair on each side that seemed to grow out of the floor like metal mushrooms. Someone had placed a white plastic lawn chair in the room, probably when the deputies realized that there would be three people instead of two at the interview. Lauren took the metal mushroom and Violanti sank down in the heavy plastic. It made a strained creak, like there might be a crack somewhere. He tried to shift his weight without splitting the chair in half.

Turning toward Lauren, who was trying to ignore his presence entirely, he asked, "Are you surprised I have a godson?"

She absently twirled her pen between her fingers. "I'd be more surprised if someone actually spawned with you."

"My wife and I are trying." He moved to the left a little, felt the chair wobble, and repositioned.

"How cute. Your kids will be so small you'll be able to carry them around in your pocket."

"Be nice."

"Believe me, I'm trying." She stared straight ahead at the door leading from the interior of the holding center, from where their prisoner would emerge shortly. "Let's just get through the next half hour."

"Agreed."

Lauren was surprised when the kid walked in. She somehow expected him to be short and dark like Frank Violanti. David Spencer was anything but. A clean-cut, good-looking kid with a shock of brown hair that fell over his eyes, he looked desperately out of place in the dirty room. David wasn't handcuffed, but he was dressed in the usual orange jumpsuit that they outfitted all the prisoners in. Even though he was tall and had an athletic build, his jumpsuit made him look sallow and small somehow. He sat down across from Lauren on his own mushroom and smiled. He had a sweetness and vulnerability about him that Lauren picked up on right away.

"How're you holding up, David?" Violanti asked.

"I have to get out of here. Can't you get me bail or something?" Despite being edged in fear, his voice was surprisingly deep and adult.

"You're being arraigned tomorrow morning; I'll have to wait to make my motion for bail then."

"I have to spend the night here?" Panic rose in his voice. Lauren noticed how he was furiously picking at the skin around his thumb nail. Enough to draw a bead of blood.

"You might have to spend a lot of nights here, kid. If anyone mistreats you—a guard, a prisoner—call me right away."

"They have me all by myself."

"That's typical for someone like you."

His eyebrows knit together. "Someone like me?"

"A white kid from the suburbs charged with a particularly mediaworthy crime. They don't want you to get molested before the trial."

He put his hand to his forehead and took a deep breath. "Thanks, Uncle Frank."

"Just keeping it real."

Lauren coughed in her best *let's get on with it* way.

Violanti focused. "David, this is the detective I told you about. I want you to answer all her questions truthfully, do you understand? Don't embellish or leave anything out. You have to be completely honest or she can't help you."

He nodded. "Okay."

Lauren waited a second for that to sink in before she started. He was staring at her intently, his eyes almost pleading with hers for something to make this nightmare go away. "I'm Lauren Riley. I work for the city homicide squad. I do cold cases, but your godfather here thinks I can help you."

"Aren't you the police? Shouldn't you be trying to put me away? The other detective I talked to, Detective Wheeler, arrested me."

Lauren sighed and explained slowly and patiently, "I work for Buffalo's Homicide squad, but I'm also a licensed private detective. You were arrested outside my jurisdiction. That means Mr. Violanti can hire me to follow up on investigative leads as a private detective, as long as your crime doesn't cross over into the city. Now, there's a little bit of conflict because the same district attorney who's prosecuting you also prosecutes my cases in the city, because he represents the whole county. But he can't tell me not to work on your case."

"You can help me?" There was hope in that question. Not the usual pissed off *mad because I got caught* attitude.

Lauren picked up on that right away. She poised her pen over her notepad, ready to write. "I don't know if I can or if I will, but let's start at the beginning. Full name?"

"David Ryan Spencer."

She wrote that down. Then asked, "How old are you, David?"

"I turned eighteen on November fourth."

He's almost the same age as Erin, she thought, as she jotted in her notebook. Erin was her youngest. He looked like some of the boys she had brought home over the years. The boy she'd gone to the prom with, the boy she helped with his paper on Shakespeare. He could be that boy. Lauren tried to banish such thoughts from her brain; she had a job to do. She went ahead with the rest of his pedigree information and then got to the point.

"Did you know Katherine Vine?"

He picked at the edge of his thumb, but kept eye contact. "No. I mean kinda, but not really."

"What's that mean?"

"She used to come into Toy City a lot, where I work. She used to buy these video games all the time and always two of the same one. I never really talked to her until last night when she left her credit card behind."

"Then what happened?" she prompted. He was going to be a bits-and-pieces interview. He'd tell her what happened, but he'd make her ask for it.

"I called her."

Interesting. "How did you know her phone number?"

"It's in the computer," he said as if this was the most obvious thing in the world. "Anyway, she tells me to bring it out to her, that she's in her car behind the building. So I did."

"Then what happened?"

David paused and looked at Violanti, who leaned toward him in his unstable chair. "Tell her everything."

His eyes darted back to Lauren's. "She was sitting in her car in the dark. She took her card back and told me to get in, then she practically attacked me."

"She attacked you?" Lauren asked, raising an eyebrow.

"No, she didn't attack me." He stumbled, trying to find the right words. "I mean, she was all over me, kissing me, ripping my shirt open, pulling my pants down, biting me ... "

"She bit you?"

David unzipped his jumpsuit enough to pull the left side down over his arm and expose a perfect bite mark on his shoulder. "Yeah, she clawed my back too. The detective who arrested me this morning took pictures."

"Did you tell her to stop when she was hurting you?"

"No. She was so into it. I've never been with someone so into it before. She bit me because she liked it." A deep blush spread across his cheek. "And I liked it."

"You're sitting here telling me that this older woman you've never really spoken to before dragged you into her car, roughed you up, and had sex with you? Is that how she ended up dead? Did it get too rough and you accidentally strangled her?"

"No! She was alive when I got out of her car. I asked her if I could call her sometime and she kinda laughed and said no. I didn't know what to do. She just sat there, so I walked to my car and drove home."

Lauren made a note on her legal pad. "Was she still in the parking lot when you pulled out?"

"Yeah, she was still sitting there with the lights off. I figured she was waiting for me to leave."

"How long were you in her car?"

"An hour, maybe more."

"You were in her car for an hour?"

"We were doing things." His eyes slid from her face, and his voice lowered. "She was doing things to me and I was doing things to her. We both were really into it. I liked her and I thought she liked me."

It was painful to hear him say that last sentence, it revealed to Lauren exactly how young this kid really was. How naïve. It was time to wrap this up. "Did you have intercourse?"

The deep blush spread to his entire face now, including the tips of his ears. "Yes."

"How many times?"

He hesitated, looked to Violanti, who nodded. "Twice."

"Did you use a condom?"

He seemed to slump a little in his seat, glancing away from her before he answered, "No."

"Of course not." She tried to control the emotion in her voice as she asked her last question. "Did she say anything to you before, during, or after sex, besides what you've told me?"

"No."

David looked expectantly at Lauren, as if she was about to spout some great, unspoken truth. And she did.

Lauren closed her notebook. "Kid, you're in a whole lot of trouble."

5

"What do you think?" Violanti asked as they walked back out of the holding center, his stubby legs still striding to keep up with Lauren's.

She stopped dead, causing him to almost collide with her. "Let's examine what they have. I think they have two people, by his own admission, who don't know each other. They have her bite marks on his shoulder. His DNA is going to be under her fingernails and all over her. I bet they have his prints everywhere in the interior of her car. I wish all my cases were this easy."

"What's the motive then? Why would he kill her?"

"Because she laughed at him when he asked for her phone number. Because he had a bad day at the toy shop. Because he doesn't know his own strength during rough sex." Lauren started walking again, not waiting for any kind of reply.

"But do you think he did it?" Violanti pressed as he tried to keep up.

"I think the prosecution already has a strong case, especially if he told that story to Joe Wheeler before he was arrested." They were back in the parking lot where this whole thing had started.

"I didn't ask you that."

She sighed. He was persistent, she had to give him that. "I need to look at everything you have. The autopsy, her background, the crime scene photos. Everything."

"So you have doubts as well?"

Lauren clicked her key fob and opened her car door. She got in and rolled down the window halfway. "I'll see you at the arraignment tomorrow. I'll decide after the felony hearing."

"I wasn't going to run the felony hearing."

"You are now."

"See you tomorrow, Detective. And thank you." An appreciative smile rolled across his boyish face. Lauren suppressed the urge to slug him.

"Don't thank me yet." She rolled the window up on him and drove off. *What the hell am I getting myself into?* she thought as she made her way home. *I should just walk away now, not get involved.* Anything to do with Frank Violanti was suspect.

But that kid, that kid, he couldn't have murdered Katherine Vine like that. To savagely strangle a woman was cold-blooded murder. Something you graduated to over time, not something you jumped to after good teenage sex, she thought. She couldn't shake the mental picture of him in his orange jumpsuit, how sad and embarrassed he was, how he was picking at himself until he bled. It was caught in her head.

There was more to the story. Of that, she was sure.

6

The City of Buffalo was your typical rustbelt dinosaur. After the grain elevators shut down and the steel plants closed, people started flocking south to escape the harsh winters. While the nation's economy plummeted, the downturn was barely a blip in a city whose fortunes were won and lost fifty years ago.

Downtown, where Lauren worked, the city's police headquarters was stuffed into a 1930s-era square building next to St. Joseph's Cathedral. A new headquarters was low on the local politician's pork barrel agenda, but there were rumors about moving into the old Federal Court building. In the meantime, Buffalo's detectives and police administration toiled in a cockroach-infested, asbestos-riddled crime of architecture. The view of Lake Erie was obscured by a raised thruway that led commuters out of the urban blight and back to their neat suburban homes, far away from city crime or politics. Every day at five o'clock, you could watch the exodus from the detective divisions' third-floor offices—thousands of cars making a break for it, escaping from the big bad city.

Lauren managed to join the flow of traffic toward the north end of the city, where Millionaire's Row used to thrive. She sped up and stopped, sped up and stopped, honked her horn, made an obscene gesture or two, all in rhythm with the rush hour traffic. Finally, she inched her way toward the entrance of her neighborhood after being cut off by a fifty-year-old woman driving a yellow Hummer. What used to be the mansions of the steel and grain tycoons was now a gated community, complete with security guard. Lauren smiled at Eddie in the guard shack as he lifted the wooden arm blocking the front of her car: city living at its finest.

It wasn't dark yet. The summer was stretching out the daylight until almost nine o'clock. Her two-story Colonial, a parting gift from husband number two as part of the divorce settlement (oh yes, she'd made more than one mistake in the love department), looked almost stately with its freshly maintained landscaping and tasteful slate gray siding with eggshell trim. The service must have been by, because stray pieces of freshly cut grass clung to her shoes as she walked around to the other side of her car. She grabbed up her bag, double clicked her fob, and officially called it a day. Kind of.

Her brain didn't work that way, like she could turn off being a cop. She never could. She might be able to pause it long enough to change her clothes and grab a bite, but then her cases came flooding back in. Without having her daughters around to clean up after, it was worse. She had managed to keep it together when Lindsey went away to college two years ago, but Erin's departure last September had hit her hard. More so than she'd ever admit. Being a single mom for most of the last two decades had conditioned her to put them first, always. Now they were gone and all she had left was the job.

Unlocking her front door, she escaped into her safe haven. The air conditioning felt like heaven as she threw her duffle bag onto the hallway chair, where it promptly slid off into a lump on the floor. She didn't bother to pick it up. Who cared if she was slightly slobby? No one else was there to complain.

That evening, as she sprawled on the flowered couch in her living room, she clicked off the flat screen over her fireplace. She wanted to concentrate without *The Real Housewives of New York* interrupting her. Lauren went over the article on the front page of the newspaper about Katherine Vine's murder.

She could have read it on her tablet, but Lauren was old-fashioned. She loved the feel of the paper in her hands, loved reading real words, not digital pixels, or whatever they were. Her fingers left little oily marks on the pages. It made her think of her father, coming home after work with his paper, drinking coffee and passing her a page once he was done with it. *You have to know what's going on,* he'd told her, *or else you'll never get anywhere.*

She sank back, put her bare feet up, and took it all in. She had facts to get to.

The picture they ran showed a beautiful blonde, tall and leggy, in some tropical paradise with the ocean behind her. Her loose hair was blowing in the breeze, she looked relaxed and happy. It was the kind of picture someone snaps at just that right moment, capturing exactly what you're feeling. She was glowing. She was alive.

The picture made her feel a heavy sadness in her chest. Katherine's life had been viciously snatched from her and now she was reduced to tabloid fodder.

Shaking out the page, Lauren continued to read. Katherine Vine, age thirty-two, had been married to Anthony Vine, the owner of a chain of gyms across the northeast. They had twin boys who were twelve years old, which explained why Katherine always bought two of the same games. Lauren's daughters weren't twins, but were close enough in age that she too had to buy two of everything when they were young to avoid catastrophic tantrums.

The article included a picture of Katherine smiling with her much older and very tan husband. Anthony Vine was something of a local celebrity due to his appearances in his own cheesy commercials. He'd walk out onto a gym floor surrounded by people lifting weights and yell his catch phrase into the screen, "If you're not fit, IT'S VINE TIME!!" His leathery orange face graced the side of bus stops, billboards, and park benches all over the city.

She saw that they had interviewed Joe Wheeler about the arrest. "We do have a suspect in custody as of noon today. He did give a statement before his arrest, the details of which I won't get into now." Just looking at the small photo of Joe Wheeler made her stomach turn. Her relationship with him had been the low point of her existence. Still reeling from the abandonment of her first husband, who had left her high and dry with two babies, she had looked to Joe for a father figure for them. She was still in the police academy when he charmed his way into her life, her kids just two and three. But his charm had faded fast to fists and beatings. She got out before her girls knew what was going on. If she could have erased those few years from her life, she would have. In a heartbeat.

She shoved that piece of the newspaper under the coffee table.

In a separate article, District Attorney Carl Church also chimed in, praising Detective Wheeler for his good work in making a speedy arrest in such a horrific case. Church's picture wasn't included in the article, but she could imagine him in his gray pinstriped power suit, looking sympathetic and outraged all at the same time. That look had gotten him elected to two terms and he pulled it out whenever it would have maximum effect. Election time was right around the corner; he'd make hay with this one for sure.

All the power players were jockeying into position for this homicide.

As she tossed the rest of the paper to the floor, Lauren could practically smell the shit that was rolling downhill directly toward her.

7

The next morning was a mob scene at the Garden Valley Town court. Every local news station, talk radio show, and newspaper had a reporter covering the arraignment. The town's court building itself was tiny; the actual courtroom, closet-sized. It was made to handle the disposition of traffic infractions and parking tickets, not homicide side shows.

Lauren came in wearing one of the fifteen black suits she had lined up in her closet for just such occasions. They were her courtroom trademark. Hair tied in a neat, professional bun at the nape of her neck, her tall black heels clicked as she crossed the floor. That normally would've made her cringe, but no one was paying any attention to her. The media people were absorbed in setting up for their sound bites. They were looking for the stars, not the bit players, in this drama. Instead of heading to the right, where the prosecution was set up, she went left to the defense table.

"You made it." Violanti was unpacking his brief case, lining up his paperwork, pencils, and legal pads in a neat array in front of him. Then rearranging them.

A touch of OCD? Lauren thought watching the shuffle. "You didn't think I'd show?"

"It's a woman's prerogative to change her mind. My wife proves that to me on a daily basis. I thought you might have a change of heart overnight. And besides, you said you'd tell me after the felony hearing."

"I heard enough yesterday."

He placed a gold pen to the right of his water glass. "He's a good kid, Riley."

She ignored that comment. "Did you make me my copies?"

Reaching into his perfectly ordered stack, he produced a manila file. "What about your fees?"

"I take it you're handling this pro bono for your godson?"

"Yes."

She took the folder from him. "I want a ten-thousand-dollar retainer. Billed hours come out of that until it's gone or the case is disposed of. Whichever comes first."

He let out a low whistle. "That's steep."

She wanted to let him know that if he really wanted her in on this, he was going to pay for it. And pay a lot. "It's less than what you would charge if he wasn't family."

"I'll cut you a check today. Did you bring me a copy of your license?"

She pulled two pieces of paper out of her pocket and slid them over to him. "One copy and my retainer agreement. I think you'll find it pretty standard."

Now he chuckled. "You're all business today. I'll have my client approve these, sign off on them, and we'll be good to go."

"Thank you."

Turning and looking into the crowd behind her, she saw Anthony Vine sitting in the back row with a man who reeked of *personal attorney to the rich*. Another burly man was standing at the head of the row, blocking it so that no one else could sit down. He was deflecting the reporters who were circling around like a flock of turkey buzzards to get a comment.

"All rise," the bailiff announced and the entire room jumped to their feet. "The honorable Judge Martin Shea is presiding over this court today."

A tall white-haired man in his sixties wearing the standard long black robe ambled out to the stand. He looked tired and pissed off. "I would like to remind our friends from the media that this is a court of law," he began. "Also, I would warn against any outbursts from the gallery. Anyone disrupting these procedures will be immediately removed from the courthouse. Please be seated. We have one case on the docket this morning. Counselor?"

A young assistant district attorney stood, straightened her skirt, and stated, "Lynn Ferro, for the people, Your Honor. We're ready to proceed."

The judge half turned toward the defense table. Violanti addressed him, "Good morning, Your Honor, Frank Violanti for the defense. We're ready to enter a plea for the purposes of arraignment and enter a motion on bail."

The judge nodded and said to the bailiff, "Have the detective bring in the defendant."

Just as the bailiff was about to retrieve David from the holding area, Violanti said, "Your Honor, in light of the strong presence of the media and your allowance of cameras in the courtroom, I would respectfully request that my client be brought in uncuffed, as to not taint the possible jury pool."

"The people object to that, Your Honor. The defendant is charged with homicide, not a parking ticket."

Judge Shea bristled at the ADA and she immediately recognized her mistake. "My courtroom always has adequate security on hand to ensure the safety of everyone involved. Whether it's a parking ticket or a murder. Request granted. Instruct the detective to uncuff the defendant prior to him being brought into my courtroom."

Lauren glanced up at Violanti from her seat and he raised an amused eyebrow to her. The prosecutor seemed to shrink down into her suit a little. Lauren had always thought Lynn Ferro looked like a pale little bird, boney and gaunt. District Attorney Church wouldn't be happy with her, and when he wasn't happy, somebody paid for it.

About five minutes later, Joe Wheeler, Garden Valley's sole detective, led David Spencer in. The fortyish detective was taller than David, with balding brown hair he slicked back with gel. His suit looked slightly rumpled, like he'd slept in it—or maybe hadn't slept at all. Garden Valley hadn't had a homicide in years and its only detective had probably been working overtime since the arrest.

A buzz rose from the courtroom as soon as they came in and camera flashes started going off. Joe pushed David forward, with his hand planted in the small of his back, toward the defense table. David looked confused for a second, then Violanti pointed to the space next to him and David slid in beside his godfather. Joe turned David over to the local court officer, who positioned himself behind and to the right of David.

"No flash photography is allowed in this courtroom," Judge Shea admonished the press. "That's my only warning."

As Joe Wheeler moved toward the prosecution side, he caught sight of Lauren sitting at the defense table. She returned his gaze without a blink. His face pinched up in a mixture of outrage and confusion, and he almost came to a halt before he regained control. He was still watching her as the judge began the hearing. Lauren turned and faced forward, blocking him out.

"Are we ready then?" Judge Shea prompted.

Lynn Ferro cleared her throat. "Your Honor, the defendant, David Ryan Spencer, has been charged in the information provided with one count of murder in the second degree, one count of rape in the first degree." She paused to look at the papers in front of her. "And one count of assault with a deadly weapon or dangerous instrument in the first degree. Copies of the people's complaint have been turned over to the defense and we are ready to speak on bail."

The judge looked directly at David. "Have you been provided with a copy of the charges against you, Mr. Spencer?"

"Yes." His voice was small and shaky.

The judge nodded and made a mark on a paper in front of him. "And having spoken with your attorney, how do you plead?"

David glanced at Violanti, who nudged him ever so slightly. David's voice was a little stronger this time. "Not guilty, Your Honor."

Judge Shea now addressed the entire courtroom. "Let the record reflect that the defendant, David Ryan Spencer, has pled not guilty to the charges as listed. A felony hearing will be scheduled for Wednesday, July 5th, at two o'clock in the afternoon."

Violanti bent forward and recorded the date in his agenda. "No conflicts, Your Honor."

The judge looked over to the prosecutor; she nodded. "The people are fine with that as well."

"I will now hear the arguments on bail."

Ferro picked up some papers from the desk and held them in front of her like a shield. "Sir, due to the nature of the crime, the people request that the defendant be remanded without bail until at least the felony hearing."

Violanti all but rolled his eyes. "Your Honor, my client has no criminal record, has strong ties to the community, and he's an eighteen-year-old kid. The defense requests he be released into the custody of his parent or at least a reasonable bail be set."

The judge sat looking down at the paperwork in front of him, made a note, and then said, "Due to the severity of the crime of which he's accused, I'm going to side with the people and have him remanded without bail. The issue can be revisited after the felony hearing. That is all." He banged his gavel on the desk and stood up as the cameras clicked all around.

Joe Wheeler jumped up, strode across the courtroom, and grabbed David by the arm. David was half twisted, trying to talk to his mother, who had been sitting behind the defense table in the gallery. Joe yanked him to his feet, locking eyes with Lauren for a hot second before she turned away.

"Whoa. Easy, Detective," Violanti warned. Joe ignored him.

"Mom?" David called back in a pleading voice. "Uncle Frank?"

"You mean he's not coming home? Frank? He's got to stay?" David's mother wailed, watching Joe march David away through the side door.

Violanti put a hand on her shoulder as she began to cry. "I told you to expect that, Sarah. We'll argue for bail after the felony hearing."

She was desperately looking back and forth between David and Violanti's face. Her whole body was shaking. "What *is* a felony hearing? I don't understand. What's going on?"

He leaned over the divider that separated the court from the gallery. "Sarah, shhhh." He was trying to get her to quiet down, as the cameras had all zoomed in on them, savoring every tear. "I'll come over to your house tonight and explain everything. Again. Don't talk to anyone on the way out."

But he was too late; reporters were already shoving microphones in her face. Violanti grabbed her and pulled her through the little swinging door set in the divider. "Bailiff, can we use the side door to avoid this circus?"

"Sure, Counselor." He swung the door open and held it for them. Lauren followed them outside, happy to escape the notice of the reporters.

David Spencer and Joe Wheeler were nowhere in sight. Joe must have turned him right over to the holding center officers as soon as they came outside. Church probably arranged for the holding center bus to be at the side door. *Nothing but the best for this sideshow*, Lauren thought.

Violanti put his arm around the sobbing Sarah and led her out into the back parking lot. It was actually the lot for a closed down hair salon next to the courthouse. Violanti had texted Lauren that morning about the secret lot. He was forever visiting different courthouses for his defense cases and knew all the tricks and hot spots for each one. They had both gotten there early to avoid the media. Lauren had played a game on her phone for a little while before going in, to let the media settle inside, like predators do when staking out their territories. The lot seemed to be deserted, except for their two cars.

Violanti turned to Lauren. "I'll get you the retainer and anything else you need tonight. Can I meet you somewhere after you've gone over the paperwork?"

She nodded. "Call me on my cell."

Lauren watched as Violanti crossed the empty back lot, gently comforting David's mother, who could only be a year or two older than herself. Lauren thought she might be forty, but a hard-looking forty. Whether that was from the stress of the last week or a lifetime of bad breaks, Lauren could only guess. Sarah Spencer was still crying as he eased her into his car and pulled out.

The media was probably clustered around the ornate front facade of the little courthouse trying to get their sound bites in. Grateful for the vacant lot, Lauren was about to jump in her Ford when she felt someone come up behind her. She turned.

"Joe."

He was standing behind her with his hands on his hips, feet planted wide apart, that look of contempt plastered on his face she knew so well.

"Shouldn't you be with your prisoner?" she asked. She was in no mood for his bullshit right now.

"He went back to lockup in a patrol unit. The better question is what the hell were you doing sitting with my arrest?"

"It's none of your business, Joe—"

She hadn't even gotten finished with her sentence when he punched her in the mouth. She wasn't ready for it and ended up on her ass next to her car in the parking lot. Her tooth had gone into her lip, blood dripping down her chin. Her hand went immediately for her gun, but it was locked in her glove box. Weapons weren't allowed in courtrooms for anyone but the deputies. Of course, he knew that.

"You son of a bitch." Spitting blood onto the asphalt, she pulled herself up against the car, head reeling. "If I had my gun on me, I'd shoot you right now."

"I don't doubt it. Lucky for me you're unarmed."

"Coward," she snapped through her bloody teeth.

"Stay out of this case, Lauren," he warned, pointing his finger in her face. "You may have everyone else believing you're some super cop, but I know you. I know you."

"You don't know shit about me anymore." She wiped her chin with the back of her hand, smearing it with blood. "Just like old times huh, Joe? Still get your rocks off beating on women."

"Yeah, except now I don't have to lie and say I'm sorry so you'll keep on screwing me." He walked away, leaving her bleeding in the parking lot.

———————

Sixteen years ago, she had met Joe Wheeler in the police academy. He wasn't the sweaty, scorned, ugly man he was now. He'd been young, ambitious, and handsome in a rugged way. He had an authority about him, and it had been comforting to Lauren then to let him take charge, to let him take care of her. She had a two- and three-year-old at home, and it had been hard, being alone, trying to take care of them. Getting the police job was like winning the lottery. Then she met Joe. When she looked at him now, she could barely see even a wisp of the man she had almost married. Over the years his bitterness had morphed him into the awful, sweaty, sadistic person he had become.

When she met him, Joe had been confident and strong. He would run behind her in the academy and encourage her. They studied together at her house while her girls played on the kitchen floor. His dad had been a high-ranking cop in the department and big things were expected of him. The two of them graduated from the academy at the top of their class. It wasn't until they hit the streets that his temper began to show.

Two years and four trips to the emergency room later, they were engaged. She kept the abuse to herself. It was embarrassing: to be a cop and handling domestics when you were getting your own licks at home. She was still new on the job, still afraid of not being taken seriously because of her looks, and Joe was well liked. He always said he was sorry afterward, and reminded her that she knew better than anyone what kind of stress he was under. He convinced her that she provoked his outbursts and that if she could just change, everyone would be happier. He told her that so many times, she really believed it.

She probably would've married him if she hadn't come in to work one night with her eye blackened shut for the second time in two months. Her partner, Earl, an older black man who had also gone to the academy with both of them, asked her what happened. She told him she fell into a door. He nodded his head at the news and left the reserve room without a word. When she went to get into their patrol car, it was gone. Earl came back an hour later. When she asked where he went, he simply said, "I was taking care of some business."

That night, after she got home, she heard Joe's car pull into the driveway of her small, rented house. They didn't live together, but he came by every night after work, usually waiting until her kids were in bed. Tonight he was early. Erin and Lindsey were playing Barbies on the kitchen floor. He turned his key in the lock and came in.

"Girls, go upstairs to your room," Lauren told them. If she thought she looked bad, he looked ten times worse. Stitches dotted across his forehead. His nose was swollen and sitting at an odd angle. From where she was standing it looked like he was missing a tooth.

"What happened to your face, Joe?" Lindsey asked. She was almost five by then, terrified at the sight of the two damaged adults in front of her.

"I fell into a door," he said flatly.

The same lie I tell, she thought studying his face. *Do I look this bad? Is this how everyone sees me?*

Then he added, "Go on upstairs so me and your mommy can talk."

For the first time, Lauren felt scared for her life. Scared of Joe and mad at Earl for making things worse. Her mouth turned to sand as she found herself melting up against the kitchen sink, trying to remember if she left the paring knife in it.

"You see what your partner did to me?" Barely speaking in a whisper, he was inching toward her, clenching and unclenching his fist. His face was twisted up in a snarl of rage. Shrinking back away from him, she tried to make herself small. She heard the engagement ring on her finger hit the sink with a dull *clink*.

Like a cell door closing on a prisoner with a life sentence.

In that second, the fear left her.

"Good," she spat.

"Good? You think this is good?" He was closer now, raising his voice.

She slipped the engagement ring off her finger, held it out, and let it drop to the floor. "Good."

"You really messed up now." He bent down and snatched the ring. "I think your partner just did me a favor. If you think I'll ever take you back, you better be on your hands and knees begging me."

He waited.

Her voice shook with rage. "Get out of my house."

"What?" Now he was a little shocked. He was the one who was wronged and she was throwing him out? This could not stand. She'd pay for that line of thought, dearly.

"Get out of my house." She dipped her hand into the sink and closed it around the knife handle. "Before I call the police and have your ass arrested."

He laughed at her for that one. This was getting comical. "If I walk out that door, I'm never coming back."

She looked at him, really looked at him, the black eye, the cuts and bruises, and thought of her two daughters upstairs. "Good."

35

The only time she flinched was when he threw the key at her.

When she told Earl the next day at work that they'd broken up he looked at her black eye and simply said, "Good."

After that night, Joe spent the next six months groveling, saying he'd get help, sending her flowers, driving by her house. She ignored it all. It was hard at first, but she knew she could never go back. She also knew she would never depend on someone else to defend her again.

She and Earl stayed partners until she made detective and never spoke of it again.

Joe left the department for Garden Valley later that year. They had run into each other from time to time over the years, but she always managed to keep a good distance from him. There was something very wrong deep in his core that told her if he could get away with it, he'd really hurt her. As she stood next to her car trying to stop the bleeding and contain her anger, she silently vowed he'd never get the chance to put a hand on her again.

8

"**W**hat happened to you?" Violanti asked as Lauren slid into the seat across from him. They chose to meet the night of the arraignment at one of those cheesy chain restaurants with rusty license plates and old movie star posters hanging everywhere. They were seated in the Marilyn Monroe booth, with a huge black-and-white likeness looming over them blowing a kiss.

The old lie came back so easily. "I walked into a door."

"My ass. What happened?"

She could tell he wasn't going to let it go. Plunking her folders down on the table, she said as calmly as she could, "Me and Joe Wheeler have some history together. I was engaged to him a long time ago. We had a run-in out in the back parking lot after you left this morning."

"A run-in? You mean he hit you? That bastard hit you?"

"Easy, Counselor. I'm a big girl. I can take care of it."

Violanti's face turned crimson. "I'll have his badge, Riley. I'll carry it around in my pocket like a lucky coin ... "

"No." She held up one hand. "It's over. The best revenge I can get is blowing his case out of the water. My lip will heal."

He paused. "You sure?"

"Let's get something straight. I'm not a damsel in distress. Joe Wheeler will never get the chance to put his hands on me again. Not if he wants to stay alive. Thank you for your concern, but our energy would be better spent on the matter at hand."

"Okay." He waited for her to say something else, but she just looked at him, waiting. "Okay." Letting the issue drop, he opened his briefcase and pulled out a stack of papers. He flipped through them, separating them into piles in front of Lauren. "David punched out at four minutes after nine on the night of the murder. One of the night security guards saw him in the parking lot at around ten thirty going to his car."

"What does the medical examiner's report say about time of death?"

Violanti tossed a copy of the report to her. She read aloud, "It says she was in complete rigor when they showed up. Core body temperature unreliable due to the extreme heat in the car. He approximates time of death between eight to ten hours before she was found. Which tells us nothing." She paged down farther. "Cause of death, ligature strangulation?" She looked up. "Was the ligature found?"

Having anticipated her next question, he tossed a photo down in front of her.

The picture showed Katherine Vine slumped forward, head caught between the steering column and the dash. Her hair partially obscured her face. Pooled on the seat next to her was a white scarf.

"She was strangled with her own scarf?"

He flipped another picture to her, an autopsy photo. The once beautiful Katherine Vine was laid out naked on a metal table. Violanti put the next picture down: it was a closeup of her head and neck. A gloved hand pointed to a faint line that ran around her throat.

"It says here her hyoid bone wasn't broken," Lauren pointed out on the report. "She was choked slowly. Maybe as a sexual thing. I've seen it before, people who get off on being choked. Autoerotic asphyxiation. Did David say she wanted that?"

"No, but I didn't ask specifically. I don't know that he would volunteer that up."

"It's no time for modesty now."

Violanti nodded. "I get that. But he's still just a kid. He'll admit to the straight-up sex, but maybe not the kink in front of you."

"Still," she said, musing over the autopsy photo, "I've seen rapists use this as a means of control. They choke the victim out and bring them back, but sometimes they go too far and kill their victims."

"I think that's beyond David."

"It's defense against murder two. If he accidentally strangled her during rough sex, it's only manslaughter."

"Riley," Violanti said slowly so there was no mistake, "David didn't do this. I'm not looking to make a deal. I'm looking to find out what really happened. Let's not jump to conclusions until we have all the evidence."

She sat back. "Okay. Fair enough. What do we know about the victim?"

"Not enough. I need you to find out everything you can about her." Now he slid an envelope to her. "Here's your check and a copy of your retainer signed by David and me. Time to start earning your pay."

She tucked the envelope in her jacket without opening it. "As it turns out, I may have an inside man on that."

9

Lauren would've lit a cigarette, if she still smoked.

Mark turned over. "I was surprised to hear from you tonight."

She had given up that habit shortly after meeting him. For some reason, after all these years, she craved one now. Lauren had dropped by his law office to talk to him. Just to talk. She caught Mark right before he would have left the office for the day. She had stood poised in the doorway for a second, hand lingering on the knob, absorbing the pictures of his second wife and son. Mark had put them up in the same places where hers had been. *A decade and a lifetime ago,* she chided herself. Then she shook it off and closed the door behind her.

"Lauren?" he had asked curiously, getting up from his desk. She made it halfway across the carpeted floor. Lauren barely had time to respond before he was all over her. She had been the one to suggest the hotel room. Mark had sprung for the penthouse suite after they found themselves bent over his desk, half naked. The desk was hurting her ass.

"An ex-wife can't call her ex-husband? I figured you'd be working late."

"You know I always take your calls, but we usually don't end up in a hotel room."

She smiled. "Are you sorry?"

He propped himself up on his elbow. "No. Just curious. I've been trying to get you in bed again for the last ten years."

"You're married," she reminded him. *You used to be married to me,* she wanted to add, *but you couldn't keep it in your pants.*

His eyes slid away. "So what changed tonight?"

"I need some information."

He groaned and rolled away from her. "I should've known this was too good to be true."

"Don't get all indignant on me. Remember who cheated on whom."

"Ughh. I don't need this." Hopping out of the bed, he pulled his pants on. Mark Hathaway was a year younger than Lauren, and he still had the ability to make her weak in the knees when he kissed her. She wanted to reach across the cover and play with his perfectly styled black hair, thick and wavy. She held back but let her eyes wander over his body, maintained by daily visits to the gym; her eyes fell on the birthmark on his shoulder. She used to kiss that mark when they were being playful. He'd spin around and kiss the freckles on her nose. She shook her head slightly. That was a long time ago.

When she was a little girl, she imagined Prince Charming would ride up on a white horse in his suit of armor. Instead, he pulled into her life in a white Lexus and an Armani wardrobe. Sleeping with him again reminded her of everything she'd lost. Truth be told, this case had been the perfect excuse for her to give in to him. She'd be lying if she said she still didn't think about him, still didn't want him. She had put Mark on a pedestal a long time ago and never took him off.

"Come on, you owe me," she teased, grabbing his arm and pulling him back toward the bed.

"I still love you, Lauren. Isn't that enough? I bought a house for you and the girls. I offer myself to you on a regular basis. And when you finally give in, it turns out you're using me?" His indignation was laughable, considering he was still married to the woman who had taken him away from her. She tried to focus.

"I'm not asking for confidential information. I just remember you mentioning you and your wife were friends of the Vines."

He shook his head. "I tell you I love you and you switch into business mode."

"It hurts less."

He sat back down on the edge of the bed and sighed. "Katherine and Tony? Yeah, we ran in the same circles. Katherine and my wife were friends. I never really liked Tony, too much of a loudmouth for me. No class. Katherine and Amanda were both involved with the same charities. Throwing fundraisers and all that crap."

"What was their marriage like?"

"Are you kidding me? Why do you want to know?"

Lauren pulled the covers up around her and sat up against the headboard. "I'm doing some background investigating for the defense."

"You want me to help you get the kid off?"

"I want you to help me figure out if he's guilty. Come on, Mark. Have I ever asked for anything?"

"No." He frowned. "That's what scares me."

"Just tell me what you know."

"I know that they've been together for a while. Since she was about eighteen, I think. It was quite the scandal at the time. He flaunted her around. He was forty and not quite divorced from his first wife. She got pregnant with the twins and a year later they got married. She was my wife's age, thirty-two."

"So young and sweet."

"Don't be catty. He was very controlling of her, which was one of the reasons I didn't like Amanda to drag me around them. He'd get drunk and loud. She'd never say boo to him. Then Jennifer came into the picture."

Her ears pricked up at that. "Who's Jennifer?"

"Jennifer Jackson, the ex-tennis pro? She's his new spokeswoman for his gyms. Swing into Vines? Come on, you never saw the commercial where the blonde is running around swinging her tennis racket?"

"I must have missed that one."

"Katherine was convinced they were having an affair. He told her she was crazy. He sent her to a shrink. Amanda said she was on about five different medications. She thought Katherine was hooked on pills."

"Is this right from Katherine? Was she just paranoid? I mean, do you know that he was having an affair with Jennifer Jackson or is it just speculation?"

"Not for sure, but all the signs were there. Between me and you, Katherine came and asked me if I knew any good divorce attorneys. I gave her the number of a friend of mine. He's good. And she would've needed someone good. Jennifer Jackson is married to Phillip Dale, the heir to the Dale Automotive fortune. It would've been messy, costly, and embarrassing for everyone involved."

"Did she follow through? Did she call your friend?"

"I don't know. I do know that the last time she went out to lunch with my wife, she talked about a private investigator."

Jackpot, Lauren thought. "She hired a private investigator?"

"Amanda said she did, but who it was I have no idea. I know she was sick about the whole thing. Katherine was a nice girl. She didn't deserve to die like that."

Lauren began pulling her clothes together. "Thanks for the information, Mark."

"Hey." He squinted at her. "What happened to your mouth?"

Just noticing now? "Don't worry about it." She knew he wouldn't.

He touched her arm, running his hand down to her wrist. "Maybe we could make this a running date. Meet once a week, for old time's sake."

Lauren picked up her bag, leaned over, and gave him a lingering kiss on the mouth, her stomach tying itself in knots. She said the exact opposite of what she felt. "I don't think so. But it was nice."

"Come on, Lauren." He was putting his shirt on, buttoning it up as fast as he could as she walked toward the exit.

"One more thing, Mark." She paused in front of the door.

"Yeah?" he asked hopefully. With his hair in disarray and shirt untucked, he looked young and sweet. The way she chose to remember him. His eyes were the exact color of the sky before a storm, a deep, dark blue you could get lost in. She suppressed the urge to go back in.

"Clear your messages often. We wouldn't want your wife to find them. I'll be in touch."

Lauren dug her cell phone out of her bag as she pulled away from the downtown hotel that was conveniently located across from Mark's office building. For a fleeting second, she wondered if he had brought other women to that hotel, but shook it off. She could act like all this was just for information, let him believe that, but the fact was she had been just looking for an excuse to cave in and be with him. She had tried taking the high road for ten years, tried to move on. But she was lonely without the girls and she missed him, missed his smile and his laugh. Missed the way he used to make her coffee in the morning and missed the way he left his shoes at the foot of the bed. Her heart still belonged to him, no matter how hard she wished it was otherwise.

A one-off, she thought. *Just once. I'll be busy with the extra case now, it won't happen again.* And now she sounded like a druggie. She dialed the phone.

"Frank Violanti." He sounded half asleep.

"Violanti, I know it's late, but I got a couple things." She ran through the little nuggets of information her ex-husband had given her without offering up her source. She could hear him scratching it down with a pen in the background.

"Good, this is excellent. I have a couple leads for you to follow up as well."

"I'm working tomorrow until six."

"Well, I'm going to need you to get out to talk to a couple of David's co-workers. I'll email you their names and addresses. I want you to talk to them tomorrow night. I need this done before the felony hearing. I don't know who Lynn Ferro is going to call to the stand yet."

"I'd be willing to bet just Joe Wheeler and the security guard, but you never know."

"Exactly, you never know. Can I count on you to get it done?"

"You got it. What's a few more billable hours?"

He laughed. "That's always been my motto. I can't say you aren't earning your money already."

"Tonight's interview was on me, no charge."

"Why's that?"

She glanced at herself in the rearview mirror, taking in for half a second the messy hair, the wrinkled collar of her shirt. "Let's just say someone else paid for it."

10

J oe Wheeler sat at his desk, holding his cellphone in his left hand, waiting for it to vibrate. He was supposed to be going over the case file. Spread out before him were pictures, reports, and statements. He had to know it all for the felony hearing, backwards and forwards.

But all he could think about was the scene in the parking lot that afternoon. He found himself staring at his cell phone, the tips of his fingers red with pressure, waiting for it to ring. Lauren always brought out the worst in him. There was something about her that provoked him every time he came into contact with her. She was like poison to him. Now she had him right where she could really screw him. He should've never popped her in the mouth. That was a mistake. He had a big cut across his knuckle that was throbbing.

Bitch, he thought. Every time he got something good in his life, she had to come around and mess it up. He had wanted to marry her and she laughed in his face. He'd had to leave the city police because of her crazy partner. Now he had the case of a lifetime, sewed up and perfect, and she joins forces with that troll of an attorney just to stick it to him.

The papers sat on his desk as he fingered his phone, turning it over in his hand. Where was the call from his boss asking what had occurred between them? Why hadn't she reported him right away? Called her boss? Called her stupid young partner? Of course, there were no witnesses; it was just her word against his. But her lip was busted when he left and his knuckle was split open.

Maybe she let it go. After all, she knew she was wrong to stick her nose into his business where it didn't belong. It was her own fault. And she'd always been good about that when they were together. She knew when she was wrong. She knew when she had provoked him into doing something he didn't want to do.

Still, they weren't together anymore. She had walked away and then married that rich attorney who knocked up his secretary. She'd gotten what she deserved. He had loved her and her kids and had been willing to take care of them all. She threw it away to marry money, showing her true colors. He'd written her off after that as the manipulating harpy she was. But now he found himself worrying about her rather than concentrating on what really mattered. His case.

She was provoking him again.

11

David lay staring up at the ceiling of his cell. A white moth bumped into the plastic light panel over and over again, making a dull thumping sound with every attempt. He was in a small room that had two hard beds, one bolted over the other, and a toilet. The upper bunk was empty and the toilet was out in the open so everyone could see you do your business. The guards had let him have some paperback books his mom brought, but they sat unopened on the ledge built into the wall that formed a little desk.

Jail wasn't what he thought it would be. Mostly because they kept him away from everyone else. He could hear other prisoners but he hadn't seen any. They sounded muffled and far away, maybe on another floor. He was told eventually they'd start taking him for recreation time in the basement but that hadn't happened yet.

A guard stopped to peer into his cell, checking on him. David gave him a little wave. He thought the guards were actually pretty decent. He didn't know that was because it was so much easier to deal with a scared kid than a hardened gangbanger. They brought him his food on a tray and took it away when he was done. One of them even asked if the food was okay because he hadn't eaten much. It wasn't gourmet, but it was edible. He just wasn't very hungry. The smell alone in the place was enough to make you sick: a mix of piss, old sweat socks, and pine-scented cleaner. But that wasn't the worst part.

The look on his mother's face as they led him away in court was heart-breaking. Of all the things that were happening to him, that was the worst. Her pain. Ever since his dad died, he was all she had. She depended on him to the point where it felt like he was the parent sometimes. She was already having a really hard time with him going away to college soon, and now this.

He listened to the sound of his own breathing and tried to concentrate on something else.

It was hot in his solitary cell, sweltering, like it had been in the car with Katherine. He couldn't help thinking about his mouth on her shoulder and the way she had cried out. Her nails raking down his back. He remembered about the sweat on her body mixing with his in the heat of the car.

He rolled over onto his side and was glad he was all by himself.

12

"**W**ho punched you out?" Reese asked as soon as she walked through the office door.

"I fell."

"Right. I may have been born on a Tuesday but not last Tuesday."

She fell into her seat and stashed her purse in her desk. "Don't worry about it. I had a little run-in with Joe Wheeler yesterday."

Reese pushed back from his computer, crossing his arms over his chest. "Joe Wheeler did that to your face?"

She and Shane Reese had been partners for the last two years. Reese was something of a rising star in the department. It had been an unlikely pairing. Almost seven years younger than her, Reese was biracial. His mom a black schoolteacher, his dad a retired white firefighter. You'd never know he was an officer by looking at him. He radiated a positive nervous energy, usually reserved for inspirational high school football coaches. He had flawless caramel skin, deep green eyes, and a smile that gave him an impish, mischievous appearance that absolutely mirrored his personality.

When he had come to Homicide two years before, other detectives had been taking bets on how long he would last. Late nights, long days, and dead bodies wore on people. Half of the detectives that transferred in asked for a transfer out in the first six months. Not only had he outlasted everyone's expectations, he excelled at the job. When he asked to do cold cases exclusively, people assumed he was having an affair with Lauren, or that he wanted to. The fact of the matter was that they were a good fit as partners. Their cases started coming together almost immediately. The rumors died off. The partnership lasted.

He was single as well, but the thought of them as a couple had never entered her mind. Lauren thought of Reese as the annoying little brother she never had. Whatever that romantic spark is between two people, they lacked it. They did, however, have a strong friendship. When her sink clogged, she called him. When there was a bat in her basement, he was there with a tennis racket and a goalie mask over his face swinging away. He was the one man in her life she could totally depend on.

She waved him off. "It's nothing. You should see what my face did to his hand."

"What do you mean, it's nothing? It's not nothing. You got assaulted." Reese's face was getting hot. "And you're not going to report it? When I see that weasel, I'm going to knock his teeth out."

"In his town? To his boss? Where he's the only detective? How much good do you think that'll do? And knocking his teeth out will only get you in trouble. I'm a big girl. I can take care of it myself, Reese." She thought if she kept repeating that mantra, eventually it would be true. And truth be told, she was embarrassed. She was a cop and should be able to defend herself. Especially from a guy like Joe Wheeler.

"You shouldn't have taken this job," he spat out. "It's a conflict. We have to work with these same ADAs. The district attorney is going to go nuts when he finds out you joined up with the dark side as a paid underling. And you're getting your ass kicked to boot."

Lauren sighed. His concern was touching, but unnecessary. "No one is more surprised than me. But I met the kid, and I just don't think he did it. My gut tells me something is wrong with the picture."

"Like what?"

"It's too good. It's too easy. It's like someone wrapped it up in a neat package and handed it to Joe Wheeler on a silver platter."

"Who else would've wanted her dead?"

Lauren shrugged. "Hard to say yet. I want to look at the husband more."

"Don't forget we have diversity training at the academy all day," Reese reminded her, then glanced at the time on his phone. "Starting in twenty minutes."

"Aren't the two of us diverse enough?" she crabbed.

"I don't think being Polish *and* Irish counts as diversity," Reese teased, but it was a tense joke, squeezed through his teeth.

"What about having boobs? Doesn't that count for anything?" Lauren knew he was genuinely concerned for her, but their dynamic was to mask it in sarcasm and insults.

"Don't even try to play that card. When I order pizza you love to remind me about my man boobs, so apparently it's not only a lady thing. Welcome to the twenty-first century."

There was a knock on the door and Marilyn, the secretary from the main Homicide office, came in. She was carrying a huge glass vase filled with long-stem roses. "These just came for you, Lauren."

She handed over the giant display and Lauren set it down on the only clean spot on her desk. Yellow and pink, her favorites. "Thanks, Marilyn," she said, looking over the display. Baby's breath dripped down onto her autopsy reports.

"Someone has the hots for you," Marilyn teased, giving a half wave and walking back out.

Reese was intrigued. "Who are those from, heartbreaker?"

Lauren pulled the little white card from the plastic prong stuck in the roses and opened the envelope. It simply read: *I STILL LOVE YOU*.

She tore up the card, dumping the pieces in the trash can next to her desk.

"Well?" Reese prompted.

She grabbed up a blank notebook to scribble down diversity notes she'd never look at again, ready to head to the training downstairs. "It was blank."

13

Riley's coffee was almost cold the next morning when she deposited the brown tote bag Lindsey had gotten her for Christmas last year on the paperwork scattered across her desk. She slugged the last of it down, eager to get a refill from the fresh pot down the hall in the break room. The aroma had hit her as soon as she'd swiped in. For some strange reason she loved the new coffee service the Captain had brought in. It reminded her of the Jamaican stuff she'd downed by the gallon when she vacationed in Montego Bay four years ago with the girls. Just the smell of it made her want to chuck the cheap swill she'd gotten from the drive-thru. So she did.

Snatching up her mug, she strolled down the hallway past the "regular" Homicide squad. She had woken up in a good mood. She had an extra ten grand in her bank account, the Fourth of July weekend was coming up, and even though she usually worked it, the holiday always marked the real start of summer for her, since it could stay cold in Buffalo well into May sometimes.

"Morning, Lauren." Mario Aquino lifted a hand in recognition as he dug through a gym bag on the floor. The sixty-year-old still hit the gym every morning before the start of his eight o'clock shift, dyed shoe-polish-black hair glistening from the shower. The squad room was already buzzing. A late-night shooting had called in half the manpower, but the victim had survived. A twenty-two-year-old gang banger shot twice in the head at point-blank range, he wasn't even unconscious in the emergency room, he just sat there with a bandage wrapped around his melon and told the coppers nobody shot him.

Still, the squad had to come in out of bed, process the scene, gather up witnesses, and start a neighborhood canvass. Now the sleep-deprived detectives were finishing up last night's shooting and jumping right into today's shift. Lauren could hear Marilyn, the squad's secretary/report technician/mother hen, deftly answering the phone lines in the main office, taking one call after another, keeping the unit smoothly floating along.

Glad I got off that boat, Lauren thought, filling her mug to the brim, taking a sip, and then topping it off again. *That pace had been killing me.*

The swipe lock clicked and Reese came strolling in. "Hey," he called lifting a bag in each hand, "can you bring me a cup? My hands are a little full right now."

Biting back her usual snarky comment, she grabbed a mug from the drying rack over the sink. "Okay, but check the messages."

He pushed back the baseball hat on his head with his forearm, almost whacking himself in the face with a plastic bag filled with God knew what. "Yeah. Two creams, two sugars, please."

She reached for the fridge handle. "I know. I know." A long time ago Lauren had been a waitress for almost a year. Sore feet, blistered hands, and a pocketful of dollar bills had helped motivate her to take the police exam. Maybe that's why she loved the smell of coffee so much—it reminded her of how far she'd come, from slinging it to pay the bills to sipping it by the ocean in an expensive resort.

"Good morning," Joy Walsh called as Lauren walked by with two steaming mugs of java. Joy was dragging herself in with the rest of the squad, her haggard face advertising her lack of sleep.

"Did you do the post from the DOA yesterday?" Lauren guessed.

Joy paused in the doorway of the squad room, short brown hair sticking up at odd angles. That wasn't lack of sleep; she always looked like she just combed her hair with a fork. "It was a natural, like I thought, but you never know, right?" *Post* was short for postmortem, or autopsy, in other words. The county medical examiner liked to do his at six o'clock in the morning, so even if you worked all day and all night, you still got to have your morning cup with Dr. Kogut, the ME, if you caught a body in the previous twenty-four hours.

"Right. Have a good one," Lauren shot back, shouldering open the door of the Cold Case office, balancing her two coffees like a pro.

The door shut behind her, cutting off any reply. Reese looked up, "Thanks." He reached for the mug Lauren was holding out to him.

"Double cream, enough sugar to let the stirrer stand up by itself."

He settled back in his seat with a satisfied smile. "You know me so well. Your lip looks better today, by the way."

"Thanks."

"Too bad about the rest of your face."

She sighed. "I work with a toddler." Actually, her lip looked worse, turning a nasty purplish color. She had camouflaged it with a shit ton of makeup that morning. Lauren was an old pro at post-battering concealment.

"Well?" she asked, waiting.

"Well what?"

She cocked an eyebrow. "Messages?"

He snapped forward, sloshing some coffee onto his desk as he grabbed two slips of paper. "Marilyn took these for us yesterday. It was so busy she must have just left them on my desk."

Lauren took the papers. "Same woman?" Carlita Ortiz. It didn't ring a bell.

"Yep. She called in the morning and after lunch. We were out. Mar said she gave her our direct number so I'm guessing we should be expecting a call any second."

Lauren sat at her desk and started unpacking her tote bag—laptop, notebook, power bars, cellphone charger. *Keep your phone close*, Violanti had told her, *I'll text you.* She stuffed her cell in her top drawer. She wanted to get Violanti off her mind and the case she'd just signed up for. The felony hearing hadn't even happened and she was already trying to think of ways to avoid direct contact with the little demon. "I'll call her after I finish my coffee."

"Good, because I have to figure out my Fourth of July plans." He bent over his phone and began rapidly text messaging.

"Could you plan on trying to figure out what's wrong with the air conditioner in here? It's supposed to be a scorcher today."

He nodded, thumbs still dancing. "Someone should tell the weather that we live in Buffalo. They're saying it might break a hundred degrees this week."

The office phone shrilled loudly at Lauren's elbow. "So much for finishing my coffee. And I'll believe a hundred degrees when I see it. It's never been that hot in Buffalo." She grabbed the receiver with one fluid movement, bringing it to her ear. "Cold Case, Riley. How may I help you?"

There was an awkward pause as the caller got themselves together. That happened. When a person thought of calling the Cold Case squad for a long time, years sometimes, and finally got the courage to actually dial the number, it seemed like they were always surprised when someone answered.

"Hello?" A lilting Puerto Rican accent.

"Cold Case," Lauren repeated, "Detective Riley. How may I help you?"

A deep breath in, a beat before the caller could push out her words as quickly as she could muster. "Yes. Hello. My name is Carlita Ortiz. I'm calling about my mother, Vinita Ortiz. She was killed in 1993 on Virginia Place near Allen Street and her killer was never caught."

"Okay," Lauren said, swinging around in her seat to grab the olive green Murder Book off its shelf. The Buffalo Police Department decided in 2008 to digitize all its Homicide files, but started from the most recent and worked its way back. Scanning one entire file could take up to two weeks, with all the notes, reports, and statements, not to mention photographs. As far as Lauren knew, they were up to January 2000, meaning everything before that was not in the computer, not entirely, but mostly still on paper.

So Lauren kept a Murder Book, a hand-typed list of every murder that had occurred in the city of Buffalo from the present on back to 1979. Some enterprising detective whose name was lost to antiquity started the murder book in the eighties and every year the squad's report technician added the last year's homicides to the book. In chronological order it listed the case number, the date of occurrence, the victim's name, the place of occurrence, manner of death, and, if an arrest had been made, the suspect's name. Without the book, it was almost impossible to find cases over twenty years old. It was one of Lauren's favorite jokes. When one of the Homicide guys asked her to look up an old case, she'd smile and say, "Let me check my computer," and start flipping through the pages, just like she was doing then.

"Carlita? I think I found it. July 29th, 1993?"

"Yeah, that's it. I was a baby when it happened. My brother was three. I just want to know what happened with her case 'cause no cop's ever called or talked to us about it."

She had that desperate sound of someone who wanted to beg, right at the start, for an answer, any answer to the questions that have plagued them for their whole lives. "This is what we're going to do, Carlita. I'm going to look up your mother's case and read it over. If you give me a phone number, I'll call you tomorrow and we'll see where we're at."

"That's it?" she asked in surprise, like it should have been harder. Like she should have had to convince Lauren to take a look at it.

We're not the enemy here, Lauren thought. But for some people the police were, she knew. "That's the start," she reassured her. "I look up the case file, give it a read. See what's been done, see what needs to be done, talk over what I've found, and then we discuss how to move forward from here, if we can."

"Move forward? Like make an arrest?"

"I can't answer that without reading the file. But this is how we start. Spell me your name and give me your number and I'll start an active case file."

Her tone had changed from apprehension and disbelief to appreciation as she gave Lauren the information. "I can't tell you what this means to me. The anniversary is coming up and every year it hurts worse. I have a daughter now and what can I tell her about her *abuela*? All these years, you know? And nobody cares. Nobody cares my mother was stabbed in the street and left to die."

"I care. I wouldn't be here in this squad if I didn't. And while I can't promise you we'll solve your mom's case, I can promise you I'll try."

"That's all I want. I just want someone to try."

That's what they all want, Lauren thought scribbling down Carlita's information, *just to know someone is trying.*

"I get choked up every time I hear you give that speech," Reese commented when Lauren hung up. He'd been listening intently to the entire conversation, baseball hat backwards, face contorted in concentration.

"This sounds like a good one. A woman stabbed in 1993."

"Before DNA, huh? Why haven't we looked at this one before?"

Lauren shrugged and dug a ring of keys out of her desk. "I'm about to find out." DNA wasn't widely used in courtrooms in Buffalo until 1996, and even then it was costly and severely limited. Cases that occurred prior to 1996 were often treasure troves of untouched evidence, left sitting in the storage lockup until someone from Cold Case had it brought up and tested, usually for the first time.

Two doors down from her office was the file room. The department had actually spent some money to protect the precious paper files, installing a locked door, climate control, and a video camera so nothing went missing. She turned the key in the lock and inhaled the dusty, cool air that swirled inside the windowless room. Some of the oldest files were already turning to dust, the pages crumbling as you held them, or had become as delicate as tissue paper, see-through and finger-stained.

Cabinet after cabinet filled every space in the room. Years were written in black magic marker on white copy paper and taped to the front of the cabinets. The newer years were up front, the oldest in the far back corner. 1993 would fall right in the middle. She'd looked up so many cases she knew where each year was housed. Some cabinets held more files than others. Some files were actually three, four, and five manila accordion folders overstuffed with paperwork, while others were thin as a church bulletin. It all depended on how much work went into the case. How much the detectives at the time had to work with. Sometimes it wasn't much at all.

She went through the files carefully, so as not to cause any paperwork to get displaced. The other detectives were sloppy with her files, stuffing everything back in and tossing them into their cabinets, most times out of order. Absently she refiled two cases into their proper spots before she came to ORTIZ, VINITA CD#93-82763589 HOMICIDE CASE #93-43.

She pulled the slim file out and smoothed down the front with her palm. Her heart sank a little. Not much. She noticed the very next file spanned two thick folders. The date was the very next day, with the word ARREST stamped across the front in black block letters. The original detectives had caught Vinita's case one night and the next night caught another murder that had yielded a suspect right away. 1993 had been the height of the crack epidemic in Buffalo. The detectives had been swamped with murders, shootings, and stabbings in a drug-fueled turf war. Low on manpower, cases got lost in the chaos. This looked like one of those to Lauren.

She signed it out by case number in the log book next to the door, stopping to smile and wave at the camera to confirm it really was her taking the file. Their captain would probably tell her not to do that again, that it wasn't a joke, but she had to have some fun in that dry, dusty mausoleum of a room, right?

Laugh or you'll cry, she thought as she relocked the door, once again dismayed at the thinness of the file she had in her hand. *This job'll break your heart.*

14

$\mathbf{B}$y the end of the day, Lauren Riley was ready to go home, wrap herself in a blanket, and fall asleep on the couch. That extra ten grand in her bank account reminded her that she had another job to do. She had to mentally put away the new case she and Reese had opened and concentrate on David Spencer now. Instead of driving to her beautiful, cozy house in her gated section of the city, she hopped on the expressway and headed out to the southern suburbs.

She had to remind herself as she fought the traffic on the thruway that being with Mark was a one-time thing. What else could it be besides a distraction from interviewing a seventeen-year-old named Amy Hooper?

Amy Hooper lived in a large, cookie cutter home in a well-manicured subdivision. She was Lauren's number-one stop on Violanti's interview list.

A chubby woman in her late forties with a ruddy complexion opened the door on the first ring. "Yes?"

"Mrs. Hooper?"

Using the door as a shield, she half hid herself behind it. Lauren could only make contact with one gray eye. "Yes?"

"My name is Lauren Riley and I'm a private detective. I was wondering if I could talk to your daughter about David Spencer."

"She already talked to Detective Wheeler."

"I'm a private detective with the defense." She flipped open her identification.

Mrs. Hooper opened the door a little wider and took it from Lauren's hand, studying it carefully.

"Amy doesn't have to talk to me if she doesn't want to, but we're trying to get a full picture of the events of that night."

She handed Lauren back her credentials. "She doesn't know anything."

"I have two daughters myself and I wouldn't ask you to put your daughter into this if it wasn't important."

Mrs. Hooper leaned against the doorframe and let out a heavy breath. "Do you think he did it?"

"If it was your son, wouldn't you want someone trying to answer that question?"

Mrs. Hooper looked Lauren up and down. While Lauren was wearing sleek, black pants and a nicely tailored jacket, she stood with her arms crossed over an old sweatshirt with kittens on the front.

Lauren tried one last time: "Please."

Mrs. Hooper turned her head and called behind her, "Amy! There's someone here to talk to you!" She moved out of the way, motioning Lauren into the living room.

It was one of those front rooms people decorate, but don't actually use. Neat and sterile as a funeral home, the cream-colored couch may as well have had plastic over it. Lauren pictured the mom dusting it carefully once a week, making sure to get the porcelain kitten knick-knacks over the fireplace.

Amy appeared at the top of the stairs that ran parallel to the living room. She stopped mid-step when she saw Lauren in the living room. Her mom spoke up, "This lady wants to talk to you."

"About what?"

Lauren chimed in, "I have a couple of questions about David Spencer. It'll only take a few minutes."

Amy came the rest of the way down and sat on the edge of the smaller couch, across from Lauren. She clasped her hands together so hard her knuckles turned white. She was a tiny girl with long brown hair and a pretty, narrow face. Amy wasn't the homecoming queen, but the girl who was on the homecoming committee.

"I'll be in the kitchen," her mother said and disappeared down the hall.

"I already told that other detective everything," Amy protested.

"I work for David, not for the prosecution. Can you tell me what you know about the night the murder occurred?" She poised her pen over her notepad.

"My parents were out of town, so I had a party in my garage. David told me at work that he was coming. I asked him myself, on my lunch break, and he said he was. Then he left through the loading docks, which was weird. He never came to the party. I kept having Jim Rensel text him, but he never answered."

"Does Jim work with you too?"

"Yeah. Him and David are really good friends. They were on the football team together. Jim thought he was coming too. He was really mad that David didn't show up."

"How long have you known David?"

"We've gone to school together since I moved here in sixth grade. He's a year older than me. He graduated on June 17th, and I'll start my senior year in September."

"Did you ever see the lady that was murdered before?"

She shook her head. "No, but they talked about her. She always bought two of the same game. Jim called her the cougar."

"When you asked about the party, how did David seem?"

"He said he was going to meet Jim at my house. He seemed normal to me. He didn't seem like he was in a hurry, or mad, or upset, or anything. There's been a million graduation parties and house parties since school ended and he went to a lot of them."

Lauren studied Amy's face. The poor girl looked on the verge of tears. "You liked him, didn't you?"

She pulled her hand across her eyes and tears fell down her cheeks. "He's my friend. But I liked him more than he liked me. I can't believe he killed that woman. I was so happy he was coming to my party. I can't believe this happened."

Lauren tried to keep her on track, to focus. "Did David have a girlfriend?"

Amy sniffed and tried to wipe her face with the back of her hand. "Not anymore. He used to go out with Amber Anderson until she ran away a few months ago."

"She ran away?"

She nodded. "Yeah. I guess she was having problems with her dad."

"Who told you that?"

"David. They went out for like, six months, and her dad didn't like it. She ran away before, when we were freshmen. They found her in Atlanta, like, two months later. She was pretty, but she didn't have the best reputation. The guys all thought she was a slut."

"Who were her friends?" Lauren prompted gently.

"She didn't really have any. She just went from guy to guy. Everyone was surprised when David started going out with her. He was too good for her. Dave could've had any girl in school he wanted. No one could figure out why he would date a skank like her."

"Is she still gone?"

Amy nodded again, a tear sliding down her nose, dangling for an instant, then splashing on her couch. "She lived a couple of streets over, on Fairview Street, in the corner house. It has a big fence around it."

Lauren wrote that down. "Is there anything else you think I need to know?"

"I just really thought … I mean, he was coming over, and the last party I had, he kissed me before he left. I thought he liked me too. Maybe a little."

Lauren reached over and patted her hand. Amy grabbed it, holding onto it.

"Do you think he did it?" Amy asked, raising her red eyes to Lauren's. All Lauren could do was tell her the truth.

"I don't know."

15

The house was just as Amy had described it. It could have been the same house as Amy Hooper's, except for the huge white stockade fence around it. It looked odd and uninviting on the well-planned street. The metal mailbox on the curb announced THE ANDERSONS in black letters. Lauren parked her car and walked up to the gate. As soon as she got within four feet of it, a vicious barking started on the other side. It was followed up by the sounds of a large dog throwing itself against the fence.

Lauren jumped back a foot or so. Her hand went unconsciously to her gun, hidden under her jacket, on her hip.

"Bart! Bart! Come here, boy! Is someone out there?"

"Hello? Mr. Anderson?"

"Yeah. Whoa boy, I gotcha. Let me put my dog away," the disembodied voice called from beyond the fence.

"Okay. I'll wait right here." Lauren was convinced the smell of gunpowder drove dogs nuts. Every owner swore up and down their pet didn't bite, but whenever a cop got near them, plainclothes or in uniform, they went into attack mode.

Lauren heard the sound of a door opening, and a screen door slam shut. A couple moments later, the gate swung open revealing a large, sweaty man in paint-stained clothes. He leaned forward, holding onto the fence as if to steady himself.

"Yeah?" His breath was hot and rotten on her face.

"Mr. Anderson, my name is Lauren Riley, and I'd like to ask you some questions about your daughter, Amber."

"Isn't it a little late for that? I filed that report months ago, and no one has bothered to ask anything, not in all these weeks." He pulled a pack of cigarettes from his back pocket, shaking one out.

"I'm not with the Garden Valley Police. I'm a private investigator."

A lighter appeared from another pocket. "I can't afford no private investigator."

"It's okay. Someone else is paying for it."

Backing up, then heading down the walk, she followed him into the house. As he held the door open with one hand, he lit the cigarette dangling from his mouth with the other.

The first thing that hit her was the smell. Dog urine and secondhand smoke. The house wasn't old, but it wasn't taken care of either. As she walked through a narrow hallway she saw a picture on the wall of a girl about sixteen. She had beautiful curly, ash blond hair and sad blue eyes with too much black makeup around them. She paused in front of it. "Is this Amber?"

"Yeah, that's her school picture. I gave one to the police." He led her to the kitchen, where the smell seemed to be concentrated. She sat at the greasy kitchen table he must have been stationed at before she showed up. It was littered with empty beer cans and candy bar wrappers. A cold beer was cracked open, and sweating on the Formica. He sat, taking a slug of it. Behind her, a small television was mounted to the wall and a baseball game was playing. Grabbing the remote from the table, he clicked it off. Ashing his butt in one of the closest beer cans, he turned his attention to her.

"My wife is out grocery shopping with the kids," he explained, as if that would make sense of the utter disgusting nature of his house. "I put the dog in the basement."

She opened her notebook again, spreading it out on her lap instead of putting it on the sticky table, "I'm working for the defense team representing David Spencer—"

"Ohhh. Hold up a minute now. I think you better leave." He dropped the cigarette into the empty can and grabbed his full one.

"What?"

He stood up with the beer still in hand. "I told my daughter that kid was no good. Now she's missing and that rich lady is dead."

"You think David Spencer had something to do with your daughter's disappearance?"

"Hell yes. But apparently, I'm the only one who thinks so. I told the cops when I filed the missing person report that he was the last person she was with. I told her David was no good. I'm glad my wife isn't here. You better get on out." His grip tightened around his beer can.

Lauren stood up. "I'll just leave my card, Mr. Anderson—"

He snatched the card from her hand and threw it at the garbage can in the corner. It missed and lay face-down on the dirty floor. "I hope that kid rots in jail. You better get on out of here."

The dog must have heard the tension in its owner's voice because it started going crazy. Lauren could hear its frenzied barking as she quickly walked out of the house. He slammed the door behind her as she fumbled with the gate latch. Safely in her car, she pulled out her cell phone and called Violanti.

"We have a problem."

16

The next morning Lauren and Violanti sat across from David Spencer at the holding center. He could sense they weren't happy as soon as he was brought in. "What?"

"Why didn't you tell us your girlfriend was missing?" Violanti demanded.

He blinked in surprise. "What?" David repeated, looking from him to her.

Lauren slid the missing person report across the table. "Amber Anderson?"

He picked up the paper, glanced at it, then threw it back down. "She ran away. It says so right there."

Violanti took a deep breath to control himself. "The police listed her as a Possible Runaway. Detective Riley spoke to her father yesterday and he doesn't think too highly of you."

"He's a drunk," David protested. "Amber said he used to do things to her. That was why she ran away the first time. He hated that she had a boyfriend. He hated me. The last time I saw her, she said he beat her up and she couldn't take it anymore. I didn't think she was going to run away, but obviously she did."

"Which begs the question, why wouldn't you tell old Uncle Frank, 'Hey, I know I'm in some serious shit here, maybe you should know my girlfriend is missing?'"

"Because she came back last time. And she's been gone a while. Her leaving didn't have anything to do with me. I didn't think it mattered."

"Didn't you care your girlfriend was gone?" Lauren asked.

"I cared, but we were sort of broken up anyway. I liked her, but I was a senior and all that. I just wanted to have fun. She wanted a serious boyfriend."

"What does 'sort of broken up' mean?"

His cheeks burned red. "She'd call me and we'd hook up. It was like friends with benefits, you know? She knew I wasn't her boyfriend anymore."

Lauren wrote that down. "When was the last time you saw her before she went missing?"

"That's the thing; I saw her maybe the last week in March. We hung out at my house because my mom was at a show with her friends. Everything was fine. That was on a Friday. I tried to call her that whole weekend because she took my favorite baseball hat home and I wanted it back. She never answered me. She didn't show up for school all week and the next week her father reported her missing. He waited at least a whole week. So I thought, if he did that, he must think she ran away."

Violanti leaned back in his seat and rubbed his eyes. "Is there anything else we should know that you haven't told us? Anything that will make me cancel my Fourth of July plans?"

"No, I swear. I didn't even know this was important or I would have."

"I want you to write down all your social media usernames and passwords. Every single one. The prosecutor's office is probably subpoenaing your accounts as we speak. No surprises, right? No pictures of your junk you sent to underage girls?"

He laughed. "No. A guy in my school did that in tenth grade. He still has the nickname Light Switch." His face turned serious. "I never posted much. You just have to be on because you'd never know what was going on if you weren't. None of my friends *call* each other. It's all texting and Instagram and stuff."

"That's good. One less thing to worry about." Violanti pushed a paper and pen to him and he dutifully began to write down the names and passwords.

"All done." When he turned his big brown eyes to Lauren, she could understand why Amy Hooper had a crush on him. He was a good-looking kid who had a way about him, a kind of glimpse you could see of the handsome man he would become, which drew you to him.

The corners of his lips turned down in a slight frown. "Hey," he said with obvious concern, "what happened to your mouth?"

17

"Look at this." Back at work that afternoon, Lauren pointed out a photo to Reese as they stood in front of the mess table where they'd spread out the entire file to look at multiple documents at the same time. She'd been right. It was a good one. Vinita Ortiz had been a twenty-two-year-old single mother of two living on Wadsworth Street in the city's Allentown neighborhood. In the early nineties a string of bars opened on Virginia Street and had become the new hotspot. On a summer night in 1993 Vinita got into a fight with another woman in the now-defunct Ozone Bar. Both women had gotten thrown out by the bouncers. Vinita ended up facedown in the street. No arrest was ever made.

The white tank top she wore was punctuated with three dark spots in the middle of her back. From one of the stains, the handle of a pocket knife stood straight up, casting a shadow across her back under the light of the lamppost overhead. Lauren tapped the close-up. "There. Right there. See? That random blood drop on the victim's skirt? And those fat drops leading away? That's our suspect. She must have cut herself."

"I see it." It was Reese's turn to take the notes, which they both hated because Reese's handwriting looked like hieroglyphics and he used the hunt-and-peck method for typing up reports.

Lauren paged through the evidence reports. Clothing seized. Bloody weapon recovered from the body. The only lab test done at the time was blood typing on the knife. Two different types. The stabber definitely cut herself. What seemed like a slam dunk now was a dead end back then. Without a suspect, a blood type meant nothing.

"We have a statement from the girl she was with that says when Vinita turned her back to leave, the other woman just stabbed her."

"No." Reese picked up the signed statement, complete with a Polaroid picture of the witness stapled to the bottom. "Luz Hernandez stated that Vinita told the woman she didn't want her man, spit on her, and had turned to walk away when the assailant jumped on her."

"Doesn't justify severing her aorta." Taking the full statement from him, she examined the picture. Before the Internet, Homicide detectives would take a Polaroid of every witness and suspect. It was the only way to know for sure who you actually interviewed that day. It showed a young Hispanic female sitting in the interrogation room, mascara running down her face, hands clasped in front of her. Her black hair was permed, sprayed, and teased up in the latest style, while two huge gold hoop earrings hung from each lobe. She looked tiny in the old office chair, like a middle school student someone had dragged in. Only the half-smoked cigarette in the ashtray next to her pegged her as an adult.

"No, but give the whole story if you're going to tell it."

She shoved the statement back at him. "Duly noted. We need to find Luz. We need to find the bartender. We need to find the bouncer . . .

Rufus ... " She shuffled through the papers until she came to the bouncer's statement. Reese picked it up.

"You don't recognize the name of the bouncer? Rufus P. Jackson was murdered two years ago on Jefferson Avenue. I got called in because we were short-handed. It was that deli robbery, remember? He caught a stray half a block away walking his dog."

"I do remember that. Shit." At least Rufus's murder had been solved right away. A car crew grabbed the two gunmen within minutes of the shooting and Reese had gotten tearful confessions from both of them.

"Poor bastard." Reese's green eyes trailed over Rufus's younger self captured in the Polaroid. "His poodle was jumping up and down next to the body trying to wake him up."

Lauren picked up another statement. "It looks like the bartender saw the most, anyway. He was at the far end of the bar in front of the big picture window."

Reese scribbled that down. He hadn't fixed the air conditioner from the day before and he had sweat puddles collecting under the armpits of his navy golf shirt. It wasn't even noon yet. "I already called Henry down in Evidence and he's going to pull the boxes. We'll get the clothes and the knife into the lab today or tomorrow."

Fanning the black-and-white crime scene photos out in front of them, details of the night started to come into focus. Facedown on the pavement of the narrow one-way street, Vinita Ortiz was sprawled with her arms out to either side. Her legs were bent together, as if she had crumpled with the blows, one high-heeled shoe lay a foot away from the body.

Reese made another note on the long, yellow legal pad. After the lab received the items from the Evidence unit, Riley and Reese would meet with the lab staff and go over the scene pictures with them.

Then they could point out exactly what they wanted to be tested and the lab techs could make suggestions as well. Paul, the deputy director of the Erie County Crime Lab, loved cold cases and always met with Reese and Riley personally before assigning a case. And for their part, they never failed to mention the outstanding work the lab had done at press conferences.

Hands on her hips, Lauren took a step back to survey the entire case file. "I think we have a really good start on this one."

Reese threw the legal pad down on the only empty space on the table. "Are you going to call the victim's daughter, or should I?"

She blew a strand of her blond hair out of her eye. "You type up those notes. I'll make the call. We've both got some research to do."

"I got a good feeling about this one," he said, starting to separate the paperwork into piles—statements, lab reports, photos, notes—so that their report technician could make working copies for them. The originals would go back in their folder for safe keeping.

"Me too, but you know it's never as easy as we think it's going to be."

"It never is," he agreed, still organizing. "If it was, it would have been solved the first time around."

18

Luz Hernandez was a hard lady to pin down. Born in Puerto Rico, she moved to New York City when she was ten, eventually following her mother to Buffalo. Over the years she had bounced back and forth between the Nickel City and San Juan, changing names twice between husbands. When she did come back to Buffalo, she never strayed far from her lower West Side neighborhood. But pinning her down to a specific address was tricky. From what Lauren could piece together through public records, her name was now Luz Hernandez Santana and her last known address was on 10th Street.

"I got a line on the bartender," Reese told Lauren, opening the passenger door to their broken down, rusty, unmarked Impala.

"I want to start with Luz." Lauren swung herself into the driver's seat, adjusting it back for her long legs. "If we can't find her, he's next."

Reese slid his sunglasses on against the glaring noonday sun. "You sound confident."

"Her daughter was so grateful on the phone when I told her we found all the evidence and had already put it in the lab. You should have heard her." Lauren inched her way out of the tight parking spot Reese had crammed their car into that morning, easing into the Franklin Street traffic.

"I have heard her. A hundred times, from a hundred victims' family members."

Lauren smirked. "Now you sound like me."

He sank back in his seat. "That would sound like this: 'All guys suck! I'm in this alone! Why is everyone against me?'"

"I don't say things like that."

H glanced at her sideways. "No, but you think it. I can see it on your face."

"Can you see what I'm thinking now?"

He laughed and looked out the window. "You kiss your mother with that face?"

Tenth Street was full of people. On that hot Friday at the very end of June, it was bustling with energy. People were excited for the Fourth of July, hanging American and Puerto Rican flags side by side out their windows, shooting off firecrackers in the middle of the road, congregating together on the front porches that graced the upper and lower levels of the houses lining the street. Cars were cruising slow with their windows down, stereos pumping, the occupants yelling in Spanish to the pretty Latinas dressed in short-shorts.

The smell of barbeque wafted into the open car window as Lauren scanned the faces they passed. Luz's picture was taped to the front dash for quick reference. She'd never had a driver's license, so she probably took care of her business on foot. The only recent photo they had of her was a decade-old shoplifting arrest mugshot. She looked older than her interview Polaroid, which was tucked safely away in the original folder, more worn out. Still, if she walked past them, they'd know.

Her last-known address was a rundown double with a sagging upper porch that looked on the verge of collapse. Sitting on a floral couch surround by plastic kid's toys were two older Latina women sipping beer from forty-ounce bottles. They looked up suspiciously when the Impala came to a halt in front. A pit bull barked furiously in the side yard, held back by a heavy chain around his neck, his jaws snapping as they exited.

"Is he secure?" Lauren called to the women, holding her door open in case she had to dive back in.

"She is. She don't bite. She only bark," the larger of the two ladies told them, knocking back some more of her beer.

"Can you put her away?" Reese was smiling but had his hand on his gun. "All dogs bite, ma'am."

"You the police?" the other woman asked, leaning forward to get a better look.

"Yes, ma'am. No trouble, we just want to ask some questions."

"We don't know nothing about nothing," the bigger lady said, extracting herself from the couch and moving towards the dog. "We mind our own business." She carefully undid the chain from the side of the house and pushed the barking dog into the side door. She folded her arms across her ample chest and stood her ground in the driveway.

Lauren and Reese approached slowly, aware of the gangbangers sitting on the porch next door taping them with their phones, making sure to catch the gold badges on their right hips as they walked toward the woman. The big lady yelled something dismissive to them in Spanish, waving them off. One of the teenagers said something back, but his friend thumped him on the chest and shoved him toward the front door. The whole flock waded inside, letting the rickety screen door slam behind them.

"They're stupid," she told them, looking toward the now empty porch. "They sit and smoke weed and look for trouble. We don't need no more trouble here."

"Ma'am," Reese began, "we're looking for Luz Hernandez. This was her last-known address."

"Yeah?" Arms still crossed, voice hard. "What she do?"

"Nothing," Lauren broke in. "We're here to talk to her about the murder of Vinita Ortiz."

The woman dropped her butt on the ground and mashed it out with her house slipper. "Now? Now you come asking about Vinita?"

"You knew Vinita?" Reese's voice took a more gentle tone.

"*Sí.* Luz is my niece. They were best friends. She had two babies left without a mommy, you know?"

"We know. It was her daughter, Carlita, who called us," Lauren said. "We need to speak to Luz about the night of the murder."

The woman looked them both up and down with a scornful eye. "*Now* you come." She shook her head. "Come with me. Luz's upstairs. She work the night shift, but I know she want to talk to you."

One of the boys from next door stuck his head out the screen and the woman let loose with a tirade of Spanish curses that made him duck right back in. Satisfied the boys would stay inside, the woman turned and tromped up the rotting wooden porch steps. Reese and Riley followed her past her drinking companion, who was still parked on the stained floral couch sipping her forty-ounce beer.

The first thing that hit Lauren's nose when they walked in was the overwhelming smell of bleach. It stung her nose and eyes, making them tear up.

"Sorry, I clean today," the woman said, looking back at Lauren's watering eyes.

"Can I get your name?" Reese called bringing up the rear. The steps were steep and narrow, every cop's nightmare—totally exposed and nowhere to go but up or down.

"I'm Erma Hildago. This is my house. Luz rent the upstairs from me." She stopped in front of a wooden door someone had painted yellow, maybe to lighten up the dark, gloomy hallway, but dirty hands and time had made it look shabby. There was no number on the door, just a handwritten sign taped above the doorbell that read: *DO NOT KNOCK DURING THE DAY! IF YOU NEED ME CALL AND LEAVE A MESSAGE. IF YOU DONT KNOW MY NUMBER FUCK OFF!!!*

Erma pounded on the door with one meaty fist. "Luz? Come open the door. The police are here to see you." There was a muffled reply in Spanish from somewhere inside the apartment and the sounds of heavy things dropping to the floor. The sound of locks turning, then the door swung inward.

It was always unsettling to Lauren, the first time she came face to face with a suspect or witness from one of their old Polaroids. In her mind's eye she saw that young girl, pretty, with teased up hair, dressed for a night out. In that split second the door opened she was faced with the fast forward of a tired-looking forty-something clutching a green bathrobe around her, lines etched like roads on a map down her cheeks, wild black hair cut short and dishwater gray.

"Luz Hernandez?" she asked.

Luz's eyes traveled to her left hip, then to the radio in Reese's hand, which squawked with a call for a car in the vicinity of the convention center. The narrow hallway made it boom and he automatically turned it down.

"These police are here to talk to you about Vinita," Erma cut in. "Talk to them." With that she turned and bumped her way back down the stairs.

Luz opened the door wider and stepped back. "Come in."

Despite being furnished in secondhand furniture and thrift store décor, the apartment was spotless. Luz motioned to the small kitchen, where Lauren took a seat on a rickety chair at a cracked Formica table. Reese stood beside her, his nervous energy better focused that way. Luz picked a coffee mug up from the kitchen counter and sat across from Lauren. It always surprised her how unsurprised people were to have two police detectives in their home. If two cops showed up at her door, she'd be firing questions at them before they set one foot across her threshold, if they even made it that far.

"I'm Detective Riley, this is my partner Detective Reese," she said and slid an official police business card across the bumpy surface to Luz, who picked it up and studied it. Reese fished his out of his pocket and set it down next to her coffee mug. "We're here because we're reinvestigating the murder of Vinita Ortiz. We want to go over the events of the night with you."

"Reinvestigating? No one investigated it to begin with. If a Latina girl stabbed a white girl, every police in the city would have come down on the neighborhood. White girl kills a brown girl? No one cares. I never even spoke to another cop after the night it happened. No one came around." She wrapped both hands around her mug, chipped red nail polish tipping her callused fingers.

"Her daughter, Carlita, called the office. I know this may seem like it's coming out of the blue, but we have restarted the investigation. We have some good leads but we need to go over exactly what happened that night."

She hung her head for a second. "Carlita. I haven't seen her since that night. She was just a baby. Vinita didn't want to go out that night, she was tired, but I begged her. I just got paid from my new job at the old Faciana's restaurant. The one on Niagara Street? It's closed now but I was waitressing there. Good money in tips. I convinced her to leave the kids with her neighbor and come to see the band playing at Ozone."

Lauren had quietly unzipped her leather folio and began taking notes on the legal pad inside. Reese jumped in, "Why don't you start from the beginning?"

"I told the cops everything that night."

"Tell us again," he prompted gently.

"It was still early, around ten, when we got there. We walked, but it was nice out—not like now, not so sticky. A cook at my restaurant was in the band. He said it was ladies' night and it would be a good time." Her brown eyes bored into the center of her mug, as if she couldn't look them in the eye because somehow she was to blame for her friend's death. "I paid the cover for both of us. It was ten bucks, ladies drink free all night, so the place was packed. The band was good and loud, it was wall to wall people. You had to squeeze in between people to get a drink from the bar. I had to go to the bathroom, and Luz stayed back at the bar because we had a tiny spot and we weren't giving it up. We were drinking rum and Cokes and laughing and not bothering anybody." .

She brushed away a tear with the back of her hand, taking a deep breath. "When I come back there's this blond woman—not nice blond like you, but bleached out with dark roots—and she's screaming at Vinita. She's trying to go after her and her boyfriend is holding her back, telling her to calm down."

"Do you remember what he looked like at all?" Lauren asked.

"He was really tall, taller than you." She motioned to Reese. "But skinny. And white. They were both white."

"Would you recognize them if you saw them again?" Reese shifted from foot to foot like he did when he got infused with nervous energy.

Luz shrugged. "I don't know. Maybe. It was so long ago."

"What happened next?" Lauren prompted.

"The bouncer came out of nowhere and grabbed both of them, one in each hand, and dragged them through the crowd to the front door. Then he just pushed them outside. Me and the guy barely squeezed out before he shut the door. But the blonde, she wouldn't stop. She was still screaming about Vinita trying to pick up her man. She was really drunk, staggering almost, and the guy was half holding her up, trying to pull her away. Vinita, she had a temper, and I guess she just had enough. She spit right in the woman's face and told her to keep her man. I grabbed her then and we turned to go. Next thing I know the crazy bitch rushes Vinita from behind. It happened so fast. I thought she was punching her in the back. Then I saw the blood. The lady's boyfriend dragged her off and there's a knife sticking out of Vinita's back."

Now the tears flowed freely as she choked back a sob. Lauren spotted a roll of paper towels next to the sink, got up, ripped off a square, and handed it to Luz.

She clutched it to her face, trying to catch her breath. "I was screaming, screaming, screaming, but the windows were open and the band was playing. No one came, she just laid there, dying. The man took off with that woman. Another couple walking to the bar saw us and came running over. The lady stayed with me while her boyfriend ran into the bar. We were in the middle of the street. How could no one have seen us? How could they let her die like that?"

"Luz," Lauren said mildly, "we're going to try to find out who did this to Vinita. Can you think of anything else that could help us? Did you hear one call the other by a first name?"

She shook her head. "It all happened so fast. One minute I was in the bathroom, the next I'm kneeling in the street watching Vinita die."

"Can you tell me anything else about the woman? How old? How tall?"

"She was maybe in her early twenties. She was my height, five-four or so, but a little chubby, like she had a gut. She wore a lot of make-up but it was sloppy, you know? The way drunks are sloppy. Him, I just remember being tall and skinny and wearing a jean jacket. I think I told the police that at the time."

"You did," Reese reassured her. "We just need to hear it again."

"I hope you find that bitch." Luz was shredding the paper towel now. "I hope you find her and she rots in jail. Vinita just wanted to listen to a band. She didn't want no white boy scarecrow. She died for nothing."

Lauren reached over the table and put a hand on her arm. "We'll do our best. I promise."

On the ride back to headquarters Reese was unusually silent. Lauren knew that meant he was mulling something over in that big melon of his. Finally, he asked her point blank, "Do you think it's true? Do you think the detectives would have tried harder if a Puerto Rican girl stabbed a white girl?"

"Then or now?"

"Either."

She sighed as they passed City Hall. "Maybe just a little true."

19

The Fourth of July fell on a Tuesday, so Violanti and Lauren spent the entire morning on Wednesday prepping David for the felony hearing. He wouldn't have to testify, but he had to be prepared for what the prosecution was going to say that day. Violanti cautioned David not to utter a word, no matter what was said on the stand, and if he had anything to relate to him, he should write it on a legal pad. The good news was that Katherine Vine's memorial service was that day, so the media would be split between covering both events and Anthony Vine and his entourage wouldn't be there.

David was nervous and Violanti went out to get him a soda to calm him down. He turned to Lauren as soon as he walked out. "Thanks for doing this for me. My uncle says you two don't like each other."

"I'm interested in the truth, David. Uncle Frank and I will go on hating each other long after this is over," she assured him. "Believe me. For now, we can put most of our differences aside and do our jobs."

"I still don't understand what today is about."

"It's called a felony hearing. The prosecution has to present just enough to convince the judge that a felony was committed. Which they obviously do. Usually the defense waives the hearing and the next step is a grand jury. Your uncle is going to run it because he gets to cross-examine the prosecution's witnesses. It's like a little fishing expedition."

"Don't they have to turn over everything anyway?"

"That's called discovery and we won't get that until after the grand jury, so this is our chance to see what they have so far and start building your defense."

He nodded. "I know Uncle Frank explained that to my mom, but she just doesn't get it. She's a wreck. I'm all she has."

"Where's your dad?"

"He died in a car accident when I was eleven. Uncle Frank was my dad's best friend since high school. He tries to be, like, a father figure to me or something. But he's not my dad, you know?"

"I'm sorry to hear that." And she was. Being a single mom was the most difficult thing she'd ever done. Being a kid without a dad was even harder, she imagined.

David shrugged. "Frank really took care of my mom after it happened. She went to pieces, just like now. He helped get her a job in his friend's law firm and he helped pay all the medical bills. I hate that he has to do this for me. He's always having to bail us out."

"I'm sure he doesn't mind. He just wants to help you."

"Everyone's always trying to help me. You don't even like him and you're still helping me. I'm supposed to be taking care of my mom. Not Uncle Frank. I'm supposed to be the man of the family." The frustration in his voice was touching. He wanted to do the right thing.

She studied his face for a second. "That's a lot to take on for a kid," Lauren replied gently.

He sighed and began tearing the edge off one of his legal papers. "I'm not a kid anymore, Detective Riley."

Violanti came in with the soda and put it down in front of David. "How are you feeling?"

He leaned back in his seat, away from Lauren. He popped open the soda and took a gulp. "Scared. But Detective Riley explained things a little better."

"I explained them to you six times already."

"Yeah, Uncle Frank, half the stuff you say sounds like legal bullshit. You're like a used car dealer or something."

Lauren sank back in her chair and smirked at Uncle Frank.

20

The felony hearing went exactly as they thought it would. First, they put the medical examiner on, who described Katherine Vine's injuries and the cause of death. Next they put Jose Franco, the night security guard, on the stand. He recalled seeing David in the parking lot approximately an hour and a half after the boy's shift ended. Violanti had no questions for either of those witnesses.

Joe Wheeler was the last one to be called up to the stand. Because he was a witness he had to sit out in the lobby during the hearing while the others testified. Now he strolled up to the front of the courtroom in his black suit, hair slicked back, with a smug look on his face. He didn't make eye contact with Lauren or even glance in her direction. The prosecutor went through Joe's case with him step by step. He secured the scene, got phone records, interviewed the witnesses, developed his suspect, picked him up, and, after consulting with the district attorney, arrested David Ryan Spencer for the murder and rape of Katherine Vine. Violanti was furiously scribbling notes on his legal pad the entire time Joe was speaking.

After what seemed like an eternity, Lynn Ferro turned to the judge and stated, "No more questions, Your Honor."

Judge Shea addressed Violanti now. "Mr. Violanti, your witness."

He jumped up in that Jack Russell terrier way he had and walked over to the witness stand. Joe looked down on him with an air of total confidence. He was convinced that he had presented an air-tight case that was only going to get better by the time Frank Violanti was stupid enough to take it to trial.

"Just one question, Mr. Wheeler."

Joe nodded in triumph at Violanti's lack of a defense strategy.

"Can you tell me what happened to Detective Lauren Riley's face?"

Lynn Ferro jumped up in her seat. "Objection! Relevance and calls for speculation."

Violanti crossed his arms, glaring at Joe as he spoke. "I assure you, his answer would be firsthand and not speculative."

Joe's face had fallen into a look of panic.

"Mr. Violanti," the judge began, "I'm aware of your courtroom antics. Miss Riley's appearance today has no relevance to the matter at hand. Objection sustained. If that was your only question for this witness, you may step down, Detective Wheeler."

"Thank you, Your Honor," Violanti said. "That was the only question I had." He winked at Lauren as he walked back to the defense table. Joe Wheeler practically ran from the witness stand, slamming the door to the courtroom behind him.

21

Bail denied again, the matter was set for grand jury. Sarah Spencer managed to hug her son before an officer came to take David back to the holding center. Joe Wheeler was nowhere to be found as Lauren and Violanti made their way through the throng of reporters to his car. Violanti wasn't taking any chances of another encounter with Joe. Picking Lauren up that morning in his private vehicle, he had parked it right in front of the courthouse, so as not to repeat any more abuse from the arresting officer.

Lauren got in next to Violanti as the cameras swarmed all around them. They both had *no commented* all the way to the car. Now Lauren turned to Violanti. "I gotta hand it to you, Violanti. I didn't see that one coming."

He grinned his little-boy smile and pulled away from the curb. "Neither did he. Threw him off his high horse, the dickhead."

"You know something, Violanti?" Lauren half twisted in her seat to face him. "You really know how to work a witness. When you do it to me, it's not so funny. Today, it was priceless."

"That's the nicest thing you ever said to me."

She smiled. "And it's the nicest thing I ever will."

Letting herself into her house a half hour later, the stillness caused a pang in Lauren's heart. When Lindsey and Erin were growing up the house was a buzz of activity. Now it seemed too big, too empty for just her. Sure, the girls called home at least once a week to tell her how things were going. But when both of them had decided to do summer internships, Lauren's heart almost broke. It was bad enough that they both were away at the same time, but that was adding insult to injury. For nineteen years she had put her daughters first, and now all she had was a great big, beautiful, empty house. Thanks to Mark.

Mark Hathaway had paid the entire mortgage off when he divorced her—out of guilt, she assumed. It had saved her a ton of money over the years, enabling her to put away for the girls' college tuition. Mark still spoke with both of the girls, which his wife, Amanda, hated but tolerated. He even came all the way to New York City to see Lindsey's Irish dance team compete in the Nationals when she was thirteen. She didn't like to admit it, but Mark was always there for the girls. In later years it was just birthday and Christmas presents, sometimes the occasional phone call, but he never cut the strings with them.

She hadn't seen the divorce coming. One day, he'd come home from work and announced he was taking them all to Disney. Lauren called into work and he had whisked them first class to Orlando. They'd stayed the weekend and come home happy and tired. The next week Mark blindsided her, telling her he'd gotten his secretary pregnant, and he was moving out. Or more precisely, Lauren told him he was moving out.

They'd had three years together: One dating, one engaged, and one married. It hadn't been enough. It still wasn't enough. She felt cheated. Hell, she *had* been cheated.

Still, Lauren couldn't help sometimes remembering how she and Mark spent their honeymoon in Paris, holding hands under the Eiffel Tower. She'd thought to herself, *How could this gorgeous, rich, wonderful man want me?* She had been under the delusion they'd been truly happy together. Just to have it all thrown in her face.

She was vaguely thinking of him when her phone rang. It was almost like he could hear her thoughts and now he was on the line. "Shouldn't you be at work?" she asked him, the old familiarity flooding back to her.

"I went to Katherine Vine's memorial today. Can I come over? I think I found out something you can use."

I can be strong, she thought after she hung up with him. *I had one moment of weakness in all these years. I'm only human. It was a mistake. We can still talk, and be friends, and that's it.*

She poured two glasses of wine as she waited for him to come over.

22

"**I** love what you've done to the place," Mark said stepping into her living room.

Stop it, she thought. *Why are you making small talk?* Watching him, Lauren could sense how at home he seemed. He had lived there with her and the girls for a little over a year.

Lauren remembered house hunting together after their engagement and finding this place. He had loved it right away. At the time, he was just starting to make a name for himself as a corporate lawyer. Mark was a trust fund kid who had never wanted for anything in his life. Walking in, holding Erin's hand, he told the realtor, "We'll take it," without even knowing the price.

"Thank you," was all she could manage to say without the bitterness creeping in.

He peeled off the jacket of his lightweight, gray pinstripe suit and handed it to her. "It was so humid in the church, a woman passed out."

"Wine?" She motioned to the table and hung his jacket in the front hall closet, just like she had when they were married, after he'd come home from the office. While she had gotten new furniture over the years, most of the house had not changed. All around were reminders of their life together, from the antique clock over the fireplace to the custom crown moldings that ringed the ceiling, to the Tiffany-style floor lamp with its ornate glass shade in the far corner. All picked out by them, together, for the life they had planned to have in that house. Now the furnishings were still there and he was gone.

He took the glass between his fingers and settled back into her couch. "I thought today was your day off?"

"I had to go to that felony hearing." She took her suit jacket off too. She didn't bother to hang it up, draping it over the back of the wing chair instead, and sat down. It felt to Lauren like he had never left, like she'd dreamed it all. There he was sitting across from her, discussing his day like they had when they were still married. The girls should be upstairs doing their homework. She would've rushed home to have dinner ready. Everything was perfect. Except it wasn't.

"What happened at the memorial?" Lauren was cradling her own glass of wine between her fingers. She was trying to snap out of it. To focus on the case and not on him.

He laughed. "All business." He took a drink and went on, "After the service at the church, there was a brunch at Carlotta's. Amanda and I went—"

"Where was little Mark?" she interrupted. Amanda's very name caused an ugly jealousy in her. Raised the eternal question: what did Amanda possess that Lauren didn't? Why were they still married whereas she and Mark hadn't even made it to their second anniversary?

"At day camp," he snapped. "Do you want to hear this or not?"

"I'm sorry. Go on." She was sorry, a little. *No need to be resentful years later,* she thought.

"After brunch, Jeffery Peters pulls me aside. He's one of the partners at Jenson, Peters and Grace. He said he saw you on television and he wants to set up a meeting with you and one of his investigators. Apparently, this guy was working for Katherine Vine. He gave me his card to pass on to you." Mark reached into his pants pocket and pulled out a business card. He set it down on the table. "He said there's more to this than some kid. The investigator's number is on the back."

"Was Anthony Vine there?"

"He was there with his sons. Poor kids. They looked devastated. Jennifer Jackson was there too. She and her husband were sitting in the front row with the family."

"In the front row? Interesting." Lauren got up and went around the table to get the card. When she reached for it, Mark grabbed her wrist and stood up. He brushed the hair back from her face and kissed her, erasing whatever thought had been running through her mind.

The house was quiet, the only sound Lauren could hear was her own heart beating. Pulling him down onto the floor, she fumbled with his buttons. His mouth was on her throat, her lips, her chest. "Lauren," he whispered in her ear, as she twisted underneath the weight of his body. He slipped her pants down and she kicked them away. The hurt, the jealousy, the questions, buried themselves in their ache for each other.

They made love on the floor as the sun sank down into evening. When they were both spent and exhausted, they lay in each other's arms, wrapped in a throw blanket from the couch.

"Why are you doing this to me?" she asked softly.

"We should try to be together, if we can manage it." He wrapped a strand of her hair around his finger, then let it uncurl off.

She propped herself up on her elbow to look down on him. "What is that? Your wife gets you and I get the crumbs? I can't do that."

"I love my son. I don't regret that. I don't regret him. And I would do it all over again just for him. You always put your girls first; you know what that's like. I have to put him first. I do love you. I always have." He slid his hand around her neck and pulled her down for a lingering kiss.

Pulling back, she studied his eyes. "You love your wife."

"Not like I love you."

"But you're not going to leave her, either."

He paused, like he was going to say something else, then thought better of it. "Not yet."

The simple truth of it was enough to make her cry. She knew she would give in to him, take his crumbs. This was what she had been afraid of, letting him back in and not being able to keep him. That was why she had resisted so long his offers of dinner or drinks. The feeling of his fingers entwined with hers brought back such memories. Memories of what they could have had.

"So now what?" she asked.

"Now I go home to my wife and son and I stay one hundred percent honest with you and we stay together until we have it figured out."

"That sounds like a great deal for you. Not so hot for me."

He kissed her again. "It's the best I can do right now."

"The best you can do is make *me* the other woman this time?"

He pulled his face up to her and looked into her eyes. "I won't hurt you. Not now. Now that I know what I lost in you. I'm here for as long as you want me."

"What if I ask you to go away? I don't want just a piece of you. I don't want this."

"If we could stay away from each other, we would have. Some people go their whole lives and never feel this way, Lauren. I know it sounds stupid. We had passion and we were exciting. I wish I had met Amanda first so I could have had this last."

"That's right off a Hallmark card. You make it sound so pretty. We weren't married long enough for it to get boring. You don't know what you did to me when you left."

"I know what I did. You don't think I know it every day? Amanda knew I wanted kids and you didn't want any more right away. You don't think I think about being weak and getting trapped by her? And I'm not blaming her because I let myself get trapped, but what do you think that does to a marriage? Amanda and I both know that if it wasn't for our son, she and I wouldn't be together."

There was a long silence that neither of them wanted to break. It was easier to pretend things were different. It was easier to think the only reason Mark left was because he accidently knocked up his secretary. It was easier to enjoy the moments of this fantasy before the reality set in again. The reality was he was a cheat. Plain and simple. He cheated on Lauren and now he was cheating on Amanda. She tried to rationalize that at least she knew. She wouldn't be caught off guard this time. She could protect herself from being hurt.

"Do you have to go?"

"Not yet."

She settled back into the crook of his arm and traced the plains of his chest with her finger. He would have to leave, just not yet. She had him again for a few more minutes. "By the way," she added, "thank you for the flowers."

His brow creased. "I didn't send you any flowers."

23

Joe splashed his face with cold water and looked in the mirror. He was in his house with the air-conditioning cranking and still sweating like a meatloaf. His shirt was almost soaked through. That runt of a defense attorney had pulled a cutie on him in the courtroom that day. A cutie, that's what the city cops call a bullshit move. Lauren's face didn't even look that bad. No stitches. It wasn't even really an assault. But that little jerk-off lawyer had pulled a cutie and caught him off guard. He'd know better next time.

Still, there was not much left to do on the case from his end except testify in front of the grand jury and get the toxicology reports. There was no defense this kid could possibly use against the evidence they had. He might as well plea to the charge and reserve his room for the next twenty-five years to life.

What he couldn't figure out, no matter how hard he puzzled over it, was why Lauren was on the case. Why Violanti would even hire her. And why she would even take it. She was supposed to be a hot-shot now. The best. What a joke.

He glanced at the time on his cell phone. It was almost nine o'clock. The sun was setting later now and he had to wait until it was dark. He walked out of his house and drove to the city. Lauren's house was in a gated community. That wasn't a problem. He flashed his badge to the security guard and he was allowed to pass. It didn't matter; he wasn't going to stop by. He was just going to do a little surveillance. The first thing that caught his eye as he passed the beautiful gray Colonial was the silver Lexis parked behind her Ford. He looped around and pulled a pen from the visor. He managed to jot the plate down without having to stop. He nodded to the security guard on the way out. It was getting late; he'd run the plate first chance he had alone at the station.

24

Mark Hathaway left around ten that Wednesday night. Lauren had crawled in bed, tired and happy. She didn't want to stop and think about what she was doing. If she did, she might end it and she didn't want to end it. She wanted Mark. Even if it was only once a week or once a month, she would settle for that. She wanted to be selfish instead of noble.

She woke up early the following Saturday morning, enjoying the sun pouring through the kitchen windows after two days of spinning wheels on Vinita's case. Truth be told, the kitchen was her favorite room in the house. She wasn't much of a cook, but the back windows overlooked her garden, which was in full bloom. Shasta daisies, black-eyed Susans, and yellow rose bushes mixed in her rock garden. They were simple sturdy plants that reappeared every year like magic. Sometimes she would take her coffee outside and sit on the back patio to enjoy the quiet in the middle of the city. A mile in any direction would take you out of her gated oasis and back into the urban chaos.

Right there, in her back garden, you would think you were the only person in the world. Watching her girls play among the flowers as they grew up had been her favorite pastime. Back there, with her watching, nothing could touch them. Now she could sit in her kitchen, sipping her Jamaican Blue Mountain, and call back those memories and her daughters didn't seem so far away.

Lauren sat waiting for the phone to ring, as it did every Saturday morning. Lindsey and Erin would call and check in. And they did, right on time. Lauren made sure that she was home for each call, waiting every weekend with coffee in hand. One would call and then the other would click in and they would three way. It was as close to being with her girls again as Lauren could get.

"I think I'm going to get my tongue pierced," Erin told her, then waited for her reaction.

"That's fine, I'll get your face tattooed on my forearm the day after you pierce it. Maybe I'll use that third-grade picture of you missing your front tooth."

Lindsey snickered into the phone. "Don't do it, Erin. You know she'll get the tattoo."

"Linds, cut it out. Mom, you wouldn't."

"I'm just telling you so you won't be shocked."

Erin wisely dropped the subject.

Lindsey was coming home for the weekend in mid-August. Erin wouldn't be back until the last week of August, right before school started, hopefully unpierced. After a half hour of gabbing, they said their goodbyes. Lauren felt the emptiness of her house creep in as she hung up with her girls.

She waited awhile after her Saturday updates from the girls to call the number scrawled on the back of the business card. She wanted to mull over the events of the last few days. Before she could start to beat

102

herself up over Mark, she decided to get back on the David Spencer case. That was the best Band-Aid she had.

When the man answered the phone, she recognized the name. Bill Kowalski had been on the Buffalo Police Department for thirty years. Now he was doing divorce investigations for Jenson, Peters and Grace. He recognized her name too; although they had never met, they ran in the same circles.

"Listen kid, she paid up front and now she's dead and I have the report I prepared for her. I'd be remiss if I didn't contact you. Can we meet?"

They agreed to meet up at a coffee shop in the theater district at one o'clock. Around noon the skies clouded up and it began to rain. Flocks of pigeons rose from the streets as Lauren drove through the steamy downpour. Caught by the surprise deluge, the birds darted into trees and bushes. Rain popped off her windshield in little bursts as her wipers furiously tried to push the water away.

The shopkeepers began rounding up the outside tables and chairs in front of the cafes and bistros as she parked her car at a meter. She checked herself in her rearview mirror. Lauren wore a blue sleeveless shirt and khaki crop pants, her hair swept up in a ponytail. It felt good to be in casual clothes after wearing suits all week. She grabbed her umbrella, then hopped out of her car and into the rain.

She made sure she called Violanti before she went to the meeting and told him about this new tip. Lauren left out the part about Mark. That was none of Violanti's business. The tinkling of bells greeted her as she pushed the door open, shaking her umbrella out under the awning before she went in.

As soon as she stepped in the door, Lauren recognized Bill. Cops, even retired ones, have a certain air about them. He was in his early sixties, sitting with his back to the wall of the small java shop, drinking black coffee. He was built like a prizefighter, his shirtsleeves rolled up over his forearms. He had his huge hands wrapped around the coffee mug, making it look like it was from a kid's tea set.

Back in the day, Bill Kowalski had been a legend in the Homicide office. He had retired from the city police force about two years before Lauren made detective. Still, his stories were repeated to the new guys in the squad. Lauren heard the other detectives tell how he used to wear his trademark black trench coat, no matter what the weather, to homicide scenes. How he'd have a cigar hanging out of his mouth during autopsies, dripping ash onto the bodies. How he refused to go to a semi-automatic when the city switched over, choosing to wear his six-shot dangling precariously from his waist in an ancient holster instead. How he once dangled a child molester by his ankles from a third-story window.

Some people said he spread that last rumor himself.

Now he sat with a shiny brown briefcase and a cell phone on his hip, instead of a revolver.

He waved her over. The aroma of the brewing coffee engulfed her as she walked toward him, making the shop inviting after the downpour. Sliding into the booth across from him, she ordered a bottle of water from the waitress who came by. Outside, the rain was pounding against the sidewalk. Lauren leaned her umbrella against the wall.

"Don't you drink coffee?"

She smiled. "I already drank a whole pot. My heart might explode if I consume any more caffeine."

He took a long sip from his mug and said, "They didn't make cops as good-looking as you when I came on the job."

"Thanks." If it had been anyone else, she might have been offended. He was from a different time, a different way of policing. "They don't make cops like you at all, anymore."

He chuckled at that one, then got down to business. "Listen kid, I normally wouldn't do this for a defense team, but I asked around and the guys I know said you were okay, and I think this stuff is important."

"You were working for Katherine Vine?"

"Yeah."

"She was divorcing Anthony?"

"That I don't know. She approached Peters and said she wanted to be sure before she made any decisions. The law firm gave her my name and she hired me about a month and a half ago."

"What wasn't she sure of?"

"She wanted to be sure her husband was fooling around with Jennifer Jackson."

"Was he?"

He slid a picture over to her. "What do you think?"

The picture was obviously zoomed in from a distance through a window. It showed Anthony Vine with his fake tan and nothing else. He was kissing a blond woman on a bed.

"How do you know it's Jennifer Jackson?"

"Look at the next one. I got a clear shot." The next photo showed Anthony Vine and Jennifer Jackson walking out a door. She had a gym bag over her shoulder. It was the same bag that was sitting next to the bed in the first picture.

"Where were these taken?"

"It's a condo he keeps on the waterfront. He bought it about two years ago. Supposedly, it's for business guests."

Lauren looked up. "Katherine saw these?"

"The day before she was murdered."

"Did she tell you what she was going to do?"

"She told me she was going to confront him. I told her it wasn't a good idea until she had retained a lawyer. She told me to hold onto these and she'd call me this week, when she figured out what she was going to do."

"What did she need to figure out?"

He held up another document he had fished out of his briefcase. "This is a copy of their prenuptial agreement. It limits her to a one-time cash payout of seven hundred and fifty thousand dollars. The poor kid didn't know any better when she signed it. She was very young at the time."

"She would've gotten child support on top of that."

"That's what I said. She told me Vine had threatened to seek sole custody of the kids if she ever left him. He'd been sending her to a shrink for two years and she was on all kinds of medication for depression. He wanted to make her think she was crazy for suspecting he was having an affair. He tried to control every move she made."

"Do you think she was depressed?" Lauren was interested in what a guy like Bill thought of Katherine's mental state.

"If I was married to a scumbag like that, I would be depressed too. She loved those kids. She wouldn't put them through a custody battle if she didn't have to. I think she would've tried to work things out first."

"So you think she confronted him about the affair?"

"I don't know. I just think it's quite a coincidence she conveniently gets murdered by some kid the day after she gets proof of her husband's affair. And I don't believe in coincidences." He pulled a stack of papers out of his brief case. "I made copies for you. She was a nice girl. She didn't deserve to be married to that guy and she sure as hell didn't deserve to get strangled. I hope it helps."

Lauren took the copies and put them in her bag, "How did she pay you, if you don't mind me asking?"

"Cash. She said she had to pawn some of her jewelry so he wouldn't find out. She only had a credit card so he would always know how much money she spent."

"What a prince."

"Yeah. But listen, I wouldn't be surprised if he was keeping tabs on her in other ways too. She said he always knew where she went, where she'd been. We had to meet behind her hair salon. At first I thought she was just being paranoid. Now I'm not so sure."

"You think he had a GPS on her car she didn't know about?"

"I do. He and that Jennifer Jackson both had a lot to lose if their affair became public. Katherine said Jackson had also signed into a prenup. And her husband is worth multimillions. A lot more than goofy Anthony Vine. I think that's why Katherine might have thought she had a shot to end the affair. Jackson had even more to lose than she did. Maybe Katherine thought if she told Anthony she had proof, he would stop making her go to the doctors and straighten up."

Lauren considered this. "Which begs the question: if I were a good-looking wife of a multimillionaire, why would I risk everything to roll in the hay with a middle-aged gym rat?"

Bill shrugged. "Boredom? The thrill of getting caught? No chance of Anthony Vine ever convincing Jennifer Jackson to leave her husband, that's for sure."

"Is there anyone else you can think of that I should talk to? Did Katherine mention any friends she might have confided in?"

"She has a sister in town. I heard she wants custody of the boys, but that's not going to happen. I don't know her name. I'm sure you can figure it out. She may be able to tell you more."

"Thanks for your time."

"Hey, my pleasure. And if you ever want to go out for a coffee for real, give me a call."

"Straight to the point, huh?"

"At my age, kid," he said, getting up with his briefcase, "I have to be." He winked and was gone out into the rain.

Lauren sat listening to the sound of the drops hitting the pavement outside and sipped her water. When the waitress came by, she ordered a muffin and began to flip through the prenuptial agreement. All around her, people were furiously typing into their laptops, taking advantage of the downpour to get some work done.

She opened her phone and called Violanti. "I just had the most interesting meeting with a retired cop."

"Another conquest?"

"You wish. I got some nice juicy photos I think you'd like to look at and a copy of a very, very unfavorable prenuptial agreement, which sent Katherine Vine into the arms of a private investigator."

"The retired cop you mentioned before?"

"You got it." The muffin was delicious.

"Are you thinking of an alternative motive?"

"Is the pope Catholic?"

"I love you, Lauren."

"Let's not get crazy." She brushed the muffin crumbs from her shirt. "I'll call you tomorrow and we can meet. I'll write you up a nice report, give you copies, all that stuff. I just need one thing from you— can you get us to see Katherine Vine's car?"

"I can start writing the motion now."

"Get on it. I'm going to enjoy the rest of my day and not think of you at all."

He snorted into the phone. "I bet you will."

"Goodbye."

Damn, was that a good muffin.

25

Joe Wheeler sat at his desk in his suburban office clutching a piece of paper in his hand. Outside the rain was coming down in steady sheets, the sound dulled by the drone of the air conditioner and the hum of the overhead lights.

Bitch. Bitch. Bitch.

She was screwing her ex-husband. Joe had come in on his day off. Taken the time to come in when he could have been enjoying himself, and ran the license plate. And it had come back to Mark Hathaway. The guy she ran off and married. His hand crumpled the paper as he thought about that. He had been keeping tabs on Lauren for a long time, but he'd never seen *his* car at her house. Why now all of a sudden? Hathaway was married, this Joe knew.

Was she that desperate for a man? He thought for sure she would call him after he sent the flowers. That she would appreciate that he remembered her favorite flowers and call to say thank you. They'd had misunderstandings before. It wasn't like he'd put her in the hospital;

she'd just surprised him, that's all. It was a misunderstanding. She even proved that by not calling his superiors. Sure, that little weasel of an attorney had brought it up in court, but he could see she was surprised by that too. He could tell she didn't approve.

So why was Mark Hathaway at her house?

He threw the paper into the garbage can. Unless it was a legal matter. Something with the house or the girls? He knew Hathaway had sprung for the house after knocking up his gold-digging secretary. His family was big money, *old* money, stretching back to the grain elevator days. The Hathaway name carried major clout in the city to this day. They had hospital wings and academic buildings named after their money. He had to be careful about him.

Outside the rain started to subside.

What to do? What to do?

Joe decided to put the information in his pocket for a while, until he knew more about the situation. He checked his watch. The strip club opened early on Saturdays. Maybe a nice lap dance with a little extra in the backroom was what he needed to take the edge off. Besides, there was a girl who worked there now who looked just like Lauren. She said she was eighteen and from Canada, but he highly doubted both those claims. If he paid her double her usual money she didn't mind when he got a little rough. That and he could always arrest her.

Being a cop did have its perks.

26

"**F**rank, you have to stop obsessing over this."

He looked up from the computer. His wife was standing in the doorway of his home office, arms folded, with that look he knew so well. She was a tiny little thing, with short black hair she kept spiked up around her face. Violanti had met her on a skiing trip when he was in law school. She had walked right up to him in the lodge and put a beer down in front of him. He remembered looking down at her and she up at him with that twinkle in her eye.

"You're the only guy in this place that doesn't have to bend in half to kiss me," she'd told him. And he did kiss her that night. And the next night and the night after that.

"I would think you would cut me a break on this, Kim. He's my godson and they're going to fry him if he gets convicted."

She floated into the room cautiously. Right away he knew where this was headed. "Don't you think," she began gently, "that you should be preparing Sarah and David for the possibility of conviction?"

111

She'd stressed the word *possibility* ever so slightly, as if it were a very farfetched notion that just had to be thrown out there.

Violanti swiveled in his chair. "Kim, I don't think David killed her. I don't. I was there when he was born. We've taken him on vacation. We went to all his football games. How can you even think David has it in him?"

"He changed when his dad died. You've tried to be there for him and he did his own thing. You said yourself, you never really know anyone."

"I wasn't talking about David."

"He had sex with that woman in the car. She scratched him up and bit him. Why would she have sex with him? He's a kid. It doesn't make sense."

Violanti sighed. "How am I going to convince a jury he's innocent if I can't convince my own wife?"

"I'm just saying that it makes more sense than some random guy coming by and killing her. Especially when you factor in that other thing."

Now he got mad. "That other thing is a nonissue. I can't believe you even brought it up."

Kim stood her ground. "I think it has to be brought up when you consider his missing girlfriend. You can't protect him just because he's your godson. If he's guilty, he needs to go to jail."

He shook his head. "No. Jail is the last place David needs to be. What would Sarah do? And what would he be like when he got out? The other situation was a misunderstanding and it was dealt with. It has nothing to do with what's going on now. Jail is not an option, so excuse me if I pour my heart into this case and take away some valuable quality time we could be spending together."

"So that's it?"

"That's it."

Kim slammed the door on the way out.

27

"**Y**eah, I bartended at the Ozone for a year. What a year that was. The worst place I ever worked at." Rodney Beamish was polishing glasses at the Lake Shore Country Club. Gone was the thick black mullet in his Polaroid; he was bald as a cue ball now. The early-nineties swagger was replaced with a middle-aged paunch threatening to burst the last two buttons on his white tuxedo shirt.

"We're wondering if you remember a particular night." Reese leaned over the shiny polished wood of the bar. "July 29th, 1993."

They were trying to make some headway on the Ortiz case while the DNA was still being processed. For a fresh homicide, you could expect results in four to six weeks. For cold cases, you went to the back of the line, taking upwards of three months. Riley and Reese tried to get as much done in that window as possible, because if a hit came back on a suspect, the case went from cold to hot real fast. Waiting until Monday for Rodney to be back in town had sorely tested Lauren's patience.

"I don't remember what I had for breakfast yesterday. How the hell could I remember what happened that night?" He began stacking the polished glasses behind the bar.

"There was a stabbing that night. A young woman named Vinita Ortiz was stabbed to death on the street outside the bar." Reese pulled a picture of Vinita that her daughter had given them out of his folder. She was sitting at a picnic table, a cake in front of her, smiling right into the camera.

Rodney took the picture from Reese, glanced at it, and handed it back with a nod. "I don't know her, but I do remember that night. It was the only time someone ever got murdered while I was working."

Lauren noticed he had a slight lisp when he talked, making *while I was working* sound more like *while I wath worthing*. Her first husband had the same lisp after he got his front teeth knocked out in a roofing accident.

"I saw the whole thing. Rufus threw them out. I could see out the window on my end of the bar, it was open to the street. They had some words and when the Hispanic girl turned around, the other girl dug something out of her purse and jumped on her. Her boyfriend pulled her off and they ran down the street. But the little girl didn't get up and I could see her friend screaming. I was trying to get the bouncer's attention, but it was so loud and crowded he didn't see me. I ran to the office to call 911 because she wasn't moving. Later I had to go downtown and they took my statement."

Lauren produced the statement from her own folder, ignoring the curious glances of the kitchen staff as they got ready to serve dinner to the membership. Mark had been a member there when they were married. She prayed none of them recognized her because she was sure they waited on the new Mrs. Hathaway quite often. "It says in your statement you didn't know the assailant, but that you'd seen her and her boyfriend in the bar before?"

He nodded. "Yes." *Yeth.* "A couple times, but never again after that. And no, I never got their names."

"What made you remember them in particular?" Reese asked.

He shrugged. "You do this long enough, you get good at remembering faces. I don't know if I'd recognize them now—hell, I don't recognize *me* now." He grabbed at his belly and gave it a shake.

You don't recognize me, Lauren thought, *but I never hung out at this bar with Mark. He'd drink scotch and smoke cigars in the lounge while we ladies sipped whiskey-laced tea on the veranda. I was never much good at being rich.*

"Is there anything at all you can tell us that could help us identify them?" Lauren asked, snapping out of her trip down memory lane.

He snapped his fingers. "There was one thing, I told the detectives this too. The guy had a tattoo on his hand. His ... " He juggled his own hands in the air trying to jog his memory. " ... left hand. This was before everyone was tatted up. It was of a goldfish, but nicer, you know? What are those fish people put in their ponds?"

"A koi fish?" Lauren offered. She had noticed in the file one of the original detectives had written the words TATTOO FISH on a piece of paper and stuck it in randomly with the rest of the paperwork.

He nodded at her. "Yes. A koi fish. Really nicely done too. Right here in the webbing between his thumb and forefinger. I complemented him on it once when he was paying me for a drink."

Lauren handed him the pad and held out her pen. "Can you make a rough sketch of it, as best you can remember?"

He took the pad and the pen. "I'll do the best I can. I'm no artist."

"That's okay. It'd be a great help."

28

The morning after Rodney Beamish did his best to scratch out a Koi fish on a legal pad, Lauren found another piece of art on her desk. Carefully arranged in the center of her desk, on top of her mounds of paperwork, was a cartoon someone had printed out. It showed a woman smiling for a flashing camera and underneath it, in bold block letters it read: PIMP MY JOB! Someone had taken the time to hand draw money signs all around the border.

She snatched it and crumpled it up before Reese could see it. She could hear him out in the hallway, bullshitting with one of the Homicide guys. It wasn't the first time someone had left a literal sign of disapproval in the office. When Richie Bystryk got caught forging overtime slips people left pigs all over his desk. Ceramic pigs, stuffed pigs, pink plastic piggy banks, day after day to let Richie know what the rest of the squad thought about that. When Richie freaked out about it, thinking someone would fess up or get in trouble, his sergeant took him aside and told him it might be better for everyone if he transferred. Which he did, right before he got fired.

This was mild compared to that, but it burned her up inside anyway. On an average day, the twenty-two other people in the Buffalo Homicide squad could give less than one shit what she did with her free time. But she takes on one case that seems to offend their shaky moral compasses and the ball busting comes out. This was only the beginning, she was sure. *Suck it up,* she told herself. *Don't let these fuckers know they're getting to you or it'll never end.*

"Hey partner." Reese came bouncing in, all energy and smiles. "What's good? What's good?"

I can't let him know. She knew he'd go ballistic if he thought someone was messing with her. She forced a smile. "You're in a good mood. Hot date last night?"

He threw himself down into his chair and popped his feet up on his desk. "As a matter of fact, very hot. I'm pleased with the way things went down."

"Will we be seeing this young lady again soon?" She slipped the crumpled ball into the trashcan next to her desk.

"What? Hell no. Let's not get crazy." He spun himself around in his swivel chair for effect. "I said I was pleased, not ecstatic."

That afternoon when she walked out to her car she noticed something stuck under her windshield wipers. As she got closer it looked like little white flags were ruffling from her windshield. She plucked up one of the little pieces of paper. Someone had stuffed Monopoly money under the blades. Keeping her face a neutral mask she casually plucked the fake bills out and got in her car. Knowing some of the arrogant assholes she worked with, whoever did it was probably watching.

That's what made you crazy—not knowing which one or ones was messing with you. Vatasha Arnold had never really liked her. She was an excellent detective but a total queen bee, and they had butted heads from the start. However, they worked completely opposite of each other and Lauren doubted she'd come in on her day off to screw with her.

Craig Garcia was a miserable prick who used to take a dump in the woman's bathroom every time Lauren worked until Marilyn, the secretary, caught him. He wasn't ashamed, said he wanted to see if Lauren's shit really didn't stink, because she walked around like it didn't. Reese hadn't come up to Homicide yet but Lauren cornered Garcia down in the gym and words were exchanged. Just words, because Garcia was a pussy who liked to pick on women behind their backs, but crumbled when he was face to face with her, alternately denying and apologizing at the same time. He would've been her number-one suspect now if he wasn't deathly afraid of Reese. He'd made a remark about Reese being half black the first week he transferred to the squad. Reese smiled and politely told him if he ever spoke to him again, he'd knock his teeth out.

Who did that leave?

Everybody, she thought angrily, pulling out of the lot. *Everybody.*

29

Katherine Vine's white Mercedes was in the Garden Valley impound lot. Lauren snapped on latex gloves while Violanti took his own photos of the exterior of the car. Against the far wall of the garage, Joe Wheeler was watching silently. While it was a standard move for the defense to want to have access to a vehicle in a crime scene, especially when it was still being held in evidence, Joe still seethed inside that Lauren had to be there. Naturally, the State Police evidence technician and Joe's lieutenant were both there, as well as ADA Lynn Ferro.

Everyone wanted to watch the dynamic duo at work. Joe couldn't help but wonder how she could be so close to him and not want to talk to him, or give some kind of sign that everything was all right. Of course, they were working on opposite sides of the field, so maybe she thought it was better that they have their next conversation alone. She could at least acknowledge him, though. Thank him for the flowers he'd sent her *nearly two weeks ago*, he fumed.

Strangely, Lauren seemed focused on the outside of the car, instead of the interior. It was like she was purposely looking for something. Methodically, she started at the front bumper. Getting down on her hands and knees and pulling out a tiny flashlight, she looked under the fender. She then had Violanti pop the hood and inspected the engine. Satisfied, she got back down on her knees and followed along the passenger side of the undercarriage. All the while Frank Violanti had his cell phone camera trained on Lauren, documenting everything she did.

She made her way around the rear of the car, laying on her back, shining her light up under the vehicle. "I found it."

Everyone stiffened for a second as she straightened up.

"Under the rear fender near the muffler. There's a GPS." She turned to the State Police evidence tech. "I want this photographed and fingerprinted, please."

Now everyone rushed forward and began bombarding her with questions.

Joe erupted, "You planted that. You came here and planted something under there. How else could you know to look for it?"

"This is a video camera too. I have it all on video. Her hands never went under the vehicle." Violanti waved his camera for all to see.

The evidence tech was on his back now with his own flashlight. "She's right. It sure does look like a GPS." He looked up at Joe. "Can you get my kit for me?"

Joe stomped off to retrieve what looked like an oversized tackle box. She didn't care about the flowers. She didn't care about his feelings or what she was doing to him. She was a selfish bitch who wanted to flaunt her tight little ass around his business. She wanted to ruin his case and throw everything they'd had together back in his face.

Joe knew she was watching him as he came back over with the box. He was seething. *She wants to see me angry*, he thought. *If that's what she gets off on, I can provide a private showing, just for her.*

120

30

"**Y**ou were right. A magnetic GPS system, available at any security store or online outlet. No fingerprints, of course, because of the constant exposure to the elements, but I've requested copies of the State Police's entire evidence report."

"Was there ever any doubt I was right?" Two weeks after their big discovery, Lauren and Violanti were sitting on a patio in a waterfront bar sipping spiked iced tea. Their truce was holding up, but still shaky. David was set to be indicted and they were killing time, waiting for evening visiting hours at the jail to explain things to him. David's mom was in the midst of a total breakdown since bail was denied. Violanti's wife had managed to get her in to see a doctor, who had prescribed medication for her. It helped a little, but he said they were still getting hysterical phone calls at all hours of the night. The strain was already starting to show on Violanti's face, even if his tone was optimistic.

"No. Not after what you found out about the way she was living. She was being tracked, which means her husband knew exactly where she was. And now I have the reasonable doubt–raising questions of 'Why didn't Anthony Vine report his wife missing when she didn't come home that night?' Or, 'Why didn't he use his little tracker and go and find her body?' And, 'Why wasn't she found until morning?' I love it."

"Can I have another ten grand?"

"I don't love it that much." He raised his glass to her and polished it off.

The waiter brought them two more drinks. As Lauren was about to take a sip, something caught her eye two tables over.

Mark Hathaway and his wife Amanda were being seated by the hostess. They were with another couple Lauren didn't know. Amanda put her designer bag down next to her as Mark pushed his wife's seat in. He looked up and locked eyes with Lauren. Mark bent down with a smile, whispered something in Amanda's ear, and excused himself. Amanda almost broke her neck whipping around in her seat to watch Mark walk away.

"Lauren, it's so nice to see you," he said in his best lawyer voice. He turned to Violanti, hand already offered. "Mark Hathaway."

He stood and they shook. "I think we worked together in the Adams case," Violanti said.

Mark's face lit up with recognition. "Yes. I knew it. Of course, Frank Violanti. You're representing David Spencer in the Vine case. I saw you on the news."

"That's me. I've retained Lauren to assist me. I wasn't aware you two knew each other."

"For quite some time." His smile was wide, toothy. The smile, Lauren knew, he used when he was putting on a show. "Enjoy your drinks. It was nice to run into you both."

He wasn't even back at his table yet when Violanti turned to Lauren. "You're sleeping with Mark Hathaway?"

"What?" She snorted, trying to stall. "He came over to say hello. I'd hardly call that basis for such an assumption. And rude too, you jerk off."

"You didn't say hello. You didn't say anything. You kept one eye on him and the other on his wife. I may be a jerk off, but I know how to read people."

A peel of laughter rang out from Mark's party two tables away.

"I was briefly married to Mark Hathaway, okay? A decade ago. He's my ex-husband."

Violanti sat back in his chair and folded his arms smugly. "So you're banging your ex-husband."

"If you say that word again, I'm going home, so drop it. Isn't it time we got going? I'm on the clock here."

He paid the bill and they made their way outside to the parking lot. They decided to take one vehicle, so Lauren left her Ford behind and jumped into Violanti's car.

He didn't even bother with a polite silence. "You and Mark Hathaway. Well, that explains the inside information you had. How did I not know you were married to one of the wealthiest men in the city?"

"I said drop it. It's none of your business."

"You were engaged to Joe Wheeler too?"

"Before I was married to Mark." Her face was getting red.

"But that's not the husband who fathered your girls?"

"No."

"And now you're sleeping with Mark again?"

She spun to face Violanti in his seat. "If you say another word, I'm going to stab you in the ear with your own pen."

"I got it. I got it," he laughed and made the turn out of the parking lot. Lauren sulked in the passenger seat the whole way to the holding center.

The line of people waiting to see their loved ones stretched out the door, down the steps, and around the block. It was Monday evening visiting and everyone who had been too busy having fun on the weekend now showed up to see their incarcerated brethren. Violanti and Lauren got to cut ahead to the attorney's line, which no one else was in. Most of the lawyers had already seen their clients during the day and gone back to their glorious new homes in the suburbs.

They signed in and waited for the deputy to take them to the attorney conference room.

David was already waiting for them. Lauren had set up this visit well in advance. Sometimes it took forty-five minutes to get people down off the blocks. Calling ahead made things easier.

He looked good. With nothing else to do, David had decided to concentrate on working out. The lines of his jaw were more angular, had lost some of the boyishness over the last month. He looked older now and less scared. More like a man.

"How are you, David?" Violanti asked as they sat across from him.

He rubbed the shadow of stubble across his chin. "I can't get a good shave in here."

"Other than that."

"How do you think? I'm sitting here rotting in a cell all by myself. I'm supposed to be starting college in the fall. I guess that's off." He gave a hard laugh. "I'm pissed off. How would you feel?"

Violanti ignored that little outburst. "Well, we got some good news for your defense. Katherine Vine was being monitored by her husband. Did you see any other vehicles in the parking lot that night?"

He sat back in his chair and shook his head. "Her car was the only one in the back lot. There were lots of cars where mine was parked up in the front. I don't remember any other car specifically."

"The district attorney is going to indict you on Wednesday. As your lawyer, I have to tell you it's your right to testify before the grand jury, but I don't recommend it."

"I didn't do it. What if I told them? What if they believed me?"

"They won't, and the prosecution will have a field day, and you'll be indicted and have hurt your defense."

"None of this makes any sense," he said and looked at Lauren. "How can that be right?"

"It is. You shouldn't testify. Trust me on this. Your uncle has to tell you it's your option by law, but if you did, all you would do is give the DA a chance to question you before the trial and tighten up their strategy."

"This is such a game. It's a joke," David spat out.

"You need to be calm, David, and put that anger away. If a jury sees you angry, we're cooked. You have to look innocent and young and sympathetic."

"This is all a load of crap."

"You got that right; however, it's crap we have to wade through if you ever want to get out of here before you look like Santa Claus." Violanti pushed a bunch of papers toward David. "Now read these and sign them."

Lauren absently leafed through some of the crime scene photos in her file as David read his grand jury waiver. A piece of blond hair had escaped from her tight ponytail and fell along her cheek. She tried to tuck it behind her ear without looking up from the pictures. It came loose again and straggled back.

Gently, David reached over and tucked it away, his finger trailing down and over her lip. "Your mouth looks much better," he said softly.

When she looked up, his eyes were locked on hers.

Lauren pushed up and back from the table as if snake had just bitten her.

"What the hell was that?" Violanti demanded, grabbing David's arm.

David jerked away. "What? What?"

Lauren hit the buzzer to get out, while Violanti went off on David. She didn't stop until she was down the stairs, out the holding center doors, and halfway down the street.

"Lauren!" Violanti called from behind. He was running up Court Street clutching all the folders they'd brought in, trying to catch up with her.

A hand came down on her shoulder and she spun around. "What just happened in there? Can you tell me? What was that?"

"I don't know, Lauren. He's a kid. He didn't mean anything by it."

"No? No kid I know ever touched me like that."

"I know what you're thinking, okay? I know. He's not a predator. Maybe you just have some kind of weird mojo that drives men wild—"

"Oh, that's rich. Blame the victim. Maybe Katherine Vine was asking for it."

"Keep your voice down!" he shushed urgently. "Let's not make more of this than it is. He's a kid and he feels like you're trying to help him. Maybe he has some kind of crush on you. That doesn't make him a killer."

"Get me out of here. I want to go home and rethink this."

31

Violanti tried reasoning with her all the way back to her car. She jumped out of his sedan without a word, got into her car, and peeled out of the restaurant parking lot where they'd left her Ford. As she headed toward home, she fished her cell out of her purse with one hand and glanced at the screen. Three missed messages from Mark. She threw the phone onto the seat. They could stay missed for all she cared. Having to see Mark laughing and drinking with his wife as if she never existed, then being hit on by a possibly homicidal—and definitely hormonal—prisoner was too much. She needed a whiskey sour.

When she was safely at home, she called her best friend, Dayla. Dayla lived halfway down the block and had been a stay-at-home mom who loved drama in any form. Now that her kids were grown and out of the house, she found Lauren's life more exciting than primetime television. Five minutes after getting the call, she was on Lauren's front steps with a bottle of whiskey and a bag of potato chips.

"How do I get myself into these messes?" Lauren asked, dumping a handful of ice into two rocks glasses in her kitchen.

Leaning a hip against the granite countertop Dayla asked, "Do you really want me to answer that?"

"No." She handed Dayla her whiskey minus the sour. "You drink your drink."

"Thank you." Dayla whisked her dark curls off to the side as she sipped her whiskey. They used to drink red wine together, but it seemed too *Real Housewives* to Dayla, so she switched to Jameson. *In her mind, detectives and their sidekicks drink whiskey*, Lauren thought with a crooked smile. *I have a middle-aged cougar for a Watson to my Holmes.*

They sat down at the kitchen table together. "I just don't get it," Lauren went on. "My gut says this kid is not guilty."

"So, you were wrong. Give back the rest of the ten grand, cut your losses, and forget about it."

"I don't think I am, though." Lauren slugged down some of her drink. "I really don't think the kid did it. He had sex with her, but I don't think he killed her. There's more going on."

"Then maybe you should concentrate on who you think *did* kill her." Dayla shook up the ice in her glass.

"Genius. Why didn't I think of that?"

"Keep the money. Solve the case. Get me another drink."

Lauren took the bottle off the table and refilled their glasses. Black hair curly and loose around her face, Dayla's eyebrows were pulled upward in a way that made her look like she was surprised all the time. Her husband was a plastic surgeon and Dayla, in her boredom, had had almost every procedure known to man done to her. Her boobs were fake, she had a chin implant, tummy tuck, eyelift, Botox— you name it. She'd gone from being a very attractive middle-aged black woman to an extremely attractive, plastic-looking, middle-aged black woman. Still, she was good people even if she did use a made up name to go with her fake appendages. Lauren thought her real name was possibly Darlene, but she wouldn't answer to it.

"Let's forget all this stuff about crime and trials and murder. Let's talk about the important things. Like who you're sleeping with right now."

Lauren couldn't help laughing. Dayla was always exactly what she needed. "It's complicated."

Dayla waved her hand around in dismissal. "Complicated! Complicated, she says! It's simple anatomy. You have girl parts and the boy has boy parts ..."

"I get it, I get it. It's just that no matter who I sleep with, it's never the right guy, you know?"

Dayla peered at her over her rocks glass, "That, my friend, is because you are an ice queen."

"I'm not an ice queen," Lauren protested.

"Ice queen ..." Dayla was singing into her whiskey now.

"How am I an ice queen? Because I don't take garbage from guys anymore? Because I refuse to settle?"

"You have gone beyond refusing to settle to a straight-up block of ice. I get that both the girls leaving for college was hard on you. I get that you've been hurt by men. I truly get that. But you refuse to give anyone a chance. It's like you want to spend the rest of your life alone in sexual happiness exile."

"Sexual happiness exile?" Lauren repeated. "Is that even a thing?"

"Yes. Yes, it's a thing in the world according to Dayla." Now she pointed a thin manicured finger at her. "You have a ripe young partner just ready for the picking. Don't tell me you've never thought about it. Those rippling muscles, those heavenly green eyes ..."

"Sounds like *you've* thought about it."

"Who wouldn't? Oh yeah, you. That's who. Raining on my sexual fantasy parade."

"Sorry to disappoint you." Lauren refilled both their glasses. They were using a lot more whiskey than ice. "He's not my type. It would be like kissing my brother."

"He's not my brother. Thank you very much." They clinked their glasses together and Dayla offered a drunken, "Cheers!"

"Reese is my partner and my friend. Besides, he's too young for me."

"Yeah, well, one of these days, that hottie will be snatched up and you'll be kicking yourself."

Dayla stayed until almost eleven o'clock and then stumbled her way home down the block. Lauren watched from her front porch until Dayla navigated her way inside, clutching the half-empty bag of potato chips she decided she had to take with her. She was feeling a little bombed herself, so Lauren crawled upstairs, pulled her clothes off, and fell into her spinning bed.

The phone buzzed on the nightstand just as she was closing her eyes. She picked it up and squinted at the screen.

Mark.

"Sorry," she whispered, turning her cell off. "No getting the milk for free tonight."

32

It was hot. Even in her bedroom with the window wide open, her white sheet stuck to her body from the perspiration. Lauren felt a cool ribbon of air kiss her side as Mark slid in beside her. He must have let himself in with the key to the lock she never changed. He reached for her and she didn't stop him. As her breasts pressed up against his bare chest she could sense the urgency in his kiss. He was on top of her, his muscular body holding her down. One hand pulled away her panties, roughly signaling that foreplay was going to be glanced over this evening.

When he pushed himself inside her, though, she knew something was wrong. He was too big. He was holding her down. She slammed her hands against his chest to break away from him, but he wouldn't stop. His thrusts were too savage, almost primal. His penetration was deep and painful and fast. She could feel his breath on her face, coming in jagged grunts as he rutted into her over and over. He was hurting her.

She opened her eyes. Instead of Mark's face hovering over hers, it was David Spencer. He smiled.

She woke up with a start. Sweat was pouring down her neck, soaking into her sheets. *Just a bad dream,* she told herself, trying to shake it off, *just a nightmare.*

She rolled onto her side and looked at the moon. The sheer panels hung limply on either side of the window. Lauren closed her eyes. With a sick feeling in her stomach, she wondered if David Spencer was in his cell dreaming of her.

33

"Can we talk?" Violanti hadn't taken the four unanswered text messages as a sign Lauren wasn't in the mood to chitchat.

"I'm at work. My regular job. I can't talk now. I'll call you later."

"When?"

"Later. Goodbye." She hung up on him and turned her cell phone off. She was doing that a lot lately.

"Problems with your new boyfriend?" Reese asked. He was holding a black-and-white photograph up to the light, examining it with a real magnifying glass, making his left eye look enormous.

"No, Sherlock Holmes. Problems with the annoying mini-counsel. Let's scour the mug machine for the boyfriend in the Ortiz case, see if we can build that up and make ourselves useful."

Putting the picture back into the file, he tossed it on his desk. It looked like a hurricane had hit it from behind. He expressly forbade Lauren from touching his paperwork. If she needed something from a case of his, she would ask him and magically the exact piece of paper would be plucked out of the pile.

"Okay. I'm sucking myself into other homicides sitting here. I don't want to get deeper into any other cases until after we finish Vinita Ortiz."

"Perfect. But first, I'm starving. And I want to get out of this building." She flapped open the sides of her jacket. "I'm broiling alive in this suit. If you're good, I'll buy you lunch today."

"I'm thinking steak."

She rolled her eyes. "I'm thinking cheeseburgers at Tony's"

"Even better." The magnifying glass was unceremoniously thrown into his top drawer.

Lauren grabbed the car keys off her desk. "Ready?"

She noticed Reese's eyes suddenly fixed on the door. She looked over. Mark was standing in the doorway. "Can I help you?" Reese asked. Mark had disappeared from her life years before Reese entered it. The man at the door in the expensive suit was a complete stranger to him.

Mark looked past Reese to Lauren. "I'm here to see Detective Riley."

Reese looked over to her for a cue. She tossed him the car keys. "I'll meet you downstairs."

"You sure?"

"Positive."

Reese brushed past Mark on his way out, looking him up and down as he did. Once he was down the hall, Mark stepped into the office. "Is this a bad time?"

Lauren walked over and kicked the plastic doorstop out. After it closed behind her she turned to him. "Are you crazy?"

He looked so desperate standing there in his Italian three-piece suit, wringing his hands together, worry line creased across his forehead. He must have been, to come to her work.

"I'm so sorry ... "

"About what? You were out with your wife. You're married. I can't pretend you don't have a wife and a life that doesn't include me."

"I don't want to hurt you."

She laughed at the absurdity of that statement. "Too late, Mark. It's my own fault. That's what I get for fooling around with a married man."

Mark came toward her and tried to put his arms around her. "I'm sorry."

She pushed back from him. "I know. Apology accepted. You have to go before someone sees you here."

He nodded his head slightly in agreement. "Can I at least call you tonight?"

Lauren's mind flashed back to the dream she had the night before. A shudder ran through her and she tried to focus. "My door will be open at seven o'clock. If you're not there, it'll be locked at seven oh five." She opened the door and left him standing alone in her office. He could find his own way out.

"Is everything okay?" Reese asked as she got into their dented, unmarked car idling in front of headquarters.

"Sometimes I think it is, other times no."

"That was your ex, right?"

She stared out the passenger window. "One of them."

"If there's anything I can do ... "

"Yeah. One thing," she said. "Just be my partner. Don't try to sleep with me, or marry me, or stalk me."

He smiled. "I think I can manage that. You still want to go out and eat? We could stay and fish in the mug machine for that witness."

"I would love to do that, but I'm still starving. Let's get a cheeseburger first."

He put the car into gear, glancing sideways at her as he pulled out. "While it's flattering that you think I might want to date, marry, or stalk you, I want you to know something," he told her.

"What's that?"

"All things considered, I really think I could do better than you."

She patted his arm maternally. "That's my boy."

34

After lunch Riley and Reese came back to the office to face the dreaded mug machine.

Since the mid-nineties every person arrested in Erie County had their mugshot and arrest details added to a database that police can use to search a suspect's prior arrests, prior addresses, known associates, and aliases. One of the more useful features is the ability to search people's tattoos. Used mostly to document gang tattoos, it still came in handy for other cases, such as Vinita Ortiz's. Not available at the time of her murder, the mug machine was loaded with tens of thousands of pictures of the usual suspects. Armed with the bartender's sketch, a bottle of Pepsi, and a candy bar, Lauren settled in back at the office for a long computer search.

Tattoos were listed specifically, but in general categories like names, flowers, gang signs, or numbers. Lauren had to specify white male, tattoo on left hand, and then go through the categories, because every intake person listed things differently. And she had to hope the guy had been arrested at all; if he'd lived a law-abiding life since the stabbing or chosen to commit his crimes in Niagara County, this search was all for naught. Lauren had once spent eight hours straight looking at mugs for a guy with a scar across his neck for a particularly sadistic rape. Sore eyes and hours later, she hit on a man who'd had his throat slit in prison. The tearful victim picked him out right away. Patience was the key.

"You think they would even take a picture of a fish?" Reese asked, looking over her shoulder.

"I'm more worried that he's never been arrested." She hit the mouse, bringing up six more close-ups of arrestees' hands.

"Keep at it." Reese gave her a pat on the shoulder. "I'm feeling lucky."

She half turned in her seat. "Then maybe you should do it," she called back to him as he sat at his desk.

"I'm feeling lucky I have you as my badass, hard-working partner." Picking up the extra tuna sub he had gotten to go since one cheeseburger was barely enough to make a dent in his appetite, Reese took a giant bite, lettuce falling from his chewing mouth back onto the paper it had been wrapped in.

"I'll keep that in mind." She turned back and kept flipping through the pictures.

———

Four hours later, after going through every left-handed tattoo picture in the database, Lauren had the bright idea that maybe Rodney had gotten the hand wrong, switched to searching right hands, and came up with the koi fish tattoo in five minutes. There, on her screen, was a beautiful orange and red rendering of a Japanese fish inked in the web of a six-foot-three white guy's right thumb and forefinger.

"Reese!" she called and listened to his chair scraping back as he rushed over to the screen.

"Holy shit," he said as she enlarged the picture. "That *is* a good-looking goldfish."

"And it belongs to Mr. Kenneth Steinmetz of Orchard Park." She clicked on a link and pulled up a mugshot. "Arrested twelve years ago for failure to pay child support."

He rubbed his hands together in anticipation. "Time for some photo arrays."

"I'll make one of his mug shot and put one together for the tattoo," Lauren said, setting up the program. "We'll get Luz and Rodney in here ASAP and do a double blind."

Departmental policy stated that the detectives working on the case could not show a photo array to a witness, in order to avoid being suggestive. They'd have to arrange two separate detectives to come in and show the arrays to Luz and Rodney. It was time consuming, but better done right than done fast.

"Do you have enough fish tattoo pictures to do an array?"

Lauren nodded. "Thank God for Pisces tattoos. Who knew so many people got their zodiac sign tattooed on them?"

"Did I ever show you my tattoo? I have a big—"

She held up a hand to his face. "Stop. If you want to keep me as a partner, you'll stop right there."

"Okay," he laughed. "Good job, Columbo. Let's get these arrays shown and pray one of them can pick out the guy or the tattoo."

35

Mark was at her house at exactly seven o'clock. He had changed out of his suit into a golf shirt and a pair of jeans. As soon as Lauren opened the door, he wrapped his arms around her and kissed her. She didn't stop him, even though she knew she should, and kissed him back.

He picked her up in his arms and carried her up the stairs to her bed. It wasn't their bed; she'd thrown that out the day after he left for good. It was her bed, in her house. He put her down gently on the duvet and then lay down next to her. Instead of trying to make love to her, he looked at her for a long time and then said, "I want this too, Lauren. It's not just sex."

Instead of delivering one of her razor sharp comebacks, she just went with it and melted away in his arms. He smelled like soap and faded cologne.

If he wanted sex, or friendship, or hugs, or a bridge partner she would give in to him. If she demanded that he leave his wife, he'd say no. If he came back over tomorrow, she'd say yes to him again. She wanted to say all these things to him, but it didn't matter. They both already knew. So she let herself be happy in the moment and hoped she wouldn't regret it.

Later, they went back downstairs and watched an old monster movie from the fifties on the couch and ate popcorn. They used to do that when they were married and the girls were in bed—snuggle on the couch and watch horror movies. Mark would laugh and tease her when she covered her eyes with the pillow during the scary parts.

When it came time for him to leave, he kissed her on her forehead. "Tonight was great."

"Yeah," she agreed, "it really was."

"I think we should go away somewhere. To a nice beach and drink big, fruity drinks with umbrellas in them."

"I can't right now. I've got too much going on, but I want to. When I close the Ortiz case or when this trial is over."

He kissed her again. "It's a date."

Why pretend to be noble? she thought to herself as she watched him drive away. *I don't care about hurting his wife. I was his wife first, after all.*

She realized that she was happy. For the first time since the girls left for school, she was happy. Even if it was a slippery kind of happy that could vanish at any minute. She was going to hold on to it as long as she could.

36

Across the street from Lauren's house there was a grand Colonial for sale. White, with stately pillars gracing either side of the entrance, it had been on the market for quite a while. The owners had moved out of state and now there it sat, vacant. The realty company had men come over to mow the lawn now and then, but the trees were overgrown and the yard was starting to look wild.

Parked deep in the driveway was Joe Wheeler's undercover car. It was hidden in the dark shadow of the house, but it wouldn't have mattered. Lauren didn't know what his car looked like. As he watched Mark Hathaway's luxury sedan pull away, his anger boiled over inside. He had his suspicions and now he knew. One time could have been a stopover for any number of reasons. But twice? No. There was only one reason he'd be there so late twice. *That* was why she wouldn't look at him when they were checking out Katherine Vine's car. *That* was why she hadn't responded to his flowers.

Because she knew she was wrong to be with Mark Hathaway, a married man. Mark had had enough of her act once already, but he was weak, same as Joe. Lauren was a good piece of ass. The best Joe'd ever had, actually. And Joe knew once you had that, you wanted more. Sweat dripped down his temple. Without the air on, the car was like an oven.

One light flicked off downstairs, then another. His hands clenched and unclenched the steering wheel. She was still so beautiful, so tempting. A woman like Lauren Riley was a prize. Something to hold on to.

Clench. Unclench.

So tempting.

Why was she still provoking him?

37

Once a day, the guards led David to a rec room in the basement of the holding center. It was a cold, gray room with stale air that smelled of mold. There were two weight benches, a chess table, a heavy bag with some old boxing gloves scattered around the floor next to it, and an ancient television set. He got one hour of rec time with the three other prisoners they had in isolation. Each prisoner had their own guard, watching them from the corner of the room, making sure they didn't kill each other. Eight people stretched across a room that could accommodate fifty made their time there seem to drag. David always started with the weight bench. He wanted to keep in shape, in case he got out of this jam and did make it to college.

One of the prisoners was a kid even younger than he was. Malcolm was a tiny seventeen-year-old who had burned his grandmother's house down, killing the tenant upstairs. He didn't say much. Sometimes he just sat in one of the chairs in front of the TV and cried softly, his shoulders hunched forward. He never said why he burned the house down, only that he was sorry he did it and wanted to go back home to his mother. David thought the kid might not be all there, that maybe he had some mental problems, but the guards didn't seem too concerned. As long as he didn't make trouble, he could cry all he wanted.

Harold was another story. He never shut up. He talked to whoever would listen, or just to whoever was in earshot, about how he was innocent and being framed by the police, and his lawyer sucked, and his girlfriend was a slut. David never heard why he was in jail or what he did exactly. Harold would slip the gloves on and beat the heavy bag as he talked out loud to everyone and no one. Sometimes the guards would tell him to shut up, but it never lasted long. He'd stop for a minute and then you'd hear him muttering under his breath. That would turn into a whisper and the next thing you knew he was back to ranting again. It got so that David just learned to tune him out.

The only inmate that seemed like any kind of a threat was Stefan. He was six-foot-two and pure jailhouse muscle. He walked over to the other weight bench as soon as he came in.

Stefan rolled the sleeves up on his chambray work shirt, revealing a series of tattoos that looked muddy and homemade. His shaved head shone under the lights like a highly polished hardwood floor. Stefan had the calculating look of a cobra. Every move he made seemed slow and purposeful, as if he was coiling to strike. One of the guards told David that Stefan had been in solitary because he'd assaulted two officers during chow when he first got to the holding center. He'd broken one guard's nose. Stefan told him he did it on purpose because he didn't like having a cellmate.

Stefan had taken a liking to David for some reason and was teaching him chess. They would sit across from each other on the rickety chairs, moving their pieces, talking softly. Stefan always talked softly so the guards couldn't hear. Not that they were plotting anything, but David thought it was just a habit Stefan had developed, having been in jail so much of his life.

Stefan was a professional at doing time. He'd bragged about it more than once. Awaiting trial on a robbery, he said he'd plea at the last minute. The food was better at the holding center than in the state prisons, he explained. He'd take the plea for one to four and be out in two and a half. Stefan had the system all figured out.

"Now with your case, kid," he said, moving his rook over, "I don't know if I'd take this to trial. They got your DNA. Juries love DNA."

"Yeah, but we had sex. I mean, we both wanted to have sex. I didn't have to kill her."

"And you told this to the cops?" Stefan's fingers rested on his queen for just a second, then moved to a pawn. On the back of his right hand, inked in black scrawl, was the name *Irma*, on his left forearm was the name *Denise*. David wanted to ask him who they were but thought better of it. Stefan shared what he wanted to share. David moved one of his own pawns forward towards Stefan's rook.

"I didn't have anything to hide."

Stefan's eyebrows pulled together as he moved his knight again. "Never speak to the cops. Ever. The first words out of your mouth should be, 'I want a lawyer.' Make them prove that shit, dawg."

David moved his bishop to block Stefan's knight. "I just can't believe this is happening to me. I bang some lady, who wanted to have sex with me, and now I'm in jail because she's dead."

"We're all innocent, don't you know that, bro?" Stefan's smile widened. "It ain't about who done this or who didn't do that; it's about who has the best lawyer, the most money, and the better connections. You think if I was a banker who robbed his own vault I'd be sitting here playing chess with you?"

146

"I have a good lawyer. And a cop who's working on my side."

Stefan shrugged. "Maybe you got a shot then. You're a good-looking white kid. The jurors will like you. Just keep sticking to the 'I didn't do it' story no matter what. Especially in here. There are a lot of snitches in jail. They'll do anything to get some time off their sentence."

"I really didn't do it."

"But you had sex with her?"

"Yeah. In her car. It was a Mercedes."

"A Mercedes?" Stefan's eyebrow arched up. "Was it good?"

A slow smile spread across David's face as he savored the memory. Stefan caught it and returned a knowing grin.

"Yeah," David assured him. "It was."

Across the room, Malcolm let out a long, slow sob.

38

"**A**re you ready to talk now?" Violanti's voice was hesitant, as if he was afraid of poking a sleeping bear.

In fact, Lauren was in a better mood that next day. She and Reese were making progress with the Ortiz homicide. She was at peace, at least temporarily, with her situation with Mark. Putting up with Violanti seemed a small price to pay when things were finally going her way.

"I am. I just needed to get my thoughts together on this case."

"What are your thoughts?"

"I looked up Katherine Vine's sister and I want to go and see her."

"Excellent."

"Don't get too happy, I could still change my mind." Her good mood didn't extend into making Violanti's life easier. She liked having him think she could walk away at any moment. It kept their playing field level.

"Well, don't. David's a good kid. He can't help it you drive men wild."

"I'm hanging up now."

"Goodbye …"

She'd had a productive day with Reese. Neither Rodney nor Luz could pick Steinmetz's face out of a photo array. However, Rodney picked the koi tattoo immediately. "That's it," he told Joy Walsh that morning as Lauren and Reese watched from the monitor in the sergeant's office. "That's the tattoo the guy had. Never seen one like it. It's like art, you know? No skulls or roses. It looks like a painting, except it's on his hand."

Luz took it a lot harder. She looked at the pictures again and again. She kept coming back to number three—which was good old Kenneth—the paper shaking in her hand, and repeating, "I want to say it's this guy. But I'm not sure. I'm not a hundred percent. But it looks like the guy … I just can't say for sure." Finally, Joy told her it was all right, gave her the box of tissues the Homicide squad kept in the interview room, had her sign the paperwork, and cut her loose.

"All we got's an ID on the tattoo," Lauren said, gathering up the paperwork from Joy and thanking her for helping out.

"It's more than we had this morning," Reese pointed out. "And he's not the stabber. All he has to do is give up his girlfriend's name."

"You think he's going to do that?" Lauren asked, popping the disk out of the machine to add to the file. The integrity of the identifications was big on defense attorneys' to-do lists as far as suppression hearings. Videotaping them made everything easier. A guy like Violanti couldn't come at the detectives and claim they influenced the witnesses at all.

"I think we should take a drive out to Orchard Park tomorrow and visit Mr. Steinmetz," Reese said as they walked back to the cold case office.

Lauren glanced down at the thin, gaunt face staring back up at her from the paper, and then thought of Vinita sitting in front of the birthday cake smiling like it was the best day of her life. "Looking forward to it."

It was a little cooler outside as she left for the day. The weatherman said a cold front was moving in from the northwest and the heat wave was breaking. It was just past six o'clock and she was heading for home, breaking the law by driving and talking on her cell phone to Mark.

He had called her twice from his office that morning and she hadn't been able to talk. As soon as she'd hung up with Violanti, Mark had called back again. Not having sex was better than getting some. At least this time. She felt like they were dating again. Any doubts or guilt were so thoroughly masked by her bliss that they were practically nonexistent. She was going to go home, take a long, hot bath, and wait for Mark. Life was good.

39

*T*wo nights in a row, Joe mused. He was spending more time there. Mark had gotten to her house at seven thirty. *Wonder what he tells his wife,* Joe thought. *Working late? Big case?* He guessed it didn't matter. With his kind of scratch, a wife would look the other way to maintain her lifestyle. Women were brutal like that. He wondered what Lauren was getting out of him. A new car, perhaps? Maybe tomorrow he'd pull into his surveillance spot and there'd be a brand-new convertible in the driveway. He focused the binoculars on her upstairs window, but the blinds were closed.

They're probably having sex right now, he thought. *He probably has her bent over the bed and she's taking it like she likes it to get her new car. Blond hair covering her face. Fingers grasping the bed sheets tight. Her breath coming in little gasps like she did when she was into it. Or pretending she was.*

Suddenly he threw the car into drive and peeled out. His tires squealed as he tore out onto the street and toward the strip club. Someone was going to get it good from him tonight. The Joe Wheeler special. No little gasps, but maybe some screams. Maybe that little bitch from Canada, if she was working. Too bad it wasn't going to be Lauren. Not tonight. Not yet.

———————

"Did you hear something?" Mark asked, looking from the chessboard set up on the dining room table.

"Probably some stupid kid." She took his last pawn with her queen and smiled wickedly. "I got you now."

40

Kenneth Steinmetz lived in a brand-new development in one of the nicer towns south of the city. Orchard Park, home of the Buffalo Bills stadium, was also home to some very upper-*upper*-middle-class residents. Given his look when his mug was taken, Lauren was surprised he'd be living out there. But then again, he could be living in his parents' basement, smoking weed and playing video games as a forty-five-year-old man.

Still, Lauren mused as the Impala rattled its way through the picture-perfect streets, it was a nice break from the noise and grit of the city. *I could never be a cop out here,* she thought. *I'd miss that constant hum, that perpetual motion.* That was one of the reasons she stayed in the house that Mark bought. She could have sold it for a nice profit, got a little Cape out here on a cul-de-sac, drove a Lexus SUV just to keep up with the Joneses, but she would have missed the vibe of the city.

Even though she lived in one of the few gated communities, the last refuges of the old money in the city, it was still not as pristine and sterile as this.

"Ugh," Reese grunted next to her. "How long do you think it'll take before we get pulled over? A black man driving a crappy car with a blond white lady?"

"Don't be so dramatic. Has that ever happened to us?"

"Not yet." His eyes scanned the street. "But I'm not looking forward to it when it does."

Lauren pulled the ponytail holder out of her hair, shook it loose, and then tied it back again. Kids were riding their bikes on the sidewalk, enjoying the summer day. People were walking their dogs, stopping to chat. *Nope.* She watched the house numbers go down. *This is not for me. I'm a city girl.*

Steinmetz's house was a tasteful blue and gray Cape Cod, complete with overflowing hanging baskets dripping from the rafters of the front porch. There was only one car in the driveway, a newer dark-colored Lincoln. They parked on the street, so vastly different from Luz Hernandez's, and got out.

"You think he'll talk?" Reese asked, meeting her on the sidewalk.

Lauren adjusted her badge on one hip and her Glock on the other. "I guess we'll see. If he's even here."

They made their way up the stamped-concrete sidewalk and climbed the three steps to the porch. No couches, plastic kids' toys, or empty forties lying around, just a handsome wicker chair set, complete with matching coffee table. Lauren pressed the doorbell, which bonged politely somewhere in the house.

A tall, thin, balding man in jeans and a tee shirt opened the door. "Mr. Steinmetz?" Lauren asked. The hand that held the knob was adorned with a very beautiful koi fish tattoo.

He backed up a step so they could enter. "Come on in."

"Mr. Steinmetz, I'm Detective Riley and this is Detective Reese with the Buffalo Police Cold Case—"

"I know who you are." He motioned them inside. "I've been waiting for you to show up for twenty years."

Reese and Riley exchanged glances as they stepped through the threshold. That was a greeting they'd never had before.

He seated them at his dining room table, excusing himself to get coffee for everyone. Reese kept an eye on him as he fussed in the kitchen, just in case he decided this wasn't the best course of action and went postal on them. Lauren got her notepad out, writing down that opening statement at the top, along with the date, time, address, and his name. Steinmetz came back holding a carafe of coffee in one hand and three mugs skillfully held by their handles interlaced between his fingers.

"Thank you," Lauren told him as he poured her a cup.

"I'll be right back with the cream and sugar," he told them and went back into the kitchen.

"Are you kidding me?" Reese whispered. "Is he going to bake us a cake now?"

"Shhh," Lauren hissed. Her eyes traveled to the family portraits on the wall. Steinmetz, a pretty lady she assumed was his wife, and three teenage girls, all wearing denim shirts and white pants on a beach somewhere. A perfect middle-class family. She wondered if he had ever told his wife about the night he left a woman lying in the street with a knife sticking up out of her back. You'd think that would come up, maybe over dinner some night; *Hey, pass the roasted red peppers and by the way, my ex-girlfriend stabbed someone to death. These mashed potatoes are delicious.*

He put the cream and sugar bowl down in front of Reese. "You look like a man who takes it sweet, like me."

Reese nodded, shoveling the sugar into his mug. "Thanks, but this wasn't necessary."

"It's no problem and I think we're going to be here for a while." His eyes traveled to Lauren's. "Or not."

"What makes you say that?" She asked.

"You're here to arrest me, right? For the girl at the Ozone Bar? This is what this is all about, right?"

Lauren didn't know if she should try to scribble all that down before he said he wanted to call his lawyer or try to remember it and keep him rolling.

"Before you say anything else," Reese jumped in, "we aren't here to arrest you, but we are going to read you your rights."

Reese produced a rights card from his wallet and carefully read both sides, making sure to ask after each line, "Do you understand?" He then dated and timed the card and had Steinmetz sign it.

"Now," Reese said tucking the precious rights card into the folder, "what can you tell us about that night?"

Steinmetz ran his hand back and forth over his bald pate, a nervous habit he'd probably had since his long hair days. Taking a deep breath, he looked up. "I don't know where to start. In my head, I've practiced what I would say a million times but now that you're really here, I don't know."

"How about the name of the woman you were with at the Ozone?"

"Shannon Pilski. Her name's Shannon Pilski."

"Is Shannon still local?" Reese asked as Lauren wrote that down and underlined it.

"As far as I know."

Lauren could tell he was trying to be 100 percent truthful, his guilt overflowing into his speech.

"The last I heard she was living in an apartment in South Buffalo near the Irish Center. She's an alcoholic. She was back then too, but I just thought she was a party girl, you know? We all drank a lot. She always just took it to the extreme."

"Was she your girlfriend?" Reese was taking the lead; Steinmetz seemed shamed when he spoke to Lauren.

"For three years. We had a son together. I *thought* we had a son together, that's why I never called the police. I didn't want our son to grow up without his parents. But that was wrong. I should have called when I saw she was dead on the news."

"What do you mean you thought you had a son together?"

"Noah was eight months old when it happened. I thought he was my son. After this happened her drinking got worse. We broke up, I started my own collision business out here, got married, but I still paid for my son. After her fourth DWI she decides she's going to take me to court for more child support but not before swearing out a warrant for not paying back support, which was bogus. I got arrested. The case was thrown out, but my lawyer decided to go hardball. Said he wanted a DNA test, my name on the birth certificate, and full custody." He covered his face with his hands. "I should have just let it go," he breathed between his fingers.

"He wasn't yours?" Reese guessed.

Steinmetz shook his head, face still covered. "No. Not biologically, but he was my son. I raised him and I agreed to keep paying child support for him. Noah was my son. But tell that to a fourteen-year-old boy whose mom's a drunk? He started getting into trouble, skipping school, doing drugs, fighting."

"Where is Noah now?"

His shoulders heaved up and down heavily. "I haven't heard from him in six years. I don't think Shannon has either. I don't know if he's alive or dead."

Lauren let the pain of the moment pass for Steinmetz. "Is that why you never came forward? Because of Noah?"

He took a deep breath and sat up straight, laying his palms flat on the table. "That's what I've been telling myself. At first I guess it was true, but then, I was just afraid. And now you're here and I'm ready. For the consequences."

"Why don't you just tell us what happened in the bar that night?" Reese told him, patting him on the hand for moral support.

"I was working at my dad's collision shop on Fillmore Avenue. Me and her planned to go out because her mom had the baby for the night and it was ladies' night so the girls drank free. But she was already smashed when I picked her up at our apartment in Cheektowaga."

Cheektowaga was a first ring suburb of the city. *No wonder they never got caught*, Lauren thought. *They came into the neighborhood and then never came back.*

"We get to the bar and she's already pissed at me because I wanted to take a shower and change and my shorts didn't have pockets so she had to put my wallet and keys and stuff into her purse. We get to the bar and she's drinking that cheap bar vodka on the rocks, one after another. It was packed and the band loud. I'm trying to squeeze in at the bar and get drinks and there's this Hispanic girl sitting there. I hand her my five-dollar bill and ask her if she can get me my drinks. It's so loud I have to repeat myself a couple times, getting real close to her ear so she can hear what I want. Shannon just loses it. She starts going off that I'm hitting on this girl. Who the hell does she think she is? Doesn't she know we have a baby together? And she's swinging. I'm trying to hold her back, the girl is yelling at her now, calling her crazy. The next thing I know the bouncer grabs both of them by their arms and marches them right out the front door. Me and the girl's friend slip out just as the bouncer closed the door on us. I thought it was over. But they kept yelling at each other. Then the Hispanic girl spit in Shannon's face. The next thing I know she's digging in her purse for my work knife and she jumps on the girl's back. It happened so fast, it was like lightning. I pulled her off, but it was too late. There was my knife, sticking up in her back and she wasn't moving. Shannon had cut her hand and was bleeding like a stuck pig so I wrapped my arms around her and dragged her away. She used my jean jacket to wrap her hand. Then we got in my car and just left. She was still screaming, ranting and raving the whole way back to Cheektowaga."

He brought the brown glazed ceramic mug to his lips and looked down into the steaming coffee. *It's the kind of mug his wife probably bought at a cute little pottery shop when they were on vacation,* Lauren observed, *when he wasn't thinking about that time his ex-girlfriend shanked someone.* He took a swallow, his Adam's apple bobbing with the coffee, took a deep breath, and went on. "I got her calmed down enough to take her to my sister Amy's house a couple streets over. She's a nurse. We told her that Shannon had broke a beer bottle in her hand. Amy had stitched her up before for her drunken falls plenty of times. She never even put two and two together when the murder was on the news the next day. I mean Shannon was a drunk, but she wasn't a killer, right?"

Except for that night, Lauren thought, *when she actually killed someone.*

Reese tried to keep him on track. "Why did you have a knife with you?"

"My dad's shop wasn't in the best neighborhood and it was useful, you know? I'm a mechanic. I used it to cut open boxes, pry lids off cans, a thousand little things. I wore it on a clip on my belt. I just threw it in her big black purse with the rest of my stuff. I never thought she would pull it out."

Lauren wrote that down. "Was it a pocket knife? A butterfly knife …?"

"It was a hunting knife with a five-inch blade. It had a little leather sheath. The sheath was gone. I think she must have dropped it."

She had. Lauren thought back to the crime scene photos: the sheath was recovered next to a car parked on the street.

"What happens now?" Steinmetz asked, leaning back in his chair. From this angle, Lauren could see that he was skinny to the point of being boney, like his shoulders were thin sticks his clothes drooped from. She had always been accused of being too thin, but this guy was gaunt. "Do you put the cuffs on me? Should I call my wife?"

"Does your wife know about the murder?" Lauren asked.

He nodded. "When she got pregnant with our first daughter I told her. When I tell you that every time I have heard a police siren for the last twenty years I thought it was coming for me, it's no exaggeration. I should have come in. After Noah left, I should have turned myself in." His whole body slumped forward, eyes welling with tears that didn't quite spill over. His thin frame seemed to bend on itself, like he was caving in.

"Sir, any charges against you would have to be brought by the district attorney," Reese told him, "but only murder has no statute of limitations. You should call your lawyer, tell him you talked to us, and be prepared to come down and give a formal statement. Why don't you give us as much information on Shannon as you can?"

Lauren marveled at how prepared Kenneth Steinmetz was to go to jail for Vinita Ortiz, even though he wasn't the one who stabbed her. The statute of limitations for being an accessory ran out years ago and even though his crime was one of omission, if his physical condition was any indication, it had weighed on him heavily all this time.

He excused himself after providing Shannon's date of birth, parents' names, and last known address. He walked over to a cherry-stained wooden cabinet and opened a drawer. Inside were dozens of snapshots that he sifted through until he came up with the one he was looking for.

"This is a picture of me with Noah and Shannon at his eighth-grade graduation." He slid the photo across the table to Lauren, who picked it up. It showed a handsome young man in a white button-down and khaki pants smiling in between who he thought were his parents. Shannon Pilski was enormous in a loud yellow dress. She had the pallor of an everyday drinker along with a protruding stomach to match. The boy was in between them, but his arm was around Steinmetz.

"Can we keep this?" she asked.

"Only if I can have it back."

Lauren slid it into the file with the rights card. "Not a problem." She looked at his hand. "That tattoo, of the fish, it's very unique."

He looked down and rubbed his other hand over it. "I got it when I was in the army stationed in Japan. I always thought it would bring me good luck." He shook his head. "Maybe I should have gotten it removed."

41

Katherine Vine's maiden name was Curtain. *Like the kind you hang from the windows,* Lauren thought as she drove to the north towns after work. She'd been excited to get the statement out of Steinmetz that morning. Now if they could just get their DNA results back they'd be ready to rock on the Ortiz case. Shannon Pilski had to submit a blood sample after her third felony DWI, so they could compare the DNA without alerting the suspect.

Until then, she still had to earn her money from Violanti. There was one Curtain listed in the phone book: Karen. Lauren was surprised to find even that. Most people just had cell phones these days. She lived out in a suburb called Getzville, only a fifteen-minute ride from downtown. When Lauren called and left a message, Karen Curtain called back almost immediately and told her to come over right away. She was anxious for someone to listen to her side of the story. Apparently, Anthony had cut her out of the entire decision-making process regarding Katherine's funeral service and the welfare of her nephews.

Packing up her file, Lauren drove out as soon as she was off the clock at work. Getzville was a nice, quiet village with one of those main streets lined with quaint shops and antique stores. Karen Curtain lived right off the main drag on Cedar Street. She had the proverbial little white house with the picket fence on a tree-lined street. The American dream.

Admiring the beautifully manicured flower beds lining the walkway, Lauren made her way to the front porch. Karen opened the door before Lauren was halfway up the steps.

"Come in, come in, Detective Riley. I'm so glad you called." She stepped aside to let her in. Karen was a tall, graceful woman in her fifties. Her hair had grayed, but her face was smooth and unlined. She wore a simple, loose linen dress that hung down around her thin frame. A natural beauty. Karen was what Katherine would've become if she had lived long enough.

"Please, let's sit in the family room." She led Lauren through her immaculate home, past the pastel-hued living room and through the rich reddish-browns of her dining room to a comfortable den full of mismatched furniture and flea market finds that worked so perfectly it may have been on the cover of a magazine.

"Do you mind if I smoke?" she asked, pulling a crystal ashtray toward her on the coffee table.

"No." Lauren hadn't seen a real ashtray in a house in years. She thought back to Amber Anderson's father, ashing in an old beer can. A rock cut crystal ashtray was a rare, exotic luxury these days. *What an old-fashioned, genteel way to kill yourself slowly*, she thought. "You don't look like a smoker."

Karen lit her cigarette with a silver lighter, probably a gift she had received for some long-ago birthday. "I wasn't. I haven't had a cigarette in twenty years, but this was too much for me. Katherine was my baby sister. Our mom and dad died when she was ten and I raised her with my own kids. I bought a pack of cigarettes on the way home from the funeral."

Pulling out her notebook, Lauren asked, "Are you her only family?"

"Me, my husband, my four kids, all grown now." Karen took a long drag. "And, of course, her sons and that man she married. I keep my maiden name for my real estate business. It's easier to put on a business card than Karen Curtain-Deushle."

Clever, Lauren thought. Curtain, like the kind you hang in a house. Nothing like a little subliminal push.

"You didn't like Anthony Vine?"

"Anthony Vine started sniffing around her when she was barely eighteen years old and lifeguarding at his country club. He seduced that child, threw his affair in his wife's face, and then married her to cover up her pregnancy. He was abusive, controlling, and spiteful. I refuse to believe that young boy murdered Katherine. I can't. Not when I know what Anthony is capable of."

"What do you think happened?"

"I know if she was ten minutes late, he would come looking for her. And he would know exactly where she was. Even if she was just visiting me. There is no way she would sit in that car in that lot all night. No way. He would've come and found her."

"Where did he say he was that night?"

"That's the thing," she said, pointing her cigarette at Lauren. "I talked to the boys and both of them said he didn't come home until they were getting ready for summer camp at six thirty that morning. Katherine had enrolled them in a summer sports camp. Less than an hour later, the cops were at the house."

"Did her sons know where their dad had been?"

"He told them he was at his office working late. He does it all the time, the boys say. I don't believe it. Not at all. And when I asked him about it, he went off on me. That's why I tried to file for custody. The day after I confronted him, he cut me off from the boys. I haven't seen them since Katherine's memorial service."

Lauren leafed through her file. "I want to show you some pictures of the car. Inside and out. Tell me if you see anything out of the ordinary."

Karen stubbed her cigarette out and took the stack of pictures. "This is her white Mercedes. Anthony had four other cars, but this one was the only one she was allowed to drive." She tapped a photo. "That's the dent she put in the back bumper two months ago. Anthony told her he'd take it to his guy, but he never got around to it." She flipped through a couple more. They were all pictures taken after the body had been removed. "I don't know why she would have her credit card up on the dashboard. That was her only means of paying for anything. Anthony never gave her cash."

She pulled the last picture closer to her face. "That white scarf. On the seat. That was a present Anthony gave her when they first met. It's a vintage Hermes scarf. He used to love it when she wore it tied up in her hair."

"Did she wear it a lot?"

Her eyebrows knit together. "No. As far as I know, it was a one of a kind. When she was eighteen, he whisked her off to Italy. He bought it for her in Milan. He was still married at the time, but she was madly in love with him. I guess it reminded her of when they were happy. She only wore it on special occasions."

"Do you have any pictures of her wearing it?"

"I'm sure I do, somewhere. I'll look tonight."

Trying to phrase the next question as tactfully as she could, Lauren asked, "Did you know your sister to cheat on Anthony Vine?"

"No. Absolutely not. That's why I think Anthony killed her, or had her killed. I think she wanted to be caught. I think she wanted him to find her in the arms of someone else for revenge. And knowing Anthony, the way he was with her, he'd do it."

"You think Anthony Vine is capable of murder?"

"There is no question in my mind. I went and talked to that investigator, Detective Wheeler? He didn't want to hear a word I had to say. He made up his mind as soon as he had an easy suspect."

"Can you think of anything else that could help me with this investigation?"

She snorted. "Besides the fact he was having an affair with that tennis player? Or that he used to knock her around? Or that he had my sister so medicated she was numb? He counted her pills to make sure she was taking them. The last two weeks, she started flushing them after he went to work. She told me she was trying to decide what to do. I told her to come live with me. I told her … " Now the tears fell down her cheeks and she reached for the cigarette pack on the coffee table. Lighting another smoke, she inhaled deeply, trying to calm herself. "Just be careful if you ever run into that bastard."

"Why's that?"

"He loves beautiful blondes. To death."

Lauren spent two hours taking notes on Katherine Vine. Two cups of tea and three cigarettes later, she felt like she finally knew the victim. Karen had pulled out photo albums, letters, and yearbooks. Everything Joe Wheeler had dismissed, Lauren collected. When she left, Karen Curtain hugged her.

"Thank you for listening to me. I hope you find enough to get that little boy out of jail. Anthony manages to destroy everything good he comes in contact with."

"I'm going to try," she assured Karen.

She wiped her eyes as tears welled up again. "I know you will. I can tell what kind of person you are. You remind me of Katherine a little. Before she met Anthony."

It was dark outside when Lauren left. The long days were starting to wear on her. She glanced at her cell phone before she drove home. Mark had left a message. The days may have been long, but the nights were too short now that she was back with Mark. She hadn't expected to stay at Karen Curtain's house as long as she had. She wondered if Mark had let himself in. If he was making a drink or relaxing on her sofa, watching baseball. She wondered if he had brought Chinese takeout over and if he would give her his fortune cookie because he said they tasted like cardboard.

Her stomach sank when she pulled in and his car wasn't there. No baseball, no Chinese, no fortune cookies. When she got inside, she checked her voice mail. "I got caught up in something. I won't be able to come over tonight. I'm sorry to have to cancel on short notice. I'll call you tomorrow. Love you."

Lauren stared down at the screen. She got the same messages from him when they were married and he was knocking up his secretary. *I deserve this*, she thought. *I know what happens when you do things like this. I didn't care and I did it anyway.*

Knowing that didn't make her feel any better.

What made her feel worse was that she still wanted Mark. She wanted him in her house with her and not with his family. She wanted what Amanda had stolen from her. "I can't do this," she whispered walking up the stairs to her empty bedroom. "I can't."

But she would.

42

The situation with Mark was still lurking in the back of her mind the next day when she went to work. Lauren found herself mulling over her life in general and especially her role in the Cold Case squad. By mid-morning she found herself studying Reese, watching how his leg bounced up and down as he concentrated on his paperwork. He was wearing the shiny black shoes his mother had given to him last Christmas. Lauren liked to tease him when he wore them and call them his tap dance shoes. But she wasn't in the mood for teasing him today. Today she was agitated and maybe even a little hostile. He pretended not to notice her staring at him.

"Remind me again. Why do we do this?"

Reese didn't look up from the old homicide report he was highlighting with a yellow marker. They still hadn't gotten the DNA results from Vinita Ortiz's murder, effectively putting that case on hold. They both wanted those results before they went after the suspect, Shannon Pilski. "Do what?"

Lauren motioned around their cramped office, with its overstuffed file cabinets and overflowing in baskets. "This. Cold cases. Why do we bang our heads against the wall every day, fishing in the same buckets?"

He kept on highlighting. "Because we speak for the dead."

"I know that. That's the standard answer. I taught you that answer, Reese. But why do we speak for the dead? Do they have a lot more to say after twenty years? Are they more chatty when their case gets cold?"

Now he put his marker down and looked at her. "Actually, I misspoke. We speak for the living. For the people left behind with no closure. We say that their loved ones aren't forgotten and that they do matter, even after twenty years."

Lauren paused to consider that for a moment. "That's very profound. You should write that down."

He picked his marker back up. "You taught me that too, dummy. You're just too full of yourself to know it."

"I'm not full of myself."

"Please. If your head were a hot air balloon, I could fly to Paris."

"Wow." She folded her arms across her chest and sat back in her chair. "Now it's coming out how you really feel about me."

He sighed. She was sucking him into her mood. "No. I'm just stating the obvious. It doesn't take a detective to see that you're attractive, and smart, and have a huge chip on your shoulder. You wish you were one or the other. Then things would be easier for you. You'd be too dumb to know men were only interested in your looks or smart enough to attract a good, decent man. As it is, you got the whole package and nothing to show for it."

"As opposed to you, Reese."

"Meaning?"

"Nice house, nobody home."

Grinning as he pulled the bright yellow pen across the page, not looking up, he said, "Stop it. You're gonna make me blush."

"Just stating the obvious."

"That's the way the chicks want guys nowadays—hot and dumb."

"You think so?" Lauren fished a mint out of her top drawer and popped it into her mouth.

"It's worked for me so far."

She shook her head. Reese kept working on the report. She knew she was just feeling frustrated at her whole situation and trying to prod Reese into an argument. He was ignoring her now, with that stupid grin plastered to his pie hole, making her even more irritated.

Lauren looked at the file cabinets that spanned the entire back wall of their office, each representing a different decade of unsolved murders. Add those to the hundreds back in the file room waiting to be reopened and you had an unclimbable mountain of murder. For every one they solved, another one cycled in. Hundreds and hundreds of families whose lives were unwhole, set off balance by a loved one stolen from them. Ripped from them. That's how they felt. She'd heard it so many times from the grieving mothers. Their child had been ripped from their lives and there was no way to patch the hole that was left. And the fact that the murder was unsolved just kept the wound fresh and open to fester every day. And when they heard the Cold Case squad was looking at their baby's homicide, it gave them a burst of hope that crashed as often as not. There was always a reason a case went unsolved and most of the time, they stayed that way. But the families hope against all odds that their situation will be one of the ones that hit the magical lottery of prosecution. And when it doesn't, the detectives are left telling the weeping families that there just isn't enough evidence, not yet. Maybe someday. For most of the families, that someday never comes.

Lauren's eyes swept across the open cases on her desk, skipping over one tragedy to the next.

"Stop brooding," Reese said, slipping the report back into one of the thick expandable manila files they used to hold their cases. "You love this job. It's your life."

"It's not my life," she snapped, sitting up straight, defensive now. Maybe she'd get her wish. Maybe they would argue.

"Easy, Lauren. It's my life too. That's why we're both still single. Well, one of the reasons you're still single."

"You're such an asshole."

"And that's one of the reasons I'm still single." He tossed the heavy folder sideways into an old metal bookshelf behind his desk, effectively filing it away under his foolproof system. Before she could say anything, he spit his pink chewing gum across her desk into the trash can to the left of it and smiled at his hole in one.

"I got news for you, Reese," Lauren replied, disgusted. "Those aren't the only reasons you're still single."

He just kept grinning, put his feet up on his desk, and leaned back in his chair. Lauren turned around to her computer. She could feel his cool green eyes, probably twinkling with evil delight, on her from behind. She didn't want to even look at him anymore.

It was exhausting, not arguing with him.

171

43

Later that night, Mark was at her house, right on time, Chinese takeout in hand. Lauren found herself in a very forgiving mood because he was so happy. Amanda had told him that she thought they were becoming distant and wanted counseling.

"What does that mean?" Lauren asked, scooping out some more sweet and sour chicken.

"I think it means she knows our marriage is on the way out. I think if we go to counseling and we really talk about it and agree, it's done. It'll make a split easier on our son."

"Or she'll convince you to stay because of your son."

"We've been living separate lives for a long time now. She does her thing, I do mine. It's comfortable and civil and my son is happy. But maybe she's not happy."

"Does she suspect you're having an affair?"

"That's the sad part. If she does, she never lets on. You'd think because I'm a proven cheat, she'd be hounding me. But she doesn't. She knows how much money she'll get, so it's almost like she doesn't care."

"She cares. She likes being Mrs. Mark Hathaway." *So did I*, Lauren thought wistfully.

"As long as my son is happy, I'll do whatever she wants to keep things amicable."

Lauren smirked. "You have that much money to throw away now?"

"Yeah." He touched his glass of iced tea to hers and winked at her. "I do."

They made love on the kitchen floor, in the front hall, and halfway up the stairs. They found themselves exhausted, lying on the landing together. For Lauren, it should've been bliss.

Pulling his pants back on, Mark asked, "What's your trial date?"

"End of October, if there aren't any delays."

"Wow," Mark said. "That's a quick turnaround for a murder that happened in June."

She shrugged. "Violanti is pushing for a quick trial, as opposed to dragging it out, which is his normal defense strategy. When you're working pro bono on a case, time is money, I suppose."

"I would charge a thirty-five-thousand-dollar retainer for a murder suspect just walking in the door and another twenty-five if it went to trial, minimum. I can't say I blame the guy. When you're a lawyer, all you have is your time. For every hour he works on this kid's case, he's losing hundreds not defending a paying client."

"I guess I didn't think of it that way," she conceded. "Plus, he's paying me out of his own pocket."

"Taking on a case like this for free would bankrupt a lot of lawyers, especially ones working on their own or in a small firm. You ought to cut him a little slack."

Lauren leaned in and kissed Mark's collarbone. "Let's not talk about Violanti. Let's talk about us."

"Beautiful. I think we should go to Maine after the trial is over. I saw an article in a magazine about this little town on the coast. It has a small lighthouse and a bed-and-breakfast over a tavern. The leaves will be changing. I think we should go."

"What will you tell your wife?"

"Just say you'll go with me. I'll make all the arrangements."

Lauren was now sitting on the carpeted steps leading to the up-stairs. All she had on was Mark's button-down shirt and some brown socks. "You don't talk like a man who's having an affair."

He pulled his tee shirt over his head. "I don't consider this an affair. The more time I spend with you, the more I realize what I gave up to get what I wanted. When I saw you sitting with that short attorney, I was jealous. All I could think about the entire meal was you. Is that fair to Amanda? Is that fair to my son? I need to fix this."

"Come on, Mark, this is the real world. People just don't dump their wives to get back together with their ex. Especially when they have as much to lose as you."

"What would I lose? Little Mark is ten now. Amanda will be main-tained in the style she has grown accustomed to. People get divorced. All I want to do is try to make the transition as easy as possible for my son."

"Why are you telling me this?"

He stretched out against the railing of the stairs. "Because I know you. You aren't going to put up with this situation forever. You'll end up with someone else and it'll be my fault."

"Don't make me any promises," she warned. "Don't get my hopes up."

"Make no mistake," he assured her, "I'm selfish. I'm not doing this for you. I want what I want."

"Even if we hadn't started fooling around, you think that you and Amanda would be heading down this road?"

"You start a marriage off like ours and I think it's inevitable. She wanted my name and my money and I wanted a kid. And let's be honest, I thought I was the man. Hotshot lawyer. Gorgeous wife and family at home, cute little sidepiece. I thought that's what men in my position do."

"I changed my mind. I don't want to talk about this anymore. Do what you have to do, Mark."

He reached over and scooped her up and carried her up the stairs. "You asked for it."

Lauren tried not to put too much stock in the leaving-my-wife speech. She knew it was normal to have remorse when you're having an affair, to try to justify it. Still, it was a nice fantasy. Mark would leave his wife and move back in with her and everyone would live happily ever after.

Lauren was a grown woman; she knew what the real deal was. Mark wasn't intentionally trying to hurt her. He might even half believe what he said. But he was a cheat and a liar, even if it was with the best of intentions. He knew that she was reaching the end of her rope with him and he was trying to tie a knot and hold onto her as long as possible. At twenty-seven, that had been unacceptable. Nearing forty, it was tolerable. Almost.

44

On the last day of July, Lauren sat in Violanti's office, surrounded by his awards and accolades. Never in her life had she seen such a moving tribute to oneself. Plastered around the office were pictures of Violanti with movie stars and dignitaries. Polished wood plaques hung between shelves filled with little glass statues. He had every acknowledgement, accolade, and honor he ever received on display. All of them proudly proclaimed Frank Violanti to be the man you wanted to represent you when you really screwed up.

"Have you been waiting long?" Violanti swept in and deposited a stack of files on his impressive-looking desk. Behind him, the view of the water ate up almost the entire wall.

"Long enough to admire your resume hanging on your walls."

He smiled slyly. "I have to impress potential new clients. The only one I don't have is a newspaper article saying I beat you."

"I'd get a nice print of dogs playing poker to fill that spot if I were you."

"Someday, Riley, someday your luck will run out and I'll be there."

Ignoring that remark, she jumped in. "What do you think about my report on Katherine Vine's sister?"

He flipped open the top file. "I need more on Anthony Vine. I sent the prosecution my witness list."

"You put Anthony Vine on it?"

"And Jennifer Jackson. I'm hoping he'll hit the roof. Or she will. Anyway, I'm hoping we'll get a call from their lawyers and be able to stir the pot."

"The district attorney is going to lose his mind when he sees that."

"I suspect he will." Violanti's smile was wide now. "It's time to get my defense on. The gloves are coming off."

"Good luck with that. I have to go to work."

"Have fun. I'll call you if I need you."

Heading for the door, she called back, "Thanks for the warning."

45

Reese was hunched over a file when she arrived at their office. He was comparing two photographs, looking at one, then bringing the other right to his nose. "You're back," he said absently, turning the picture sideways.

"I had to meet up with Napoleon for a minute. He's been hounding me. And he's paying me, so why put off the inevitable?"

The picture was now upside down and held out at arm's length. "Kelly from the lab called. The DNA from the Ortiz case is in. It's a match to Pilski's sample. I left a message with Kevin King about indicting."

"I can't believe the luck we've had with this case."

"I know, right?" Reese agreed. "It's never this easy. I almost think we're being punked. I had Marilyn make another copy of the file for us, including all of our updates and new reports."

"You've been a busy boy." Lauren stashed her purse in her desk and stuffed her handcuffs through her belt, so that one shackle dangled over the small of her back. The phone rang at her elbow. "Cold Case, Riley."

It was Linda from downstairs. "Lauren, the district attorney is here to see you."

She put her feet up on her desk, knocking a pad of paper to the floor, "Which one?"

"The *district attorney*, not an ADA. Carl Church is here in the lobby and he wants to come up and see you."

Trying to hide her surprise, she swung her feet down and snatched up the fallen pad. "Buzz him in." Lauren hung the phone up and stared at it for a second, gathering her thoughts.

"Who was that?" Reese asked.

Putting her hands behind her head, she sat back in her chair.

"Who was that?" he asked again, sliding the DNA reports back into their envelope.

"I'd take a ride right now, if I were you. Give me a half hour."

"Why?"

"Because Carl Church is on the way up."

Reese slammed his hand on the desk. "I knew it. I knew this case would get you in trouble. We have a ton of work to do on the Ortiz case. I don't have time for this. Damn it, Lauren."

"I don't want you involved. Why don't you take off? Please?"

"How can you be so cavalier about this?"

She sighed. "Because the die is cast. I'm already in up over my head and it's too late to change it now. Just go. I'll deal with it. I don't want you to suffer any of the fallout from my adventures."

He stood up. "This is not how a partnership works, Lauren. We're supposed to be on the same page."

"I'm sorry." It sounded feeble, even to her.

Grabbing up his portable radio, he stalked out.

I manage to complicate every relationship I have, Lauren thought, making sure no sign of the Vine case was on her desk. *Nothing can ever be simple.*

Training her eyes on the door, she sat waiting for Church to come in like a prisoner waiting for the executioner. *If I'd known he was coming, I would've tidied the place up*, she thought to herself as she absently rifled her fingers through a random file in her stack.

Less than five minutes later, there was a single knock on the door. Before Lauren could say anything, it opened. Carl Church didn't wait for invitations.

A former marine, Church kept his salt-and-pepper hair cut high and tight. Still fit in his early sixties, his suit hung perfectly pressed over his impressive frame. A proud black man born, raised, and educated in the City of Buffalo, he surprised everyone fifteen years ago when he swept the mostly white suburbs to clinch the job as the County District Attorney. He backed the right candidates, went to the right fundraisers, and prosecuted the right cases. Now he was arguably the most powerful elected official west of Albany.

Flinging a piece of paper on the desk in front of her, he demanded, "What's this?"

She picked up the document and examined it. "It looks like a defense witness list."

"Funny," he said in a voice that said there was nothing funny about it. "It was faxed to my office this morning. Can you tell me why your name is on it? Or how about Anthony Vine and Jennifer Jackson? Can you explain to me what's going on?"

"I thought you knew the defense hired me after the felony hearing."

"I didn't know what to think. With you and Frank Violanti's track record, I couldn't believe you'd even speak to the man, let alone work for him. I thought maybe you were some half-ass relative of the kid or something. I want to know. Right now. What's going on?"

He was standing over her, looming almost, in his expensive suit and power tie. "It is what it is, Carl. It's a witness list. Violanti hired me as a private investigator and I took the case. Anything else, I can't say."

That set him off. Lauren knew he wasn't used to having his loyalty snatched out from under him. Or being told no. "Have you forgotten all the times I've gone out on a limb for you with your cold cases? How many weak cases I let you run with because you had a hunch? How many nights I spent writing you search warrants and losing sleep over your trials?"

"No. And I haven't forgotten how much publicity those cases got you, and how you used them in your re-election campaigns, either. I think the kid is innocent. I think there's a lot more to this story. I think the detective rushed to make an arrest, maybe under pressure. And I have a hunch who that pressure came from."

"You really want to make an enemy out of me? After all the good work we've done together?"

"Enemy? Did you really use that word just now?"

"What would you call it?" he challenged in his deep baritone voice. "Either you're with me or against me. Understand?"

"No. I don't."

"I'm trying this case, personally."

"What about Lynn Ferro?"

"Second chair."

She paused, letting that sink in. "Oh."

Carl only personally prosecuted the most high-profile cases. Everything else was farmed out to a lesser assistant district attorney. He hadn't taken a case himself in over two years.

"After all the times we stood together on the podium, we're going to be sitting at opposite tables in this case. How's that going to look?"

She couldn't help but smirk a little. She was tired of him trying to bully her in the name of their so-called friendship. "I guess it will look like one of our careers is going to end."

He drew back, shocked that Lauren could even insinuate that she might be able to win against him. He took a deep breath, trying to control his temper. "I'll forget you said that. And we'll see how this plays out. But I'm warning you now, as a friend, to watch your step. I think you backed the wrong horse on this one and I won't defend you when you're proven wrong." He stressed the word *friend*, as if to off-set his previous use of the word *enemy* and how easy it was to change from one to the other.

She wanted to say she wouldn't defend him either. She also wanted to say that they weren't friends. She wanted to tell him to go screw himself. For one of the first times in her adult life, she filtered her thoughts and words and simply said, "I appreciate you coming down and talking to me face to face."

He picked the paper off her desk. "I won't let this affect my office's prosecution of your other cases." He was already rereading the paper, waiting for her to apologize or something absurd like that.

You are so full of baloney, Lauren thought as she stood to face him.

He put on his best politician's face and stuck out his hand. "I'm really quite fond of you, Lauren. It's just a shock to me that you would do something so damaging to your career."

It's only damaging if you arrested the wrong person, she thought as she shook his hand. "Thanks, Carl. I'm glad you were straight with me."

"Sorry to barge in. You know me. I have to get to the bottom of things. Know where I stand."

"I know, Carl. It's okay." Because as far as she was concerned, he was standing in a huge pile of crap.

He seemed to pull himself together and added, "Let me know what we can do about the Ortiz case. I heard you got good numbers on the DNA."

"Will do," she called as he walked out the door. He let it slam behind him. Lauren was all alone in the Cold Case office. She debated whether to call Violanti but thought better of it. She called Reese's cell phone instead and told him, "Everything is taken care of."

"The coast is clear?"

"For now."

"I'll swing around and pick you up for an early lunch. That'll get your mind back on track."

She said okay, but she wasn't that hungry anymore.

46

Violanti called Lauren about two hours later to have her clear a space in her calendar. Both Jennifer Jackson's attorney and Anthony Vine's attorney wanted a meeting with him. He made two appointments for the next evening, one after the other. The two attorneys were demanding to know why their clients were on the defense witness list.

Violanti was in his glory. This was the part he loved. Putting the squeeze on people. The defense had no obligation to tell the prosecution anything, while they had to turn over everything to him as part of discovery. He was working on the assumption that Vine and Jackson had not yet revealed their affair to Carl Church. He had no intention of letting on that not only did he know, he had proof. He'd hold that card up his sleeve for a while. Especially since he hadn't received his discovery material yet. He wanted Lauren there so she could listen in and maybe catch some detail he might not think important. She would be listening with a detective's ear, not a lawyer's.

Violanti looked down at the entries written in red ink in his agenda. This was going to be good. Sometimes he loved his job.

47

Lauren hung up. She hadn't mentioned Carl Church's visit. Violanti would've loved the chance to exploit that social call as a threat, which it was, but in the end would have no bearing on the outcome of the case. It would only make the DA angrier and more determined to personally eradicate her as the traitor she had proved herself to be. See how it plays out, that's what Church had said. She was willing to do that without throwing fuel on the fire.

As she fiddled with the phone, switching it from ear to ear, she called Mark. Answering on the first ring, Lauren didn't tell him about the run-in with Carl either. The two men were friends and she didn't know what he would make of it.

She told him instead not to come over that night, which shocked him a little. Said she had a lot of work to do. Secretly, Lauren enjoyed the disappointment she heard in his voice. She was glad it was Mark and not her for once. Later she'd think about that and how sad that was. How ironic that she was the one having second and third thoughts about their relationship. How this case had drawn them back together and how it was tearing her police career apart.

She was starting to have second thoughts about a lot of things.

48

For the second day in a row Lauren was in Violanti's office. This time she didn't get the carved chair in front of the desk, but a smaller wooden one in the far corner to take notes.

Anthony Vine's attorney was first. He was a big, overstuffed, balding man whose jacket button looked like it was ready to burst at any moment. He sat straight up like the overpreened peacock Violanti knew him to be, chest puffed out, and demanded to know the meaning of his client's name on the defense witness list.

"I'm sure he'll be on the prosecution's list too," Violanti cooed at him soothingly.

"I want to know right now if you intend to point the finger at my client as an alternate suspect."

"I have no intention of telling you my defense strategy."

"It's despicable. A grieving husband. Have you no conscience?" His round face was rapidly turning a stunning reddish purple.

"I assume he has cooperated with the police?"

"Fully."

Pouring it on thick, Violanti asked mildly, "Then what could he possibly fear from me on cross examination?"

Ignoring that, the attorney snapped, "I don't even know if the district attorney plans to use him at trial."

"Exactly why I have to put him on my witness list. You answered your own question. You could have saved yourself a trip, Robert."

"You're a prick, Violanti," he spat as he got up and grabbed his brief case. "A heartless little prick." He stormed out the door without so much as a good day.

Violanti turned to Lauren, who was smirking. "What?"

"He hit the nail on the head. What could I possibly add?" She laughed and scribbled on her notepad.

"Mock me all you want, Detective, but now I know I have his camp rattled. I want Anthony Vine furious on the stand."

"Oh, I believe you. I know how you work." She'd been on the receiving end of his shenanigans more than once.

"Now I'll let Jennifer Jackson's attorney stew for a little while." He reached into his desk drawer and pulled out a fat cigar. "Want one?"

"No thanks. I'm trying to cut down."

"You sure? They're Cuban."

"I can smell it from here. You're going to stink and smell me up too if you light that thing."

"It's a new world, kid." He blazed up, curls of smoke encircling his head. "Smelling like a Cuban cigar should be the least of your worries."

Lauren made a noise that was somewhere between a cough and a gag.

He happily puffed away. He couldn't wait to read Anthony Vine's statement. Violanti had a little mole over in the DA's office, a file clerk who knew his aunt, and she'd given him the gist of it. He had people everywhere. Some he paid, some he helped out when they were in trouble, and some did it because they had a grudge. Violanti didn't care about motives, just results. He would have the statements as soon as the prosecution turned them all over on discovery anyway. It was just nice to be ahead of the game.

Violanti mulled over what they knew so far.

Vine said he called his wife around seven that evening and told her he'd be working late, maybe even staying in his office. His personal office was at his headquarters downtown. He said he fell asleep and didn't get home until six o'clock in the morning. Katherine wasn't there. He woke the housekeeper, who told him Katherine had left around eight the night before. She had put the boys to bed around nine thirty, when Katherine didn't come home.

Violanti found that interesting and wondered if the housekeeper tried to call Anthony. If she did, he didn't mention it. He made a mental note to add her to the witness list. He also wanted Anthony Vine's phone records subpoenaed. Violanti wasn't sure how much that would really tell him. Vine would have an extra cell phone in someone else's name. Guys like him always did.

Anthony Vine had said he was just about to call the police when they showed up at his house. They wouldn't tell him anything there. He was taken to the police station and told the news.

Interesting.

"Well?" Lauren prompted, breaking him out of his thought bubble.

He hit the intercom button on his phone. "Send in Mr. Hoffman, Ruth."

Mr. Hoffman did indeed come strolling in, but with Jennifer Jackson in tow. "Ms. Jackson," Violanti said, trying not to sound surprised. "I wasn't expecting you."

"I'll do the talking," Hoffman prompted. As opposed to Vine's attorney, Mr. Hoffman was thin and sickly looking. His pale skin stretched across his cheeks like he'd had one too many facelifts. The only thing that looked sharp on him were his eyes, dark and beady, like some kind of nocturnal animal.

Hoffman pulled a chair out for his client with one bony hand. She slipped into her seat meekly, off to the side, while he sat directly in front of Violanti. Clutching her thousand-dollar designer bag, Jennifer Jackson looked on the verge of tears. Her blond hair had been cut severely short, almost to the point of a buzz cut. *Interesting*, thought Violanti. Her athletic body looked constricted in the black suit she was wearing. She seemed on the threshold of a full breakdown.

"I've received word that my client is on your witness list. She's a business associate of Anthony Vine, she does not know the accused, and can offer nothing in the way of your case."

Violanti smiled. "Are you sure about that?" He handed the attorney the pictures of her and Anthony Vine at his condo.

Jackson took one look at them, covered her face, and began to cry. Her attorney leaned over and whispered something in her ear. Straightening up, he gave the pictures back.

"Mr. Hoffman, consider this fair warning. If Anthony Vine gets on the stand and says he was in his office that night, I may have to call Ms. Jackson to impeach him. And I certainly wouldn't want her to commit perjury by denying their affair."

She began to sob; Hoffman put a reassuring hand on her back. "There is no denial to the affair."

"Was she with him that night?"

"We choose not to answer that question at this point."

"Because you have to call Vine and get your story straight?"

"Because Ms. Jackson is a public figure. Her husband does not know about the affair. We aren't going to make any more statements to you until her personal affairs are in order. If ever. I will have to trust that you use good taste and conscience in making those photos public. I don't know where you got them, but it's disturbing to Ms. Jackson and myself that she may have been followed." He leaned over and whispered something in Jackson's ear, who nodded emphatically as she tried to control her tears.

"I thank you for your enlightening photos and fair warning. Consider this meeting over." Hoffman stood up and held a hand out to Violanti.

Giving it a pump, he politely averted his gaze from Jennifer, who was going to pieces in her seat. "Always a pleasure," Violanti said. "Goodbye, Mr. Hoffman."

Hoffman didn't even attempt to shake Lauren's hand. Just tilted his head stiffly her way and turned his eyes toward his client. He crooked his arm under Jennifer's, helping her up. She seemed fragile and small, not the confident athlete who was always swinging into Vine's Gyms. She cried all the way out the door.

Leaning all the way back in his chair, Violanti put his hands behind his head. "That went well."

Balling up a page from her notebook, Lauren tried to make a basket and failed. The random paper sat squarely in the middle of the floor. "She was with Anthony Vine that night."

Resisting the urge to get up and grab the paper, Violanti added, "She has every reason in the world to want Katherine out of the picture. Especially if Anthony mentioned to her that Katherine knew about the affair and there was a threat of them being exposed."

"Maybe more than Anthony," Lauren started flipping through the file that she'd amassed on Jennifer Jackson. "Says here she had a two-million-dollar endorsement deal with a sneaker company. Vine was giving her half a million yearly plus a profit percentage to represent his gyms. Her husband is close to a billionaire. She was on the cover of three magazines last month. Should I go on?"

Violanti shook his head. "No. But for the life of me, I don't get the attraction between her and Vine."

"She could do better," Lauren agreed.

Violanti was still trying to wrap his head around it. "What's the draw? She has money. Her husband isn't repulsive. Why fool around with Anthony Vine?"

"If we could figure out why people cheat on one another, we wouldn't be working for peanuts in this dump of a city."

"True," he agreed. Then: "And what's with the hair?"

"You noticed that too?"

"I am a man."

"Well, that's debatable." Violanti was not amused. Lauren shrugged, continuing while relishing the burn. "Maybe some self-punishment. Maybe she knew all this would come out in the wash."

"Maybe. This is good. Now we have two possible alternate suspects. If they were together that night, then they have no alibi, not really. Either one could have gone off and done it, and the other would have to cover."

"Anthony Vine's headquarters is in the Larkin Building. I know they have security cameras there."

"Got any contacts there?"

It was Lauren's turn to smile. "The head of security. Mel Goodman used to be my lieutenant."

"I love this town. Make the call." He pushed his landline toward her, returning the grin.

Less than five minutes later, Violanti's face was twisted in disgust.

"Erased? At whose request?"

She shrugged as she pushed the phone back across the desk. "One guess."

Clutching some papers, Violanti's secretary stuck her head in the office and he viciously waved her away. Shrinking back, the door closed with a soft click.

"Is your old boss willing to testify to that?"

"If you subpoena him, yeah. But I bet he would rather not."

"Has Vine ever requested a tape be scrubbed before?"

"Not in the three years Mel has had the contract. At least, that's what he told me."

"That son of a bitch."

"Mel said Anthony Vine's head of personal security came three days after the murder and had them erase every tape from the week of the homicide."

"How could he do that?" Violanti demanded. "He destroyed evidence."

"Vine owns the building. And David Spencer was under arrest, not Vine. Mel didn't think anything of it, really. Why would he?"

Violanti tapped his pen against his cheek. "Son of a bitch," he repeated, pleased. "This is getting better and better."

Violanti watched as Lauren documented the time and substance of the phone call in her notebook. Later, when she got home, she'd have to type it up and add it to the file. That's what he was paying her for, after all.

While she was meticulously making her notes, Violanti sat mulling over these latest developments. He kept tapping his fountain pen on his cheek, on his desk, making little ink blots on his day planner.

Lauren asked, "How are things with our hormonally driven client?"

"He's going stir crazy. Lifting a lot of weights, doing pushups. He's trying not to dwell on the trial. He just graduated high school for Pete's sake, he should've gotten a reasonable bail. So much for competing with the rich and powerful. Anthony Vine says in he stays and in he stays."

"How's his mom?"

"On the verge of a nervous breakdown. She realizes there's only a fifty-fifty chance her son is coming home."

"That's still better odds than when we started," she pointed out.

"That doesn't comfort her. When David's dad died, she went off the deep end. I'm the closest thing they have to family. This is killing her." Deftly switching the subject, he went on, "I want your friend Mel in here. I want him on paper." He hit his intercom button again. "Alice, get in here. I need to revise my witness list for the Vine case."

"I'm out." Lauren stood with her files.

"Stay within reach. I may need you." He picked up his cell phone and started to stab the numbers with his finger like he was mad at them. Brushing shoulders with Lauren as she left, poor Alice hurried in still holding the papers she had tried to bring in before.

49

Finally in the confines of her home, Lauren poured herself a drink and lay down on the couch. It was getting dark and she was tired. Not ready to go to bed, but tired of the case. Violanti was almost right when he gave it a fifty-fifty; she thought it was really more like forty-sixty to the prosecution. A few sympathetic mothers might hold out. It was hard to say.

She loved coconut rum, pineapple juice, and milk. Her own fake version of a piña colada. She even bought plastic straws to drink it with. Flicking off the lights, she propped her pillows up under her head and prepared to watch some trashy TV. Out of the corner of her eye she noticed a light. For a moment, she thought Mark was pulling in the driveway. She sat up. A car had pulled in across the street in the Mullins driveway. That house had been for sale forever.

Drink in hand, she walked over to the window without turning on the light. She didn't move the curtains but peeked through a crack in the fabric. A dark car was parked far back in the driveway. Its lights were off, making it barely visible. She couldn't make out the driver. He or she was still in the front seat, the car in park.

For a hot second she thought Anthony Vine might have hired someone to follow her. She dismissed that. No private investigator would be that obvious. Someone was watching her house, because from that vantage point, her house was the only thing to watch. She waited another minute.

Time to call the police, she thought as she crept over to the phone. With the lights out, whoever was inside the car had no way to see what she was doing. Lauren dialed 911, told them her address, and said there was a suspicious vehicle in the driveway of the empty house across the street. The dispatcher said they would put it out right away. She hung up and carefully made her way back to the window.

As if they knew Lauren called the police, the dark-colored car came ripping out of the driveway. The driver had ducked down so Lauren couldn't make out a face. She tried to get the plate, but it was obscured by something, maybe a rag.

Within a minute, two police cruisers were at her house. Lauren met them outside. They were young guys, cops she'd never worked with on the street, but who had heard of her. Every cop on the force had heard of her. They took her more seriously than they usually would have. A single woman thinking men were watching her? Normally, it was a blow-off call. But Lauren Riley was something of a police legend, especially now that she was taking on the district attorney. If she thought something was up, these two cops were going to handle it. It made Lauren feel better. She gave them a description of the car and the direction of flight. After they told her they'd check it out and keep an eye on her house, a thought flashed through her mind.

As the red and white lights of the patrol cars faded around the turn, Lauren wondered what kind of unmarked car Joe Wheeler had.

50

Luckily Joe had his police scanner with him. Usually he didn't bother because with Lauren in the throes of passion, she wasn't likely to notice his car. Lover boy didn't come over that night, so she made him right away. He forgot how smart she could be. Thankfully, he had covered his plate after he went through the gates. The security guard didn't bother with him anymore, thought he was on some kind of long-term investigation. He'd pull through the security gate and drive around the corner then pull over and cover his plate with an old black tee shirt. He never thought anyone would notice him because, to be in the neighborhood, you had to belong there. The guard at the gate said so, right?

Now he'd have to give up his surveillance of her house. The cops would go right to the gate and see who came in. He wasn't worried, he hadn't done anything wrong. If he was asked he could say it was part of the Vine case. He was surveilling Lauren to see if she was meeting with possible defense witnesses. She wouldn't press it, though. She never had before. The time would have been when he punched her in the parking lot. She only called the cops because she didn't know who it was. He wondered what would've happened if she had known it was him. Would she have invited him in? Made him some coffee and talked it out? He didn't have a wife and kid to go home to. Joe actually had something to offer her.

Maybe she would've taken his hand, told him everything was okay. There was nothing that couldn't be fixed. He would say nothing, just take her right there. Once she had him again she'd remember why she'd wanted to marry him. She'd forget all the garbage she let get in the way of their love.

He found himself driving to the strip club again. He hoped his favorite girl was back to work. She hadn't been there in a while. He was a little rough on her the last time.

51

"The Invisible Man wants to see us. He cornered me on the way back up from the gym." Reese tossed his gym bag in the corner by his desk and wiped his hands on his dockers. His face was flushed from the shower and he still had droplets of water clinging to his close-cropped hair.

Lauren pulled the cellphone from her ear and hit end in mid-ring. "Right now?"

"That's what he said. Both of us. In his office. I literally haven't seen him around in two weeks. It's like getting an audience with the Queen."

"Okay, then," she said getting up. "Let's do this." She knew that sooner or later the brass would haul her in because of the Katherine Vine case. A million scenarios raced through Lauren's head, none of them good. The commissioner was pulling the plug on her side work, she was getting transferred, they were both suspended. She dug her fingernails into her palms the entire way to the Invisible Man's office at the far end of the Homicide wing, almost drawing blood. This had to be bad, very bad.

Captain Maniechwicz, aka the Invisible Man, was the administrative Homicide captain. Since the squad was supervised on a day-to-day basis by its three sergeants and one lieutenant, all Captain Maniechwicz really had to do was sign off on case clearances, go to high-profile scenes and press conferences, and reassure the commissioner that all was well. It was rare to actually see him in the Homicide wing on a regular working day when nothing hot was going on. It was even more rare that anyone got called into his office. He had a hands-off policy, which he claimed let the detectives do their jobs, but which everyone in Homicide really thought meant absolving him of liability if anyone messed up. He lived by the mantra of plausible deniability.

Lauren had worked in her first precinct with the Invisible Man when she was on patrol. He'd been a lieutenant on the day shift and since she had worked nights usually only saw him in passing when she was leaving and he was coming in. He had been a strange bird even then. He liked to talk in riddles, ask questions when you asked him a question, cock a skeptical eyebrow when you gave him a report—all of which made you feel somehow inferior to his self-proclaimed staggering intellect. Tall, broad, and seventy-five pounds overweight with white-blond hair that gave him a frail look, he seemed more like a bored college philosophy professor than a police captain.

A couple of heads turned as they stood outside his office door, Reese rapping the metal with his knuckle. No one went to see the Invisible Man. His main form of communication was email and memos, asking for more emails and memos, which he sent to the commissioner. Commissioner Bennett loved it because it kept the chain of command documented without either of them being directly involved in anything even remotely controversial.

"Come in," Maniechwicz called. The office was tiny, with bare beige walls. A pair of newer filing cabinets and a printer/fax/copier combo took up the far corner. The captain was sitting in his mammoth office chair, gut spilling over the front of his pleated black pants. Piles of papers were stacked neatly in front of him, some marked up with red pen, others with green stickie notes slapped on them. His system of filing reports was obviously more sophisticated than Reese and Riley's, or at least he gave a great appearance of efficiency. *But that's the Invisible Man,* Lauren thought, *all about the illusion of work.*

The only wall decoration was hanging behind his desk. A huge Buffalo Bills flag in all its red, white, and blue glory was tacked into place, covering the window, making the room take on a reddish tinge. A Jim Kelly bobble head stood sentry at the top of his desk, nodding along occasionally with the conversation.

Reese cleared his throat. "You wanted to see us, Captain?" There was only one armless chair positioned in front of his desk, so they both stood side by side.

He looked up from his city-issue iPad. All the top brass had gotten them that year, with the promise the detectives would inherit them as soon as the newer version came out. The department's own version of the trickle-down economics. "The commissioner called me. Seems that Carl Church is concerned you're working as a private investigator on the Garden Valley homicide. He thinks it could conflict with your duties here in the Buffalo Homicide squad. Are you working a second front for a defense attorney? Is that true?"

The term "second front" was used in the department to describe a second job. It originated with the World War II veterans who had to take a second job to make ends meet back when officers were barely making a living wage. The police job was their first front, the moonlighting job was their second front. The term had just continued being used, with less and less officers remembering its origins every year.

Lauren nodded. "Yes, sir. But I filed all the required second employment forms—"

He held up his meaty hand, cutting her off. "Is that investigation impeding your work here in the Buffalo Homicide squad?"

"No."

He looked over to Reese. "Is her investigation impeding your work here in the Buffalo Homicide squad?"

Reese shook his head. "No."

The Invisible Man clapped his hands together. "Then what you do in your off hours has no bearing on me or my squad. If the DA has a problem with your outside employment, he should take it up with the Police Union. I shall file a report stating such and send it off to the commissioner."

"Is that it?" Lauren asked when he went back to pecking at his iPad.

"Do you want there to be more?" he asked, but he didn't look up from whatever he was doing. Lauren noted the middle button of his Oxford shirt was precariously close to popping off against the strain of his gut. As it was, the material stretched wide, allowing his white undershirt to peep through the gap.

"No, sir."

"Good. Then you two can get back to work." He made a dismissive motion with his left hand and turned his iPad sideways, squinting at it.

Lauren and Reese glanced at each other and retreated from the office. As Lauren was about to close the door behind her she heard him call, "Hey, Lauren."

Freezing in the doorway, she looked back. "Yeah, boss?" He was still hunched over the tablet, poking at it with two meaty fingers.

"I thought Joe Wheeler was an asshole while he was here on the job. I'm sure that hasn't changed. Good luck."

She gave the top of his head a grateful smile. "Thanks, boss." And closed the door behind her.

52

Two things happened after their meeting with the Invisible Man: all hell broke loose and the Vinita Ortiz case got put on hold for the second time by the Buffalo Police Homicide squad.

As soon as Riley and Reese walked back into their office they found Carrie Warnes from Crisis Services pacing around wringing her hands. One of the regular Homicide guys must have let her in. The victim advocate was a frequent flier to the third floor of headquarters, acting as a liaison between victims and the cops. Carrie was a short, squat, matronly twenty-something who wore pink glasses and long, flowy maxi skirts. Her face flushed, eyes wide as saucers, she looked like she was about to have a nervous breakdown in the middle of the Cold Case office.

"We have a situation," she stated, rather dramatically, even for a victim advocate. "It's the Stenz case."

The Stenz case was huge. Twenty-eight years ago, Martha Stenz had been found behind the botanical gardens with her head almost cut off. No blood left in the body. No blood on the ground. No blood anywhere. That was easily explained by the fact that she was killed elsewhere and driven to the scene postmortem by her killer. But the press had put their own spin on it. They dubbed it the Vampire Slaying and it made headlines for weeks.

The main suspect, her husband Freddie, lawyered up right away. The case went cold.

And it would have remained cold if his new wife, Arlene, hadn't come forward just that very morning and told her domestic violence advocate that Freddie had admitted to her he murdered his first wife, Martha.

Arlene, Carrie said, had woken up that morning determined to leave Freddie. She told him she wanted a divorce, and he had fallen on his knees and begged her to stay. She had to, he said, because he had killed Martha to be with her. Arlene was the love of his life, not Martha, and he had killed her to prove it. Despite her obvious terror, he went on to tell Arlene that the wedding ring that Martha had been wearing, along with the knife he used to kill her, was still stashed up in their attic.

After an hour or two, Arlene finally convinced him she was going to stay and he went off to work. She ran like hell to Crisis Services on Main Street, where she'd been secretly receiving help to muster up the courage to leave. Demanding to see Carrie Warnes right away, she was still in her pajamas as she stood in the lobby. Carrie ushered her into her office, and Arlene had broken down.

Crying and carrying on, Arlene said that Freddie told her how he cut his wife's throat, drained the blood into the sump pump in their basement, and dumped her at the botanical gardens. He waited two days to report her missing, giving him plenty of time to clean up. The cops hadn't even looked in the attic when they served their search warrant on the house, Stenz had bragged. They just kept rifling through their bathroom and his car, not bothering to check any of the junkers on his lawn out back to see if they worked. The rusted Chevy Nova had, but by the time the detectives showed up, he had burned out the interior and it was just a shell. Suspious, but not enough to charge him with.

As their conversation went on, Carrie learned that Arlene and Freddie were having an affair at the time of Martha's murder. She had never believed he had done it, even when it first happened. He had convinced her that Martha had been running with some shady people, that he was being framed. Now, all these years later, Freddie dumped this on Arlene and she had to live with the thought she was responsible for Martha Stenz's death.

And that she could be next.

Carrie realized right away Arlene's problem was way above her pay grade. She made Arlene stay put, took her notes, and ran every red light on Main Street to get to headquarters.

Lauren and Reese managed to get Carrie calmed down and Arlene brought over from the Crisis Services building. They spent the rest of the day taking statements, going over the crime scene photos, and nailing down Freddie Stenz's routine.

Even though they had arranged to put Arlene Stenz in protective custody and were proceeding cautiously, they had to make a move soon. Martha Stenz's death had made a huge splash back in the day, and if word leaked out that they had a break in the Vampire Slaying, it could ruin the case. By seven o'clock that evening Reese was putting the finishing touches on the search warrant. Their victim advocate was prepping Arlene to go in front of the judge, who they had pulled out of a fancy dinner party to meet them at the Homicide office, to give a sworn statement in support of the warrant.

It happened like that with cold cases—long stretches with no movement, then a big break. And when that happened, it was like a snowball rolling downhill. If the witness didn't crap out, there was no stopping it. Because of the immediate danger Freddie Stenz posed to his wife, Arlene, an arrest would have to be made right away. An avalanche was getting ready to come down on Freddie Stenz and he had no idea it was about to happen.

53

Kevin King was at their office the next day to go over the developments in the Stenz case with Lauren and Reese. Kevin was a homely red-haired man in his late forties who wore bow ties and loud suits. He called himself the Kinger when he got drunk at the DA's Christmas party every year. He was actually one of Lauren's favorite ADAs to work with. Unfortunately, that night he wasn't his usual wisecracking self, but more reserved and formal.

They sat around the worktable, charts, photos, and statements strewn about. Kevin wouldn't so much as look at Lauren when she spoke. Finally, Reese had enough. "Kevin, if there's a problem with this case, tell us right now. If there's a problem with something else, go screw yourself."

"Come on, Reese, you know when Church isn't happy, nobody's happy."

"Lauren's side work has nothing to do with this case. We are doing this search warrant tonight. I want to know if you're on board one hundred percent."

"You know I am. Church just makes it tough, you know?"

"No, I don't," Lauren chimed in. "Enlighten us."

"Church is friends with Vine. This is personal with him. And with you."

"Really?"

"Carl Church has been milking your cases for years. It's a dirty little joke around the office. If you win this case, when he's personally trying it, his ego will be crushed. He can't have that. He loves standing on the podium with you at press conferences. He is all about appearances. This doesn't look good for him. He hasn't said anything to me, but right now you are a sore subject."

Reese threw his pencil on the table. "I told you this would happen. I told you."

"Shut up, Reese," she shot back. "So, you're telling me my disloyalty is breaking Carl Church's political heart?"

"More like his balls," Kevin admitted. "But you didn't hear it from me."

With the air cleared, they managed to get the search warrant put together. The special term judge who looked it over and signed it praised the detail that had gone into it and wished them luck. Kevin started to get excited, the way you do when a crappy case turns the corner. He wanted to head over to Carl Church's office and give him the heads up on the case. "It's always good to let the boss know what's going on," he said. "Especially when he's in a foul mood."

They broke up the party and agreed to meet at headquarters at eight p.m.

As she finished up some loose ends, Lauren thought about what Kevin had told her. She and Church had stood together for the cameras. He'd thrown his support behind her cases. She hadn't cared why at the time. What was good for him was great for her. Victims' families who had thought their loved ones were forgotten now found closure with arrests and prosecutions. It was a case of one hand washing the other, and it had never mattered to her until now. If it got the killers off the street, then everybody won.

The fact that there were rumors about her around the DA's office bothered her. Granted, when you've been married as many times as she had and been involved with a few cops and attorneys, things were bound to get around. This was different. This was professional. Her reputation as a detective was fragile. Being a woman, it always was. Church was ruthless, this she knew. He didn't defeat his opponents, he destroyed them.

Was that the reason he hasn't taken the gloves off with me yet? Because he's confident he's going to win and wants to teach me a lesson? Make an example out of me? She'd expected fallout from taking the case. A man like Church was a force to be reckoned with, and in all honesty, he really had been good to her over the years. Had she made herself poison to the DA's office for good? Even Kevin King, who had worked with her for years, was tiptoeing around her. And now she had someone watching her house. This was bad.

All because of her unholy alliance with Frank Violanti.

She had to put it out of her mind today because she had a job to do. The search warrant was going to make or break the Stenz case and she had to be on her game. She didn't bother to go home. By the time she got there, she'd have to turn around and come right back. Lauren and Reese had already arranged to have patrol assist them while they did the search warrant at Fredrick Stenz's house that night. Hopefully, after the warrant, it would be case closed on Freddie Stenz.

She and Reese decided to grab some food to kill time. Eating was Reese's favorite pastime; he was constantly hungry. *If I ate as much as him, I'd be a whale,* Lauren thought as they pulled out of headquarters'

211

parking lot. They went to Janice's, a little diner that was open twenty-four hours a day. The place was mobbed with people stopping home after work. He was such a regular, the waitress knew Reese and gave them a big booth in the back.

He perused the menu. Reese was one of those people who always had to ask the waitress for another five minutes to decide. He didn't need another five minutes; he just liked looking at the waitress's ass as she walked away. He was shameless.

"Are you going to tell me 'I told you so' again? I know you can't wait to throw it in my face," Lauren pressed.

He glanced over the top of the menu. "Oh, is that bothering you now, Ice Queen?" He looked back down at the entrees. "Sorry. I was just being sarcastic."

"You're a child, you know that, Reese?"

"Don't hit on me, Riley. You know I'm not into cougars." He smiled up at the waitress who had come to take his order. "I'll have the double cheeseburger basket with a strawberry milkshake."

"I hope you get fat," Lauren huffed and ordered a chicken salad.

Handing the menus over to the waitress, he scoffed, "The ladies will still want me. It's a curse."

"You're cursed, all right," she agreed.

That set the tone for the rest of dinner. She'd say something and he'd come back with a snarky remark. With rough, nervous energy, he tore a napkin to shreds as they talked, his arm muscles working without conscience thought, creating a little pile of paper in front of him. His Army tattoo peaked out from under his shirtsleeve, memorializing his time in the Gulf. His fervor was contagious at that point, charging up Lauren as well. He was invested in this case now and everything was going to come together tonight.

54

At eight o'clock they met with the patrol crews and the lieutenant. An unmarked police car had been sitting on the house for the last five hours. Freddie Stenz was supposed to be at work. There was no sign of his rusty old pickup truck. If all went well, they'd grab him up at the brass factory after they executed the search warrant, pull him right off the line, and march him out in front of all his co-workers. Justice served after all these years. The Vampire Slayer in custody. That was the plan.

Sitting in the backseat of their car, Kevin King wouldn't go in until after they made entry. The assistant district attorneys never did. He'd wait in the car until they cleared the house, room by room, and then supervise the search. Someone had lent him a bulletproof vest two sizes too small for him. The sides flapped open because he couldn't pull the Velcro around his beer gut.

"You know the drill, right?" Lauren asked as he yanked at Kevlar.

"This ain't my first time at the rodeo. Let's just get this over with. My kid has to be at hockey practice at five in the morning."

"Good to know. You're on a deadline."

"Cut it out, Riley."

"Okay." She spun around to face the dash. "Let's do this."

With everyone now in place, Lauren got on the radio. "Car 1077 to car crews on Seaward Avenue? I'm going to approach the front and Detective Reese is going to approach the back. This is a no-knock warrant, so whoever is doing the ram, come with me."

Cops began to drift out of their cars, in position all along the street. It was still light out, the long summer days pushing the twilight back. Seaward Avenue was a lonely street on the Buffalo River that backed to a defunct mill. Most of the crumbling, broken-down houses were abandoned. After the paper mill closed, a lot of the homes were condemned as contaminated. Only a few people stuck around. Fredrick Stenz was one of them. He had inherited the house from his parents, so Arlene said, and refused to move even though he had a good job at the brass factory. He was a pack rat as well, Arlene had told them. He never threw anything away.

Except, it seemed, his first wife.

As Lauren and Reese exited their vehicles, the cops converged on them, and they split into two groups.

"Don't hit the back door right away," Lauren reminded Reese's crew. "Arlene said he has crap piled in front of it. We'll try to navigate around it and let you in."

As if giving a preview of what they'd find inside, the front lawn was littered with ancient lawn mowers and broken shopping carts. Steering her own group of four up the front walkway, Lauren saw Reese's group snake around the garbage in the yard to the back of the property. At least three rusted-out cars were parked in the driveway, end to end. Their parts and pieces were scattered next to them or piled on wooden pallets. Random car doors were stacked against the garage. There was a small lag as both clusters waited for the other to be in position.

Trying to avoid the holes in the rotted wood porch, Lauren situated herself across from Jim Daniels, a powerhouse of a cop, who held the ram. He stood about six-four and was nothing but muscle. Looking at him holding the heavy ram, the random thought went through her head that he might work out at Vine's Gym.

When Lauren calculated everyone had time to get in place, she gave a nod to Jim. Taking his cue, he boomed, "Police! Search warrant!" His voice was thunderous as the ram hit the door, shattering the lock and raining pieces of dry, rotted wood down on them. It seemed to implode in on itself, crumbling into an opening. With guns drawn they entered the house.

They weren't alone.

Standing naked in the middle of the filthy living room with a shotgun pointed at his chin was Freddie Stenz. Beer cans littered the carpet around him. Newspapers were stacked from the floor to the ceiling along the walls. Cockroaches darted in and out of the breaks in the garbage, sent into a panic at being disturbed.

Hands wrapped around the stock, finger on the trigger, Freddie's white, doughy, middle-aged body shook violently.

All five cops stopped dead in their tracks.

"Don't come in another step," Freddie warned.

Lauren held out a hand in a calming gesture, "Listen, Fred. Let's just relax, all right? There's no need for this, okay?"

"I knew when she left me yesterday," he blubbered, the gun bouncing up and down. "I knew she'd tell. I've been waiting here since she left. I knew you'd come. I killed my wife for her, to prove it to her that

215

I loved her. I did it for her." His body was wracked with sobs, tears running down his face, splashing onto his hairy chest.

"She loves you too." Lauren scrambled for words to buy time. Her heart was pounding under her vest. "She wouldn't want you to hurt yourself. Listen, we can work this out, really. Just put the gun down."

"Where's Arlene?"

"She's somewhere safe. Somewhere close. Just put the gun down, then we can talk. You and me. We can work this out."

"Can I talk to her?" he asked hopefully.

"We'll see, okay? Let these guys go outside and call some people—"

Just then, the sound of a boot kicking in the back door rang out through the house.

"What the hell is that?" he screamed, whipping his head around, trying to locate the source of the noise.

"It's just my partner," Lauren explained quickly, trying to calm him back down. "We didn't let him in the back and he's kicking in the door. Don't look at him, look at me. He doesn't know what's happening."

"Stop it! Stop him! Stop!" he screamed.

From behind, the sound of a door splintering filled the room.

"Stay back, Reese! Stand down!" Lauren screamed. But they couldn't hear her. The sound of their boots pounding up the hallway caused a wild look in Freddie's eye as he turned and saw the other cops charging in. That second was all it took.

He pulled the trigger.

Reese stopped up short, blood spatter hitting him full in the face. Freddie's body slumped down like a sack of wet cement.

"Ahhh, no, no, no!" Reese yelled, dropping his gun and trying furiously to wipe his face with both hands. One of the cops he was with bent over and threw up all over the floor.

"What the hell is going on in here?" Kevin came bounding up the front steps. He took one look at the scene before him, his bow tie poking out from his too-tight vest, and went right back out. He had just effectively removed himself from the crime scene.

Suddenly, Lauren had ten pairs of eyes on her, including the lieutenants'. Everyone was looking to her for the next move. She holstered her gun but kept her hand on the grip to stop it from shaking. The other she buried in her pocket.

She took a deep breath to keep it together. "Call the Homicide office, get evidence, and photography. I want this scene taped off." She started giving the various officers tasks. "No one gets in this house but the people already here. We still have a search warrant to serve. Reese, go clean yourself up and check the attic. I'll wait for the ME's office ... "

Just like the cockroaches they had disturbed, the police began to scramble around the garbage and the headless body, careful not to look at the wall where most of the brain matter had hit, intent on doing their assigned task.

Lauren watched as a blood-spattered Reese found the filthy little bathroom off the kitchen. For the first time ever, she had nothing she could say to him.

55

Reese filled the sink with brown water and tried to scrub the gore off him, only partially succeeding. He grasped both sides of the stained porcelain and steadied himself. He could feel his heart pounding in his chest, his ears ringing from the shotgun blast. *I'm wearing this guy's brain,* he thought and fought back the bile that immediately rose in his throat.

Reese knew he still had to serve the warrant, to do his job. He had to suck it up, pick the pieces of skull out of his hair one by one, and get back to business. Slowly, the dizziness evaporated. He could hear Lauren's voice in the living room giving instructions. Looking in the ancient mirror over the sink, he could still see a spray of blood across his nose and cheek. Holding his breath, he splashed more of the dirty water on his face. *I saw worse in the Gulf,* he reminded himself, wiping a grimy towel over his face. *Coward. Frigging murdering coward.*

Dropping the bloodstained towel to the floor, he walked out of the bathroom. All around him cops were rushing back and forth, following

Lauren's orders. The original plan popped in his head; she'd search the downstairs, he'd take the attic. Without going back into the living room, he doubled back and found the stairs. He had to be professional. He had to be thorough. And he had to keep it together in front of the other cops.

Methodically, he started his search at the top of the attic stairs, pulling on latex gloves from his pocket, careful not to touch anything.

"You need some help, Reese?" one of the patrol guys offered from below.

"No, thanks. I got this." He pulled himself all the way up, shining his mini Maglite around the unfinished attic. More boxes, trash, and debris littered the cramped space. "I got this."

Choking back the dust, he checked out the ceiling. Wedged in the rafters were more boxes, skis, an old artificial Christmas tree with silver tinsel dripping from it. The discards of Stenz's entire life.

At ten thirty that night, clothes still dotted in Fredrick Stenz's body fluids, Reese found a bloody knife wrapped in plastic, up in the rafters at the very back of the attic. Freddie had placed his items on the beam carefully, in a neat row. Even though they were hidden from sight if you were floor level, the display was in full view once Reese was eye level, standing on a rickety metal kitchen chair. Like maybe Stenz came up there once in a while to look at his trophies.

The blood was so old it was black. Covered in dust and mouse droppings, next to the wrapped knife, a wedding ring sat in a black velvet jeweler's box. In a handy zippered bag, Reese found a list of how to clean up a crime scene. Also, tucked into the yellowing plastic, was a copy of the life insurance policy Freddie had on Martha Stenz, spotted with his wife's blood.

Complete with a perfect black fingerprint.

Reese called out to the police photographer to come up to the attic to document his find. As he set up his equipment Reese looked over the entire stash.

Freddie didn't even have the decency to wash up, Reese thought as he pointed to the policy with his gloved hand for the camera, *before he looked to see how much he was getting.* He bagged the document after the photographer snapped a photo.

Case closed.

56

Carl Church didn't know what to do about the Stenz case. As he sat in his large, open office he considered the possibilities. Unlike Violanti's, the DA's office was sparsely furnished and bare walled. He wanted no distractions. The previous district attorney had had a monstrously dark, paneled, old-world cave lined with legal books and hung with antique world maps. When people came to see Carl Church, he wanted them focused solely on him. He had county workers rip the paneling out and put in the four stark, white walls. The only decoration was a brass stand in one corner, sporting the American and Marine Corps flags.

He had the perfect opportunity to publicly humiliate Lauren Riley for Fredrick Stenz's suicide. Sloppy police work, he could say. On the other hand, she had gotten a confession out of Stenz before he pulled the trigger, and found the corroborating evidence to clear the case once and for all. All from schmoozing the second wife, who had refused to talk to the police in the past.

Two perfectly sound ways of looking at the outcome of the Vampire Slaying case.

Church had the cell phone in his hand on vibrate. The calls had been coming in since last night from the media, and his voice mail was full. He had to make a statement one way or the other, and he had to do it soon. This was what the press considered a juicy case. Love, sex, the ultimate betrayal, a catchy killer name. They'd be eating this up until the Vine case came to trial.

The Stenz case could influence prospective jurors in the Vine case. Husband with a new lover offs his wife. That hit a little too close to home in favor of the defense. If Church made hay out of this, it would only draw attention to the cheating spouse who'd do anything to get rid of his wife. Violanti would love to quote him during summations.

Carl Church rushed into nothing. He would bide his time and pick his moments. Lauren did everything right at that scene and he certainly didn't want to make her look like a sacrificial lamb when it came time for trial. No, he'd hold off. Winning the case against David Spencer would open up a new door for him; then he could close Lauren Riley's.

He picked up his landline and had his secretary get a hold of his number-two man, Samuel Washington. Washington would give the press conference. He was good at talking a lot and saying very little. *Low key,* he stressed, *we are still looking into the incident. Too soon to comment. All the forensic evidence has not fully been processed and submitted for our office's review,* and so on.

Lauren Riley's greatest asset was that she'd always been lucky. She'd always managed to come out on top. But all things come to an end, eventually.

57

Lauren put on a strong face in the wake of the Stenz suicide, but when she got home, she scrubbed herself raw in the shower. She didn't like to win at any cost. The coward had killed his wife and now he made a victim out of Lauren because she couldn't stop him from pulling the trigger. Reese had left the scene with the same drained look on his face. There was no victory in a suicide. Just more blood and death and brain hanging off the ceiling.

She had days of paperwork ahead of her. She and Reese would have to bring in every single cop for a statement. They'd have to get a rush on the DNA from the knife at the lab. They'd have to get counseling for their star witness, who just about lost her mind when she found out old Freddie'd killed himself. Worse, Frank Violanti had been blowing up her phone, so she'd put it right to voice mail. Talking to the weasel would only make her feel worse.

It wasn't until the next day she realized she hadn't thought of Mark once during the entire episode.

Riley and Reese went about the aftermath professionally. There were no words of comfort or hugs. Maybe they would talk about it later, or the next week, or after they took the last statement. Maybe not. Lauren liked that she didn't have to talk to Reese, that there was no pressing need to fill the silence with small talk. There was no elephant in the room for them. Just paperwork, and that was comfort enough. Somehow they both noticed a slight shift in their relationship. What was once equal had infinitesimally tilted to one side, throwing them off balance.

When she saw Samuel Washington's press conference that afternoon, she was relieved. She knew Church could have played it another way. Lauren also knew he wanted a fair fight. He wanted to beat her on the evidence and use his force of personality to persuade the jury that his side was the right side. And when he did, Lauren figured, that was when the other shoe would fall.

As soon as he saw the press conference, Mark called. He wanted to come over and see her right away, but she held him off for a couple nights to decompress. Seeing Mark would make her feel worse, not better. She stalled him as long as she could, but he was in her bed by the end of the following week.

He had come over right after work on Friday. They ordered a pizza and sat at her dining room table. She broke out the good china they had gotten as a wedding gift from his aunt Judy, wondering if he would notice. He didn't.

"Does your wife suspect anything yet?" she asked bluntly.

"I think she does now," he admitted. "She's been looking at condos on the waterfront. I don't know that I want my son living there, but I don't want to start battling at this point in the game."

"Why wouldn't she live in your house?" Lauren wanted to call it *the estate* but held her tongue.

"I was willing to move to the waterfront and give her the house. Now she says she wants a change. She says the place we have is too big for just her and little Mark. She wants to be closer to downtown and the arts as well."

"She's a patron of the arts now?"

"She loves the galas and gallery openings and crap like that. At least she won't have to drag me along with her anymore."

Lauren studied his face carefully. "You really are going to do this? Divorce your wife?"

"What have I been telling you?" He took a bite out of his pizza. "Damn, this is hot," he sputtered, cheese dripping down his chin.

Later, after they made love, she thought of all the things men did to get and keep the women they wanted. Beat them. Buy them. Kill for them. She thought maybe it had very little to do with love or sex, but power. Power over their women. Mark had all the power in their relationship. He always had. After all that happened in light of the last few months, that didn't bode well.

"Hey, Mark."

He rolled over onto his side. He'd dozed off on the bed, arms outstretched over his head. "Yeah?" Rubbing his eyes, he half sat up.

"I don't think you should come over any more until she really leaves and you've broken up."

"What?" He was sitting straight up now. "Why?"

"Because you're a cheat and a liar. You don't want to hurt anyone's feelings. I get that. You don't want to be the bad guy. But you are the bad guy. If you really want to be with me, move out. When you do, call me and we'll start all over from scratch."

"Are you kidding me? Haven't you been listening to what I've been saying?"

"Very carefully. Get your shit together and then we'll talk. I don't like being your sidepiece anymore. I deserve better than this. And your wife deserves better than this. I got my petty little revenge, I don't have to twist the knife."

"You're serious?"

"Get your clothes on. I love you, but don't come back until you're ready to start over."

Lauren watched him get dressed and listened while he protested, but she wouldn't be swayed. She walked him to the door but wouldn't kiss him goodbye. "Don't do anything rash and hurt your son. Make the transition easy, like you planned. Or stay, if that's what you want."

"I can't believe you're doing this." He pulled the door open.

"Someday, Mark, you'll thank me for this."

And then, like an old-fashioned vinyl record skipping back, he was gone.

58

The next Monday at work Reese noticed the change in her. "You break up with that guy?"

"You can't break up with a married man. But yes, I ended it. How very observant of you to notice."

She almost didn't hear it, so softly said under his breath, but as Reese moved away from the file cabinet she caught the word tumbling from his mouth: "Good."

It didn't feel good. Inside, she ached for Mark. Doing the right thing felt like crap. Especially with the trial coming up. Thankfully, Lindsey was coming home. That just about saved her sanity. Otherwise, she might have caved in to his phone calls. And his text messages. And his emails. She had to tough it out. Lauren had waited ten years for Mark to come around in her life again. She gave him ten years to give up his self-centered lifestyle. She knew people only changed if it benefited them somehow; if the change got them what they wanted. If Lauren was what he really wanted, then he had to show her. She had enough going on without having to wait for him to knock on her door or count the minutes before he left. She thought she could, she thought it wouldn't matter. And it didn't, not at first. Now she wanted all or nothing. It was time to see if he would call her bluff.

Lauren took the weekend off to spend with Lindsey. She usually worked overtime now that both girls were in school, but not this time. The date was circled in red pen: Friday, August 18th. Her first born, her little angel, now at Penn State studying criminal psychology. Lauren waited, watching expectantly out the front window, when Lindsey texted her she was ten minutes out. After what seemed like an eternity, a small green Ford turned into her driveway. Lauren tried not to run out the door, controlling her stride as she walked down the front steps.

The first thing Lauren noticed when Lindsey got out of the car was the weight she had put on. The thin waif was gone and replaced with a curvy woman. She was the spitting image of Lauren, down to the freckles across her nose. Lauren still had a few inches on her, but that was the biggest difference. Erin took after her father, dark hair cut pixie short, chocolate brown eyes. She was a slight, tiny, studious type; the perfect art student. Erin had wanted to study art history in New York City, but decided it was too close and jetted off to Duke. Daughter number two would get her own smother treatment in a couple of weeks.

Screw it, Lauren sprinted across the lawn and hugged Lindsey in the driveway. *My baby's home.*

"Easy, Mom," Lindsey laughed. "I'm in Pennsylvania, not Tibet."

"It seems that way sometimes."

She pulled two bags out of the back seat. "It's only a six-hour drive. You can come visit any time you want."

"Will you take me to a frat party? I've never been to one."

"No." Lindsey slung one of her bags over her shoulder and handed the other to her mother. "I wouldn't want all the hockey guys hitting on my mom."

They walked together into the house. It seemed more complete now with her there, more like the home they'd shared together all those years. Lindsey raced up the stairs to make sure her bedroom was intact. Lauren went into the kitchen to get some iced tea.

Lindsey came back down and walked into the kitchen with folded arms. "Okay, Mom, who is he?"

"Who is who?"

"Who is the guy you're dating?"

"I'm not dating anyone."

"Then why are a bunch of your dirty clothes on my closet floor? You don't fast clean your bedroom unless someone else is going to see it."

"Is that what they teach you in college?"

"Among other things." She sat facing her mom and took her glass of iced tea. "It's not a big deal, Mom. Is he nice? Do I know him?"

Lauren hesitated. Lindsey picked up on it. Now she was going to be relentless. "Who is it?"

"It's Mark. I was seeing Mark for a little while, but now I'm not."

"Mark? You mean Dad? Mom, he's married."

"Yes, daughter, I'm aware. That's why I referred to the dating part in the past tense."

Lindsey slapped her forehead. "I should've known. I'm so stupid. He sent me front-row seats to a concert in Pittsburgh a few weeks ago. The card said he was thinking of me."

"He always sends you and Erin things."

"No, this was different. The tone was different, the wording, like he was wondering if I knew."

"Now you know."

"Why'd you stop seeing him?"

She paused, not really believing she was having this conversation with her daughter. "Because he's married and I don't do those things, and I don't want you or your sister to think that kind of thing is okay."

"Oh, come on, Mom." She laughed. "Don't blame this on us. If you really wanted to date him, you would. Why'd you actually break up?"

She sighed. Lindsey was just like her. "I stopped seeing him because he's married. I wanted him to end it with his wife. I told him to get his act together and then we'd see what happens."

"Very brave, Mom."

"I don't feel brave."

Lindsey sipped her iced tea and reflected on this. "Do you love him?"

"I've always loved him. That's not the point."

"Then what is?"

"If he left his wife for me today, he'd still be a cheat and a liar. I'd never be able to trust him and I know I still haven't forgiven him, so what kind of a future would we have?"

She shrugged. "I guess. But you two have never really let go of each other."

"Maybe that's the problem." She looked around. "I live in the house he bought me. My daughters call him dad. Maybe I need to cut all ties with him and live my life."

Lindsey smirked. "Let me know how that works out for you."

"You'll be the first to know, Princess Lindsey." She decided it was time to change the subject. "What do you want to do today?"

"Can we go to the mall or something? Get our eyebrows waxed?"

She looked at her daughter. "What?"

Lindsey smirked. "Mom, you can't let those things grow wild. It looks like you have a caterpillar on your forehead."

Lauren reached up and felt between her eyes. "Is it that bad?"

"Don't you have any friends that will tell you these things?"

"Dayla, but she's usually drunk."

"Waxing is no joke, Mom." Lindsey put her hands on her hips. "And if you're letting those things sprout, what else are you neglecting to maintain?"

"I never thought I would be having this conversation with you." Lauren grabbed her purse with a wicked smile. "Let's go."

They spent the rest of the day in retail therapy and wax treatments. About three o'clock in the afternoon, Violanti texted her that he had received the discovery material. She didn't bother to answer him because she was trying on flowery summer hats at an absurdly expensive store downtown. *I'll be damned if Violanti thinks I'm working for him today*, she thought, twirling in the mirror. Lindsey pulled out her cell and they took a selfie with their hats and sent it to Erin.

They decided to go to dinner at an Italian place on Main Street. Lauren was in a ridiculously good mood. Being with Lindsey was exactly what she needed after what happened with Mark, coupled with the Stenz incident. It was still hot as the sun was going down, so they decided to eat outside on the sidewalk patio. A cool breeze was blowing off the lake as they enjoyed watching the people strolling by while they ate.

Halfway through their entrees, Lauren noticed a familiar face. "Hey, Reese," she called to her partner, who was walking along toward them.

"Hey, Lauren," he replied. He was dressed casually in a pair of jeans and a tee shirt, his short brown hair covered with a baseball cap. Reese played in college and was obsessed with stats and standings. Lauren removed the considerable pile of shopping bags from the third seat at the table and invited him to join them.

"I was just going to meet my friends down the street for a beer," he explained as he slid in, forming a triangle at the little round table.

"Lucky for us. Reese, this is my oldest daughter Lindsey. Lindsey, this is my partner, Shane Reese."

"Hi, Shane." She reached over her ravioli to shake his hand.

"It's nice to finally meet you. You can call me Reese, everyone does."

Lindsey blushed and looked down into her glass. "Okay. But Shane is a great name."

Oh no, Lauren thought, watching the dynamics of the moment, *my daughter is flirting with my partner.* He smiled. A full, toothpaste-commercial smile. "Thanks. When you're done, why don't you two join us down at Flannigan's?"

"She's not twenty-one," Lauren reminded him.

"She doesn't have to drink. They put those little wrist band things on if you're underage. Don't be such a stick in the mud. My friends have been waiting to meet my famous partner for years now."

Lauren looked at Lindsey, who was urging her with her eyes to accept. She knew she didn't have a good reason to say no, other than that she didn't want her partner to hook up with her daughter. "When we're done, we'll walk down."

"Great. I'm already late, so I'll see you there. Lindsey, fantastic to meet you. See you both in a little while." Jumping up, he waved good-bye as he headed towards the bar.

As soon as he was out of earshot, Lindsey squealed, "Mom, why didn't you ever tell me your partner was hot? And young?"

"I don't look at him like that." She'd done her best over the years not to bring work home with her. Even when she'd needed Reese to come over and help with one fixer-upper problem or another, she always made sure the girls were at school.

"Is there any other way to look at him? Did you see those green eyes?"

"Are they green?"

"Mom..."

"Okay. I get it. He's good-looking," she admitted. "I want you to know that I'm not really comfortable with this. He's been my partner for two years but if he hits on you, I'll have to shoot him."

Her hands went to her hips. "Mom."

"He's too old for you."

"I don't want to marry him. Can't we just go and have a good time? Remember what that is? A good time?"

Lauren knew when to admit defeat. She motioned to their food. "Well, finish your dinner at least. I know he'll still be there when we're done."

Stowing their bags in the car after dessert, they walked the two blocks down to Flannigan's. The baseball game was on and the bar was packed. It was a typical sports bar with signed jerseys on the walls and girls with tight black tee shirts waitressing. The long polished bar was two deep with patrons drinking heavily and watching the game on the big screens. A burly bouncer proofed them as soon they crossed through the door. He glanced at their IDs. "She's underage."

"She's not drinking," Lauren told him. "I'm her mother."

"Damn." He looked them both up and down and handed their licenses back. Snapping a bright yellow wristband around Lindsey's arm, he reiterated, "Damn. I mean, welcome. Please." He motioned them forward into the bar.

Lauren rolled her eyes and Lindsey giggled. From across the bar, at a back table, Reese stood up and waved them over. He was sitting with three other guys in their early thirties, surrounded by pitchers of beer. Lauren and Lindsey threaded their way through the crowd to get to them.

They rearranged themselves so the ladies could sit. "I got you a pitcher of soda." Reese pushed a glass in front of Lindsey. Lauren folded her arms as he set a beer in front of her. "Guys," he announced, "this is my partner, Lauren Riley, and her daughter Lindsey." Hands were shaken all around and Lauren sat herself between Lindsey and Reese as a pre-emptive measure.

As much as she didn't want to, Lauren ended up having a great time. Spilling beer on Reese's friend, she found herself jumping up and cheering with the crowd after a grand slam in the ninth inning. Lindsey rooted for the other team, just to spite the guys. She even managed to snag one of their baseball hats and wear it backwards as a sign of protest.

Once the game was over, Reese and Lauren entertained the group with war stories and good-natured bickering. "So I told her, 'This guy is a total pervert and a runner. We're going to knock on the door and he's going to run right out the back.'" Reese loved telling that story. "And she says, 'No. I got this. Follow my lead. I'm a pro.'"

"Those words have never come out of my mouth, ever," she corrected, trying to get him to stop, but he was on a roll.

"We get to the house and it's a double, right? And dude lives in the upper. We start up the staircase and she says, 'Wait here', and I'm just standing there like, what? This guy always runs. Always. But she's the boss so I stand there."

"I just want to state, for the record, I have never been the boss."

Ignoring that he plunged on, "So she gets to the door and I'm still halfway down the staircase. If this dude looks out the peephole he'll see her, but not me, and I think, okay, now he'll definitely run because he'll think he can get the jump on one female detective. But I forgot one thing."

"What was that?" Lindsey leaned forward, enjoying the moment at her mom's expense.

"That she was in plainclothes. And she had her badge tucked into her shirt and she was wearing jeans. So when our boy heard the knocking he got up from his computer, where he was conveniently watching porn, and saw a good-looking blonde standing there. He must have thought the porno gods had granted his every wish that day—"

"Reese," she warned, but she was laughing too.

"Sorry. Anyway. He throws open the door and says, 'Hey! Who are you?' And Lauren doesn't miss a beat, even though he's got nothing on but a pair of cut off jean shorts, she grabs him by the arm, flips him around, and cuffs him before he even knows what's happening and says, 'I'm the police. Nice to meet you.'"

Everyone roared, clinking their glasses, even Lauren. One of Reese's friends, a guy named Dean, had somehow managed to rearrange the group and sit himself next to her. "That's a great story. He probably thought he was the luckiest guy in the world."

"I don't know about that."

He draped his arm along the back of her seat, leaning in close when he spoke to her, "I know I would have."

"Answered the door in cut-off jean shorts?" Lauren teased him.

"Hey, whatever it takes." He was a physician's assistant who worked for an orthopedist. They kept talking. The pitchers kept coming.

Dean was shorter than Lauren liked, but very smooth and extremely funny. Whenever he laughed, his whole body shook and the laugh reached his soft, brown eyes. She found herself moving closer to him until his arm was around her shoulder, watching his lips and wondering if they were as soft as they looked.

Excusing themselves to the bathroom, Lauren and Lindsey inspected themselves in the mirror while they washed their hands after using the facilities. "Mom, you should totally hook up with Dean."

"I'm not having this conversation with you." She ripped a piece of paper towel from the hanging roll and dried her hands.

"Come on, you just got everything waxed! It's perfect timing."

"You're not too old to ground." She wadded up the paper and threw it into the trash can.

"You can't ground me," Lindsey shot back, pushing open the door, the noise from the bar all but drowning her out, "for speaking the truth."

Maybe I should, she thought as they made their way back to their table. *Why not have a one-night stand?* Reese came into view and Lindsey slid in next to him, laughing at something he said about the bathroom. *Because I care about what they think of me,* she reminded herself, *that's why.*

But there was no harm in flirting, she decided. When last call came, Dean asked for Lauren's number and she was just about to give it to him when another of Reese's friends, who had been doing shots and swiping on Tinder all night, passed out facedown onto the table.

The bartender went nuts. "That's it, folks! You have to go!"

The bouncer rushed over, helped Reese hoist his friend from his seat, and together they got him out of the bar. The whole crowd found themselves out in the street, laughing, trying to get the friend into a cab. In the chaos, Lauren and Lindsey found themselves detached from the group and walking to their car alone.

"Are you going to go out with Dean?" Lindsey asked, taking the car keys from her mother. Lindsey had witnessed firsthand how many of the pitchers Lauren had helped drink.

Lauren had been so engrossed in her conversation with Dean that she'd forgotten to block Reese's access to her daughter. "Are you going to go out with Reese?"

"He didn't ask me," Lindsey pouted.

Pouring herself into the passenger seat she smiled as she closed her eyes. "I told you he was stupid."

59

The next morning Lauren was in a world of hurt. Drinking draft beer in large amounts didn't agree with her keeping food down and she spent most of the day between the bed and toilet. She tried to cover her head with her pillow because it seemed like the phone never stopped ringing. Luckily, Lindsey was there to take messages for her. *I'm too old for this crap*, she thought as her stomach flip-flopped, *this is why I don't socialize anymore.*

Around three o'clock Lindsey came up to her room with a cup of black coffee in her hand. "Frank Violanti called. Wants you to call him right away. The lawn guy called, he's coming over at five, not four. Dean called, left his number ... "

"I didn't give him my phone number."

" ... Reese called and asked if it was okay that he gave Dean your number. And Dad called."

"You mean Mark."

"You've had me call him Dad since I was eight, and now because you're pissed at him you want me to call him Mark? Anyway, Dad called and he's taking me to dinner with little Mark."

Sitting up, Lauren waved the coffee away. "He's using you to get to me."

"Don't flatter yourself. He calls me, we do things, that's why he's my dad."

Lauren didn't feel like fighting this one out so she changed the subject. "Did Reese ask you out?"

"Not yet." Gone was last night's pout, replaced by a confident head tilt.

She rolled over and pulled the covers over her head. "Don't flatter yourself."

60

She waited until she was driving to work on Monday to call Violanti. He was steamed she hadn't returned his phone calls, but she kindly reminded him that her daughter was in town and to butt out.

"We need to get this done as soon as possible," he told her. "I have boxes of discovery material to wade through."

"All right, I'll come over after my shift and we'll go through the discovery material. Don't have a cow. Or in your case, a calf."

"Just be here." If he could have, he would've slammed the phone down in her ear. All she got was a brisk beep.

Reese was crumpling paper up and shooting baskets when she walked in.

"Bored already? It's only eight thirty in the morning."

"It's the Bronstein case." His voice was laced with frustration. "The suspect died yesterday. All that work for nothing."

"The case was thirty-seven years old. We did the best we could. Sometimes we just can't put it together in time."

"I know." He stuffed his notes into the garbage can. "I know. So, did you and your daughter have fun Friday night?"

"We had a lot of fun. Thanks for inviting us."

"My friend Dean is in love with you now."

"He's nice," she said noncommittally.

"I told him to not bother, but he insisted on calling you anyway."

She swiveled around in her seat. "Why would you tell him not to bother?"

He dumped another manila folder into the trashcan. "Because you only date losers and guys who treat you like crap."

"Thanks a lot, partner."

He looked up at her now. "Isn't that the truth? You could go out with Dean. He's a great guy. He's not married, wouldn't beat you up, won't cheat on you, but you wouldn't like that, would you? You want someone more broken than you are."

Lauren sat in stunned silence for a second. "Where the hell did that come from?"

He tore a stack of papers in half. "Never mind. Forget it. It doesn't matter." He threw the last of the papers away, grabbed his jacket, and walked out of their office. Lauren waited. They needed to talk this through.

For the rest of the day she stewed, perplexed about the scene with Reese. Reese was the one constant in her life. She thought they had an almost perfect working relationship. She knew he wasn't happy about her working for Violanti. She also knew he was still messed up from the nasty turn the Stenz case had taken. Having a second suspect die in the same month was shitty luck, but that wasn't anything he could blame her for. Maybe he did want to transfer out. Maybe she wasn't the perfect partner. She'd wait for him to return and they'd talk it out, trading insults and jabs, like they always did.

He never came back to work that day.

61

Lauren met Violanti at his office, still in a twist about Reese. She walked past his secretary without a word and presented herself.

Violanti picked up on her mood as soon as she walked in. "What's eating you?"

"Nothing. What's so important that you had to blow up my phone all weekend?"

He pulled a big cardboard box out from behind his desk. "I can make a lot of hay with this stuff. I got the maid's statement. I got Vine's statement. He lied and said he fell asleep at his office. I got the security guard seeing David walking, not running, from the car. I got Vine's phone records, Katherine's phone records, and Jennifer Jackson's phone records. This stuff is beautiful."

"You're going with the theory that the husband did it?"

"Look at this." He pushed a stack of papers toward Lauren. "This is one month's worth of phone calls to Katherine Vine's cell phone. Anthony Vine called her an average of twenty times a day. Twenty times a day. The only other phone calls were made by her sister, her hairdresser, and the one call from the toy store on the night she was murdered."

"You think that's enough for reasonable doubt?"

"Combine that with a lack of alibi, a hell of a motive, and a tracking device. I think I got something here."

"What do you want me to do?"

There was a pause as Violanti studied her face. "What's wrong? Is something bothering you?"

"Oh, come on," she snapped. "As if you didn't know what this case would do to my career. You sit in here like King Shit of Turd Mountain and bask in your cleverness and I have to wallow in everything rolling downhill."

"Hey," he shot back, "you're a big girl. You're getting paid for this."

"And now I'm a whore just like you."

"No, now you're working for me instead of Church."

"I ought to slap you in your smug little face, Violanti."

"No need for violence, Detective Riley." He pushed back from his desk. "I have a list of things for you to follow up on. I never expected us to become friends, but you will keep your hands to yourself. You have work to do." He held out a piece of paper.

Lauren knew her face was flushed. She snatched the list out of Violanti's hand. "Screw you."

"Yeah well, screw you too. Do your job."

She stormed out of his office, clenching the paper in her fist. She was tempted to rip it to shreds and be done with the whole thing. The problem was, the truth hurt. She took the money, she signed on the dotted line, and she had no right to complain. Lauren Riley had never hated herself more than she did at that moment. As she crossed the plushly carpeted lobby of Violanti's building, she whipped out her cell phone. *I might as well be a total screw up,* she thought as she punched in the number.

He answered on the first ring. "Mark?"

62

Lindsey was eating popcorn and lounging on the sofa when Lauren got home. She had on a pair of short-shorts and an old tee shirt with her fuzzy pink slippers. She looked up as Lauren threw her bag in the closet. "I was getting worried, Mom. Why didn't you call and say you'd be late? I was waiting."

"Did you eat?"

"I made some frozen lasagna I found in the freezer. There's a plate for you. It's in the fridge."

"Thanks." Lauren walked into the kitchen, away from her daughter. She wanted to go take a shower, but she was starving. She nuked the plate and sat at the table with a glass of water. There was a bottle of zinfandel in the fridge, but her head still held the echoes of her hangover from the weekend.

Lindsey walked in holding the popcorn bowl on her hip. "Dayla called. And Dean again. Are you going to call him back?"

"I don't think so."

"Why not?" she demanded.

Lauren sighed and looked up. "I just don't want to, okay?"

"You still want to be with Dad."

"Mark. And it doesn't matter what I want. Some things are beyond our control."

Sitting at the table with her mother, Lindsey put the bowl down and folded her arms. *Like looking in a mirror*, Lauren thought, *or a time machine*. It was like seeing herself at twenty again; thinking you knew everything, your whole life in front of you. "Besides, I want to focus on us while you're home, okay?"

"I just hate seeing you look so sad."

It must be written all over my face, she thought, and suddenly lost her appetite. Calling Mark was a mistake, she knew that from the second she dialed his number. Meeting up with him at his office was Lauren's way of punishing herself. She wasn't vain enough to think it might punish Mark too. The sex had been fast and angry on his desk. The phone next to them kept ringing until she threw it against the wall. Mark took that for excitement instead of rage. When she left, he looked satisfied and she felt empty. What bothered her the most was that she wasn't sure who she should be mad at—Violanti, Reese, Mark, herself, or all of the above.

"I'm just tired of this case I'm working on. It's really starting to wear on me. And the suicide didn't help. I just need to take a break from all this."

"Why don't you take off tomorrow and we'll go somewhere?"

Somewhere. Anywhere was better than where she'd been lately. "That sounds fantastic. Anywhere you want, just as long as there's no police work involved."

Lindsey reached over and popped a forkful of lasagna off of Lauren's plate and into her mouth. "Don't stress. I'll think of something."

They ended up going to the movies, something they hadn't done together in maybe ten years, eating fake, buttery popcorn and drinking soda from jumbo-sized cups. The movie was a romantic comedy and it was passable. Lauren had forgotten how much more enjoyable going out to the movies was. When you shared it with someone special, when you were laughing together.

Inevitably, on the way to the restaurant after the show, her mind drifted to the list Violanti had given her. There were no municipal cameras in Garden Valley; it was a safe suburb with very little crime. Most of the surveillance cameras were privately owned by businesses. Violanti had the brilliant idea that if Anthony Vine left his waterfront condo, he'd have to pass by the city's camera, stationed at the intersection in front of the Naval Park. There was no other way to leave the complex and head south out of the city. If it had been one of her city cases, all she would have to do was walk downstairs and ask to see it. Because she was technically acting as a private citizen, Lauren would have to file a request under the Freedom of Information Act to get the camera footage from that day. That was the drawback to private detective work: more red tape. *But not today*, she thought as she pulled into the Blackthorn. *Today, I'm enjoying my daughter.*

The Blackthorn was her favorite Irish restaurant on Buffalo's South Side. Some beer cheese soup would take her mind off things, and a shot of whiskey. Maybe two shots.

After a fabulous meal of thin sliced corned beef and potatoes boiled and salted to perfection, they sat at the bar enjoying the air conditioning. Unlike Flanagan's, which was a fake Irish bar in the downtown theater district, the Blackthorn was as authentic as the imported polished wood figures carved into the intricate molding along the bar. Lauren's friend Kevin had owned it, but he had passed some years ago, and his brother and sister had taken it over, keeping the feel of home and safety. She'd always taken the girls there to eat, or to celebrate St. Patrick's Day, but this was the first time Lindsey sat at the bar with her.

Sean, the aging bartender, knew how old she was and put a black coffee down in front of her. "Come see me in a couple years." He winked at Lindsey and then set Lauren's Irish coffee on the dark wood.

"Come on, Mom," Lindsey pleaded as he walked away. "I'm not a kid anymore."

"You're my kid and believe me, the longer you wait before you start drinking, the better off you'll be."

"I drink at school all the time."

"Maybe I should have you change schools."

"Mom."

"You're lucky I let you drink coffee." She extracted herself from her stool. "I have to go to the bathroom. Don't touch my drink."

"Mom." She rolled her eyes.

63

Joe Wheeler watched from the corner of his eye as Lauren rose and headed upstairs to the bathroom. The bar was pretty full with the after-dinner crowd, so Joe had planted himself over in the farthest corner with his back to Lauren and Lindsey. Thankfully, two other couples had pulled a table up right next to him, blocking most of Joe from view. He had followed them from his new observation point. Across from the guard shack at the entrance to their neighborhood, there was an access road to an old library that was being restored. Joe could pull onto the road and watch who was coming and going without having to worry about covering his license plate. He sat there until he saw Lauren's car pull out and had waited patiently as they went to see the chick flick. The Blackthorn was a perfect spot to surveil them because it was naturally dim due to the extensive dark woodwork that adorned the bar.

He paused for just another second to make sure Lauren was all the way up the stairs and rose from his seat. He took his empty pint glass up to the bar and squeezed in next to Lindsey.

"Shot of whiskey," he told the bartender and pushed the empty glass forward. The man took it and plunked the shot glass down with a hard thunk. Lindsey looked over. "Nice and cool in here," he said to her as the bartender poured his shot straight from the bottle.

"I guess," she replied noncommittally and turned her back on him.

She doesn't recognize me, Joe thought, enraged. *I was like a father to her for two years and she doesn't even know who I am. Lauren erased my memory from her kids' minds.*

"I said, it's nice in here," he tried again.

"I'm just waiting for someone," she said over her shoulder, not bothering to turn around.

He downed the shot with one gulp and smashed the heavy shot glass upside down on the bar.

"Easy on the wood, pal," the bartender admonished. Joe flicked a twenty at him and stalked out of the bar.

————

Lauren returned five minutes later, settling into her barstool. "What'd I miss?"

"There was the creepiest, sweaty old guy here. He tried to talk to me. Ughhh."

"What happened to him?"

"He got mad and left."

"Good." Lauren scanned the bar, just to make sure. "Sometimes it seems like a girl can't even enjoy a drink without some psycho hitting on her."

"You should've seen him, Mom. He was gross."

64

Lauren was sad to see Lindsey leave, but Erin came home in short order and that took her mind off things again. Lauren had accrued a lot of vacation time and she took it. She and her youngest daughter went shopping and out to dinner and to the movies, just like she had with Lindsey. Erin was more the artsy type and, thankfully, was not interested in going to bars. Instead they went to galleries, where Erin explained light and texture and theme to Lauren. She was impressed with how much Erin had grown since she'd gone away to school the year before. Her baby was now teaching her things.

"Mom, you really need to get a hobby," she told Lauren as they sat in a new seafood restaurant at Canalside. Off to her left, out of the oversized window, she could see the remains of the terminus of the Erie Canal the city had dug up and built an amazing entertainment spot around. Restaurants, bars, the Erie County Naval Park, and masses of actual sightseers surrounded them. If someone would have told Lauren that Buffalo had the potential to be a tourist attraction fifteen years ago, she would have laughed in their face. Now, rising out of the ruins of the grain elevators, abandoned buildings, and broke-down factories, there was a glimmer of hope.

She sipped her diet soda. "Yeah, I could join a book club. I'd be the only lady packing a gun and watching the exits."

"You have to do something." Erin picked some of the salt off the top of her beef on weck. "Doesn't anything interest you?"

She shrugged. "I guess I never thought of it before. I've never had the time. But now that you and Lindsey are gone, I admit, I'm a little bored." Lauren longed for the days when it would be just the three of them again. Probably at Thanksgiving, definitely for Christmas. "I promise I'll find something besides work to keep myself busy. Don't you start worrying about me."

The puppy? she thought. *Maybe after the trial.*

When Erin went back to school the first week of September, Lauren found herself feeling more alone than she ever had in her life, and the golden retriever puppy was sounding better and better. Something had changed between her and Reese, something small, but important. Lauren had felt it the night of the Stenz suicide, and the vibration of it carried over into their everyday work. Reese had come in the day after he stalked out of work and acted as if nothing had happened. Lauren went along because she would rather ignore the situation than deal with it. She consoled herself that everything would be better once David Spencer's case went to trial. Once it was over, she was convinced, things would go back to normal between them.

―――――

By the time they picked up the Ortiz file again it was the first week of October. It was time to try to talk to Shannon Pilski. Time to try to put Vinita Ortiz to rest.

"You want to do this today?" Reese asked.

Lauren began to thread her belt through the loops on her pants, stopping at the last one on her right side to slide her holster on. Buckling up, she adjusted her waistband, now weighted down by her gun. "She lives in my old neighborhood now."

"Want to stop by and visit the relatives?"

"My folks are in Florida now, you know that."

"I did know that. I was hoping to see some of your less-talked-about extended family."

"Like my daughters' aunt, who hasn't seen them since they were in preschool?"

"Now, now," Reese cautioned. "Let's not open up any old wounds while we're out in South Buffalo."

She grabbed the radio. "Isn't your dad from South Buffalo?"

"He was the captain at the station on Hollywood and Abbott Road, right down from Mercy Hospital, but he grew up in the Ward."

South Buffalo was officially known as the Irish heritage district, but the old First Ward was the real ancestral home of Buffalo's Irish community. People who came from the Ward wore their roots like a badge of honor. They were the real Irish, the original immigrants, the seat of Celtic power in the city. Reese liked to rub the fact in that even though Riley grew up on McKinley Parkway, in the heart of South Buffalo, his people were from the Ward and therefore profoundly more Irish.

"I'm sorry, I forgot you were royalty."

He laughed. "It used to mean I was tough, back when the Ward was dumpy. Having a black mom and a white dad wasn't exactly celebrated.

Now the developers are snapping up the land and building high-end condos. Who knew anyone would want a view of the grain elevators?"

The high temperatures of the summer had faded at the end of August, breaking Buffalo's record heat wave, and melted into a spectacular September. By the third week of the month the leaves had already started to change. Lauren hung her hand out of the Impala's window to catch the breeze as they drove over the Skyway. She loved the fall. The weather had chilled, but the nights stayed warm. The breeze off the lake felt like a deliciously cool kiss after the blistering summer. The turning of the page on her kitchen calendar that morning had reminded her that the grand finale was getting near. The trial would start soon, and once it was over, she could concentrate on what to do about Mark. Her life could be her own again.

But first came Vinita Ortiz.

They turned off onto Tifft Street, past the nature preserve, past Bishop Timon High School's football field into the heart of South Buffalo. Every street held a memory for Lauren, from waiting for the bus on South Park Avenue to take her downtown, to the beautiful tree-lined McKinley Parkway, where she'd grown up with her parents and sister. Shannon Pilski lived past Mercy Hospital, where both of Lauren's daughters had been born.

"I want to drive past Dad's old station," Reese told her, heading down McKinley Parkway and cutting up Kimberly Avenue to Abbott Road. "He used to bring me there all the time when I was a kid."

"Sure." Lauren nodded. They continued down Abbott Road, rolling by Reese's father's old firehouse. The firefighters were sitting in lawn chairs out in front, drinking coffee, enjoying the sunny day while a young guy, probably a rookie, polished the brass on the rig just inside the bay doors. Lauren pictured Reese as a kid, climbing on the trucks there, his dad's fire helmet on. The look on his face as they passed by told her it was a good memory for him, maybe one of his best.

Past Mercy Hospital, Abbott Road was starting to get a little rough. There were some closed businesses, run-down bars, and, Lauren realized as they pulled up to the curb, rooming houses. Those had never been there when she was growing up. *Things change,* she thought, climbing out of the car. *I can't complain. I don't even live here anymore.*

They made their way into the two-story building that needed a guy from Code Enforcement to pay a visit right away. Pilski's address was thankfully listed as one of the ground-floor rooms. All the lights in the hallway were smashed out, making them pick their way through a maze of debris to Shannon Pilski's door. Instead of knocking with her hand, Lauren banged the butt end of her radio against the wood. No way she was touching anything in that place.

The smell of stale beer and unwashed clothes assaulted Lauren's nose when Shannon Pilski cracked open her door. Trying not to brush up against the garbage bags that overflowed next to Pilski's door, Riley and Reese were forced to stand single file in the hallway of the rooming house. Shannon's face, now ruddy and bloated with her alcoholism peeked through the door. "Yeah?" she demanded suspiously, looking Lauren up and down.

"Shannon Pilski?"

"Who wants to know?" A cockroach scuttled across the floor behind her.

"I'm Detective Riley and this is Detective Reese. We were wondering if we could come in for a minute and talk to you."

Her eyes narrowed. "About what? I didn't call you. Are you from Child Protective Services?"

"No, ma'am. We're from the Buffalo Police Department. Can we come in and talk?"

"Buffalo Police? What's this about?" The door closed a hair.

"We want to talk to you about an old case." Lauren inched a little closer, trying to get her boot in the crack. "Can we come inside out of the hallway? It's pretty cramped out here."

"What old case?"

"We could go downtown if you don't want to talk here," Reese offered up.

Her eyes focused in on Reese. Her lip curled up, revealing two rotten front teeth. "What do you want to talk to me about?"

"You don't want your neighbors knowing your business, do you?" Lauren asked.

"Fuck you. Talk to my lawyer." With that Pilski slammed the door in Lauren's face, deadbolt turning with a solid *thunk*.

"That went well," Reese laughed, backing out of the garbage path.

"Maybe you should have used your magnetic charms on her." Lauren's face burned as she tried to control her anger.

"I don't think I'm her type."

She half turned back toward the door. "I should just arrest her right now."

"This was her one chance to talk. The DA will get her a lawyer and offer her a preindictment plea," Reese reasoned. "Don't rush things because she told you to screw off."

"I think she told us both to screw off." Lauren stomped down the steps and out into the changing autumn air. It was warm out, but that leafy tinge now hung in the atmosphere. She thought of the copy of the DNA report she had in her folder, stating that the unknown female blood found on the knife, clothes, and street matched the sample Shannon Pilski had to give when she got her third felony DWI. With the statements from her former boyfriend, the bartender, and Luz, it was more than enough to put the cuffs on her. The district attorney liked to take cold cases slow, though. And at this point in the game, with every-thing going on, she wasn't about to rock the boat. She'd let the DA make the preindictment offer, especially if it would save Luz from hav-ing to testify about that night. Opening this wound again had almost given the woman a nervous breakdown. She called Lauren's cell and left a message every day asking for an update, saying she thought she had seen the woman at the mall or that she had strange blocked numbers showing up on her phone. Lauren couldn't imagine Luz on the stand.

"It'll feel good when you get to put those handcuffs on," Reese told her as they approached the car.

"If you say so," Lauren replied, trying to get the feeling of cock-roaches crawling on her to leave. "But remind me to disinfect them afterwards."

65

It was during this down time, while Frank Violanti was preparing for the start of the trial, that his wife Kim knocked on the door of his home office. September had bled into a dazzling October, with red and orange leaves blazing in the trees and Buffalo Bills football frenzy reaching its peak. As he had helped his wife put up the Halloween decorations earlier, like she did every October 1st, he knew he had been spending too much time alone, too much time obsessing about the trial. He knew he had been neglecting her. So when she came in with two big glasses of iced tea, he accepted his with a smile and not the usual scowl for her interrupting his work.

"Thanks, babe," he said and sipped it. She made perfect iced tea, complete with lemon slices floating in the glass, and just the right amount of ice.

"You're in a good mood," she commented, taking her usual seat across from him in the floral easy chair. It had been in their first apartment and survived the move into the new house. Its matching sofa had not been so lucky.

"I see the light at the end of the tunnel. Pretty soon this trial will be over and I can have my life back. We can have our lives back."

She nodded in approval. "I was hoping you'd say that because there's something I need to tell you."

"Oh, yeah? What? Are we going to Aruba for Christmas like you've wanted to? Anything you want, Kim. You've been a saint about all this." He smiled because he meant it. He knew he could be hard to live with and distant when he caught a big case. All she'd ever done was support him. Now that the hard part was coming up, he needed her to know how much he appreciated her.

"Not Aruba. Not this year, Frank." She traced the flower pattern on the armrest with her index finger.

"We're not? Then what?"

"I'm pregnant."

It took a good five seconds for the words to sink in. They'd been trying for over four years. The doctors had found nothing wrong with either of them. These things sometimes take time, they'd been assured over and over. Every month, Kim cried as she got hit with another slap in the face. They'd taken fertility drugs, gotten treatments, but nothing seemed to work. That past April she had turned thirty-eight, which seemed to be a kind of milestone for her. *No more treatments,* she said, *no more shots. I'm done. If there's nothing wrong, maybe we weren't meant to have a baby.* Violanti knew better. Every month when he heard her sobbing in the bathroom, he knew better.

She saw his puzzled look and repeated herself, "We're having a baby."

"We're having a baby?"

Now tears were running down her face. "I wanted to be sure. I waited to tell you."

"When? When are we having a baby?'

"I'm four months pregnant."

"Four months?" Had it really been four months since he'd heard her crying? Or hadn't he been paying attention? He got up and wrapped his arms around her. "I love you. I love you so much. I love our baby ..." Now he was crying too.

His next thought was, *I have to call my mom.*

All the frustration and tension melted away like chocolate on a hot sidewalk. After this trial was over, he was going to be a father.

66

While Frank Violanti was overcome with happiness at the news he was going to be a dad, Joe Wheeler was internalizing all his feelings about Lauren and morphing them into rage as the trial got closer. He was hearing rumors, whispers about a plausible defense. That his cut-and-dried case was not so cut-and-dried. He sat in his office, mentally rehashing the last meeting he had with Church. The trial was a little more than a week away. The case was strong, but Violanti was a smart little bastard. He could twist things.

He toyed with the file in his hand. He had been holding it back, like an insurance policy. He had thought the kid looked familiar when they scooped him up. He remembered looking at David as he sat in their interrogation room and asking himself, *Where do I know this kid from?*

He was too busy with the murder case to follow up on his gut then, but the feeling kept gnawing at him. Now that he had some down time, a little digging into the old files produced his answer: another case starring David Spencer.

He hadn't brought the old file to Church's attention at first because, in reality, he could have done more of an investigation back then. Now, he thought he should give Church the file—he might be able to use it as leverage somehow, if only to make that little turd Violanti sweat about his client.

He tapped the manila folder on the corner of his desk. Thin file. Not much of an investigation. When the situation went down, it had seemed a waste of his time and resources. Just a case of boys being boys. He had disposed of it and relegated the case to closed status as quickly was possible.

He'd take the hit on that. He had bigger fish to fry.

67

The conference room on the sixth floor of the district attorney's office was stifling. With floor-to-ceiling windows that didn't open, it let in the light, trapped the heat, and turned the air inside to a thick soup. Despite the crisp October air outside, in that room it was stuffy as hell.

"Five DWIs, two petty larceny convictions, three assault and harassment charges, two possession of a controlled substance." Kevin King let the papers of Shannon Pilski's rap sheet flutter to the table. "Seven to fifteen years on a manslaughter one charge is a gift."

"My client has three children ... "

"Two of which she lost custody of years ago and another no one can locate." The Kinger had asked that this case be assigned to him. After the disaster at Freddie Stenz's house, he clearly wanted this slam dunk. If Shannon Pilski's young, hippyish court-appointed lawyer thought he could sway Assistant District Attorney King with an appeal for mercy, he was dead wrong. "Let's stop playing games. If she takes it to trial she's looking at twenty to life."

Lauren and Reese sat on either side of King, across the conference table from the public defender and his client. Pilski was slumped in her chair, radiating the smell of booze from every pore. Lauren's mind flashed back to family parties as a child. Her grandmother would get drunk every holiday and berate everyone in the room, including her, the same smell rolling off her in waves. She died of a massive heart attack when Lauren was fourteen, and they never spoke of her again, except in the most general of terms. In Lauren's Irish/Polish catholic family, her grandmother's disease was not to be talked about and the damage she had caused the family was buried under denial.

Pilski's lawyer tried to play that angle. "My client has a serious alcohol problem dating back before this crime was committed."

"And I see she walked out of court-mandated rehab after her last DWI. And never went to her outpatient treatments for her prior convictions, which is why she spent a year of weekends at the county jail in 2014."

"I have a problem!" She slammed her hand on the table. Her ponytail-wearing, patchouli-scented attorney tried to shush her. "How can you charge me for something that happened so long ago? Like it even matters now."

"It matters to Vinita Ortiz's children," Kevin snapped, the flush of anger making the freckles across his cheeks stand out.

"That bitch spit on me! What was I supposed to do? Huh? What the hell would you have done?" She was trying to get up out of her seat, her lawyer practically throwing himself on top of her.

"If your client can't control herself, I'll have to call in the deputies," Kevin told him.

"Call in the deputies. What about these two right here?" She leaned forward, spittle flying from her mouth in a spray. "I guess this one has nothing better to do than go around arresting white people.

Isn't that right?" She turned her venom on Reese. "I bet you love locking up white people, don't you?"

When Reese just sat there looking calmly at her, she picked a pencil off the table and threw it at him, barely missing his head. He didn't even flinch, which pissed her off even more. Lauren marveled at his self-control.

"Fuck you!" Pilski thrust the paperwork in front of her at him, sending reports flying around the room.

"Enough!" Her lawyer yanked her up and shoved her toward the door. "I'll be in touch," he hollered, trying to get her into the hallway. Reese and Riley exchanged glances. The commotion continued outside, with drunken shouts and threats and the sound of the court deputies running up.

"Detectives," Kevin said, shoveling his paperwork into his polished leather briefcase, "I think we'll have a plea agreement shortly."

Lauren walked out of the DA's office with her head full of lists of things to do. She had to get all the paperwork straight in case Pilski did take the plea. She would still have to go through the arrest process, only her lawyer would deliver her to the court.

Reese decided to go meet with an old informant over at the holding center, probably to walk off the urge to punch Shannon Pilski, so Lauren agreed to take the file back to the office. The DA's office was right across the street from police headquarters. Lauren crossed the four lanes of traffic at the crosswalk, cutting through the side parking lot that ran alongside her building. She had a lot to put together. The Invisible Man would want all the details when Kinger indicted. Ticking them off, one by one in her head, she pulled out her phone and started making notes. The older she got, the more she found herself relying on her To Do list. It was as if she'd reached maximum storage in her brain and now needed an external hard drive to keep everything in order. As she walked through the lot, a shadow fell across her.

Anthony Vine was standing in front of her.

What is it with me and parking lots? she thought, stopping up short.

He was blocking her way, beefy hands folded neatly in front of him, like a middle-aged nightclub bouncer with badly dyed black hair. His red tee shirt was stretched across his oddly muscled torso. It was like someone had sewn an old man's head onto a young man's body. That didn't concern her as much as the guy standing ten feet away, also muscled, but young and thuggish.

"Mr. Vine." Lauren asked, "What can I do for you?"

"Why are you poking around in my life?" His voice was soft and flat.

"Excuse me?"

"Your little runt boss of a defense attorney put me on his witness list. Me. Why are you looking at me and not David Spencer? Why would you do that? Do you need the money that bad? Are they not paying you enough on the city payroll?" He didn't sound threatening, just genuinely puzzled.

"Mr. Vine, if you want to sit down and have a conversation, we can go right to Mr. Violanti's office. With the trial starting next week I'm more than willing to listen to what you have to say—"

He raised a hulking arm and waved that thought away. "I'm just trying to wrap my head around a person who took an oath to protect and serve, who then tries to get killers off and frame innocent victims."

She took a step back. "Mr. Vine, this is not the time or the place for this." The smell of the car fumes in the lot started to make her feel lightheaded. It was as if every car decided to leave the lot simultaneously and needed to exhale as much carbon monoxide as possible.

"My wife," he continued, moving forward to match her step, "was a sick woman. She was diagnosed bipolar and suffered from paranoia. I tried to help her."

"By drugging her up and putting a tracker on her car?" Lauren's temper started to rise. Even though his tone was more condescending than threatening, she was tired of getting bullied, tired of getting pushed around.

"I was trying to get her back to reality. Did you know she bought ten thousand dollars' worth of crystals a month before she was murdered? She thought they could cure the voices that told her to do things. I was trying to save her life."

"Having an affair was saving her life?"

He gave a hard laugh. "I never said I was a good husband. But I didn't kill my wife, and you're trying to make me look guilty instead of that kid."

"You've done enough to make yourself look guilty, I didn't have to do a thing."

Now anger seeped into his voice. "Watch your mouth. When you make accusations, you better have something to back them up with."

"What if I said I do?"

Not used to having women stand up to him, he sputtered, "I'd say you better quit this case and stay with the police department while you still have a job."

She cocked an eyebrow, hoping to piss him off even more. "That's not how this works. David Spencer deserves a good legal defense. I'm just following the evidence."

"Follow something else. You're making a mistake, Detective." He suddenly turned and snapped his fingers. The younger version of him jumped in the driver seat of a sleek black sedan and revved the engine while Vine headed for the passenger side.

"I'm just doing my job!" Lauren called after him.

"Whatever helps you sleep at night," he tossed back, getting in the car and speeding away, leaving Lauren standing on the sidewalk.

Parking ramps, she thought as she walked toward her building. *Or maybe I'd have better luck with buses.*

68

The next day Lauren dropped by Violanti's office with copies of the disk he had asked for, which showed the intersection activity outside of the condo the night of Katherine Vine's murder. She's been so caught up with the Stenz and Ortiz cases she hadn't gotten around to bringing them over. She also wanted to tell him about the weird little run-in she had with Anthony Vine, but Violanti was hustling out of his office as she crossed the threshold.

"I can't talk right now. I'm due in court. Drop those off to my secretary."

"What case?"

She turned and followed him back to the elevator. He was definitely avoiding her. "It's a suppression motion in David's case. It's nothing." He stabbed the button on the panel with one short finger and looked up at the numbers descending over the door.

"What's Church trying to suppress?"

"He isn't," he said, still looking up. "We are."

"What are you trying to suppress?" The doors slid open. Two women were already in the elevator, business dressed, but with sneakers on so they could walk on their lunch break.

Violanti sighed. "It's nothing, okay? It's a witness who has no relevance to this case. They added her on the witness list two days ago. The trial starts Monday. I had to schedule this fast." The door opened and he walked out without checking to see if she was following him, which she was. She'd wanted to tell him about Vine's visit, but that took a backseat now to whatever Violanti was up to.

"Who's the witness?" she pressed as they crossed the lobby, his short legs doing double duty to stay one step ahead of her.

"Someone who was dealt with two years ago and should never have been brought up."

"Violanti." They hit the revolving door and spilled out into the street. "What aren't you telling me?"

"Just go do whatever it is you do and let me handle this, okay?"

"Do you mind if I watch?"

He stopped and faced her. "I do mind. Please, just let me handle this."

She studied his face. "Who's the witness?"

"Please, Lauren? Sometimes ignorance is bliss."

"Now you know I'm coming."

The stand-off lasted another second before he stomped off toward the courthouse. "Suit yourself. I'm trying this case in less than a week. I don't have time for this."

Lauren followed him from a distance to the courthouse. It was an odd-looking mashup of old and new architecture. When you caught a case at the Erie County courthouse you never knew if you'd be in the 1800s with soaring ceilings twenty feet high, the boxy 1970s, or the airy open 1990s. Today they were in the '70s.

As Violanti unloaded all his files on the defense table, Lauren found a seat in the gallery. Hard plastic chairs were linked together so no one could throw them. There was a woman she'd never seen before sitting in the front row with a young girl. The girl was cute and a little chubby, with a bob haircut and black glasses. She looked nervous and the woman with her, presumably her mother, looked ready to pass out. Her face was flushed and her hands were clenched around the bamboo handle of a straw bag. The only other person in the courtroom was a single deputy until Lynn Ferro came in with her briefcase. Church didn't handle such mundane tasks as suppression hearings. Not enough splash for him.

Another deputy came in, whispered to the first, then they both disappeared down a side hallway. As if on cue, the court clerk and stenographer came in together from the right side of the judge's bench and took their places. The bailiff came in, looked around, and then announced, "All rise. The Honorable Judge O'Keefe presiding."

The three women in the gallery stood as the judge made his way from behind his seat and slid into place. "You may be seated," he said. The three women sank back into their plastic chairs.

His court clerk pulled a file from a stack on her desk, handed it to the judge, and announced, "This is docket number 324567 on the calendar. A hearing to suppress the testimony of Samantha Godwin pursuant to the case of the People versus David Ryan Spencer."

The judge opened the file and leafed through the motion. "This is a last-minute witness for the prosecution?"

"It is, Your Honor," Lynn Ferro piped up. "We apologize for the delay, but her existence was only made known to us by Garden Valley Detective Joe Wheeler five days ago."

"And it is your contention, Mr. Violanti, that this witness should be suppressed on a number of grounds."

"These are unproven allegations that were dealt with by the police two years ago. They found no evidence to support her claim. No charges were ever filed. The report was sealed. These allegations have no relevance to the matter at hand and would be extremely prejudicial to the jury. I'd also like the record to reflect that this matter is set for trial starting this Monday, October 23rd."

"Sir, the people contend that this shows a pattern of conduct and a propensity for violence against women—"

"Objection! The girl herself never alleges my client physically hurt her in any way."

"Enough," the judge said wearily. "Bring in the defendant. Are the people ready?"

"Yes, Your Honor."

"Mr. Violanti?"

"Yes, sir."

There was a long moment of silence as everyone waited for David to be brought out. He was wearing the jail uniform; presumably because the hearing was scheduled so fast, Violanti didn't have time to prep him. Lauren knew he wouldn't be testifying anyway. Not here. Not yet.

Looking a little confused and scared, David sat at Violanti's table. He closed his eyes tightly together, as if he hadn't fully processed what was going on yet, then opened them while releasing a heavy breath. David whispered something to his godfather, who silenced him with a small sweep of his hand.

The judge addressed Lynn Ferro, "Call your witness."

"Sir, the People call Samantha Godwin."

Rising from her seat in the gallery, the teenage girl came forward and walked through the gate that one of the deputies held open for her. She passed David without looking at him and let herself be guided to the witness stand. The court clerk held a Bible out to her and asked as she placed her hand on it, "Do you swear to tell the truth, the whole truth and nothing but the truth so help you God?"

She nodded. "Yes."

"You'll have to speak up," the court stenographer admonished.

"Oh, okay," she stammered a little. "Sorry."

"Have a seat." The judge motioned her to the witness stand. Sinking down onto it like it was an electric chair, she sat on the very edge, her mouth almost touching the microphone in front of her. Her simple pale blue dress seemed to make her look younger, along with her chubby cheeks and studious glasses. Lauren wondered if Church had suggested that outfit. He was a stickler for dramatic detail.

Lynn Ferro rose and crossed the courtroom. She went through the usual pedigree information: name, age, address. What grade was she in? Where did she go to school?

Then she got to the meat of the inquiry. "Do you know the defendant, David Spencer?"

"Yes."

"From where do you know him?"

Her eyes darted to David then back to the prosecutor. "From school. He was a year ahead of me in school."

Ferro walked over and leaned her arm on the edge of the witness box. A classic lawyer move. "When did you first meet David Spencer?"

"When I was a sophomore and he was a junior."

"How did you meet him?"

"Everybody knew who David Spencer was. He was the best football player in school. He made varsity his freshman year."

"He was popular?"

"Yes."

"How did you meet him?" Lynn prompted.

"My friend invited me to a party in the quarry—"

"What quarry is that?"

"Oh, it's the old abandoned quarry off of Lakeshore Road. I don't know if it has an official name. Kids have parties there. Beer, fires, and stuff. They were having a party there because it was homecoming that weekend and we had won the game and everyone was happy and celebrating."

"You and your friend went to the party?"

Samantha nodded. "Kaitlyn Kelly. She's a cheerleader and she knew a lot of the guys. We got there just when it was getting dark. Some of the guys went and got firewood and built a fire. Everyone was drinking beer. David had pulled his Jeep down to the quarry and had music playing from it. He knew my friend Kaitlyn, she introduced us."

"What happened next?"

"The cops came. Everyone scattered because we could see the flashing lights coming from the road. David said for me and Kaitlyn to get into his Jeep and we did. He drove out the other way, up onto the tracks. He followed them to a back road and then we got back onto the main road. He said he would take us home."

"Did he?"

She nodded. "He took Kaitlyn home first because she lived the closest. He dropped her off at the top of her street and then we watched until she got in. I told him where I lived and he asked if I wanted to hang out for a little while longer."

"What did you say?"

"I said okay, but I had to be home by ten thirty. He said okay and we started to drive around. After a while, he pulled over under an old railroad bridge by the school. He said he wanted to talk."

"What did you talk about?"

A tear slid down her cheek. "Nothing. He kissed me and at first I kissed him back. Then he tried to take my shirt off and I said no."

"He tried to take your shirt off and you said no? Clearly said no?"

"He stopped and we kept kissing and then he did it again. And I said no again. And he stopped for a while. Then he tried to put my hand on his penis and I pulled away and told him to take me home. He just kept kissing me and kept trying to get me to do things, then he just went ahead and had sex with me."

"What do you mean, 'he had sex' with you?"

Samantha sputtered, clearly distressed. "He pulled his pants down and just went ahead and had sex with me. I just lay there because I didn't know how to stop him. When he finished, he started up the Jeep and dropped me off. I was so shocked, I ran upstairs and took a shower. I was freaking out because he didn't use a condom. I didn't know what to do." Her tears were free flowing now. The judge held out a box of tissues he kept on his desk for just such an occasion. She took one and wiped her eyes and sniffed.

"For the record, Samantha, did you say the word *no* to David Spencer when he tried to have intercourse with you?"

She sniffled. "Yes."

"Did you say *no* repeatedly to David Spencer?"

"Yes." The pain in her voice was heartbreaking to Lauren.

"Did you want to have sexual intercourse with David Spencer?"

"No."

Lynn's voice dropped a notch. Lauren knew this was the part that Violanti would come back to later to attack. "Did you report what happened to anyone?"

Samantha shook her head. "I told my mother and she took me to the doctor and they called the police."

"How much later did you tell your mother?"

"Two months."

"Why did you wait so long?"

"I was scared. He was really popular and I was afraid no one would believe me." She sniffed again and wiped her nose with the tissue.

Lynn Ferro turned to the judge. "No further questions for the witness, Your Honor."

She turned on her heel and walked back to the prosecution table. Violanti got up slowly, holding a file in front of him and walked toward the girl, keeping a polite distance.

"Are you ready to continue, Miss Godwin, or do you need to take a break?" Violanti asked kindly.

She shook her head. "No, I'm okay."

"Good. Just let me know if you need to stop. I only have a few questions."

"Okay."

"You testified that when David tried to take your shirt off, you said no, correct?"

"I said no."

"And you testified that when he tried to put your hand on his penis, you said no, correct?"

"Correct."

"But you testified that you kept kissing him, correct?"

"Yes." Her answer was just above a whisper.

"And when you testified he had sex with you, you didn't mention you said no again, is that correct?"

"I'd already said it."

"But you continued to kiss him?"

"He knew I didn't want to have sex with him." Her voice sounded mad and confused now. She was getting defensive and scared.

Lauren's gut twisted. Sexual assault victims always ended up defending themselves.

Violanti leaned in closer. "How did he know? If you didn't say it, how did he know?"

Lynn Ferro jumped up. "Objection!"

"Withdrawn. Samantha, what made you decide to tell your mother about what had happened between you and David?"

"I needed to go see a doctor. I thought something was wrong with me."

"You thought David had given you something?"

She nodded. Her cheeks flushed red, a tear rolled down one cheek and soaked into the front of her blouse.

"You have to say yes or no, Samantha."

"Yes."

"Did he give you something?"

"No, I had a yeast infection."

Violanti took a step back now, putting distance between himself and Samantha. "The doctor called the police, correct?"

"Yes."

"You didn't call the police?"

Her voice was getting smaller. "No."

"Your mother didn't call the police?"

Almost inaudible: "No."

"What did the police do?"

Barely a whisper now: "They took a report and a detective came to my house. He said since there was no evidence it would be my word against his."

"Was this Detective Joe Wheeler?"

She nodded.

"I'm afraid you're going to have to speak your answers out loud."

"Yes."

"Was it Detective Wheeler who contacted you for this proceeding?"

Louder: "Yes."

"Did you continue to go to school with David Spencer after the night at the bonfire?"

Samantha's eyes slid over to David, then quickly back to Violanti. "Yes."

"Did he threaten you at all?"

"No."

"Did his friends threaten you?"

"No."

"Did David ever speak to you again after that night?"

"No." More tears, now her shoulders were shaking.

"How did that make you feel? When he didn't speak to you?"

The prosecutor leapt to her feet. "Objection!"

The judge pounded the gavel, but Violanti quickly said, "Withdrawn. Your Honor, I have no more questions for Samantha."

She was slumped over in the witness box, sobbing and clutching the tissue the judge had given her. Judge O'Keefe made a motion and the bailiff let her mother approach the box and remove her gently from the stand. The mom glared at David as she passed, arms wrapped around her daughter.

Like a lioness protecting her cub, Lauren thought as she walked Samantha right out of the courtroom.

"Your honor…" Ferro chimed in, hoping to make a point quickly, but the judge shot her down. He held up one hand, and she stopped mid-sentence.

"Miss Ferro, we don't have to go any further. Your office knows that Miss Godwin could never be used as a witness. While I have no opinion as to whether or not the event actually occurred the way she described it, you know and Mr. Church knows that you cannot use an unproven allegation of a juvenile against another juvenile at trial. I can only surmise that Mr. Church was hoping that this would leak to the press somehow. I'd expect a stunt like this from Mr. Violanti, but not you, Miss Ferro. I'm sustaining the defense's motion to suppress this witness. Furthermore, I'm instructing you and your office to make no mention of this witness at trial and to have no comment about this witness should you be asked about her by the press."

"Your Honor—"

"You skated on some thin ice this time. No more stunts, Miss Ferro." The judge got up and walked off the stand without another word.

Violanti turned toward Lynn Ferro. "Nice try." He smirked.

"Asshole," she shot back and gathered up her paperwork. Violanti patted David on the shoulder. His face was as white as the paper his motion was written on. The deputies came forward and led him out through a side door, back to the lockup.

Lauren waited until Violanti passed her before she got up. She followed him silently out of the courthouse onto the street.

"Go home, Lauren," he called without turning around.

"No, I think you and I need to talk."

"Nothing to talk about."

She caught up to him and matched his stride. All around them people were streaming by, on their way to lunch or back to work or home for the day. "When were you going to tell me about this?"

"I wasn't. You heard the judge, it's an unproved allegation."

A really huge unproved allegation, Lauren thought, *you conniving prick.* "You should've told me."

"I get it. I get it. I'm a bastard. I tricked you into this. Blah, blah, blah. Give me back the money and go home. If not, I have work to do."

Lauren suppressed the urge to punch him in the throat. "It's a good thing for you I found Jennifer Jackson's car on tape rolling through the intersection at 9:50 that night and returning at 10:45."

Violanti stopped dead in his tracks, causing a woman to walk face first into his back. He apologized as she brushed past him, swearing under her breath. "What?"

"The windows are too dark to tell who's driving, but the plate on the Lexus comes back to Jennifer Jackson."

The astonished look that had spread across his face was replaced with a wide smile. "Motive and opportunity. Son of a bitch."

She slapped him hard in the stomach with the package containing the disks she'd been carrying the whole time, knocking the wind out of him. She hadn't suppressed the urge to hit him very well after all. "Merry Christmas, asshole."

69

David was fifteen minutes late getting down to the rec room because of the hearing. The courthouse deputies had turned him over to the holding center guards who, in turn, had to take him back to his cell to put his paperwork away once the side show was over.

None of the other guards took notice of him as he shuffled with an attitude to the empty weight bench at the south end of the room. The other bench was occupied by Stefan, who was already shiny with perspiration. With his shirt off, David could see the rest of Stefan's lean torso, covered over in tattoos and scars. One particularly nasty one ran from his collarbone to his belly, red and puckered, like someone had taken a jagged piece of glass and sliced him with it. Maybe someone had.

"Where you been?" Stefan asked through gritted teeth as he pumped the bar over his head. "They picking your jury?"

"No. Not yet. Tomorrow and the next day, my uncle said. I had a hearing this morning," David said, pulling a ten-pound disk off the bar and replacing it with a twenty. "Frigging cops."

"What'd they do, bro?"

David laid on the bench and gripped the bar above his head. He sucked air in and out, in and out, and then pumped the weights up. "They found this girl and wanted to use her at my trial. My lawyer got it all thrown out, but I can't believe all the bullshit," he huffed between reps.

"Who's the girl?"

"A nobody. A loser. A freaking lame ass who wanted to screw someone on the football team. Then after we did it and I never called her, said I forced her to have sex with me."

"When was this?"

"Like, two years ago! I can't even believe the girl had the nerve to get on the stand and say that shit. She was lucky to even get me to talk to her, let alone have sex with her. She should be thanking me for being too drunk to care what she looked like." As David began working out, he shifted his anger from the weights to her. He began to think of all the things he'd like to do to that bitch now. He'd make what happened on the way home that night seem like a peck on the cheek.

Stefan nodded solemnly. "Broads are like that. They drink too much and it's your fault. You have to be careful. They say, 'I said no'. But you're already half undressed. You can't go halfway with a man and then take it back."

"That's what I'm saying." David was pumping the bar rhythmically now. "She knew exactly what was going to happen the minute she got in my Jeep."

"I had a girl try to press charges against me for some shit like that before." Stefan hooked the weight bar onto the bench and sat up, sweat trickling down the sides of his face.

"What happened?"

"Nothing. The detectives came and questioned me. It was my word against hers."

David smiled for the first time since he walked in, beads of sweat starting to pop on his forehead. "And that's a beautiful thing."

70

The press conference for the Shannon Pilski arrest was scheduled for one o'clock. They had eight minutes to walk down to the second floor. "How do I look?" Reese asked, adjusting his navy and red striped tie. "Any bats in the cave?" He turned his nose up for Lauren to inspect.

"No. But you have to trim those nose hairs."

"My trimmer broke. Is it bad?"

Lauren scoped out the inside of his nostrils. "Not terrible, but keep your chin down."

"Shit."

"And have a mint." She held the little metal tin from her desk out to him.

He scooped out two, popped them in his mouth. "You're going to give me a complex. Fix my stupid tie, please."

Standing directly in front of him, Lauren undid the mess at his neck and expertly tied a Windsor knot. "There." She brushed off his shoulders. "Perfect."

"Are we ready?" He picked up the nice brown leather folio he liked to hold in front of him as a prop for just such occasions.

Snagging her own paperwork shield, she took a deep breath. "Let's do this."

Mario Aquino and Joy Walsh looked up from their conversation in the hallway. "Good luck, guys," Joy called to them. "Great job."

Reggie Major, in on overtime, came walking out of one of the doorways. "I worked on that murder when it first happened. I was brand-new up here. Glad you two could finally make an arrest. Sincerely."

"Great job, Cold Case," agreed Mario. "If all my cases keep going south, I'll have a few more for you by the end of the month."

"Thanks," Lauren laughed, hitting the exit bar on the door with her hip, "but I'm afraid we're booked up to the New Year."

A couple more "good jobs!" were called out from the inner office as the door fell shut behind them. Lauren had to smile. As much ego as there was floating around the office on a daily basis, so did a lot of heart. The approval of her peers still meant something to her, even when she tried to convince herself it didn't.

They walked down the narrow staircase from the fourth to the second floor. As soon as you walked out, you were face to face with the commissioner's office, which was full of the top brass waiting to walk down to the police academy's auditorium. They made a left, walking past the old-time police photos one of the photographers had the genius idea of blowing up, framing, and lining the hallways with. They passed a patrol car from the fifties, its two occupants standing next to it, squinting into the sunshine with their eight-point hats on. Another showed a beat cop perched on top of a two-story snow mound during the Blizzard of '77 surveying a frozen city street. The last picture before you walked through the double doors was a portrait of a 1960s traffic cop, smiling with a silver whistle clenched between his teeth. He was waving cars forward with one leather gloved hand. It had become a sort of superstition to touch Uncle Ron's face before you entered the academy. No one knew what that old-time copper's real name was, but over the years countless officers had claimed he was a relation of theirs; grandfather, cousin, father-in-law, but by far the favorite was uncle. Hence Uncle Ron.

Reese reached over and touched his whistle. "Wish me luck, Uncle Ron."

Lauren, who usually didn't pay attention to the tradition, even brushed her fingers over the glass. Nothing, literally nothing, scares cops more than having to go in front of news cameras. A barricaded suspect? Chasing a double murderer? A drunk waving a butcher knife? *Child's play,* Lauren thought, *compared to having to get on the stage in the auditorium with the hot lights blinding you, trapped there by the reporters and their questions.*

But she also knew it was necessary. For the police department, for the DA's office, for the public, and especially for the victim's family. This was a rarity: a Cold Case that was solved without lengthy searches, complications, or excessive drama. The double failures of the Stenz and Bronstein cases back to back were the most common results of opening a case. Vinita Ortiz's homicide seemed almost too easy. All the dominos fell exactly where they'd wanted them to. That almost never happened. But when it did, there was a satisfaction to it that sometimes, once in a while, justice was finally served. Knowing that she and Reese were a part of that fueled Lauren with a sense of purpose. She wasn't leaving Cold Case, no matter what the outcome of the trial next week. Church would have to force her out.

Off to the left, standing on the very corner of the stage was Carlita Ortiz and her brother, Vincent. The resemblance to her mother was striking—same dark hair, same wide smile. The son was tall, at least six-one to his sister's five-two, and fidgeting, pulling at the collar of his button-down shirt, jaw clenching. A woman from the mayor's office was with them, talking to them, trying to keep them calm.

Lauren smiled as she approached them. "Hey guys." They had met in person three times before this, but it didn't make it any easier for them. They got what they had always wanted—their mother's killer arrested, something many families never got—and yet their relief was marred by the reality that nothing had changed. Their mom was gone and even though Shannon Pilski was getting seven to fifteen in prison, they still had a life sentence without her.

Carlita hugged Lauren to her, breath coming in ragged gasps, trying not to cry. Lauren hugged her back, waiting until she was ready to let go.

"Ms. Riley," Vincent said, leaning forward to shake hands with Reese, "Mr. Reese."

"How you two holding up?" Reese asked.

"It's hard on my wife, you know?" Vincent said, tugging at the top button again. "She doesn't know what to say to our kids. They're so little. She stayed home."

"What about your kids?" Lauren asked Carlita.

Carlita managed a smile and pointed down into the rows of seats lined up in front of the stage. "That's my husband, Juan. And that's Vinita. Named after her *abuela*. And her brother, Marcelino." She waved to her family, sprawled across three seats, the little girl kneeling in her white dress to walk her dolls to each other across the metal chairs as her little brother tried to grab them. Her husband waved back, giving her an encouraging smile. Lauren knew from Carlita that their uncle had gotten him and her brother both jobs at the Ford Stamping plant out in Woodlawn, south of the city, where Lauren's own father had retired from ten years ago. *Vinita would have been so proud of her kids,* Lauren thought as the department's media officer started placing everyone in their designated spots.

Mayor Patrick Karnes took the stage, along with DA Carl Church, ADA Kevin King, Police Commissioner Barbara Bennett, and the Invisible Man. They got arranged around the lectern, with Riley and Reese off to their left and the family to the right.

The Invisible Man walked up to the microphone, tapped it once to make sure it was working and began. "I'd like to thank all the members of the press who have come out today. I am the Administrative Captain in charge of the Homicide division, Captain Stanley Maniechwicz. Spell it like it sounds." A titter went up among the reporters as he paused a moment for them to adjust their cameras. "Before we begin I'd like to introduce the people with me on the stage, starting on my left ... " He went on with the introductions, spelling each person's name after they waved or nodded in acknowledgement. When he was finished, he motioned Commissioner Bennett forward, who lowered the microphone to her red lips.

"I'm Buffalo Police Commissioner Barbara Bennett and I'd like to welcome you all to our academy. Yesterday I was informed by the Erie County District Attorney Carl Church that a plea deal had been reached in the Cold Case homicide of Vinita Ortiz. Ms. Ortiz was brutally stabbed to death at 469 Virginia Place, July 29th, 1993. The case went cold." She paused for effect, looking out over the cameras. Bennett knew how to work a crowd. The city's first black female commissioner, there had been a lot of expectation for her to fail. Brought in from New York City, she'd neither messed up nor made a splash; utterly boring for the scandal-loving press.

"This summer, after being contacted by family, Cold Case detectives Lauren Riley and Shane Reese diligently followed up on their mother's death, culminating in the identification of a suspect, Shannon

Pilski. Yesterday, Thursday, October 19th, through the efforts of the district attorney's office, a plea deal was worked out, sparing the family the pain of enduring a trial." She stepped aside, inviting Church to come forward. "District Attorney Carl Church would like to speak on that."

Shaking her hand before turning toward the room, he stood squarely in front of the mike, his charcoal gray suit accented with his trademark red power tie. Also a practitioner of the pregnant pause, he eyed the room for a moment before he spoke. "After more than twenty-four years, the district attorney's office is pleased to announce the successful resolution of this case. It's a testament to the teamwork and collaborative effort of the Buffalo Police Department, Erie County lab, and district attorney's office that these cases, thought to be unsolvable, can be reopened and justice served to the victim's families. I commend all the men and women involved for their hard work and diligence. And I'd like to remind the public, as far as cold cases are concerned, there is always hope."

Nice touch, Lauren thought as he turned the lectern over to Carlita Ortiz, who nervously ran through a litany of thanks to everyone involved. When she was done, the Invisible Man stepped forward again and opened the floor for questions. Most were expected: Who is the suspect to the victim? Why did it take so long for justice to be served? How did the case get reopened? Typical softball questions that Maniechwicz handled without batting an eye, until an older reporter from the *Buffalo News* stepped forward, tape recorder held out in front of him and asked, "Jury selection for the Katherine Vine homicide is going on right now. Aren't you personally trying that case, Mr. Church?"

Church's face clouded over with anger for a split second before he managed to pull himself together. "Yes, I am. Yes, it is. And my second chair, Assistant District Attorney Lynn Ferro is more than competent to pick the jury."

"Sir, isn't Detective Riley working for the defense in that case? Isn't that a conflict of interest?"

Church stepped back to the lectern, elbowing the Invisible Man aside. "There is no conflict of interest. Whatever side of a case we are on, we are both professionals. Presenting a case to a jury isn't about picking sides, it's about getting to the truth. And the jury decides that. Not me, not Detective Riley."

Every hand in the room shot up, questions fired up at the stage, but Captain Maniechwicz stepped forward, waving his hands, and shut the press conference down. Church stormed off the stage behind a thick blue velvet curtain with the Kinger following him. Lauren and Reese exited the other side of the stage, slipping through a door that took them into the camera room. Fifteen heads swiveled around as the door shut behind them.

"Nothing to see here, folks." Reese raised his hand in a friendly wave to the light duty officers who manned the city's hundred surveillance cameras. They strode through the center of the double banks of screens on either side and went out through another door leading to the stairs.

"I didn't see that coming." Lauren exhaled when she was sure they were finally alone.

"Really? Because that's what I've been warning you about since day one."

"Reese, please ... "

He held up a hand, shushing her. "Shannon Pilski still needs to be processed. Kinger told me she's in custody over at the holding center. Let's do the arrest paperwork, run it over, get her mugged and printed, and call it a day, okay?"

She studied his expression for a moment, trying to gauge where his head was at. Was this the final straw in their partnership? Come Monday, when the trial started, would she even have a partner?

"Okay," she sighed. "Let's go."

71

On Monday morning, after the jury selection, there was nothing left but the trial. After little more than four months of preparation, investigation, and researching, the case was going before a jury. Everyone involved wanted different things. Joe Wheeler wanted his moment in the spotlight. Frank Violanti wanted his godson's name cleared. Carl Church wanted justice at any cost. David Spencer wanted freedom.

Lauren just wanted it to be over.

In a criminal trial, the prosecution always gets the first and last word. They represent the people and for this reason they get to make the first opening statement to the jury and the last closing argument. In between those two monologs, the prosecution presents its case, methodically calling witnesses, presenting evidence to the jury, and hammering home their theory of the crime. The defense gets to cross examine those witnesses on their testimony, to poke holes in the prosecution's case, and when they are done the prosecution get to redirect or re-question their witness to mitigate the damage done by the defense. Then the prosecution rests and the defense gets to put their witnesses on and the process is reversed. The defendant may or may not testify. The defense can recall the prosecution's witnesses. The judge presides over the battle of the objections on both sides, remaining neutral, in theory maintaining the flow of the trial.

This complicated dance goes on hundreds of times a day, every day, all across the country. A thousand little dramas battle out in the court system, some for things as mundane as a parking ticket, others for mass murders, but always the same no matter how the television crime shows warp the perception.

It always starts with *The People*. The People versus David Ryan Spencer. And both sides were ready.

Lauren sat ramrod straight in the hard wooden seat as the courtroom began to fill. First it was the court deputies, then the stenographer, the court clerks, some interns. The huge room shrunk with every person that came in, until it felt like she would suffocate from all the bodies pressed around her. This trial was the hottest ticket in town. And she had a ringside seat.

"Is this chair taken?"

Dressed in his lone gray "court" suit, Reese was standing in the aisle smiling down at her.

Looking up in shock, Lauren asked, "What are you doing here?"

Plunking himself down next to her, he tugged at his tie a little. "Supporting my partner. You really think after watching what you've gone through in this case I'm not going to see how it ends?"

He was sitting next to her like it was the most natural thing in the world for him to put his career in jeopardy right along with hers. "What about work?"

He shrugged. "I have vacation time."

Then he just looked forward, waiting for the trial to start, like everyone else. Even though the October day was cool, the angry hum of the air conditioners on full blast made it seem like the courtroom was a plane ready for takeoff, which in a way, it was.

"Thank you," she whispered.

He threw an elbow into her side. "Shut up. It's about to start."

She sank back in her seat and shut up.

72

Absent from the courtroom was anyone who was going to testify: Anthony Vine, Jennifer Jackson, Joe Wheeler, the medical examiner. Witnesses were not allowed in the courtroom to hear other witnesses' testimony. Somewhere in the courthouse, they were milling around, separated, waiting to be called.

The jury was brought in and seated. Twelve unlucky souls and two alternates who had tried their damnest to get out of serving at any cost. Picking the jury had taken almost two days. Violanti had wanted all the young men he could get, who could identify with a horny teenager, while the prosecution wanted old ladies who would see a victimized mother. In the end, it was split pretty evenly. Neither side was completely satisfied, but then again, the system was set up so they never really were. The jurors listened raptly to the judge as he instructed them; this was the point in the trial where they were still interested. Their eyes would dart over to David every time the judge mentioned *the defendant*. After what seemed like an endless list of dos and don'ts, the judge announced that the people could make their opening statement.

Carl Church took his time rising from his seat, holding a fountain pen in one hand, making his way toward the jury box. "Ladies and gentlemen of the jury," the DA began, standing straight and tall, impressing the jury with his cool demeanor and smooth baritone voice. "This case is simple. It's not a whodunit. It's not a television show with twists and turns and a surprise ending. Contrary to what the defense is going to hurl at you, the evidence will show a simple case. This case amounts to the evidence. It doesn't lie, it has no agenda, it just is. And what the evidence will show is that the defendant and the victim were acquainted. She came into the toy store where he worked quite often. And that Katherine Vine, the victim, was a beautiful woman; the kind of woman men desire. And that's what the defendant did, he desired her. The evidence will show that he pulled up her rewards club information two weeks before she was murdered. The evidence will show that information listed her address and her phone number. The evidence will show that on the night she was murdered, he called up that information again. He called her cell phone less than five minutes after she left the store. The physical evidence will show that the defendant had waited for his opportunity, the victim leaving her credit card behind, and jumped on it."

He turned and pointed the pen at David. "He brought it out to her car, forced his way inside, and raped her. When he was done, he strangled her with her own scarf, left her for dead, and casually walked away. I'm not going to go over every bit of evidence with you now; I'll let the witnesses do that. And I'm confident that in the end you will see that there is no vast conspiracy. That the evidence is clear." He leaned up against the jury box so they could get an up close view of his sincerest expression.

Damn, Lauren thought, *he really is good.* Watching Church work the jury slammed home how tough this was going to be for Violanti. *They can't tear their eyes from him.*

"David Ryan Spencer worked in a toy store. Katherine Vine was a wealthy wife and mother, the beauty he couldn't have and could never have. She was his fantasy. As soon as the chance made itself available, he got himself alone with her and he took her. He took her body and he took her life. He left a grieving husband and two little boys without a mother. Once you've heard all the evidence, I'm confident there is no other verdict than guilty. Guilty on all counts, it's that simple."

Church walked briskly back to the prosecution's table as Frank Violanti jumped up. Church was known for his openings and closings. He liked to make a short forceful opening and a point-by-point closing. Violanti had said he planned on mirroring that strategy for his own case. He ran his hands over his suit, took a deep breath, and looked at the jury.

"Mr. Church is one hundred percent right: this case is simple. I agree that the evidence will show that. What I don't agree with is that it will point to my client as the killer. Ladies and gentlemen, I submit to you, what is more simple a motive than jealousy? Or money? Or greed? Because that's the motive we're talking about here. You are going to hear from a lot of witnesses in this trial. A lot. But the one person who won't take the stand is David Spencer. Why, you may ask? Because David already gave a sworn statement and told the truth. Just hours after Katherine's body was discovered, he was making a voluntary statement to the police, which you will hear. There's no need to put him on the stand because the truth doesn't change.

"My client had sex with Katherine Vine in her car. Consensual sex. When they were done, he left and she was alive. He told that to the detectives less than six hours after her body was found. My client gave a full, honest, and complete statement to police. He freely gave a swab of his DNA. Why? Because he had nothing to hide. What would be David's motive to kill Katherine Vine? I know what Anthony Vine's motive would be. To get her out of the way so he could continue his affair with tennis star Jennifer Jackson. To get her out of the way so he wouldn't have to pay her a fortune once she sought a divorce. Anthony Vine knew where his wife was every second of every day. Katherine Vine had a tracking device on her car. The evidence will show that. And Anthony Vine saw his opportunity to get rid of her as soon as he saw David walk away from her car. And now that man would let a teenager go to jail for his crimes.

"Ladies and gentleman, I'm glad he brought up the evidence. Look at it carefully. It will show who the killer is. Absolutely. But that killer is not David Ryan Spencer."

When Violanti was seated again, Lauren watched David lean over and whisper something to him. Violanti reached over and gripped his godson's arm lightly, replying in an equally quiet tone. Lauren narrowed her eyes on the lawyer and the boy, who looked older to her now despite his comically large suit. What were they talking about?

The judge looked from one counselor to the next. He nodded to himself and then declared, "Mr. Church, call your first witness."

73

The first few witnesses in a homicide trial usually just set the stage: the store manager, Julie Densmore, who found the body; the ambulance attendants who determined Katherine Vine to be dead at the scene and called the medical examiner's office; the first officer at the scene. Violanti's cross examination was sparse, as they had nothing terribly damning to say about David. They added the background needed to forge on with the rest of the case.

It wasn't until the end of the first day of the trial that DA Church started to get to the meat and potatoes of the case by putting the ME on.

Church circled around the medical examiner, surely so the jury could see his face while the doctor testified. It was still early in the trial and Violanti knew the jury was focused and engaged and eager to hear what the ME had to say.

Dr. Daniel Kogut was the county medical examiner and had been for twenty years. He was comfortable on the stand and confident in his examinations. Katherine Vine was strangled with her own white silk scarf, he testified. Besides the ligature mark to her neck, she had three bruises to her person, one on her left thigh, one on her upper right arm, and one on her left shoulder blade. She was in good health when she died, no abnormalities were observed. The doctor testified to these facts as they pertained to the autopsy he performed. He then explained the word *asphyxia* to the jurors and told them it was the cause of Katherine Vine's death. She had been asphyxiated, the blood had been cut off to her brain. He explained how he had taken fingernail scrapings and submitted the swabs for DNA testing. He also had performed anal, oral, and vaginal swabs for the same purposes. He went over the photographs taken at the autopsy and reviewed his findings step by step. It was all very straightforward and routine.

Then Violanti rose and approached the doctor. Dr. Kogut still looked calm and relaxed, wearing a navy golf shirt and dark pants, as if testifying was no more stressful than a round of golf. His white hair was neatly combed over his balding head and his brilliant white teeth screamed of being dentures. Violanti had two pictures in his hand.

"Doctor, I know you just went over the autopsy photos with Mr. Church for the jury, so I only have a few questions for you. I want you to look at People's exhibit 5A and 5B." He handed the oversized pictures to the doctor. "Can you tell the jury what these pictures are of?"

"Those are Katherine Vine's hands at the time of her autopsy."

"And do they accurately depict the state of both her right and left hands?"

"I would say so."

He took the photos back from the doctor. "Thank you." He held them and looked down at them. "Doctor, you testified that you took fingernail scrapings from the victim during your autopsy. Is that correct?"

"Correct."

"How many of Mrs. Vine's fingernails were broken?"

"What?" The doctor looked confused.

Violanti asked his question again slowly, speaking each word with a deliberate calmness. "How many of Mrs. Vine's fingernails, under which you found my client's DNA, were broken off?"

"None."

He held up both the photos to the jury. "None. So it's fair to say that during this violent attack, not one of her perfectly manicured nails snapped off?"

"None of her nails were broken."

"You testified that you found three bruises on the body. Can you tell the jury in layman's terms how big each of those bruises were?"

The ME flipped through the copy of the autopsy report he had brought with him to the stand. "The one on her forearm was the size of a nickel approximately. The one on her thigh the size of a quarter, and the one on her shoulder the size of a half dollar."

"Was there any bruising to the face or head?"

"No."

"Any to the wrists? Like she was being held down?"

"No."

Violanti leaned in for the jab. "Is it possible those bruises could have come from sex with an eager eighteen-year old boy?"

"Objection, Your Honor," Church said. "Calls for speculation."

The judge nodded. "Rephrase the question."

Violanti smiled apologetically at the judge, then turned back to the doctor. "Could those bruises have been caused by something other than homicide?"

"None of them were fatal."

"Were any of them even serious?"

"Given their sizes, I would say no."

"Doctor"—Violanti brushed a piece of lint off his sleeve—"did you note any bite marks on the victim?"

"No."

"Any scratches on her?"

"None of significance."

"Interesting," he muttered as if to himself, but it was for full effect on the jury. "Doctor, you testified that she died of asphyxia, correct?"

"That's correct."

"By strangulation?"

"Correct."

"With a ligature?" Violanti raised an eyebrow.

"Correct."

"Was the hyoid bone broken in her neck?"

"No."

Violanti feigned curiosity. "Isn't it common in strangulations for the hyoid bone to be broken?"

Doctor Kogut sat up straight and crossed his arms. "It's not uncommon for it not to be."

Body language is everything, Violanti mused to himself. "And the blood vessels in her eyes were not broken, but yet she was asphyxiated?"

The doctor sounded exasperated now. Violanti's way of questioning was meant to grate on his nerves. "Yes, with the silk scarf found in the car. The silk fibers found on the body confirm that."

He was circling the doctor now, knowing he was getting under his skin. "So this was not a violent choking out? This was someone who slipped the scarf around her neck and slowly squeezed the flow of blood off to her brain."

"I don't know if I would characterize it exactly as that."

"But you could."

The prosecutor called out, "Objection! Calls for a conclusion."

"Your Honor." Violanti spread his hands wide. "This doctor has seen hundreds of murders and is an expert witness. I'm asking, in his professional opinion, how would he characterize the way Katherine Vine was asphyxiated."

The judge took a moment to consider the point, then motioned to the doctor. "You may answer the question."

The ME seemed to be searching for the right words. "In my professional opinion, the evidence points to a slower strangulation, but a strangulation none the less."

Violanti stepped back, let that sink into the jury's collective brain, and smiled. "Thank you, Doctor. No more questions."

Church jumped up for the cross. "One question, doctor. Was Katherine Vine strangled with her own scarf?"

"Yes." He sounded relieved.

"Thank you. No further questions."

The trial adjourned for the day after the doctor stepped down. *I did okay*, Violanti thought as he gathered up his materials. *Neutralized a little of the damage of Church's opening statement at least*. He looked for Lauren, but she was already gone. Her and that partner of hers.

74

David was allowed to meet with Violanti to go over the events of the day. David had to be calmed down, then yelled at, then calmed again. When he finally got David to listen and not freak out, Violanti told him what to expect. The first witness for the next day was going to be the security guard, then Detective Joe Wheeler would take the stand. Violanti wanted David to be prepared. This was where it got interesting.

"One more time," Violanti prompted in the little room that the court officers had provided for them off of the main courtroom. It was boxy and painted a pale blue, almost like David's cell, except for the matted and framed painting of pink roses hung on the far wall. The picture looked ridiculously out of place in the monotone room, an absurd splash of color in the utilitarian space. "What was Joe Wheeler's demeanor towards you?"

David paused, thinking. "At first, he was nice. He said he had to talk to everyone that worked that night. The more we talked, the more mad he seemed to get. And sweaty. The guy was sweating like a meatloaf by the time we were done, it was gross."

Violanti ignored that. "He didn't threaten you or yell at you or anything like that?"

"No."

"And the statement you gave was truthful. No lies?"

"I didn't have anything to lie about." David shrugged his shoulders. "We had sex. I left. She was alive."

Violanti circled a question on his yellow legal pad with his black felt tip pen. "Good answer. Good. Did Detective Wheeler ask for your DNA?"

"Yeah and I gave it to him. I knew it would be all over her anyway."

"Good. Good." He was furiously scribbling notes, rethinking questions and adding new ones. All of this was very, very good.

David looked over Violanti's shoulder toward the door. "Is Lauren coming to see me today?"

He stopped in mid-question, putting his pen down on the table hard. "Are you kidding me? I'm trying to save your life and you want to ogle my private detective in the middle of your trial?"

"I was just wondering if she was coming, that's all." There was a hopeful hitch in his voice.

"She doesn't exist, okay? For the rest of the trial, she's a ghost to you. I need you to concentrate on the matter at hand, stupid."

"Don't have a fit, I was only asking."

"Really, David. What's the matter with you?"

He put his head in his hands and wound his fingers through his hair. "Not you too, okay? I have to listen to it every day from my mother. Just once, would someone have some faith in me?"

He studied David's face. "When this is over, you and I are going to have a long, serious talk."

"About what?" David looked genuinely baffled.

"You know about what. I think you have a problem. I think you need help."

David shrugged again, as if Uncle Frank was suggesting he take tennis lessons. "As long as I'm not behind bars."

Violanti shook his head. The disregard in David's voice shocked him. He hoped that it was just a reaction to the stress of jail and the trial, but after his father's death, David had changed. The kind and gentle little boy had been replaced with something else. Something more fierce. Somehow, in the back of his mind, Violanti had always known that David could be cold. Maybe dangerously so.

"Don't count your chickens, kid." Violanti picked up his pen and started writing again. "This is going to be a very uphill battle."

75

Joe Wheeler was behind Lauren's house. He had parked his car a good four blocks from the main gate and jogged in through a cut he had found. He wore a drab gray running suit, with what looked like an MP3 player, but was, in fact, a police scanner. Joe weaved in and out of backyards and side lots until he hopped the fence, unnoticed, into Lauren Riley's backyard.

She had a rock garden installed by the far wall with flowering shrubs all around that provided just the right amount of cover. He knew she had a motion light on her back door, but he was prepared for that. Underneath his jogging suit was a pair of dark cargo pants and a black tee shirt. His Glock was holstered to his thigh. He withdrew a black air pistol from his waistband, double checked it to make sure it wasn't his Glock, and then aimed it carefully at the ornate glass. He squeezed the trigger and there was just the tiniest tinkling sound of broken glass on the back steps.

He had watched her come home, watched the lights flicker on in various rooms, and out again, all the while waiting patiently on her back patio next to a garden gnome. When her bedroom light finally went out, he waited another hour to be sure she was asleep before he made his move. He had been planning this for a long time, and now that the trial was in full swing, it was time to act.

Golly, I was back going over my notes when it happened. Ask the guards; my car never came through that gate. He ran over the words again and again in his mind, rolling around to the final volley: *You know what? Talk to my lawyer.*

He was counting on the fact that she lived alone and that the crime wouldn't be discovered for at least a day. But maybe there would be no crime, if things went the way he hoped they would; maybe it would be a happy ending for all involved. All she really needed to see was that he was the one who would do anything for her. And once she got a taste of what she'd been missing all these years, she'd melt right back into his arms. He was stronger now and more practiced. He could give a woman what she needed. Hadn't he proved it again and again? And those were professionals. He'd taught them some lessons and they still came back for more, because when it was good, it was good.

And he was going to give it to Lauren good.

He carefully stuffed the air pistol back into his waistband, didn't want to be leaving that around. He looked behind him to make sure he hadn't dropped anything, patting his pockets to make sure everything was in place. Turning back around, he was just about to reach inside his jogging pants for the Glock when he felt a ring of cold steel touch the side of his head.

"Move. Please. So I can kill you." Lauren stepped back so the muzzle was still aimed at his temple, but not flush against his skin.

Smart move, he thought. *Now I can't take it away from you.*

"What are you doing here, Joe?"

He didn't say anything; he kept his hands up, waiting for his move. All she had to do was let her guard slip for one second...

"You really should get a better deodorant; I could smell you through the kitchen window. You dirty, sweaty pig."

He said nothing.

"Did you really think I didn't know it was you sitting across the street from me all those nights?"

From a distance, a police car's siren sounded. It was getting closer. His eyes shifted toward the sound.

"I already told them it was you in my backyard. I told them not to put it out over the air."

So *now* she'd done it. She'd gone ahead and told.

"You have nothing to say to me? After all this effort?"

He looked her square in the eye. "I was going to chop your fucking head off."

Lauren took another step back and almost stumbled, because there was no doubt, whatsoever, that he meant it.

He was actually smiling about it.

The police cars pulled up, car doors slammed.

"You're going to jail," she whispered.

"For what? Jogging and standing in your back yard?" he asked with mock innocence.

"You just said you were going to kill me."

The cops came up the driveway and started yelling for her to drop her weapon.

Now he grinned. "Prove it."

———

In the end, she pressed charges on him for trespassing in her yard, a mere violation, the same as a parking ticket. He told the cops he had done nothing more. "Listen," he insisted as he sat on the hard, plastic back seat of the police cruiser, "I was just jogging around her neighborhood. I like to jog in this gated neighborhood because there's almost no traffic and it has nice views of Delaware Park."

"Aren't you a little far from home?" the young cop asked him, clipboard open, taking notes.

"With the trial going on downtown, this was closer. I got a late start and I wanted to clear my head."

"How'd you end up in her yard?" the older, black female cop asked. *She might be a problem*, Joe thought, trying to angle himself for a better look at her.

"I heard a noise and saw the light in the back yard go off so I went back there to investigate it. I found the pellet gun and I was waiting in the dark for whoever dropped it to come back."

"You always go jogging with your gun?" The younger cop was twisted around in the front seat, the plastic barrier between them dirty and scratched. Joe was sitting on the very edge of the seat, God only knew what bodily fluids were festering on the plastic.

"I always carry my Glock on me, what cop doesn't?"

"I don't," the female cop said sharply. *Officer Lewis*, Joe remembered reading from her nametag when she put him in the car. He tried to catch her eye in the rearview mirror, give her a wink to melt the ice. It didn't work.

"Did you know this was Detective Riley's house?"

"Of course. That's why I went back there. To make sure she was okay. I didn't expect her to come out threatening me with a gun."

"I think I'd come out with a gun too, if I found a man all in black creeping around my backyard," the woman cop pointed out.

That's because you're an ancient old hag and what man would want to sneak a peek at you? Joe thought, but caught himself and smiled. "She's just a little hysterical right now. We have that trial going on and it's a lot of stress. That's why I was so worried when the light went out. She's working on the defense for that kid who murdered Katherine Vine."

"I know," the old lady police officer with the big mouth informed him. "It's just a hell of a coincidence you were here to save the day."

"We have a history, me and her, you know." He gave a sly smile to the younger cop, a kind of *wink, wink* that men do in locker rooms. "And what the hell is that smell back here? It's making my eyes water."

"Sorry about that," the bitch in charge finally caught his eye in the rearview. "Our last prisoner pissed himself."

He didn't even have to go to the stationhouse. He could tell by the look on Lauren's face that she couldn't believe they were buying his crap. Well, she'd have to believe it. He was issued a ticket and sent along his way to pay his thirty-dollar fine whenever he got around to it.

Funny thing was, in his mind, he accomplished what he had set out to do. Now Lauren Riley knew he could have her anytime he wanted. The events of the night had proven to him that she wasn't worth it. She had her chance to put him out of her misery, but she didn't pull that trigger. He couldn't respect a woman who wanted him in her life so bad she was willing to risk hers.

As he walked back to his car, tucking the ticket into his cargo pants, he thought about winning the trial. He smiled. Then her humiliation would be complete. All in all, it was a good night. He was ready to testify.

76

Lauren was still shaking with anger when she locked her door behind her. The cops wouldn't lock him up, and if she had been in a clearer state of mind, she would have had them call Carl Church. She knew the lieutenant who responded to the call; he was a good guy, listening patiently while she ranted about what was going on. Then he reminded her that if Joe Wheeler got arrested, there might be a mistrial and did she really want that? He was right, of course, but it wasn't fair. Joe could make up a fairy tale and walk away with what amounted to a parking ticket because he always knew when to play his cards. The next day she was going to have to watch him on the witness stand smugly give his testimony, like he didn't have a care in the world. She'd report him to his boss, after the trial, but that seemed too little too late.

When she finally settled into her bed, she was exhausted, mentally and physically. She tried to close her eyes, but she hadn't been sleeping well to begin with. She had taken the whole week off from work for the trial, but there still weren't enough hours in the day, especially now that she had a crazy ex-fiancé trying to chop her head off.

But he hadn't. She'd caught him in the act. She got the drop on him and could have taken him out. She was mad, but she wasn't afraid, not anymore. She played the scene over and over in her mind, like a movie stuck in a loop. Staring up at the ceiling, she tried to plot out what she should do next. She could go right to the judge with her incident report. She could call his supervisor. She could file for a restraining order right away. But all that would change nothing right now. If he really wanted to get her, no piece of paper would stop him from trying. The next time he wouldn't be so lucky. Next time, she wouldn't wait for the cops.

For the life of her, she could not remember the sweet guy who had picked her up for the police academy every morning, even though it was out of his way. She couldn't picture him holding her hand when they graduated, but she knew he had. That guy had changed into someone else when they were dating, and he was all but unrecognizable now.

When the trial was over, she was going to go to his supervisor, her supervisor, Carl Church, whoever would listen, and expose him for the thug he was. That was the thought that finally rocked her into an uneasy sleep that night.

———————

Lauren woke still filled with a dulled rage. She opened her eyes, knowing what the lieutenant had said the night before about the mistrial was right. Stalking a member the defense team seemed to be universally frowned upon, and it could be cause for a mistrial. She didn't want to wait another six months and have to go through this all over again.

As she slipped out of bed, she noticed her hand was shaking a little. She'd have to take something for that.

She padded across the floor to the bathroom and popped open the cabinet. Her doctor had given her the happy pills two years ago for stress. She only took them when she was really anxious. This situation seemed like it qualified.

Now I'll have to watch him get on the stand like some superhero who saved the day by locking up David, she thought as she got undressed. *But I know what he really is—a pathetic, brutal monster.*

She turned the water on as hot as she could stand it and let it run down over her, trying to wash the blind anger away. It helped; she felt herself start to relax. The tension in her muscles began to melt down the drain with the rage.

After her shower, she walked back in her bedroom to get dressed. She slipped a dark coral blouse on to wear under one of her fitted jackets. She wanted to look sharp as a knife for court that morning.

She may have been a weak person once, but that was done. She had proved that over and over again in her life. She raised two kids on her own, managed to pull through after two divorces, and survived her relationship with an abusive boyfriend. She had flourished at work, had good friends, her daughters were healthy and smart. She had truly succeeded in life. Grabbing her black pumps, she started down the stairs to get her cup of coffee.

Except for Joe Wheeler. *Well,* she thought heading toward the door, travel mug in hand, *I could have put a bullet in his head, but didn't. That's not weakness. That's being stronger than him.*

77

Joe looked professional—almost handsome, if he did say so himself—as he took the stand that next morning. He had waited patiently while the security guard testified about seeing David crossing the parking lot. Violanti got him to admit on cross that David wasn't running or acting suspiciously, but just walking. Joe was convinced that Violanti had done no damage. Fishing, that was all, he was fishing for a defense. That's what you did when you had nothing.

Joe's dark suit was perfectly pressed, worn with a tone-on-tone shirt and tie that brought out the flecks of gold in his eyes. He had gone to the most exclusive men's store in the city and told them to give him their best suit, spare no expense. Prior to his adventure the night before, he had gone and gotten his hair cut. He even splurged and had gotten a manicure. He had to look good for the cameras.

He crossed the gallery without so much as a glance toward Lauren, who today was sitting in the back row with her partner. Of course she would want to be as far away from him as possible. Walking toward the stand, he wondered if she was thinking about taking that trespass report to his boss after the trial ended. And that it wasn't too late to report the assault in the parking lot.

Joe found it laughable. As far as he was concerned, she might as well have been a potted plant. Let her sit there with her pretty boy partner. This was his moment. It was time to make his case. And when David Spencer was found guilty, his boss would give two shits about what his scorned ex-lover had to say about him.

With the courtroom caught up in rapt attention, DA Carl Church went over Joe Wheeler's investigation step by step, from the time he arrived at the scene to the moment he put handcuffs on David Spencer. A quick check of the computer showed Katherine Vine's purchase, which led to the phone call to her cell, which led to David. At ten thirty on the morning in question, Joe Wheeler picked David Spencer up from home, where he was enjoying a nice bowl of cereal with his mom. Joe had explained to him there had been an incident at the toy store the night before. He asked if they could both come back to the station with him and they did. Joe even let his mother sit up front in the unmarked car. Joe had asked David's mother to wait in the lobby, then laid it all out for him. David went over the story of her leaving her credit card in the store. He gave a blow-by-blow account of everything: the kinky sex, the biting and scratching. He admitted it freely. The only thing he wouldn't sign off on was the strangulation. David said he never even touched the scarf, that she had pulled it out of her own hair.

Joe testified that David seemed neither scared nor intimidated. Church made hay out of that as a sign of his guilt, that he was proud of what he did, but too cowardly to actually say it. Objections were thrown around. Church had Joe read David's statement into evidence, which Joe did with dramatic flair. If he had written a screenplay, Joe couldn't have set it any more perfectly. Especially since he was the hero of the story. Case cleared with arrest that same day. Perfect.

Carl Church thanked Joe and told the judge, "No further questions for this witness." He was practically beaming when Violanti stood up for the cross examination.

Violanti approached Joe slowly. He took his time. *The longer he holds back and draws this out,* Joe thought, *the more he thinks I'll be off my game.* He knew Lauren hadn't told him about the events of the night before. Joe had counted on that. If Violanti had known, he would've moved for an immediate mistrial and investigation. Lauren was still good at keeping her mouth shut. What good had calling the cops done for her anyway? Violanti's pause was amusing to Joe. Adorable, even. It added to his enjoyment of the moment, prolonged his time in the spotlight.

"Detective," Violanti began, standing slightly off to the side so the jury could see Joe's face, "you testified that you read my client his Miranda warnings, correct?"

"I read them to him and he signed the Miranda waiver indicating he understood and waived those rights."

"You told him he could have a lawyer present during questioning, if he wanted one?"

"I did."

"And he understood that?"

"He indicated he did."

"He just graduated from high school. He works at a toy store. He lives with his mother. How sure are you he understood?"

Church stood up and objected. "This was all covered in the suppression hearing on the statement, Your Honor."

"Agreed. Sustained. Move on, Mr. Violanti."

Violanti nodded and rephrased: "Even though he seemed to understand his rights, he didn't want an attorney?"

"He never asked for one." There was a calculated smugness in his answer.

"Did you know that I'm the defendant's godfather?"

Joe felt the color drain from his face. That smugness dissipated for a moment. That wasn't a question he'd anticipated. "No. I did not."

"Don't you agree, Detective, if my client thought he'd done something wrong, he would've called me right away?"

"Objection!" Church jumped up. "Calls for speculation. How would the detective know what the defendant would or wouldn't have done?"

"Sustained."

Church sank back down, but on the edge of his seat, ready to bounce up again.

Violanti seemed not to notice and went on. "And the bite marks on my client's shoulder were proven to be from the victim?"

"Yes."

"Did the bite marks break the skin?"

"Her dental pattern was clearly visible."

"I didn't ask you that," he admonished. "I asked did she bite hard enough to break the skin. Did my client need stitches? Was there any of his blood found in her mouth?"

A moment of stony silence, then, "No."

"Could that bite mark have been a passion mark? Like a hickey?"

"Objection!" Church called out. "Calls for speculation."

The judge nodded. "Sustained."

Violanti moved in closer. "David Spencer gave you everything you asked for, correct? Swabs, a statement, he let you take pictures?"

"Correct."

318

"Did you ask Anthony Vine for any of those things?"

"No." Joe knew his face was stone now.

"Did you ask anyone else for those things?" he pressed. "Anyone?"

"No."

"So, what you're telling me and this jury is that you never followed up on the possibility of any other suspect?"

Joe's voice was tight when he answered. *Keep it under control.* "He was the only suspect."

"Really? How long after the discovery of the body did you make an arrest?"

"Approximately seven hours."

"Seven whole hours." Violanti let that sink in with the jurors. "And you call that a complete and thorough investigation?"

The veins were bulging in Church's neck now as he yelled, "Objection!"

Violanti was unshaken; he was doing some damage. Joe wanted to reach across the witness stand and throttle him.

"Withdrawn. Detective Wheeler, how many homicides have you investigated since you've been with the Garden Valley Police Department?"

"There have only been two homicides since I started, both committed by the same suspect."

"You've only handled one other homicide case in your entire career, correct?"

Heat crept up Joe's neck. "Yes."

Violanti nodded along, as if trying to do the mental math. "With your limited experience, you believed seven hours was enough time for a proper investigation?"

"Objection!"

"Overruled." But the judge sounded interested. "Answer the question."

Joe took a deep breath. "I think I'm a very experienced detective. I've worked on hundreds of other types of cases. The district attorney consulted with me on all the evidence before David Spencer was charged."

"I rode in a plane once. Does that make me a pilot?"

One of the young female jurors burst into a snort of laughter and Joe felt an urge to punch that bitch in the mouth.

"Objection!" Church slammed both hands on the prosecution table. "Your Honor! I move to have that statement stricken from the record!"

The judge looked down his glasses at Violanti. He was not amused. "Mr. Violanti, no more of that. The jury is instructed to disregard that last statement."

Stricken, Joe thought, *what horseshit. It's already out there. And the little prick knows it.*

"Sorry, Your Honor."

"Continue, but carefully, Counselor."

"Of course," he said, trying to look sheepish, like a kid caught with his hand in the cookie jar. "Sorry, Your Honor," he repeated.

"Get on with it."

Joe could tell the judge was getting frustrated with Violanti's shitty tactics. Hopefully, the jury was too.

Violanti jumped right back in. "Detective, are you aware that a tracking device was found on Katherine Vine's vehicle?"

"Yes."

"Were you present when it was discovered at your police impound, attached to the underside of her vehicle?"

"Yes."

"Did you ever follow up as to how such a device came to be placed on her car?"

"No."

"No?" Violanti asked as if he were shocked.

"No," Joe said, trying to control his voice, his demeanor. The jury wouldn't like it if he came off as a hothead.

"Did you ask Mr. Vine if he placed it there?"

"No."

"Why not?" Violanti asked, as if this mystified him.

"It didn't seem connected to the crime."

"A tracking device, reporting her every move, didn't seem important?"

Beneath Joe's expensive suit coat, puddles were forming under each armpit. He felt an irritating drip down his side. "There was no way to trace it. I looked into that. And no way to say when it was placed under the vehicle."

"But you never asked Anthony Vine about it?"

"No."

"Because you arrested my client?"

"Yes."

"And your investigation was over when you put the cuffs on David Spencer?"

"The investigation wasn't over, per se, but the case was cleared with arrest."

"It wasn't over?" Violanti's eyebrows shot up. "What follow-up did you do?"

"We still needed the DNA reports, the autopsy findings, a background investigation—"

"Wouldn't you want to have those things before you rushed out and made an arrest?"

Joe looked to Church as he was rising to object to the question. Violanti stepped in between their lines of sight and pounded his fist down on the edge of the witness stand. "Don't look at him. He didn't ask you a question, I did!"

"Objection! Objection! Objection! Badgering the witness, out of order—"

Violanti overrode Church's objections with his own. "Your Honor, this investigation was a sham, my client was arrested before they even had all the evidence—"

"Objection! The defense attorney is now testifying—"

"Not another word!" the judge boomed, drowning them out. "Both of you! In my chambers now!"

The three of them trooped into chambers. Like children caught fighting in the school yard, Joe knew both attorneys were getting chewed out by the judge. After a few minutes everyone came back and the judge declared that unless Violanti had any other points to make with the witness, Joe was stepping down. He instructed the jury to disregard the outburst.

Violanti told them, "I'm done, Your Honor. The witness can step down."

"Respectfully, Your Honor, I'm not," Church snapped. "I have some redirect for the witness."

"I'll agree to the redirect, as long as you made it quick," the judge advised, his tone telling Joe that his patience was worn thin by both of the attorneys.

A half hour later Detective Wheeler was off the stand and sitting in the gallery along with the rest of the spectators.

He was furious. His undershirt was soaked straight through with sweat, making his shirt stick to him. His eyes stayed locked on Violanti, as if he was sizing him up for target practice. This was supposed to be his day. His star moment had been tarnished by the little bastard. He looked over at Lauren, who was whispering to her partner. *That bitch is laughing at me,* he thought. *Laughing with another guy she's screwing. She wouldn't have been laughing last night if things had gone my way.*

He faced forward again. *This was supposed to be my moment.* The runt had actually stolen the spotlight from him. He had waited so long for this. He dug his fingernails into his thighs through his pants, savoring the pain. Even when David Spencer was found guilty, Joe's victory would be incomplete.

It was criminal.

78

The trial moved on.

Lauren wanted to kiss Violanti for the show he put on at Joe's expense. He had made him look like a mean, incompetent asshole. Now he was sitting out in the gallery with a pissed off look on his face that wasn't going to endear him to any of the jurors, that was for sure. After last night, any doubt had been erased as to what a psychopath Joe Wheeler really was. Seeing Violanti reveal a glimpse of it on the stand was a small victory for Lauren. Still shook up from their run-in, she tried to focus on the trial, not Joe sitting across the aisle.

The next witness was the Vines' maid. Anita Perez was a stout, smart, efficient woman. The type that not only worked for a household, but became part of it. Anita was olive-skinned and dark-haired, with the faintest trace left of her Madrid accent. Dressed in a simple yellow blouse and black pants, she clutched a patent leather handbag to her bosom. She twisted a frayed piece of the shoulder strap as they swore her in. It was probably her way to keep her hands from shaking, but it was distracting. The more questions she was asked, the harder she twisted and pulled.

Anita stated that she had worked for the Vines since the twin boys, Jacob and Andrew, were born. Church took her through the events of the night and next morning step by step. Her testimony was exactly what Lauren expected it to be. No bombshells were dropped.

After Church established his timeline, he went into the Vine family's home life. Anita stated as she twisted that it was not out of Mr. Vine's character to not come home some evenings. "Most of the time," she said, "Miss Katherine didn't seem bothered by it, but she was on a lot of medication and nothing seemed to bother her too much."

Katherine was a loving mother to her two sons, spoiling them and treating them with gifts whenever she could. "A good woman," Anita declared as she began tearing up. "A good woman taken too soon." The boys were devastated at the loss of their mother and Mr. Vine hadn't been the same since. The house was not the same. She broke down on the stand and the judge let her have a few moments to collect herself. Lauren's heart went out to her, watching her have to display her grief on the stand.

Church declared he had no more questions.

Violanti had no questions for her. Lauren knew he didn't want to anger the jury by appearing to squeeze a poor, grief-stricken woman. Anita stepped down and practically ran from the courtroom, dabbing an old-fashioned handkerchief to her face. Lauren absently wondered if she had sewed the hanky herself.

The prosecution then called the man Lauren had been waiting for: Anthony Vine.

Vine stepped to the witness stand with the appropriate look of grief on his face. He wore a black suit coat over a white tee shirt with tan pants, like some sort of *Miami Vice* throwback. His hair was unnaturally black, to match his unnaturally tanned complexion and his overly muscular build. He was a man in his fifties trying to look like he was still in his twenties. The results were both sad and comical at the same time. Lauren thought his only saving grace had to be his money—why else would any woman be seen with someone like him? *Power*, she thought as she studied him on the stand. *He has a lot of power around this rusty city. He holds the keys to a lot of doors. And maybe he also locked some of them.*

Carl Church was no fool. He put the affair with Jennifer Jackson out there right away. He led Vine step by step through his movements of the day of Katherine's murder. Vine had gone to work, caught dinner with two business associates at Fiamo's steakhouse, then met Jennifer Jackson at his condo on the waterfront. They drank some wine, made love, and fell asleep, not to wake up until the morning, when he rushed home to find his wife missing. Church rested.

Frank Violanti walked toward the witness stand with the same deliberate slow stroll he used for Joe Wheeler. His fingertips dragged lightly over the polished desk as he made his way around it. Lauren admired Violanti's nerve. He knew how to push all the right buttons. Anthony Vine sat glaring down at him from his seat. He was visibly becoming angrier with every second Violanti wasted. Finally, he stood before Vine, a tiny David to his tanned Goliath, and smiled.

"How are you today, Mr. Vine?"

"Am I supposed to answer that?"

Violanti waved his hand, as if he was not concerned at Vine's obvious hostility. "Withdrawn. Mr. Vine, you just went through your whereabouts with Mr. Church on the night your wife was murdered. You and Jennifer Jackson were at your condominium that night, correct?"

"I already said we were."

"Of course you did. We all heard you say it." He made a sweeping gesture toward the jury box. "And how long were the two of you together that night?"

Church jumped up. "Objection, Your Honor, asked and answered."

"Sustained. Rephrase the question."

"Mr. Vine, at what time did you and Mrs. Jackson arrive at your condominium?"

"I said about eight o'clock."

"And what time did you leave?"

"About six thirty in the morning."

"You never left? The two of you stayed in the condo the entire time?"

"Objection! Asked and answered!" Church was getting red in the face again.

He's going to stroke out by the end of this trial, Lauren observed. *It looks like his head is going to explode.*

The judge dismissed him this time. "I'll allow this line of questioning."

Violanti practically beamed. "Thank you, Your Honor. Mr. Vine could you please answer my question?"

"No. We never left."

"Never?"

"Objection!"

"Overruled. Move on, Mr. Violanti," the judge cautioned.

Anthony Vine clenched his teeth together. "We never left."

"And did you call your wife?"

Vine nodded. "I told her I'd be working late."

"What time was that?"

"About eight o'clock."

Violanti whirled around and went back over to the defense table. He grabbed a stack of papers and asked they be moved into evidence. Church asked to see them, bobbed his head once in agreement, and he passed them to the court reporter to be marked as exhibit 23B. Finally, he turned to Anthony Vine and handed him the papers. "Do you recognize these?"

Vine ruffled through them. "Yes. They look like my phone records."

"Judge, let the record reflect that Exhibit 23B is, in fact, certified copies of Anthony Vine's phone records for the month of June."

The judge looked at Church. "No objections." Lauren watched Church lean in, no doubt wondering where Violanti was headed.

"So entered," Judge O'Keefe said. "Continue."

Violanti turned back to Anthony Vine. "On the evening your wife was murdered, do you see any calls or texts made to her cell phone? I believe I highlighted them for you?"

He flipped through the pages and then stopped. "Yes. I see calls I made."

"How many calls did you make on that day to her phone?"

He counted with his finger, carefully going down the column. "I made sixteen calls to her phone."

"Sixteen." He paused and looked at the jury. "How many texts?"

His lips moved as he counted. "Five texts."

"What time was the first call?"

He squinted at the page. "8:39 in the morning."

"And what time was the last call?"

Once again, he fished around the page. "8:02 p.m."

"No calls after that?"

Vine looked again. "No."

"How about that night into the next day? What's the next call you make, according to that?"

He seemed to stiffen up. "To Carl Church at 7:53 a.m."

"Objection!" Church roared. "Relevance?"

The judge looked annoyed with Church now. "I'll allow it. Move on, Mr. Violanti."

"What time did you get home in the morning?"

"About six thirty."

"Was your wife home?"

"No."

Lauren noticed sweat forming at Vine's temple. She hoped the jury was close enough to see it.

"Who was home?" Violanti asked.

"My two sons and our housekeeper, Anita."

"We've already heard testimony from Anita that she tried to call your wife on her cell phone repeatedly that night and tried to reach you. Correct?"

"That's what she said."

"Why didn't you try to call your *wife* on her cell?" Violanti stressed the word *wife* for effect.

"Objection!"

"Overruled!" the judge barked, and Church sank back into his chair.

"When I got home, Anita said she had been trying all night. I was about to call the police when they knocked on my door. When the officers said to come with them, I called Carl. I wanted to know what was going on."

Violanti seemed to digest this and moved back over to his table. He fiddled around with his folders for a second, checked his notes, and looked up. "Can you look at Exhibit 23B again for me? Look at the day before the murder?"

Grudgingly, Vine flipped through the pages again.

"Can you tell me how many times you called and texted your wife's cell phone the day before the murder?"

Once again his finger moved down along the column. Vine cleared his throat before he spoke. "Twenty-one times."

"Twenty-one times." It wasn't a question. "You called and texted your wife's cell phone twenty-one times the day before she was murdered. What time was the first call?"

He looked down at the page. "8:21 in the morning."

"And what time was the last call?"

"11:02 p.m."

"Where were you the night before she was murdered?"

Now the path of the questioning was clear and Vine looked over toward Church. "Don't look at him," Violanti prompted again. "Look at me. Where were you at 11:02 the night before your wife's murder that you had to call her cell phone?"

"Objection!"

"Sit down, Mr. Church!" the judge admonished. "No grounds for objection. Answer the question, Mr. Vine."

"I was with Jennifer Jackson at my office."

"And you still called your wife at 11:02?"

"Yes. I wanted to let her know I'd be later than I thought."

"But the night she was murdered, your last call was at 8:02? You didn't think to call that night to say you'd be spending the night away again?"

"Objection!"

"Sustained. Rephrase."

Vioalnti kept up the barrage. "Why didn't you call your wife again that night? Or text her the next morning? Why was your next call to Carl Church?"

"I already said Jennifer and I had fallen asleep. I tried to rush home so Katherine wouldn't know what time it was when I got in. Anita said she'd been calling her all night—"

"You expect me to believe a man who calls and texts his wife twenty-one times on a typical day, from the minute she gets up until the second she goes to bed, would conveniently fall asleep and forget to call her on the night she was murdered?"

"Objection!" Church was starting to sound a little desperate to end this line of questioning.

"Sustained."

Violanti crossed back over to the defense table and retrieved a small round object encased in a plastic evidence bag. He had the court clerk number it and enter it into evidence. He held it out to Anthony Vine. Vine made no move to take it from him.

"Do you know what this is?"

"No."

Violanti practically shoved it under his nose. "Why don't you take it and examine it before you say no?"

Vine took the bag, gave it the slightest glance over, and handed it back. "I don't know what it is."

"Your Honor, let the record reflect that the people have already stipulated to the State Police Forensics lab's report that this device marked Defense Item 47 is a Global Positioning System tracking device that was found attached to the underside of Katherine Vine's Mercedes."

"So noted."

Violanti now held the bag up high, so the jury could see. "Mr. Vine, do you have any idea how a tracking device became attached to your wife's car?"

"No, I do not."

"You didn't have it put there to keep track of her?"

His voice was full of red hot hatred for the little defense attorney. "No, I did not."

"You've never seen this device?"

"No."

Lauren could practically see the steam coming out of Vine's ears. Violanti had him enraged.

"Did you ever drive the Mercedes your wife was killed in?"

"Once in a while, not often, like to unblock the driveway or put it in the garage. I want to sell it, but they said I should keep it until after the trial."

Violanti ignored that last part. "She was the primary user of the vehicle?"

"Yes."

"So she would be the most likely target of someone tracking the movements of the car?"

"Objection," Church said. "Calls for a conclusion."

The judge agreed. "Sustained."

Violanti repositioned himself to give the jurors a better view of Anthony Vine's expression. "Mr. Vine, are you aware that devices such as this can transmit their data to a cell phone with Internet capability?"

"No, I wasn't," he snapped, "but that's very informative."

"Does your phone have such capabilities?'

"I have several phones, but yes, they all have Internet access. I have to stay connected with my business."

"Do you sometimes carry more than one phone?"

"Sometimes," Vine admitted. "I have some strictly for business and one that's personal."

"Were you carrying more than one the night your wife was murdered?"

Vine looked him straight in the eye and growled. "I don't remember."

Violanti nodded, as if that was the answer he expected. "Mr. Vine," he continued, "did you have a life insurance policy on your wife, Katherine Vine?"

Vine's eyes darted from Violanti to Carl Church, who knew better than to object to the question. Even a lowly detective like Lauren knew it was definitely fair game. "Yes."

"And how much does that policy pay out, Mr. Vine?"

Vine swallowed hard. "Two million dollars."

Violanti leaned in. "I'm sorry, I didn't hear that. Could you repeat that for the jury?"

"Two million dollars," he choked out roughly, contempt dripping from his voice.

"Two million dollars," Frank Violanti repeated. "Did you receive the money yet?"

Vine took a deep, stuttering breath. "No."

"Is that because the insurance adjustors want to know the outcome of the trial first?"

"Objection!" Church called out.

"I'll rephrase," Violanti volunteered. "Isn't it true that if you were a suspect, the insurance company would withhold payout?"

"But I'm not a suspect," Vine shot back.

"How convenient for you." Violanti stepped back from the stand before Church could object. "No further questions at this time, but I would like to recall the witness later."

"Granted." The judge made a note on the paper in front of him. "Call your next witness."

Violanti turned to Lauren sitting in the gallery as Anthony Vine stalked off the stand. He gave her a wink and retrieved his papers from the witness stand.

All things considered, Lauren thought, *this was a very, very good day.*

79

The prosecution rested on the third day of the trial. Church presented Dr. Mazur from the county lab to testify about the DNA evidence as their last witness. Lauren considered Dr. Mazur a friend, as he loved to go over cold evidence with her and Reese. He would pore over the crime scene pictures with them, picking out items to test, commenting on the latest breakthroughs. He always told them the DNA was the icing on the cake but they were the ones who had to bake the cake, meaning put the case in context for his DNA grand finale.

Dr. John Mazur was a tiny, shriveled man with a large port wine stain birthmark that stretched from his left cheek to his ear. He hated to come out of his lab, much less to testify. He never looked Lauren in the eye when he talked, always somewhere up and to the left. He loved his numbers and data and charts; people, not so much. Now he squirmed nervously in his seat, picking at imaginary lint on his lab coat, refusing to look at Carl Church. First, he explained to the jurors how DNA was collected and stored. Then he went on to educate them on the process of extracting DNA from items submitted to the police. Church rolled around to the specifics of the Katherine Vine case. He went over the reports in painstaking detail.

Mazur testified that the DNA found under the victim's nails was a match to David Ryan Spencer to the tune of 1 in 26 quadrillion. Quadrillion. Lauren knew that kind of number would blow the juror's minds, especially when the doctor explained that 26 quadrillion people was billions more than had ever lived on the planet and probably ever would. He then went on to testify that no other male DNA was found under her nails. Mazur quietly told the jurors about the semen found in her body that came back to David Ryan Spencer with the same startling numbers. The jury now looked over at David, eyes narrowing. When Carl Church was finished with him, Violanti had no further questions. Lauren knew his reasoning. Science was science. Why do more damage?

When Dr. Mazur stepped down and shuffled out of the room, Church declared that the prosecution rested. Judge O'Keefe asked Violanti if he was ready to proceed. With an affirmative answer from the defense, the judge then declared, "Call your first witness."

"The defense calls Jennifer Jackson."

A ripple went through the crowded courtroom as everyone turned to watch Jennifer walk in. She had on an expensive-looking silk dress. Lauren took in the sleeveless black sheath that showed off her muscular arms, toned from years of tennis. Her painfully high heels clicked all the way to the witness stand. Jennifer's short-cropped hair was carefully gelled away from her face, but her eyes were puffy and red. If Lauren had to guess, she would've said that Jennifer must have taken something medicinal in preparation for this cross-examination. If Jackson was expecting to see Anthony Vine, he was tucked away in a conference room two floors down, waiting to be recalled to the stand. Jennifer stole a glance at Vine's people, who were taking up an entire row near the middle of the courtroom. They stared her down as she took the stand. They were all big, muscular, middle-aged hangers on who did Vine's bidding. Jennifer didn't look at them after she was sworn in, but stared straight ahead at Frank Violanti, as if waiting for a guillotine to chop her head off.

"How are you today, Mrs. Jackson?"

"Fine." Her voice was barely a whisper. Violanti adjusted the microphone so that it was closer to her mouth.

"Mrs. Jackson, do you know Anthony Vine?"

"Yes."

"From where do you know Mr. Vine?"

"He employs me as a spokesperson for his gym franchises."

"Do you have a relationship with Mr. Vine other than professionally?"

"Yes."

"What kind of relationship do you have with Anthony Vine, aside from your professional one?"

"Objection! Mr. Vine's relationship with Miss Jackson was fully disclosed by Mr. Vine himself."

Violanti looked at Church, then back to the judge. "Its relevance will be made crystal clear if you allow me to continue."

"I'll allow it, Mr. Violanti, but don't beat a dead horse."

He turned back to Jennifer Jackson. "Please answer my question."

She shifted in her seat. "We were lovers for a year."

"Were lovers?"

"I broke it off with him after his wife's death."

"At the time of his wife's death, you were lovers?"

Her voice was small. "Yes."

"And Mr. Vine testified that on the night of his wife's death, he was with you?"

"Yes."

He went on gently, "You were with him at his waterfront condominium?"

"Yes."

"Your Honor, if it pleases the court, I'd like to play Defense Exhibit 34. It's a time- and date-stamped video of the intersection of Lower Terrace and West Eagle Streets taken by the city monitoring system. I'd also like to move into evidence this custody control sheet."

Lauren knew that was her cue. Getting up, she walked to the back of the courtroom and rolled a video monitor toward the stand. While Church objected and the two lawyers argued about the admissibility of the tapes as evidence, Violanti had Lauren set up the monitor to face the judge, jury, and witness. Working slowly and carefully, Lauren retrieved a second one, placing it against the wall, so that the prosecution and gallery could see. The judge allowed the tape into evidence eventually and made Church sit down with the copies of the paperwork Violanti had provided for him. Handing Violanti the remote, Lauren returned to her seat in the gallery next to Reese.

After everything was marked and noted, he powered up the screens. Lauren had made sure the video was cued to the Lexus approaching the intersection and being stopped at a red light. Although the license plate was clearly visible, the driver was obscured by the reflection of the darkly tinted glass.

Violanti paused the tape. "Can you tell me, Mrs. Jackson, whose vehicle this is?"

She blinked her eyes, trying to fight back tears. Her voice was choked. "Mine."

"I'm sorry, could you speak up?"

"It's my car," she blurted out.

"From eight o'clock on the evening in question until six thirty that next morning, did Anthony Vine leave that condominium for any reason?"

"Objection!" Church was on his feet. "May I approach?"

The judge motioned both counselors up to the bench. It was supposed to be out of earshot of the jury but both attorneys were so worked up their voices carried loud and clear throughout the courtroom. *Maybe,* Lauren thought, *a little purposefully on Violanti's part.* "Sir," Church practically panted in rage, "I have a sworn statement from the witness that says Mr. Vine never left. Mr. Violanti is supporting perjury of this witness—"

"If I may be allowed to continue with my questioning and present my evidence, Mr. Church can feel free to cross examine the witness as to what she lied about."

"That sounds about right, Mr. Church. Have a seat."

Violanti floated back toward Jennifer Jackson unruffled. "Did Mr. Vine leave the condominium?"

Jackson slumped into her seat. "He said he had to get condoms."

"What time did he leave?"

"I'm not sure, before midnight."

"How long was he gone?"

"About an hour."

"Doesn't that seem like an awfully long time to get condoms?"

Church sounded to Lauren like he was about to lose his mind: "Objection!"

Violanti didn't miss a beat. "And can you tell me who is driving this vehicle at that time?"

"Anthony Vine took my car because he said his car was too noticeable."

"Why would his car be too noticeable?"

"It has the words VINE TIME! written in red letters across the rear bumper."

Violanti nodded, then fast-forwarded through the video, allowing the jury to see the minutes ticking away. The car came into view again, but this time it caught a green light. The back of the car was clearly visible as going through the intersection. Violanti paused the tape again. "Is this your car?"

"Yes, that's my car."

"Who is driving it?"

"Objection!" Church called out. "You can't see from that picture who is driving the vehicle!"

"Sustained."

Violanti pressed forward. "Did Anthony Vine return from buying condoms?"

"Yes." Her voice was small and pinched.

"Did your car return as well?"

"Yes."

"What was Mr. Vine's demeanor like the night of Katherine Vine's murder?"

"Objection. Calls for speculation."

Violanti cocked an eyebrow. "I think Ms. Jackson is in a unique position to accurately gauge Mr. Vine's mood at the time of the murder."

The judge nodded. "I'll allow some leeway. The witness may answer."

"He kept checking his phone," Jackson replied. "He has one of those smart phones with all the crazy apps on it. He kept playing with it and checking it."

"Was that before he left?"

"Before and after. When we finally laid down to catch some sleep, I had to tell him to put it away. The next thing I knew, it was morning and he was gone."

"Was that usual for him?"

"Yes. He always tried to leave before his wife would wake up, but he always left a note for me. That morning, he didn't."

"What time did you wake up on the morning in question?"

She dragged her forearm across her nose, soaking her sleeve with snot. Lauren wanted to hand her the box of tissues sitting on the court clerk's desk. "About eight."

"What time did you learn about the murder?"

"As I was driving home. I heard it on the radio."

"You heard it on the radio? He didn't call you right away?"

"Why would he?" she sniffed. "I was just his girlfriend. His wife just got murdered. I guess he had other things on his mind."

"When did you last speak to Anthony Vine?"

"That night. He was crying and we made a date to meet after the funeral."

"So it seems, at some point that day, you were on his mind." Before Church could jump up he went on, "Did you keep the meeting?"

"I did. We met at his office. I told him I didn't think it was a good idea if we saw each other for a while. He agreed."

"Did you know that Katherine Vine had a tracking device on her car?"

"No, but he always seemed to know where she was."

Church cut Violanti's next question off. "Objection. She is in no position to know what Anthony Vine knows."

The judge agreed. "The jury will disregard that last statement."

Violanti continued, "Did you give a sworn statement to Detective Joseph Wheeler?"

"Yes."

"In that statement, were you asked if you or Anthony Vine ever left his condominium that night?"

"Yes."

"What was your answer then?"

"I lied and said no."

"Why did you lie?"

"I didn't want to make it seem like Anthony could be a suspect and hurt the case against David Spencer."

"Did Anthony Vine tell you to lie?"

"Objection! Hearsay!" Church's face was almost purple now.

"Sustained." Judge O'Keefe's voice had a warning tone in it. But Lauren could see Violanti was going for the full effect and wanted to push the envelope as far as he could with this witness.

"Did you and Anthony discuss the case against David Spencer?"

"Yes."

"Did he ask you how you were going to testify today?"

"Yes."

"And did you tell him?" Violanti asked. "That you were going to tell the truth?"

"I told him I didn't know. Not for sure. I mean, he thought you might call me, but he wasn't sure. I didn't know what to do. I'm so sorry for his wife." A tear fell from her nose onto the wooded rail of the witness box. "I really am. I can't believe someone killed her."

"Are you still in a relationship with Anthony Vine?"

More tears spilled down her cheeks. "No."

"Why not?"

"Like I said, I broke it off. Right after the murder."

"Have you spoken to Anthony Vine since you broke it off?"

"Yes."

Better to let the jurors' imaginations run wild with that last statement, Lauren thought. *Sometimes what's left unsaid does more damage.*

Violanti smiled sympathetically, "Thank you, Mrs. Jackson. No further questions." He wheeled around. As he went to sit back down at the defense table, he brushed shoulders with Carl Church, who was marching toward the stand.

"Mrs. Jackson, do you recognize this piece of paper?"

He handed her a white sheet of paper and she looked it over. Then she nodded and handed it back. "It's the statement I gave to Detective Wheeler."

"And did you sign this statement?'

"I did."

"But now you're saying that some things in this statement are untrue?"

"Yes."

"How do we know that you aren't lying now?"

"Objection!" It was Violanti's turn to spring up, palms pressed flat on the polished wood of the defense table.

Church looked toward the judge. "Your Honor, this is fair game. The defense brought it in."

The judge looked at the defense table. "Sustained. You opened the door, Mr. Violanti."

Lauren saw Violanti start to protest, think better of it, and sit down.

Church picked up as if he'd never been interrupted. "Are you lying now?"

"No."

"But you lied to Detective Wheeler?"

"Yes."

"And you lied to your husband when you were having an affair with Anthony Vine?"

"Yes."

"And the only reason you came clean about the affair or your car was because you were confronted with evidence by Mr. Violanti?"

"That's not the only reason." Her eyes cast downward.

"It's not? Are you still married?"

"We are in the process of a divorce."

"Who served whom with the papers?" Church pressed.

"My husband served me." Her voice was a whisper now, full of shame.

"So, you didn't want a divorce?" Church's voice became softer, almost sympathetic.

"No."

"And now you're concocting a story to put your lover in jeopardy by committing perjury?"

Jackson actually sat back startled, like he'd slapped her.

Violanti could barely contain himself. "Objection!"

"Sustained."

Church glanced at the witness, who was all but doubled over in the stand now, crying. His gentle tone evaporated into contempt. "No further questions. This witness has no credibility."

Lauren couldn't help but feel for Jackson, as the woman practically crumpled in on herself with that last remark. If Church's aim had been to crush her spirit, he had succeeded.

"Mr. Church," the judge admonished, "another outburst like that and I will declare a mistrial. The jury will disregard that last remark. Redirect?"

Violanti shook his head. Lauren knew Church had scored some points on that one and Violanti was at least sympathetic enough to let it go.

The judge turned to the witness box. "Mrs. Jackson, you may step down."

Carl Church's satisfied smile lasted all the way back to his seat. Jennifer Jackson marched tearfully through the crowded gallery and out the door. Despite his heated objections, Violanti didn't seem bothered by the cross, now that it was over. Lauren believed he had done some damage to the defense for sure, but Church could have done worse to Jennifer Jackson on the stand. Violanti certainly would have. He just had to keep chipping away at the prosecution's case.

"Next witness, Counselor?" the judge asked.

Frank Violanti was more than ready. "The defense wishes to recall Anthony Vine."

Judge O'Keefe nodded. "Recalling Anthony Vine."

Church's smirk disappeared from his face. In the heat of his cross of Jennifer Jackson, Lauren could tell he had forgotten all about Violanti's intention of recalling Vine. "Your Honor"—he stood facing the judge—"I would like to request we break for the day, start fresh in the morning."

The judge glanced down at the gold watch on his right wrist. "If the defense has no objections?"

Lauren could tell Violanti had plenty of objections, but to hold the jury would make him extremely unpopular at this stage of the game, and jury opinion was everything. "I have no objection."

"We'll resume testimony tomorrow at ten a.m."

Hitting the desk with his gavel, the signal sent everyone to their feet before the bailiff even got out his "All rise."

Lauren watched Violanti gather up his case file, whispering to David the whole time. *If nothing else*, she thought as she followed Reese into the aisle, *tomorrow is going to be the prize fight.*

80

Lauren and Reese met up early the next day and had an almost silent coffee together before heading over to the courthouse. She was too tense to make small talk and he didn't push it. No flirting with the waitress, no weight jokes, just minimal speech and a five-dollar bill left on the greasy counter.

Coming into the courtroom early again, they took their same seats, watching the scene assemble itself. As Lauren watched, she felt the pang of a headache start behind her left eye. All the stress of the last few months felt like it was suddenly drowning her, pulling her under. She bent forward, pinching the bridge of her nose, eyes closed, willing it away. Reese's hand on her back nearly made her jump out of her seat. He said nothing, just held his hand between her shoulder blades, practically soaking the pain in with his touch. She leaned back, opened her eyes.

She could do this.

At exactly ten a.m. the judge took the bench, surveyed the court-room, called both attorneys up, and took care of the formalities. Lauren watched the jury: some were alert, pencils and paper in hand, some looked bored, and one young man yawned for what seemed like a full minute. Satisfied that everything was as it should be, the judge sent the attorneys back and started the proceedings.

"Mr. Violanti?" the judge promted.

He stood. "The defense would like to recall Anthony Vine, Your Honor."

He nodded. "Recalling Anthony Vine."

It took a few minutes for the court officers to bring him in. Vine's jaw was set in outrage, his features clenched and tense, as he made the trip back up to the stand. Violanti snatched up the remote for the video monitors that were still in place as he approached the stand.

"Mr. Vine, it was your testimony that you never left your water-front condominium on the night in question after you made the last phone call to your wife, was it not?"

"Correct."

Violanti clicked a button on the remote and both screens lit up with the image of Jennifer Jackson's car at the red light. The color drained away from Vine's face. "Who does that vehicle belong to, Mr. Vine?"

He didn't answer.

"Does that car belong to Jennifer Jackson?"

"It looks like her car."

"Can you read the date and time stamped on the bottom of the screen?"

"I don't have my glasses on."

"Would you like me to bring the television closer?" he asked help-fully.

"No."

"Did you, in fact, leave the condominium at 9:50 p.m. on June 25th of this year?"

He looked at Church.

"Don't look at him. Look at me," again Violanti had to tell him. "He doesn't have the answers, you do. Mr. Vine, did you leave your condominium in Jennifer Jackson's car on June 25th at 9:50 p.m.?"

"What do you want me to say?" Vine barked.

"The truth," Violanti snapped back. "Is that, in fact, you in that car on the screen?"

"I can't believe this—"

"Answer the question!"

"Yes," he spat out. "Yes, it was me. I went to get condoms and some OxyContin. That's why I fell asleep and I didn't wake up until the morning, instead of going home."

"Now your story is that you were in a drug-induced coma while your wife was being killed?"

Church rose to object, but the judge impatiently waved him down. *You can't object just because you don't like the answer that's coming,* Lauren thought as the prosecutor sank back into his seat.

"I've had a pill problem for a while—"

"I didn't ask you that, Mr. Vine."

Anthony Vine sat back in his seat as if bracing for another blow.

Violanti got right up into Vine's face, which was not such an easy thing for him to do, considering his lack of height. "Did you kill your wife?"

"Objection!" Church burst up from his seat.

Violanti pressed on, ignoring Church's objection, "Did you kill your wife, Mr. Vine?"

"Your Honor!" Church pounded his hand on the table.

"Answer the question, sir, and no more of that, Mr. Church," the judge admonished, motioning for Church to sit down again.

"No. I didn't kill my wife." Vine snarled. "I got condoms and drugs."

"From where?"

"A guy I know on the west side. I'd been buying from him for a few months."

"He gave you condoms and drugs?"

"No." Vine shook his head as if to get everything straight. "He gave me the pills. I stopped at a store on Niagara Street and got the condoms."

"What's the guy's name?"

"I don't know his name. He's a short Hispanic guy. He stands on the corner of Maryland and West. He's probably there right now."

"Anthony Vine, the millionaire, has to buy his drugs on the street like a common junkie? Don't tell me you don't have people to do that for you?"

"Objection!" Church called from the prosecutors table.

"Sustained." The judge was starting to lose patience with Violanti's ambush.

"Withdrawn. What was the name of the store you stopped at?"

"I don't remember." Vine was flexing and unflexing his left hand. "It was one of those small, little Spanish markets."

"There are about twenty of those up and down Niagara Street. Was it on the left or right hand side?"

"I don't remember."

Violanti nodded, seemed to consider that answer, and asked, "Did you stop before or after you got the pills?"

"Before ... no, after."

"Which is it?"

Anthony Vine stopped for a moment. "After."

"Are you sure? That night is kind of fuzzy for you, isn't it, Mr. Vine?"

"Objection!" Church jumped up.

Violanti didn't even break pace. "Withdrawn. Did you drive to Garden Valley and kill your wife?"

"No."

"Are you sure? You seem a little off about the events of the night."

"Objection!" Church was going to have a heart attack if he kept leaping from his seat.

"Sustained."

Violanti tried again. "Did you drive to Toy City that night?"

"No."

"Did you see your wife having sex with David Spencer?"

"No."

Violanti cut right to it. "Did you lose your temper and strangle her with the scarf you bought her in Italy?"

"No, I didn't! I did not kill my wife. I didn't kill her!" Vine started to rise from the witness stand, causing the bailiff to come over and gently ease him back down.

Violanti paused while Vine tried to control himself, breathing in and out, clutching the sides of the witness box, his oversized arm muscles bulging under his shirt.

Then he started out again softly. He was almost done. "Did you share your drugs with Jennifer Jackson that night?"

"No." His face fell from the rage of Violanti's questions to a deep sadness. "I didn't tell her about getting the drugs. Very few people know about my habit. It's something I'm deeply ashamed of. I hurt my back three years ago and got addicted to the pain pills. Now my doctor won't give them to me anymore. I don't know how to stop. I

351

never thought I'd be that guy, you know? Katherine knew. Sometimes I'd steal some of her meds. After she got diagnosed bipolar, I kept sending her to other doctors to get more prescriptions."

Lauren wondered if Vine came up with that story himself or if Church had helped. A sad tale, to be sure, but Violanti wouldn't let himself get derailed. "So, you could have told Mrs. Jackson you were going for condoms, killed your wife, and now here you are with this made-up story. Is that the truth?"

Church was pleading now. "Your Honor, please."

"Enough, Mr. Violanti." The judge's voice loomed ominous now. "Either move on or stand down."

"I think I've made my point. No further questions."

81

With the end of Anthony Vine's testimony, the defense rested its case. Church tried to do damage control, a lot of it, lasting into the late afternoon. Vine looked exhausted and shrunken to Violanti as he finally exited the stand. He'd been on the stand all day, and Violanti knew what it was like to take that kind of beating, although it didn't garner any sympathy for Vine. Maybe it was wrong of him, but Anthony Vine was a bully and Violanti was glad to see him be on the receiving end for once.

The judge adjourned for the day and set closing arguments for the next morning, Friday. Frank Violanti spent most of Thursday night scouring his trial notes, honing his closing argument to head off any damage Church could do at the pass. The prosecution always got the last word in a criminal trial. Always. Violanti had seen enough of Church's closings in the past to prepare himself. He liked to use charts and props, PowerPoint presentations, and physical re-enactments to get his point across. He was dramatic and dynamic and juries were mesmerized by his even, reasonable voice. The voice of justice for the people. Because wasn't he, District Attorney Carl Church, elected to represent the people? Violanti would have to anticipate his closing and neutralize it with preemptive strikes.

While Kim slept quietly on the couch next to him, he furiously scribbled and reworked his closing, over and over again until he was satisfied that he could do no better. He fell asleep on his desk, facedown in his notes, like a college student cramming for exams. Funny thing was, he slept like the dead.

———————

The next morning Frank Violanti found himself in the courtroom again, looking at those same jurors, wondering if he had poked enough holes in the prosecution's case. Now he had to point out each and every hole, remind the jurors of the prosecution's weaknesses. He felt that the closing he'd written was his masterpiece. With his own PowerPoint presentation, he painted a picture of a flawed investigation from the very start. He laid out in living color all the things he had hit on during the trial. That it was a rush to judgment without a proper investigation. The lack of experience of the lead detective. He walked them through Anthony Vine as a viable suspect. The husband had means, motive, and opportunity. He reminded them of a lack of criminal past on the defendant's part and David's willingness to talk to the police. How David cooperated fully from the beginning. How Anthony Vine concealed more than he shared. All these things he wove into an intricate portrait, pointing away from David Spencer and toward Anthony Vine.

Lauren and Reese watched from the gallery, looking impressed. Violanti had the jury's attention, they were leaning forward, taking notes. He walked through the case against David point by point, refuting every bit of evidence in one way or another. Even Joe Wheeler, who he was watching out of the corner of his eye, started to look worried. At the end, when he humbly thanked the jury and assured them that they'd do the right thing, Violanti was convinced it was a wrap. Not only had he created a reasonable doubt, in his mind the jury could have nothing *but* doubt. Frank Violanti had hit it out of the park.

Then Carl Church stood up.

There were no PowerPoints or blown up photos, none of the stuff he was noted for using in his closings. There was just him in his navy blue power suit, looking handsome and strong and reassuring, standing in front of the jury.

82

"Ladies and gentlemen," Carl Church began. "This case is simple."

Lauren watched as he ran a finger down the left of the rail that separated the jury from the courtroom floor, as if inspecting for dust. He strolled in front of them as if he had all the time in the world. Looking up thoughtfully, he addressed them like they were old friends. "Mr. Violanti has pointed out alternate theories for every bit of evidence I presented to you. He gave a different interpretation of each witness's testimony. He might have raised a doubt in some of your minds, because he's a good defense attorney and that's his job."

Finding herself inching to the edge of her seat, Lauren's breath caught in her throat as Church held off a moment with a well-timed pause.

"Ladies and gentlemen, these are the facts. David Ryan Spencer is the last known person with Katherine Vine. David Ryan Spencer had sex with Katherine Vine. That's a fact. Katherine Vine bit David Ryan

Spencer. Katherine Vine was strangled with her own scarf, in her own car, the same night she had sex with David Ryan Spencer. These are facts not even disputed by the defense. Was Anthony Vine having an affair? Yes. So what? He was with his mistress the night his wife was murdered. He left for condoms and drugs, so he says. Did he? I don't know. What I do know is there is not one fact that puts him at the scene of his wife's murder. Not one. Not a witness, not a piece of video, nothing. You must judge this case on the facts. Not speculation from the defense. Because that's what it is."

He twisted his torso to glare at Violanti, to drive home who was raising these ridiculous theories. "Speculation. Frank Violanti is pointing the finger at Anthony Vine because he has nowhere else to point it. He asks you to look for a person with a motive. But I submit to you this was an absolutely senseless murder. Senseless. There is no motive you could supply me with to make sense of killing Katherine Vine. She was a beautiful wife, a devoted mother, a beloved sister, and a good friend. To try to put a reason on her death is as pointless as her murder."

Turning back to the jury, he grabbed the jury box rail with both hands, his voice raising in righteous indignation. "Ladies and gentlemen, David Ryan Spencer wanted Katherine Vine. He wanted her in the worst way. He saw her on numerous occasions and lusted after her. He said it in his own statement. David Ryan Spencer saw an opportunity and he took it. To say Katherine Vine randomly had sex with him and then another person showed up moments later and killed her is something that happens on television, not in real life."

He let that sink in a second, his eyes skipping from one juror's face to the next. "This is real life. David Ryan Spencer wanted to have sex with Katherine Vine. So he concocted a plan. He tricked her into leaving her credit card, he had sex with her, and then strangled her to death. It's that simple."

With those words, and the expression on the faces of the jurors, Lauren's hopes sank.

83

At 11:23 in the morning on the fifth day, the trail was over. Unlike the O.J. Simpson case, which played out for weeks, most murder cases are presented and wrapped up in a matter of days. When Carl Church finished his simple—yet brilliant—summation, the judge charged the jury, issuing them the detailed instructions on how to go about their deliberations, then sent them into the jury room. It was a Friday, the day most feared by prosecutors and defense attorney's alike for beginning deliberations. While some juries took longer to reach a verdict than the trial itself took, Friday juries were notorious for quick verdicts. The jurors wanted their weekend. They didn't want to be sequestered. They wanted their family and friends and their lives and to be done with the case. While the judge let the bailiffs order in food for them, the rest of the cast of characters agonized in the wings, waiting for the verdict. All the months of preparation, hearings, motions, and testimony boiled down to this. What Lauren had come to think of as The Wait.

"I hate waiting for things."

"I thought I was the impatient one between the two of us," Violanti replied, squirming in his seat. Lauren fought the urge. The chairs in the conference room that the judge had provided them were cushioned, but still uncomfortable. The two of them sat facing each other, sweating out the jury deliberations together. She wished Reese could have come back there with them. It gave her some comfort to know he was still out in the courtroom, waiting. He was a hell of a friend to stick it out with her. They both knew the jury could be out for six hours or six days.

Five hours into it, Violanti was starting to get antsy. If they didn't reach a verdict by six o'clock, the judge would send them home. Lauren felt a bumping motion shaking her chair.

Violanti's leg had begun to bounce up and down. He knew better than anyone what a Friday meant. The anticipation was becoming agonizing.

"Stop it," she hissed.

He immediately clamped a hand over his nervous leg. "Sorry." Violanti looked at his watch. "It's five fifteen now."

"Fifteen minutes later than the last time you checked." But she glanced at her phone too, just to be sure.

He had his notes spread across the table in front of him. He kept going over and over the testimony, looking for what he could have done better, what he would change. Lauren wanted to tell him that he had done everything he could, that he gave David a great defense, but she couldn't muster the energy. She wished he hadn't banished his two assistants to wait in the courtroom in case there was any activity he should know about. Outside the door of the conference room, she could see David's mom hunched over with a woman holding her

360

shoulders. Better for the both of them to hide out in the little room next to the courtroom and pretend to look busy and not worried.

One of the bailiffs had stuck her head in the door. "Mr. Violanti?"

"Yes?"

"The judge wants to see all the attorneys in his chambers immediately."

Lauren and Violanti looked at each other and both jumped up. This was not usual. The first thing that ran through her mind was juror misconduct. A mistrial. The thought of having to do it all over again made her stomach twist into a knot. *All of this*, she thought, *the trial, reconnecting with Mark, getting stalked by Joe Wheeler, could have just been a first act, a dress rehearsal, a Goddamn run-through.*

They followed the portly little deputy back into the courtroom and into a hallway that ran behind the bench. The judge's chambers were full.

"Counselor." Judge O'Keefe motioned to a seat next to the district attorney. Violanti shook his head. Lauren tried to melt into the background. Something was very wrong. The tension in the room was electric. It played across every face packed in there. Lauren could tell, whatever it was, it was not good news. Carl Church was already making a pitch to the judge.

"Respectfully, Judge," the district attorney began, "I think this calls for a recess so we can access the situation."

"What situation?" Violanti demanded. "The jury is already out. How can we recess? What's going on?"

The judge held up his hand, silencing them both. "Mr. Violanti, the state police have just notified this court that a body believed to be that of Amber Anderson was just discovered in a wooded area sixty miles south of the city. The district attorney wants a continuance to investigate any relevance to this case."

There was a stunned silence. Those who had walked in late had the wind knocked out of them. Lauren looked at Violanti, but he was already approaching the judge's desk to stand next to Church.

Joe Wheeler was leaning up against the back wall with a satisfied look on his face. *The wind is back in that prick's sail*, Lauren thought. *As far as he's concerned, this was all the proof he needs that David Spencer is a murdering sexual predator.* When Lauren tried to catch his eye, he looked away. She didn't know what she would have said exactly if he hadn't been basking in this perceived triumph, but it was nothing ladylike, that was for sure.

"Whoa, hold up here, Judge. This case has already been tried. The district attorney doesn't get to go fishing just because a body has been found. We won't even know if it is Amber Anderson for days. Even if it is her, it has no bearing on the matter at hand."

"I disagree, Judge. If we were allowed to examine the preliminary findings, we might—"

"I object to any delay in the outcome of this case." Violanti held his ground.

Church pulled himself up to his full height, so that he towered over Violanti. "And I submit that this is a significant event that warrants further review." The two men began arguing, the room erupted in shouts and curses. The judge yelled for silence. In all her years on the department, Lauren had never seen anything like this before. Two of the deputies wedged themselves between Church and Violanti, trying to break things up.

At the moment, another deputy stuck his head in the door. "Judge O'Keefe, the jury has a message for you." As if on cue, the room suddenly went silent. The intruding deputy reached over and handed a folded piece of paper to the judge. His face was red and blotchy from trying to regain control of his chambers. He took the paper with aggravated relief. Opening it, he read it and tossed it onto his desk.

"Well, ladies and gentleman, the point is moot. The jury has reached a verdict."

Everyone in the room seemed to hold their breath.

Lauren was numb. There was no more shouting. All the grandstanding was done. With the verdict in, the die was officially cast.

She flashed back to the picture of Amber Anderson on the wall of her parent's filthy house. She thought of the way David Spencer had described having sex with Katherine Vine. She could feel his hand on her face. A shudder ran through her. This could not be happening. She needed more time to process this information, but there was no time. This was it. What they had all been waiting for. Violanti and Carl led the way and she followed the small crowd out of chambers and filed back into the courtroom.

Five and a half hours. Not long. That was not long to deliberate. There was no way to tell which way it was going to go. And now there was a body of a young girl who may or may not be David's ex-girlfriend. Had David killed Amber Anderson? Had he killed Katherine Vine? Had he raped Samantha Godwin?

What had she done?

For the first time in her life, Lauren wished she didn't have to hear the verdict.

She took her seat behind the defense table. "What's going on?" Reese pressed when he saw her face. "What's wrong?" All she could do was shake her head and stare at the empty jury box. She fought back the bile rising to her throat as the players made their way back to their places.

The district attorney and his second chair stood at the prosecution table, ready. Church looked tense, standing with his fingers splayed over the table, jaw set, as the courtroom deputies opened the doors for the public.

Reporters began to flood in, excited by the quick verdict, knowing that tonight would be a good news night. David's mom entered with her friend and sat behind Lauren. She could hear Mrs. Spencer breathing to the point of hyperventilation, her friend trying to calm her down, unsuccessfully.

Across the aisle, Anthony Vine sat with a stony face, surrounded by his entourage. His meaty arms were folded across his chest. One of his men leaned over and whispered something in his ear. He nodded, but his expression never changed. He stared straight ahead, waiting for the show to begin. Joe Wheeler sat down next to him, his face a tense mixture of anticipation and anxiety.

Lauren couldn't accept the possiblity that Joe may have been right all along, that she had been duped, fooled. Every ounce of her common sense had told her not to take the case in the beginning, but she had anyway. Now she questioned if that was because she had thought she could prove David was innocent or because she could not allow Joe Wheeler to be right. With all the particulars she'd seen, all the people she talked to, she was still conflicted. Was it because of the hard evidence or just the feeling there was something off about David? Because the facts she had dug up certainly created reasonable doubt. Vine had the means, motive, and opportunity to murder his wife. What was David's motive? What possible reason did he have to kill Katherine Vine? The only person who benefited from her death was her husband. So why was she physically sick to her stomach?

The deputies brought David in, sat him at the defense table, and took his cuffs off. He glanced back at his mother, gave Lauren a half smile, then turned to face forward. Staring at the back of his head, she fought the bile rising up in her throat. *Who is this kid?* she thought. *Who is he really?*

The bailiff surveyed the courtroom, made sure all the appropriate people were where they were supposed to be, then called out, "All rise."

The courtroom rose in unison. Judge O'Keefe came from the left and stepped up to his seat. There was no hint in his demeanor of the drama that had been unfolding in his chambers not fifteen minutes before.

All the players were in place.

The judge admonished the crowd that no outbursts would be tolerated. Everyone sat back down.

"Bring in the jury," he instructed.

There was no sound as the group of four men and eight women shuffled into the jury box, no reading their faces. They looked blankly toward the judge. After only five and a half hours, they looked tired and worn out. *That's not a good sign,* Lauren thought as she scanned each juror. *Weary people don't deliberate, they just want to go home.*

"In the case of the people versus David Spencer, Madam Forewoman, have you reached a verdict?"

The forewoman, a black lady with smooth ebony skin and short cropped hair, had on a flowered dress that seemed too bright and cheerful for the occasion. Her attitude was anything but cheery as she rose and passed a piece of paper to the bailiff on her left. Her eyes looked red rimmed, like she'd been crying. "Yes, we have, Your Honor."

The bailiff handed the paper to the judge. He read it carefully and looked up. "Was this verdict a unanimous decision?"

"It was, Your Honor."

"I would like to thank the jury for their service and diligence in this matter. It is no small thing to pass judgment on another person, especially in a case such as this. You should all be commended for your hard work and diligence." He turned away from them and toward David. "Would the defendant please rise?"

David rose slowly from his seat. His hands were shaking.

"On the first count of murder in the second degree how do you find the defendant?"

"Not guilty."

"On the second count of rape in the first degree how do you find the defendant?"

"Not guilty."

A rush of sound rippled through out the courtroom and the judge pounded his gavel.

Anthony Vine stood up. "Not guilty? Not guilty?"

One by one the jurors were polled. Each one said in turn the same thing: not guilty.

Deputies started to swarm toward Vine, but his people hustled him back into his seat. The man who had whispered into his ear earlier was now forcibly holding him down. Vine's face was red and orange at the same time. One of the deputies said something inaudible to Joe Wheeler. He nodded and the five men Anthony Vine came with got him out of his seat and removed him from the courtroom.

David's mother broke into sobs as Violanti hugged him tight. All around them flashes popped off.

The judge kept talking, but no one was listening, the courtroom was lit up like a Christmas tree. The last thing Lauren made out clearly was Judge O'Keefe telling David he was free to go.

Free to go.

Now David was hugging his mother as she cried, leaning over the waist-high divider. Her shoulders heaved up and down as she clutched at him, like a castaway saved from a sinking rowboat. He was smiling. Happy. They did it. He won.

Lauren sat like a stone. She couldn't move. She could barely breathe.

The reporters started to crowd around, microphones extended, looking for sound bites. Lauren pushed the microphones out of her face. Reese grabbed her arm. "No comment. No comment!" he said, over and over as he pushed a path through the parasites, pulling Lauren along with him out of the courtroom into the hallway towards the elevators.

She passed a distraught Anthony Vine sobbing against the wall, while his friends tried to shield him from the media. They were trying to swarm him too, arms outstretched, yelling questions at him, snapping pictures. Joe Wheeler was nowhere to be seen. With the verdict came the taint of suspicion on Anthony Vine. The reasonable doubt of David Spencer's guilt meant that they had cast a reasonable doubt on Anthony Vine's innocence. Joe had jumped ship right away, like others were sure to do. Maybe Anthony Vine really was a broken man, now that all his dirty little secrets had been exposed for the world to pass judgment on. But Lauren couldn't be concerned with that now.

She just wanted to remove herself from the building. From this side show that had taken over her life and destroyed so many others. The elevator's door slid open and Reese pulled her inside, stabbing the close button, sending them to the lobby.

Maybe it was her imagination, but when Reese was leading her out, she thought she heard David call after her. Call her by name.

84

The day after the verdict Lauren walked into Frank Violanti's office for the last time. She looked tired and drawn. He was sitting at his desk, still surrounded by his self-made memorial, but instead of his cocky winner-take-all attitude, he was visibly subdued. She hadn't called, but she could tell he had been expecting her.

She unceremoniously dumped all her files pertaining to David Spencer on his floor. White paper fluttered out and swirled around her ankles.

If she thought he'd react with anger, she was wrong. He merely looked at the mess she'd just made and said softly, "We don't know that David killed that girl. Her body was too decomposed to even give a cause of death. They haven't even identified the body yet."

"We don't know that he didn't kill Katherine Vine. We just stirred up some reasonable doubt."

"Then we did the right thing," he countered. "That was our job, Lauren."

That underlying truth stung more than any insult he could have hurled at her. "I can't help you anymore. If the State Police charge David, don't call me."

"I wasn't planning on it. And they won't be able to charge him. He didn't do it."

She studied his face. "You really believe that?"

He hesitated a second too long. "I have to, he's my client."

"That's no answer."

"It's the only one I got."

There was a long silence as the two faced off against each other. Seagull after seagull flew past Violanti's head, framed by the giant picture window. His hair still spiked up, his suit still looking like it came from his father's closet. Nothing had changed.

"We uncovered a boatload of evidence that points directly at Anthony Vine. He had motive, opportunity, and now no alibi. How can we just discount that? How can you? Because David gave you the creeps one day?"

"I don't know what to believe."

What Lauren knew was that they'd be back on opposite ends of the courtroom, but she wasn't sure he'd ever be able to go after her again like he used to. Now he knew she was a true believer. He was not. He played the game and played it well. The fundamental difference between the two of them was never more clear or disturbing to her. Lauren Riley wanted justice; Frank Violanti wanted results.

Lauren looked him dead in the eye. "I'll never stop watching David Spencer. If he did this, he's only just getting started. And when the time comes, I will be the one that takes him down."

She turned and walked out without another word. There was nothing left to say between them. Their truce was over.

Lauren exited the building feeling unburdened for the first time in a long time. Her next stop was an appointment with Joe Wheeler's lieutenant and the chief of the Garden Valley Police. She was bringing copies of the police report and pictures of her black eye. She didn't know what good that would do, maybe none, but she wanted it on record. She wanted him exposed for the brutal bastard he was. Once that was over, she could get on with her life and get back to normal. *Whatever that is*, she thought as she twisted through the revolving doors to the sidewalk.

Her unmarked car was idling on the curb outside Violanti's building with Reese waiting for her behind the wheel. He revved the engine a little as she walked up and gave her a crooked grin. As tired as she was, she managed a sad little smile for Reese. Because he was there for her.

Lauren's phone vibrated as she opened the passenger side door. It was Mark. She hit ignore.

———————

David was flipping through the photos on a dating app while he waited for Detective Lauren Riley to emerge from Uncle Frank's law firm building. It had been just his luck to see her exit the loud wreck of an unmarked police car and disappear into the building as he pulled up. He parked his mom's maroon sedan on the opposite side curb and watched. He was supposed to talk to Uncle Frank about the new allegations that had come about, but that could wait. He wanted to know what Detective Riley was up to. She had been carrying a load of files. *Probably my paperwork*, he mused and sat back. He had all the time in the world now.

Too thin. *Swipe.* Too much make up. *Swipe.* Too educated. *Swipe.*

As he paged through the sea of pictures, his mind drifted back to that night with Katherine.

The sound of the car door opening startled her.

She had looked up.

"I'm sorry," she stammered, surprised that he had come back. She had slid her credit card up on the dashboard while she rifled through her purse for something. He had stood on the driver's side, door open, sweat making his hair stick to his forehead. "Did you forget something? Because I—"

David lunged at her.

The shock of him ripping the scarf out of her hair made overpowering her easy. As she struggled against the silk pulling against her neck, he could feel her breath on his face. She kicked out at the seat, her feet still bare from when she'd kicked off her shoes. Her hands reached out, trying to grab onto something, some life ring she could use to bring her to the surface, gasping for air. But there was nothing. He was on top of her, his full weight pressing her down. He was pulling the scarf tighter, but slowly. Slowly.

Her fight weakened. He took his time now, savoring the moment. Her eyes begged for answers she'd never get, then clouded over.

David let the scarf slip from his fingers, looking over her body, taking stock of his work. She had been hot, all right. On the backseat was the bag from the toy store with the woman's two games. She always got two of the exact same game. Vaguely, he had wondered why she did that. Had she been trying to get his attention? She had gotten his attention all right. He propped her up a little, so she didn't look so disheveled. He wanted her to look nice. He straightened his shirt, closed the door, and walked right to his car.

His uncle had showed him the crime scene photos during the trial. She had slumped forward somehow. Very nasty looking. Oh well. He had tried to be nice.

The memory snapped away when Detective Riley came out of the building without the files she had gone in with. He gripped the steering wheel and watched her move toward her car. Blond hair done up in a ponytail, bobbing as she walked, his eyes were glued to her. The guy driving had been with her at his trial. He had to be her partner. David heard him gun the engine a little as she got in and they were off.

Detective Riley had gotten his attention.

She would be tough. A lot of thought and planning. It had been the lack of thought and planning that had almost been the end of him this time. But he was in better control of himself since he went to jail. Jail had taught him the value of patience and timing. His girlfriend had been a necessity, Katherine had been opportunity, but Lauren would be a pleasure.

But that was his long game. He needed something else to fill the void in the meantime.

Swipe. Swipe. Swipe.

No, no, no.

Wait a second. He paused to examine the picture in front of him more carefully. Young, red hair, freckles, loves dogs.

He gazed down at his phone. She was perfect. He hit CONNECT and the screen to her mail box popped up. He put the car in drive and tossed the phone on the seat next to him. He'd message later.

He smiled to himself.

This was getting easier for him.

Acknowledgments

I would like to thank everyone who, over the years, has taken this journey with me. First and foremost, my family: Dan, Natalie, and Mary Grace, you are the inspiration and motivation for everything I do. My mom and sister, dad in heaven, my in-laws—without your help, this book would not be here.

To the writers in my critique group, John, Mike, Eric, Elisa, Rick, Barb, Lisa, Lynn, Shannon, my partner in crime, Stephanie Patterson—thank you for the comments, good and bad, the encouragement and the great company over these last few years. A special shout out to Mike Breen for giving my draft of this book the once-over and helping me with my comma problem—now get back to writing!

A shout out to the members of the Western NY Chapter of Sisters in Crime-Murder on Ice, who helped me with my query, told me what to expect, and have rooted for me every step of the way.

To the incomparable novelist Dinitia Smith, who on my worst days told me to suck it up and never let me give up on myself, thank you for all your support.

A huge thank you to my agent Bob Mecoy, for taking a chance on me.

To my fellow coppers on the Buffalo Police Department, thank you for providing me with enough ideas for a hundred books. You are truly heroes in my eyes, especially everyone I was partnered up with at one time or another over twenty-two years. And no, that character is not you.

John Gilmour, Esq. gave me so many wonderful insights into working for both the prosecution and the defense. Any procedural legal mistakes in this book are definitely mine and not his.

Dr. Joseph Bart took time out of his incredibly demanding schedule to answer all my medical questions for me. Once again, any mistakes in this story are mine and not his.

Thank you, Tracy Gallagher Reid, for the awesome gift of your friendship. I count myself blessed that you were a part of my life.

I'd be remiss if I didn't mention fellow writer Jess Lourey, who met me at a SinC workshop and suggested I send my manuscript to her editor. Everyone should buy a copy of one of her books. Right now!

And last but not least, my editor at Midnight Ink, Terri Bischoff, who changed my life with an email I opened on the road somewhere in the hills of Pennsylvania. Also to Nicole Nugent, for ironing out my mistakes. Thank you both for all your time, patience, and effort to help make this book a reality.

© Short Street Photographers

About the Author

Lissa Marie Redmond is a recently retired Cold Case Homicide detective with the Buffalo Police Department. She lives and writes in Buffalo with her husband and two kids. *A Cold Day in Hell* is the first novel in her Cold Case Investigation series.